ALL
WE
NEED

RONNIE MATHEWS

Cover Design by Melissa Doughty at Mel D. Designs

Editing by Paisley McNab at Perfectly Write

Proofreading by Caroline Palmier at Love & Edits

ASIN: B0DXD6HWYV (Ebook)

ISBN: 978-1-0683210-1-6 (Paperback)

To my husband.
The sweetest man I've ever met and who I'm lucky enough to call mine. Thanks for giving me my own personal love story, putting up with my grumpy ass, and constantly cheering me on.
Love you to the moon and back.

author's note

Thank you so much for deciding to read All We Need. I hope you love Booth and Alessandra's story as much as I loved writing it.

All We Need is the third book in the Sutton Bay series and can be read as a standalone. All books in the series will be interconnected standalone stories, but I suggest reading them in order to get the full feel of the stories.

This is an open-door romance and intended for readers who are eighteen years or older. All characters written are consenting adults and you will find explicit, on-page sexual content, explicit language, and real life situations. I ask that you always look after yourself, and if you wish to see a full list of content and trigger warnings, please visit: www.ronniemathews.com

playlist

Mind Over Matter (Reprise) - Young the Giant
Bitter Winds - Dylan Gossett
This Life Ain't Easy - Jonah Kagen
Mood - Lofi - Yagih Mael
Kiss With A Fist - Florence + The Machine
Unravel Me - Sabrina Claudio
Wildfire - Cautious Clay
Power Over Me - Dermot Kennedy
Secret Smile - Semisonic
Woman - Mumford & Sons
Bloodsport '15 - Raleigh Ritchie
Only You - Orchestral Version - Zara Larsson
Electric Love - BØRNS
Lost & Found - Darren Kiely
Cherish You - Mikky Ekko
Eurydice - Vincent Lima
Never Better - Wild Rivers
Craving - James Bay
Godlight - Noah Kahan
faith - Camylio

Troubled Waters - Alex Warren
Snow On The Beach - Taylor Swift, Lana Del Rey
Stubborn Love - The Lumineers
Beautiful Things - Benson Boone
Freezing- Wild Rivers
All My Love - Noah Kahan
Love You 'Til Death - Forest Blakk

Scan QR code below to listen on Spotify.

CHAPTER ONE

booth

"You can tell Mrs. Stewart to shove that complaint right up her—"

Eyes as wide as saucers, the nervous server stares at me from the other side of the stainless steel pass. I swear the staff here is getting younger and younger. Or am I getting older? Last I checked, there were no gray hairs.

I'm a dick for not remembering her name. She tiptoed in here, during the height of dinner service, quiet as a mouse, to tell me that Mrs. Stewart—the town's official Karen—found her clam chowder "subpar" and "cold."

I explained, "Yes, it would be cold. Considering she ran the dish over thirty minutes ago."

I'm cranky, hot, and exhausted. I've been at the restaurant since seven a.m. and running the pass for nine hours.

Flashing a smile, I wipe my hands down the dish towel flung over my shoulder. "Tell her we'll send out two blueberry pies on the house. That usually does the trick."

"Yes, sir. Um, Mr. Sadler?" Her voice wobbles, and she fidgets with the notepad clutched between her trembling fingers.

Jesus.

"Chef will do fine. Or Booth," I tell her right as the sound of a ticket printing out buzzes in my ear. Ten minutes before the kitchen closes.

Tracy? Tammy?—shit, I need to learn her name—leaves the kitchen as Patrick, my oldest brother *and* bar manager, strides through the swinging door.

"Sorry! Sorry!" he shouts, palms upturned in apology. "We have a new team member tonight and they forgot we stopped taking orders at nine thirty."

Apart from our height and last name, we're nothing alike. I have shaggy, dark brown hair; his is wavy and a similar shade of dark blond to our middle brother, Graham. They both share the same green eye color, whereas mine are light blue. Patrick is levelheaded; I'm hilarious and handsome.

Most people would hate the idea of working with their family. After a grueling day like today, it's usually good to see his face. *Usually.*

Snatching the ticket from the printer, I scan it over and groan. Holding eye contact while flipping him the bird, I read out the order. "Last one of the night. I need one seafood platter, two Teddy's lobster rolls, half a dozen oysters, one extra portion of fries, and two calamari."

A round of halfhearted "Yes, Chefs" echo around me.

Patrick winces and mouths, *Sorry.*

"The team has been killing me tonight, Pat." I grab a stack of plates and flip on the heat lamps. "Have any of the new staff ever worked in hospitality before?"

His shoulders drop, making me feel bad for grating on him.

"Forget it. I'm burned out and still have prep to do for the fair. Just promise me you'll get them trained up ASAP."

He straightens. "We're already on it. I swear..."

Tomorrow, our small town of Sutton Bay is hosting its annual Fall Fair. It would be blasphemy if a town hidden away in coastal New England didn't throw an event in honor of the season.

My family's restaurant, Our Place, has had a table at the fair since opening almost thirty years ago. Specializing in seafood cuisine, if you come to this corner of the country looking for the taste of Maine, this is where you'll find it.

When my father, Ted Sadler, opened the restaurant with his closest friend, George Thomas, they imagined somewhere folks could sit down with family and enjoy a meal that tasted like it was whipped up in your grandmother's kitchen. The second they step through the doors, they're greeted by a warm, homey welcome.

As the head chef, I pride myself on maintaining that legacy —even if it isn't where I saw my career headed.

But things don't always go according to plan. My father passing away suddenly—leaving us all lost and heartbroken— almost seven years ago was definitely one of those things. My brothers and I banded together to keep this place going in his honor. Only, things continued to not go to plan, and earlier this year, Our Place was in deep water. Patrick and his now-girl-friend, Johanna, did all they could to stop the restaurant from being sold to a greedy corporate monster.

Ultimately, we had no choice but to sell.

Fortunately—or not so fortunately—a *mysterious* bene-factor stepped in and bought the restaurant. Who, after dotting the i's and crossing the t's five months ago, hasn't bothered to reveal themselves.

"Tomorrow should be good. I can't believe the owner signed off on it." Skepticism drips from his words.

I divert my attention, shuffling around the bottles of oil and sauces lined up on the pass.

"Booth. You got permission, right?" Patrick's tone grows serious. He's got that dad voice nailed down. Too bad my five-year-old niece doesn't bend to it.

"Hmm? What was that?" Right on cue, my sous chef, Simon, slides two lobster rolls in front of me. "Actually, no time for chitchat, sorry, bro."

"You stubborn prick." He's laughing now. He knows I'm not kneeling for some faceless dude whose shirt is probably too tight and wouldn't know how to run a restaurant even if it slapped him in the face. This is *our* restaurant.

Our Place.

"Better hope this doesn't come back to bite you. I'm not holding your hand while you whine about one of their emails again."

Chucking a rogue fry at his head, I shrug. "*Only* when they pull their head out of their ass and show their face around here will I take them seriously. For now, they sign my paychecks. That's all."

He rolls his eyes. "Whatever. Get finished in here and I'll buy you a drink."

An ice-cold IPA sounds heavenly. My lips smack together as I imagine the hoppy bubbles on my tongue. Then I remember the to-do list the length of my arm and throw my head back, sighing. "Can't. I still need to prep for tomorrow and then I'm up at six to set up. Rain check?"

"Next week." He jerks his chin at me. "See you later."

After he leaves and we send out the final order of the night, the team and I whizz through the clean down until the kitchen sparkles from top to bottom. Once I give everyone permission to head home, I drag myself to the back office, collapse into the rolling chair behind the desk and stretch out my aching joints. They crack so loudly, I'm surprised I don't glow in the dark.

Rubbing my eyes roughly, I mentally go through everything I need to do before powering up the computer. While browsing for the stock sheet, the cursor pauses over a folder I haven't looked at in months.

Menu ideas.

Since I was promoted to head chef after Gloria, the restaurant's longest-serving member of staff, retired, I've wanted to spice up the menu a little. There are no complaints about what we currently offer, and all the dishes are a staple in most households in Maine, but it's out of date. The idea of an exciting, modern menu, where I could put my own flare on it, has always been a dream. I tried for months, only to be shot down by George and my mom, who took over when my dad passed.

It's not what the people of this town are looking for.

This might be a little unconventional.

I understood what they were saying, truly, but it still stung.

I can't see myself doing anything else, but sometimes I wonder if this is the future Dad saw for the restaurant. For me.

The role wasn't handed to me on a silver platter. Like anyone else, I started as a dishwasher and worked my way up the ranks. Not wanting to go too far for school, I enrolled in the local community college for culinary classes.

That once-burning passion has fizzled out over the years. Especially since the new owner took over.

What if...

No, I scold myself, cutting off that internal voice that creeps into my head occasionally.

This is where I'm supposed to be.

What Dad would have wanted.

SPICES AND SUGARY GOODNESS ASSAULT MY NOSE, MIXING WITH the fresh, salt air blowing in from the bay. It doesn't matter if this is the first or hundredth time, the smell of fall is nostalgic and comforting.

With the restaurant's table setup for the fair, Dex, Patrick's best friend, and I are helping my brother, Graham. For such a quiet, reserved guy, he's really going all out for his "fake girlfriend." Quinn owns Just Brew It, the small bakery in town, and because my brother is a complete simp for her, he's surprising her with her own table after he found out she couldn't afford it. Thanks to my genius idea, Graham and Quinn have entered into a faux dating arrangement so he doesn't have to attend his ex's—who is the worst—wedding alone. The best part: he's fucking crazy about Quinn.

The town hosts four main fairs every year: fall, winter, spring, and summer. They all started off as small gatherings, put on for the local kids and businesses. Now, huge crowds from all over flock to Sutton Bay. It's a great way to give back to the community and honestly, a nice change of scenery. I'll be manning the restaurant's stall with Simon, Jo, and Pat most of the day.

Currently, Graham stands in front of Quinn's table, eyes blown wide in panic behind his glasses. "She's going to hate it." He groans and shrinks away.

"Nope!" I shout and drag him back. "Quit doubting yourself. This is nice—really nice. If I were a chick and a guy did this for me, I'd be buying a one-way ticket to pound—"

"Booth Elias Sadler!" I'd recognize that strict tone anywhere. She's usually a pint-sized sweetheart, but as we turn to find my mom strolling our way, with Patrick and my niece, Lottie, in tow, I cower at her stern glower. "I raised you better than that."

"Sorry, Mom," I mutter.

"*Sorry, Mommy,*" Patrick mocks.

I fix him with a *fuck off* glare. "I didn't even call her 'Mommy.' Get your ears checked, old man. Don't even ge—"

Something shimmers in my peripheral, distracting me. Following the flash of light, I find the source of my distraction.

A watch.

The watch hasn't left me speechless, though. It's the person it's attached to.

I'm not shallow. Shit, I don't even have a type. Some would call me a playboy—my brothers do. But I don't jerk women around. I make my intentions very clear. If they're interested in having some fun while in town, I'm more than happy to oblige. I respect them—unless they ask me not to. I'll cook them breakfast. Let them use my shower. Pay for their cab. Wish them all the best.

Both parties know exactly what a night together means.

The fair is the perfect place to find women who are here temporarily. If I'm honest, it's been months since I've had the time or energy to pursue anyone. I've exchanged a couple of numbers and bought a few drinks, but that's as far as it went.

Suddenly, I'm very energized.

I take in the inky-black hair falling in thick, shiny spirals. Porcelain skin, smooth like velvet. Even the curve of her upper lip as she pouts at the table in deep thought is enticing, and I've only seen her side profile so far. The long, beige duster coat she's wearing hides her figure, but she's at least half a foot shorter than my six two.

I'm on the move before I know what I'm doing, and catch Dex mutter, "Does he ever take a day off?"

Not today, buddy. Because I want to see this little show-stopper face on.

Maybe it'll put an end to this dry spell.

The fair isn't open yet, but already the smell of candied apples, cinnamon treats, and chili fills the air. Right now, I'm grateful for the lack of crowds. My eyes stay glued to the stranger as I stride across the gravel path, lined on both sides with small tents and marquees.

When I'm ten feet away, I see what grabbed her attention. Small canvases are propped upright on the table, each painted with a picturesque scenery. Deep oranges, pale blues, vibrant greens. They're beautiful, but when I'm close enough to get a good look at this woman, they're quickly forgotten.

Shit. She really is gorgeous.

Right, art. I can chat nonsense about paintings for a few minutes, impress her with my "knowledge," ask her out for dinner, and then...

Clearing my throat, because I'm not one to creep up on women, I sidle up next to her. "Pretty good, huh?"

She doesn't turn, just nods slowly with a low hum.

"I'm more of an oil paint kinda guy. It's daring. Unique." Squinting at the table, I think of something artsy-fartsy to say. "I love when an artist uses this...brushstroke. Are you a collector?"

Her head tilts a fraction. "You're a fan of the *grisaille* technique?"

I don't know what the fuck she said, but I like the way she said it.

Her sultry voice drips over me like warm wax. She'd make the prettiest of noises, I'm certain.

Focus, Booth. Put your dick away.

What was that word she said again?

"Huge fan. The *grizzly* is very contemporary." *Nailed it.*

"Is that so?" Finally, she twists her body to look at me. A pair of striking gray eyes—like rings of mercury—pin me in place. There's something familiar about the shade, but I'm already scanning the rest of her face. A straight nose slopes down to two rosy-pink lips. Thick, coal-black lashes and brows frame her piercing orbs, and there isn't a mark on her flawless skin. Her face is cut with sharp lines, matching the scrutinizing gaze she levels me with.

I'm a little intimidated by the way she crosses her arms over her chest with a quirked brow; intimidated *and* oddly turned on. I'm man enough to say I'm disappointed her eyes don't rake down my body like most women's would.

"Tell me more." She waves a graceful hand between us.

"I'd love to." I step closer, giving her a half smile. "How about over dinner? I'm dying to hear your thoughts about your favorite artists. Impressionism versus what impression I'm making on you."

Her mouth doesn't even twitch. Nor is she blushing. *Weird.* A smile and a cheesy pickup line usually do the trick. Her expression gives nothing away, but I'm not giving up.

With a flat tone, she says, "There's no time like the present. And I think the artist is due back soon. I'm sure they'd love to hear your opinions."

I'm running out of bullshit things to say and I'd rather jump into the ocean than talk with some hoity-toity know-it-all.

Carefully, I pick up a painting, admiring the orangey-pink sunset behind a city skyline that appears 3-D with the way the paint is layered. It's impressive, clearly done by a professional, but that's as far as my keen eye goes. "Not really my thing. Kinda basic, if you ask me."

I have no fucking idea what I'm saying, and sweat begins to trickle down my spine.

This calls for the big guns.

Lowering my gaze to my white sneakers, I pop out my partners in crime and raise my head to look at her.

Her features are so cold, I shiver. Not the normal side effect when I flash my dimples. They rarely make an appearance this early on—she should be flattered.

She's anything *but.*

The second thing to surprise me is when she rounds the table to stand on the other side. She props her hands on her hips and hits me with a stony look. "I'm sorry you find my work so *basic.* I'll take that criticism into consideration."

I blink back my embarrassment and a nervous laugh slips free.

Oh, but she is far from finished.

"And for your awareness. *Grisaille* was created in the fifteenth and sixteenth centuries. It is associated with oil paint, though. Gold star to you. Now, if you'll excuse me, I have to finish setting up." Her tone is dismissive.

I'm stunned silent, which is rare. So is making a fool of myself, and my brain spins as I think of how to salvage this.

"Listen." I pull my beanie off and comb my fingers through my static hair. "Maybe we got off on the wrong foot. Yes, art is not my thing, but when I see a pretty girl, I have to speak to her."

"*Girl?*" If looks could kill, god rest my soul.

"No, no. Not girl. Grown woman. Old woman. Shit, no, you're not old. Actually, how old are you?" My T-shirt sticks to my back as I dig my grave deeper with each stupid comment. I drop my head in my hands. "This isn't how I imagined it was going to go."

A murmur of voices sounds behind us. The gates are open, and in minutes, crowds of people will swarm this place. Last chance, because Momma didn't raise no quitter.

"Let's start from scratch." I do a 360-degree turn, hold out my hand, and grin so wide my jaw is close to dislocating. "Hey. I'm Booth Sadler. Head Chef at Our Place. Local to Sutton Bay. Happy to be your tour guide. Nice to meet you. And you are?"

To my surprise, there's a tiny flare in her eyes, but it quickly disappears. I don't know her name, let alone how long she's in town for, yet I'm desperate for any crumb of detail about her.

Wait, what? No, that sounds like something my lovesick brothers would say.

"Well, *Booth.*" She brushes some lint off her shoulder. "This has been a pleasure, but I have customers to serve. Take care now."

Twice she's dismissed me. She's a feisty little thing, but in a cunning way that makes me hard when it shouldn't.

Chuckling softly, I shove my beanie back on. "Okay, okay. Point taken. Let me ask you one thing." I lean forward and gift her with a megawatt smile and circle my mouth. "You're telling me these did nothing for you?"

Her eyes drop, and slowly, with a manicured finger, the tip stained purple, she pokes the dent in my left cheek. "This little thing?"

I smile harder.

"Hmm. I've seen my fair share of dimples." She drops her hand. "They really aren't that impressive."

My mouth falls open, and before I have the chance to shoot my shot—for what feels like the hundredth time—she busies herself with a box of canvases behind her.

I'm not sure if I should laugh at her candidness or cry at my expense.

As I turn around, ignoring the amused faces of my family and friends, my fingers brush over my deflating dimples.

The fucking audacity.

alessandra

ONE MONTH LATER

Deep ruby liquid swirls in my glass, moving precariously closer to the rim with each flick of my wrist.

I'm so mesmerized by the garnet-colored whirlpool, I almost miss my phone flashing with an incoming call. Seeing my mother's name light up the screen has me smirking.

Reaching over to snatch it from the coffee table, I tap the screen before the call drops. "You couldn't go one day, could you?"

"Pfft. Is it illegal for me to want to speak to you, *thisavré mou*?"

Hearing my mother use the familiar term of endearment —*my treasure* when translated from her native Greek—has a trickle of warmth seeping into my chest. After two rowdy boys, my mom's dream to have more children came to a halt following a complicated birth with my middle brother. Until I came along a few years later.

"You spoke to me three hours ago."

"I got bored waiting for your father to stop talking business with his friends," she retorts sassily.

"You're always bored. Maybe we should find you a hobby?"

"I had a hobby. Now, I am a lady of leisure." She sighs happily, even though I know retirement is driving her kooky.

There's shuffling through the phone. She's probably traipsing through the hallway of her and my father's home, draped in an elegant robe and sipping on a full-bodied merlot now that their dinner guests have gone. Glancing down at my satin robe and glass of red wine, I snort. I am my mother's daughter.

"I didn't realize being a glamor puss was a hobby," I tease.

She gasps. "That's an awful word, Alessandra. Shameful."

"It does not mean—forget it." I shake my head, holding in my laugh. The woman has been in the States for over four decades, but there are still some phrases that throw her for a loop. I'm glad she's never lost the lilt in her voice, pitch rising and falling with each syllable. "How was the party?"

"Oh, you know." I don't know. "You were missed, it wasn't the same without you. At least we will see you at Christmas."

"You're still traveling to the cottage tomorrow?"

"Yes. But if your father starts playing his murder podcasts, I'm driving myself." My parents mostly reside in their Greystone in the West Village, but in late November, they stay at their "cottage" in the Hamptons until New Year. A seven-bedroom, four-bathroom, fully staffed cottage. "Now, enough about that. How is it going?" Her voice lowers, and I picture her leaning forward as she waits.

I glance around the tiny apartment; my unpacked suitcase and the few boxes I had shipped from New York sit in the corner. Since arriving four days ago, the only items I've taken out are my painting supplies. This is home for the next couple of months. Quite the contrast to my apartment in SoHo.

It's been a month since my first trip to Sutton Bay, a small fishing town hidden by the towering pine trees of Acadia National Park. Four weeks to prepare, yet I feel more unprepared now that I'm here. My little espionage at the Fall Fair only feels like yesterday.

My eyes roll so far back in my head when I think about meeting *Dimples* I go dizzy. Never has someone hit on me in such a cliché yet enthusiastic way. Nothing deterred him. He didn't make me uncomfortable, and I quite enjoyed his performance, but I'm not here to make friends, especially with Booth Sadler. If I had known who he was, I wouldn't have entertained him for so long. There's too much at stake to be getting overly familiar with people here.

Three months. That's how long I've given myself. I'm here for one reason only: answers.

"Tell me what you're thinking." It's not a question, and there's no hiding from my mother.

"Is this a mistake?" I whisper. I'm a confident, driven woman, and I never make rash decisions. So upturning my life like this is very out of character.

My wine glass clanks against the coffee table as I place it down hastily.

"It is your decision, thisavré mou. I am proud of you for this. As is Papa. But remember, if you change your mind and want to come home, that is okay. You can join us here. Do what is right in your heart and try to turn that big brain of yours off for once."

"What if they don't want to know?" I hate how small my voice sounds.

Being vulnerable makes my skin itch. There's something unnerving about being unprotected like that; waiting to be weathered by the scrutinizing stares of unfamiliar people. Not even my brothers see this side of me. Only my parents. And even then, it's rare.

We're a close family. I see my parents often, with them only living a few blocks away. My brothers less often. Andres, the oldest child, lives in Florence, Italy, and oversees the European side of our family's business. Alexis, my middle brother, is based in California and is due to be announced as the CFO any day now. We make the most of video calls and always get together on the holidays. Apart from today. Instead of spending Thanksgiving with my family, I'm alone in a strange town.

I also work for our family's business, Argiros Enterprises. The glittering skyscraper in downtown Manhattan is where I thrive. It's rare you'll find me working from home, so the fact I'll be working remotely while here is going to be a challenge. I inherited my mother's bluntness and hardheadedness, and from my dad, his unwavering work ethic.

"Oh, Alessandra..." My mother sighs. "Give them time. I wish I could tell you how they'll react or what you'll find, but I cannot. Take however long you need and enjoy your time out of the city. You deserve a break."

Her honesty is welcome, the last thing I want is to be placated.

The sound of a door opening sounds through the phone and I hear my father's deep voice as he greets my mom.

"Is that my wonderful daughter?" His cheery question makes me smile.

"Yes, darling. Would you like to say anything?" Mom asks.

His response is louder, likely leaning over my mom while he hugs her hello. "Tell her that I love her and I'm very proud."

My eyes sting.

"I love you both too," I say slowly so my voice doesn't crack.

Before my emotions get the better of me, my stomach gurgles.

"Mama, I'm going to go. I need to make dinner."

"Eat, eat," she sings, and I know she's shooing her hand as if standing right in front of me. "Happy Thanksgiving, Alessandra. *Na prosécheis. Filákia.*" *Take care. Kisses.*

"Happy Thanksgiving. Na prosécheis." Smiling, we smack our lips together through the phone before hanging up.

Stretching toward the ceiling, I stand from the sofa and head to the small kitchen.

Renting this apartment was risky, but it was the only place available. The rent is incredibly fair—not that money is an issue. Not wanting to speak to the landlord, Martin Willis, needlessly, I didn't question if he was undercharging me.

Opening up the fridge, I groan at the sight of the bare shelves. I'd kill for the banquet my parents put together every Thanksgiving.

I really need to do a grocery run, but until then I'll be surviving on chips and salsa.

With my girl-dinner in tow, I move to the window in the living room that overlooks the main street running through town. It's been dark for hours and the streetlamps illuminate the fat snowflakes as they dance from the clouds. Winters in New York aren't the same. The snow quickly turns to gray sludge, causing havoc on traffic and sidewalks. Here, it's whimsical.

I make a mental note to see if I can find a small cabin to stay in for a few days—somewhere undisturbed and off the beaten track.

Sitting on my stool, I secure a fresh canvas on my easel and stare at it vacantly as I munch on my food.

There's something cathartic and freeing about starting a new piece. No rules. Free to do as I please.

Thanks to my busy schedule, I've hardly painted in months. Maybe the silver lining to me being here is that I'll find some spare hours to finally start and finish a painting.

A flash of light pulls me out of my relaxing haze as a truck rolls by. The headlights bathe the white-dusted street in a yellow glow. Snowflakes cling to the windowpane until they slide down the glass, racing one another.

Inspiration strikes.

My hands wander toward the cobalt blue, titanium white, and lamp black. Squeezing out a generous amount of each color onto my palette, my arm moves with effortless grace thanks to muscle memory, and I slather on the first layers of paint.

The tension in my muscles eases with each stroke. The doubts about being here dissolve as the different shades blend and melt together until it matches the deep gray-blue clouds outside.

It's not grisaille, but a technique known as *impasto*—where layers of oil paint are applied to the canvas for a three-dimensional effect.

Despite my annoyance at meeting Booth, my lips quirk just thinking about his stupid grin and misplaced determination to pursue me. If I were someone else, I might have gone along with it. He's not my usual type, with his boyish charm and unruly hair, but there was something genuine and inviting about him. He definitely wasn't *boyish* either. His height dwarfed mine, and though he was clean shaven, there was something virile in his devastatingly handsome face. All sharp lines, dark brows, and wide frame.

Maybe I should have given him a chance?

I'm quick to tamp that the *fuck* down.

While attending the fair wasn't great for keeping a low profile, it gave me the opportunity to scope out the town and get an idea of what the people are like.

The last thing I need is an overeager playboy thinking he can woo me into bed. Booth looks like the type to ask questions. Ones I will not be answering. Forgetting his dimples and sky-blue eyes will be easy.

But how long can I avoid him?

The simplest thing for me to do would be to keep my head down.

Too late for that.

I needed a genuine reason to be here. No one would question a starving artist wandering into town, but pulling that off will be difficult. I'm smart, persuasive, but a shit actress. Plus, I pride myself on my work. Love it, in fact.

I appreciate my mother reassuring me I can take my time here, do what I need to do, but I'd much rather rip off the Band-Aid and see this town in my rearview mirror before New Year.

I'll treat it like any normal business transaction. In and out. Straight to the point. Once I have my answers and this trip goes as expected, I can forget about Sutton Bay and its people.

My hand hovers above the canvas, creativity fading.

As quickly as it struck me, the inspiration quickly dwindles into the nothingness.

With my walls down, I'm bombarded by questions.

Why me?

Why not *me?*

Is this pointless?

What will they say?

Will they turn me away?

The paintbrush clatters to my palette and I take in the half-hearted streaks of paint.

I forget my food, forget the wonderland beyond the window, and forget all the reasons this is a good idea.

I'M JOLTED OUT OF MY DEEP SLEEP WHEN A SCREECH CUTS through my dream.

Sitting upright, I grip the bed sheets and scan my surroundings in a panic.

When I reassure myself I'm alone, the same high-pitched noise sounds. It's coming from outside.

Tiptoeing to the window, I slowly pull back the drapes and peer out onto the street below.

A woman paces back and forth, hands flailing in frustration as she shouts the same thing over and over.

Quinn.

I don't know who that is, but the longer I watch, the more irate she becomes.

She gets louder, banging her fists on the window of the coffee shop and bakery my apartment sits above.

Is no one else hearing this racket? There isn't a single soul outside, which makes sense, but I don't want to be the person to handle this.

I stomp over to my bedside table, unplug my phone, and open up my contact list until I find the number I need.

My finger hovers above Martin Willis's name.

We've only communicated via email and all I know about him is that he lives on the outskirts of town, provides local businesses with freshly grown produce, and owns several commercial and residential properties in Sutton Bay.

Quite the businessman.

It's ten p.m., on Thanksgiving. He must be with his family. He won't want me bothering him over some—

"Quinn!" The woman's bloodcurdling scream slices through the silent night, shaking the windowpanes. When the sound of glass smashing and a large thud follows, my thumb taps Martin's name without hesitation.

It rings a few times before his sleepy voice greets me. "Hello?"

Unease swirls deep in my stomach, but I push it aside. "Hi, Martin. It's Alessandra Argiros. I moved into the apartment abo—"

"Oh. Yes. Alessandra." I hear rustling. "Is everything okay?"

"It's, umm, no, it's not actually. There's a woman here. I'm not sure who." I peek outside again and hear her murmured grumblings. "She threw something through the window of the bakery."

"Shoot. Right, stay upstairs and call nine-one-one. I'll be there in five."

He hangs up before I can respond, and I do as he says.

By the time I've finished explaining to the police dispatcher, a truck pulls up outside. The cops are close behind, and the situation is deescalated—though the woman doesn't go down without a fight.

I stay put, peeping out of my window in my pajamas, when the buzzer to my apartment has me jumping out of my skin.

Crap. What if it's Martin? I'm not in the mood to meet him in person today. Or ever.

Pleading that it's the police, I unlock the front door, jog down the stairs, and unlatch the door leading onto the street.

My eyes go wide, and so do my visitor's when the door swings open.

Booth's mouth slackens before his gaze tracks slowly down my body. My skin warms and nipples pebble under his stare. It's then I remember I'm in a skimpy set of silk pajamas. Sans robe.

"It's you." His brows furrow in confusion, snowflakes cling to his lashes as he points up the stairs. "You live here?"

"That's correct." I roll my shoulders. "And why are you standing outside?"

He huffs a laugh of disbelief. "Martin asked me to check on the tenant upstairs." His head jerks to the right, and I follow to see the shards of glass strewn across the sidewalk. "My brother's girlfriend, Quinn, owns Just Brew It. We're here to help."

A pang of guilt strikes me. That explains the name being shouted through the street. "Oh. Right. Is she okay?"

He shrugs wearily. "Shocked, which isn't surprising.

Graham will take her home once they're finished up with the sheriff."

It's then I see a small figure, draped in a large coat, with a tall man hugging her tightly while they chat to the police.

"Is there anything I can do?" My eyes remain on the couple.

"Nah. We've got it. But a buddy of mine, Dex, he'll be doing some work tomorrow morning to cover up the window. It might get noisy."

"Right. Yeah. That's not a problem."

I rub my hands over my biceps, and despite the biting cold, neither of us makes a move.

"This isn't normal." His voice is timid as he shifts awkwardly on his feet. He sees the question in my face. "People smashing windows and screaming through town. You're safe here. In case you were worried. I know the town, and I live close by...if you ever need to call someone."

My face heats for a totally different reason. We're complete strangers, yet he's out here trying to look after me.

Except for my father and brothers, men have always had a habit of seeing me as the weaker sex. Through college. During my internship. Once promoted to senior associate.

My passion makes me emotional. My drive makes me controlling.

And I refuse to be seen as helpless right now.

"I don't need saving. I'm more than capable of handling myself." My voice rises in volume, and Booth's expression morphs from sheepish to defensive.

"Whoa, that's not what I was implying." He raises his palms. "You're new here. Alone. I don't doubt you could handle yourself."

"Who said I was alone?" I huff.

I'm exhausted, fed up, and I know I sound like a bitch right now, but I'm in no mood to backtrack. Especially with Booth.

With tired movements, he scrubs a hand down his face.

"Clearly I'm fucking this up. *Again*. I'm sorry to have disturbed your night. Let me get Martin, and you can be on your way."

My heartbeat races, but before I can stop him, he disappears into the bakery.

A minute later, a tall, slim elderly gentleman—looking to be in his late sixties appears.

"It's nice to finally meet you. I'm sorry it's under these circumstances." He speaks formally, but there's a New England twang to his accent. Turning toward Booth behind him, he says, "You've met Booth, I see. Good lad."

I try my hardest not to look at the man in question, but even in the dimly lit streets, I see him mouth, *I'm a good lad* before winking.

"It's good to meet you, Martin." I shake his offered hand. "It's no problem. These things happen. I see it's all sorted, so I'll leave you to it. Sorry you had to end your Thanksgiving like this."

My voice is steady, and I press my shaking hands to my thighs, my sweaty palms heating my cold skin. Slowly, I back away as Martin stares at me curiously.

Booth has the same look.

Who's blaming them? I'm acting peculiar, but I don't like curiosity.

Curiosity led me here.

CHAPTER THREE

booth

I LOVE A CHALLENGE.

Since I was a kid, I'd jump at the chance to try anything once, no matter how difficult. In middle school, I tried out for the soccer team even though the offside rule hurt my brain. It didn't faze me getting benched almost every game; I was happy to be there.

Failing classes? Fine. Put me in summer school and I would work my ass off.

Teaching my little sister, Florence, how to ride a bike, even though she has the balance of a one-legged donkey. Piece of cake.

Going to a local college none of my friends are attending? No problem. Making friends came easily to me.

Quitting wasn't an option until I'd given it my all.

I'd somehow stumbled across an unsolvable puzzle. Hot one minute, ice cold the next. She had me eager for the burn and the frostbite. Never have I fucked up so tremendously when speaking to a woman. Let alone twice. She's fiery, smart, and clearly out of my league.

Which entices me more.

I'm strolling up Robin Road as I recall our last run-in.

Before the door opened, the identity of the tenant above the bakery was a mystery.

Then a goddess was revealed, clad in black silk that covered nothing. Long legs, the gentle slope of her breasts, and tight nipples poking through the thin camisole. Face bare, eyes heavy with sleep; she looked delicious. Her hair was a wild mess of curls, sticking up in all directions, making her appear younger.

Struck dumb. Again. I barely managed to say two words. *It's you.*

It had been a whole month since we met, and I hadn't seen her once. When we parted ways at the fair, I presumed she was only there to sell her artwork.

Like our first interaction, her defensiveness was off the charts. Too bad it didn't do the trick in discouraging me.

Sutton Bay is a small town. We're bound to run into each other again and they say the third time's a charm.

The snow has been coming down hard since Thanksgiving. I trudge through the uncleared drifts piling up on the sidewalk until I reach the restaurant, surprised to see the light on inside.

Pulling out my keys, I unlock the door and scurry inside before a flurry of white powder tailgates me.

"Hey. You're here early," a voice calls from behind the bar.

As I unzip my coat and hang it up, I nod at Patrick. "And you're here earlier. You good?"

He nods with a sigh. "Yeah, I was up early to deliver a letter to Quinn."

"Ahhh. How's she doing?"

For the past week, we've been helping Graham. He's still holding onto some old baggage from his previous toxic rela-tionship, and after attending his ex's wedding, it was clear he hadn't unpacked it all. He and Quinn are taking some time apart, which I think is good for them both, but he's enlisted us to deliver her letters every day.

"Better. Much better. I think they'll be seeing each other soon," Patrick says confidently.

"Here's hoping. Mom is still in panic mode and driving me up the wall."

He snorts. "Yeah, and trying her hardest not to get involved."

"That'll be the day." Separated by the driftwood bar our dad built, I stand in front of him. "Speaking of our meddling mother, I'm going to move back into my house tomorrow. With Florence back, she can keep an eye on her. I love her, but good god, I need my own space. Two Sadler women are enough to drive any man gray."

Last month, my mom slipped on her driveway and broke her leg. My siblings and I freaked out as flashbacks of our dad's sudden passing were dragged to the surface. I turned the tables on my mom—moved in with her and smothered her while she healed.

"What? Is sleeping in your childhood home making it difficult to bring women back? Is the poster of Pamela Anderson staring at them off-putting?"

"I took that down years ago." *After my college girlfriend complained.*

Plus, I haven't tried to take anyone home in weeks. Not since—

"You're pulling a weird face. Are you in pain?" He laughs while polishing a pint glass.

"Yeah. Because of you. For almost twenty-eight years." I drag my beanie off and throw it at his head. "I'll be in the back if you need me. I'm not on shift, but I've got some admin to do."

His face drops, and he gently places down the glass. "Okay, but I have to warn you...there's going to be an email in your inbox you will not like."

My eyes fall shut as I take a steadying breath, knowing exactly what I'll find.

For months it was radio silence from the owner, and only recently have they given their input. Or ruled with an iron fist more like.

When it was announced we were officially being sold, I thought this was my chance; I'd finally get to showcase my talent and ideas.

Big fat fucking no.

Email after email, the new owner shot me down. And that was before I even mentioned changing the menu.

Can we get a new oven? *It's not within budget.*

Can we hire a second line cook? *The sales don't back this up.*

Can we change our bread supplier? *The current one is cheaper.*

I'm being micromanaged to my last nerve by some faceless idiot sitting behind a desk.

It's becoming harder and harder to let it slide, and with the manic rush of the holidays on the horizon, I'm at the end of my tether. I understand we have budgets, but I want to see the whites of their eyes when they tell me no.

Today's email is hopefully their letter of resignation.

"Don't start a fight with them."

Throwing him a wink, I saunter to the back of the restaurant. "I'll be nothing but cordial."

A couple of minutes later, I'm reading over their email before typing away furiously on the keyboard. I only feel an ounce of remorse toward the recipient of the email, Larry, who is the unfortunate escrow agent responsible for all transactions between the owner and us.

From: l.schumann@js.williams
To: booth.sadler@ourplace.com
Subject: RE: New supplier

Dear Mr. Sadler,

I trust this email finds you well.

After some deliberation, my client has provisionally declined your request to enter into a contract with Ms. Jackson of Just Brew It. Once a review of the supplier's services and quality of goods has been completed, they may reconsider, should everything be found satisfactory.

My client also asks that any future proposed business contracts are to be approved before any verbal agreement is given.

Kind regards,

Larry Schumann - Lead Escrow Agent

JS. Williams Solutions

From: booth.sadler@ourplace.com

To: l.schumann@js.williams

Subject: RE: New supplier

Good morning, Larry,

Please inform your client that Ms. Jackson is a member of the family, and such things do not require approval.

They would know that, had your client familiarized themselves with Our Place's ethos.

Have a good one.

Booth

I've never met Larry, but I suspect he curses me out whenever my emails land in his inbox.

Quinn's a talented baker, reliable, and is hoping to expand her business. Even if she wasn't family, why would we say no? Our current supplier has been tardy for the last few months, and the bread delivered isn't what it used to be.

Too bad I've already canceled the contract with our old supplier and Quinn is set to deliver freshly baked goods to us in the new year.

My smug smile melts off my face when I realize this doesn't change anything for me.

I'll be doing what I always do; cooking from the same menu we've had since the '90s. It's what tourists expect when they spend their vacations here. Lobster rolls. Clam bakes. Bean-hole beans.

I love my job. I love my job. I love my job.

I need to remind myself *why* I love it and to take some control back. I'm the head chef. Not Larry. Not the owner. *Me.*

Excitement bubbles in my chest and my spine straightens as an idea takes root.

Nothing has worked so far, but if they saw a tiny change to the menu, maybe they'd finally show up.

I'm sick of being bossed around through a computer screen.

If they want to say no, they can come here and say it to my face.

I open up the menu saved on the desktop and, without second-guessing myself, delete three of our least popular items and replace them with dishes I've been itching to try out. Bluefin Tuna Tartare, Grilled Swordfish, and a Smoked Tofu Burger.

A grin slowly stretches across my face like a scheming villain when Johanna appears in the doorway. One glance at my expression and she flinches.

"That look is never good. Ew, stop waggling your eyebrows at me like that." She laughs as she settles in the chair across from me.

I give her one last waggle then steeple my fingers under my chin. "Could you arrange a new menu tasting for next week?"

"A new menu tasting?" Her brows rise in surprise. "What have you done?"

Johanna has worked in the industry longer than me, so she knows what I mean.

Leaning back, I shrug. "Something I should have done a

long time ago. I understood why we couldn't make menu changes when the restaurant was struggling, but we're not anymore. Jo," I groan, tone pleading. "I'm *tired* of cooking the same shit every day. It's three items. One of which we trialed on the specials in the spring."

She shakes her head but can't hide her smile. Jo's known me my whole life thanks to our dads being in business together; she's like a second sister. I even dated her little sister, Harriet, until senior year of high school. There isn't much she doesn't know about me; including it's futile trying to convince me once my mind is set.

"You're gonna get in trouble." She sings like we're in the playground.

"Yeah, well, whoever is behind these emails can come to Maine to give me a spanking."

"Gross. Didn't need that visual today." She grimaces before eyeing me skeptically. "Wait...is that why you're doing this? So they show up?"

My mouth hangs open. I don't want to lie, but I can't exactly tell her I'm bored of my job. Plus, it's not a total lie. "Don't tell Pat."

"I'm not lying to him if he asks, Booth."

I wave a hand in her direction. "Fine. Fine."

She hesitates for a beat, studying me closely before she stands. "Leave it with me. If this comes back to bite us, you're taking the blame. I'm not in the mood to piss off Mr. Moneybags when I'm buttering them up for a new dishwasher."

"Oh great. The bar gets spoiled but I can't get a double oven to make my team's life easier." I fold my arms with a *harrumph.*

"Maybe if you were nice to them, you'd get shiny new toys too. Email me over the new menu and I'll print them." She heads toward the door but spins before she reaches it. "I hope you know what you're doing."

"Nope." I kick my feet up on the desk and lean back. "But that's why this is going to be so much fun."

CHAPTER FOUR

alessandra

"You had one job."

I glare at the internet router.

Every Thursday, I meet with my team. We go over upcoming proposals, reflect on recent investments, and check in with each other. Most of them are based in New York, and this is the first meeting we've held virtually.

Everything was going fine until it wasn't. The buffering symbol has been taunting me for an hour, and the service isn't strong enough to connect to my hotspot.

Stupid small towns.

I was already behind thanks to moving last week and Thanksgiving.

Some would call me a workaholic. From the few men I've dated in the past, apparently being career focused is an unattractive trait to have as a woman.

Boohoo, to their masculinity.

Argiros Enterprises is a huge, multinational company. My mother's father started it in the sixties and it quickly grew into the multimillion-dollar organization it is today. We're well known for our chain of boutique hotels across the globe, but we have our hands in a few other pots too.

My parents met when my dad moved to Athens on a whim, working for my grandfather fresh out of college. What started off as a summer romance quickly turned into a transatlantic love story until my *pappoús* gave his blessing for them to wed. They married two months later, and to many people's surprise, Dad took my mom's name. When my father was offered the opportunity to take the company stateside, my mom didn't hesitate to follow him.

We're always looking for new investments, keeping track of up-and-coming markets. Which is where I come in as senior associate. I've traveled the world hunting for new opportunities, and I'm itching to get back out there.

Admitting defeat, I pack up my laptop, headphones, and water bottle before heading downstairs. Living above the bakery was inconvenient at first, but not now I remember they have free Wi-Fi.

Five steps is all it should take for me to enter the bakery. Only I barely make it inside thanks to the line of people backed all the way to the door. It's busy. Really busy. There isn't a free table, and from the frazzled look on Quinn's face, serving customers as quickly as she can, there won't be space for a while.

Stepping back outside, I hike my scarf up over my ears to fight off the bitter temperatures.

While coming up with a new plan, I take in the surrounding buildings.

Mismatched brickwork and brightly colored storefronts line either side of the street. Dark blue state flags flap in the wind. Everywhere you look, there's signage about fresh lobster or fishing trips, a nod to the town's backbone. The streets are quiet, but a few people stroll down the hill toward the sparkling bay.

I've always loved the ocean. After spending my summers on the island of Paros, where my mom was born, the smell of salt air and strong winds blowing through my hair always calms me. Here, it feels different. It's clean and crisp like Greece, but without the stifling heat, you can take in the other scents. The subtle smell of pine, salty tang of low tide, and fresh seafood.

Suddenly I have a hankering for oysters.

I know exactly the place I can get them. It's more spacious than the bakery, but as I make my way toward the redbrick building, I pray it's as busy so I have an excuse not to go in.

The glass door swings open, the bell above my head notifying the hostess of my arrival, and my prayer goes unanswered. It's almost three p.m., so the lunch rush is over, leaving plenty of unoccupied tables.

The decor is exactly what you'd expect to find from a seafood restaurant in coastal New England. The whitewash paneled walls and exposed brick create a rustic vibe, with the fishing gear and vintage photos giving it character and authenticity. The wooden bar is clearly handmade and unique. Everything about the interior is cozy and welcoming.

I straighten when the smiling hostess jogs my way.

"Table for one?" she asks jovially. She's young—fresh out of high school young.

Nodding, I point to a two-seater table adjacent to the bar. "That one would be great, if that's okay?"

"Sure thing." She grabs a menu and escorts me to my seat. "Theresa will be your server today. She'll be right over. I can get you started on a drink now if you know what you want?"

I quickly scan the laminated menu. "I'll get a ginger beer with a slice of lime, no ice, please."

"Perfect. If you need anything, my name is Sandy."

Once seated, I unpack my laptop, connect to the internet, and flinch when I see the number of unread emails. One hour offline and I'm swamped with requests. I dive straight into reading, flagging, forwarding, and responding.

My drink arrives, and I order half a dozen oysters with horseradish ice.

It's easy for me to switch off and give my undivided attention to my work. Within forty minutes, I've conquered almost half of the emails as the noise of customers and silverware fades.

That is until a booming, carefree laugh pulls my attention to behind the bar.

And my eyes land right on Dimples.

I already knew he worked here, so I'm not surprised to see him, but I slump down in my seat, using my laptop as a shield. He's dressed in a fitted gray athletic T-shirt, hair hidden under a backward baseball cap. He chats and jokes with the bar staff, easily making them laugh. His attention snags on the few tables in here and he greets them cheerfully, like old friends.

You wouldn't dare make eye contact with someone on the subway back home. When the server dropped off my food, it was hard not to grimace when she asked me a slew of questions about where I'm from, how long I'm here, and what my plans are.

Small towns are hive inducing.

Booth nudges a man a little older than him and they talk in hushed voices. The other guy pulls out his phone and shows Booth something on the screen, immediately changing his demeanor from happy to pissed. He rips the cap off his head and pulls at his hair in frustration.

"Are you fu—" Booth's eyes dart around the room before his volume drops, but still loud enough for me to hear. "This is the fourth time this month they've bypassed me and gone straight to you, Pat. I'm sick of it."

Subtly, I lean forward to eavesdrop some more. The blond guy—Pat, which I presume is short for Patrick—remains calm.

"Don't worry about it." He lays a hand on Booth's tense shoulder. "I'll email them back and ask them to reconsider."

"I *am* worrying about it. This is *our* restaurant; not theirs. That oven was only two hundred dollars above the budget," Booth seethes. "I'm not sure how much longer I can continue doing this."

Patrick's face drops. "What do you mean?"

Booth shakes away his annoyance. "Nothing. Forget about it." He bends the bill of his hat and fits it back on his head. The movement causes his forearms to flex and I'm ashamed to say I salivate a little as I lean forward to get a better look.

Theresa, my server, chooses that moment to come clear my table.

"How was everything?"

Smiling, I tap the metal bowl filled with empty oyster shells. "They were divine. When were they caught?"

"Oh, I'm not sure." She nibbles her lip. "Let me ask Chef."

Panic sets in. "No, no. It's fine. Don't bother him." For the love of god, don't let him know I'm here.

She smiles, and collects my empty dishes, unblocking my view of Booth.

His lower half is hidden, until he shifts to the right, giving me a glimpse of everything. And I mean *everything*. Tight, black spandex highlights every sinewy muscle, curve, and dip of his thighs, ass, and...bulge. The cycling shorts stop above his knees, showcasing toned calves dusted with dark hair. It's almost unfair that he's able to pull them off. On anyone else, they might look ridiculous.

I realize I'm ogling and turn to find Theresa watching me, watching Booth.

"He's *so* hot. He and my older cousin were in the same class," she says with flushed cheeks.

Voice even, I ask, "Can I get the check, please?"

"Sure?" She juggles the dishes with one hand, while reaching into her apron. The dinging of the bell from the kitchen distracts her, and in slow motion, I watch as she clips the edge of my glass and the fizzy, cloudy liquid spills over my laptop and legs.

The smash of the glass on the floor and my loud "Fuck" draw everyone's attention in my direction. Including a pair of bright blue eyes.

"Oh my god, oh my god. I am *so* sorry." Theresa stares at the mess with wide eyes, lip trembling. This industry is going to eat her alive if she cries over a spilled drink.

The hostess dashes over with hands full of paper towels, and my cheeks heat. Nothing about this is low key.

Ginger beer soaks my jeans, no amount of rice is going to fix my laptop, but all I'm concerned about is getting out of here.

"It's fine. You're fine." I grab some money from my purse—leaving them a generous tip—and stuff my belongings away. Not daring to look up, I throw my coat on and go to hightail it out of here when a tall frame blocks my exit.

"Shit. Are you okay?" Booth asks, concerned.

Poking him in the chest, I huff. "You owe me a new laptop."

He freezes, perplexed, then has the audacity to throw his head back in laughter. "Me? What the hell did I do?"

Shit. I'm basically admitting that his muscles distracted me and that is something that would inflate his ego to an immeasurable size.

Not wanting to look ruffled, I purse my lips.

"Seriously, though." He steps forward. "Leave your details and we can cover any repairs and your dry cleaning bill."

"That's not necessary," I say flatly. "And neither are those shorts."

The dramatic rise and fall of his eyebrows does nothing and slowly his smile disappears. Booth stands there, hands fisted on his hips, proudly jutting out his lower body like a male peacock. "Do you like men who cycle?"

"I prefer my men silent." I cross my arms over my chest, annoyance heating my blood. "Don't you have a job to get back to or the Tour de France?"

"You're funny." He nods down. I raise my chin. "I'm flattered you remember where I work."

This guy.

"Is there something more I can do for you?" I say, ignoring his flirting, just as he goes, "You don't like me, do you?"

I frown at him. "I don't know you."

With a casual shrug, he pulls out his phone. "How about we change that?"

"Oh my god, you're trying to chat me up, even now?" I scoff and step forward, close enough that the scent of his body wash and something smoky fills my nose. "The dimples didn't work on me. This isn't working on me. And whatever you have planned next *definitely* won't work on me. Quit while you're ahead."

A coy grin stretches across his face. "You didn't forget about my dimples. That says something."

"Good lord. Is there a repellent I need to buy to get rid of you?" I step back until there's a healthy amount of space between us. "You're insufferable."

"My mom says it's endearing. Plus, you intrigue me."

"Become *un*-intrigued. Fast." He doesn't budge as I skirt around him. "Goodbye, Booth."

"Hey, hey. At least tell me your name." He cocks his head.

He could've easily asked Martin for my name the other night, and there's a morsel of respect that he didn't.

Ugh. Why am I still standing here?

"That's not going to happen," I tell him bluntly.

"All right then. I'll take a guess." He taps a finger on his chin, gaze tracking me from head to toe, only to linger on my face. His obvious perusal makes my skin tingle, and I absolutely shouldn't care what's going on in that dumb brain of his. "How about...Silver?"

My mask of indifference slips. "*Silver*? Why would you call me that?"

"Your eyes. They're beautiful. The way they shone in the sun that day..." Shaking his head like he's getting carried away, he rubs his palms together. Dare I say, I detect a little bashfulness.

A bit of my armor falls away at his compliment. The irony of the nickname isn't lost on me. Not that he'd know that. Goddammit, he's making me soft. "I was half expecting a cheesy pickup line."

"Well, I was going to save them for our date."

"There will be no date," I correct and take another step toward freedom.

"But I suppose you've earned it," he continues, like I haven't spoken, following me toward the door. "Is your dad a robber? Because he must have stolen those stars in your eyes..."

His voice fades as my face drops, spine going ramrod straight. It's a silly reaction and I'm quick to brush it off, just not quick enough.

Worry riddles Booth's features, and he takes a tentative step forward. "Shit, did I say something wrong? That was insensitive of me. I should know better tha—"

My hand shoots up, halting his apology. "I appreciate you coming by the other night to check on me. I should have said thank you. I'm not trying to be rude, but nothing I've said so far seems to work. You're not my type. I'm only here short term. I'm busy. Understood?"

It's like shouting at a naughty puppy with the way his shoulders deflate, though I think it's more to do with the fact he thinks he's upset me than the rejection. As much as I want to shut this conversation down, I can't leave him thinking that.

Hoping to ease his mind, I soften my voice. "My dad is *not* a robber. He works in private equity and will probably never retire. But seriously, this"—I gesture between us—"is never happening."

I could probably do with getting laid. It's been a couple of months, and the last guy I was with had his head so far up his ass he forgot to locate my clitoris.

Booth has nice hands. I bet he'd find it.

No, no, no, no, no.

This isn't on the agenda.

The hopeful gleam in his eyes eases my guilt and worries me. Clearly nothing I say is going to deter him and now I regret being nice. It has no benefits. He's like a pesky bug. A very handsome bug.

"You know what they say…" he drawls.

"No. I don't. And neither do you. Don't say it. Don't be that guy." I'm practically begging as I point a finger at him in warning, which he ignores.

"Never say never."

CHAPTER FIVE

booth

THE LAST THING I SEE IS HER WILD MANE OF CURLS WHIPPING IN the wind before she disappears from view.

Should annoying her get me hard?

Patrick watches me with amusement.

"Who was that?" he asks, brow raised.

"No one." Eyes lowered, I run my hand along the bar.

It was one of the first things installed and handcrafted by my father and George, who spent hours collecting and salvaging driftwood they found washed up on the shores of Piper Beach. I was too young to remember it being built, but Patrick says he learned a lot of new swear words that year.

He considers me for a beat before his eyes pop out of his head and he bellows with laughter. "Holy shit. That's the girl from the fair, isn't it? I can't wait to tell Graham. Booth with a crush. How fucking adorable."

"It's not a *crush,* you prick. I wanted to...ask her a question." He sees right through my lie.

"Was the question 'Why don't you like my dimples, *wah wah*?'" Then, he gapes at me and gestures to my outfit. "Is this why you're wearing this atrocious getup?"

I avert my gaze. "I was gonna go for a ride."

"Bullshit," he hisses. "You're trying to impress her with the bike shorts, aren't you?"

I cough into my fist—barely muffling my "Fuck off" —before storming away. Statistics have proven that women like my bike shorts. Did I put them on today in the hopes I'd bump into her? Perhaps.

I'm headed toward the kitchen when Jules, our assistant manager, waves me down.

"Hey, do you know the woman who just left?" She points toward the table Silver vacated.

"Umm, yes?" *Kinda.*

"Great." She shoves something into my chest. "Give this back to her, would you? She must have left it in her rush to get out of here. Tell her we have her dry cleaning bill covered too."

She disappears, leaving me to stare at the small wallet in my hand. I continue to study it as I walk through the swinging doors, the aromas and heat hitting me all at once. Simon nods at me before returning his attention to Kyle, our line cook and newest hire. His skills aren't where we need them to be and from the frustrated sigh Simon releases, he's fed up already.

I'd be more patient if his attitude didn't stink and he wasn't continuously late.

I stand outside the large walk-in refrigerator, tossing the wallet up in the air.

Surely the waitstaff has to look at the ID whenever they're handed a lost wallet or purse? Slowly, I slide out a card until the edge of a driver's license appears, and I pause.

I feel slimy.

With anyone else, this would be normal, but it feels invasive considering she wants nothing to do with me. Deciding I have no other choice—and curiosity eats away at me—I reveal a New York driver's license. Then, her name.

Alessandra Argiros.

Of course her name is sexy.

I bet it would sound just as good coming from my mouth.

You look pretty today, Alessandra.

Why don't you like my dimples, Alessandra?

Get on your knees, Alessandra.

Yeah, it definitely has a ring to it.

I recall her comment about her stay here being short term.

How long is short? Long enough for me to get on her good side?

If I allowed myself to think rationally, I'd reason with myself that this is ridiculous. That I'm wasting my time.

Suddenly a crash sounds from the front of the kitchen, followed by a flourish of *"Fucks."*

I peek my head around the corner to find Kyle surrounded by cooking oil.

I absolutely do not have the time.

But I've never been one to turn down a challenge.

"PHONE BOOTH, YOUR HAIR IS WAY TOO LAME FOR YOU TO HAVE SO many styling products."

"You fucking take that back." My cry of protest meets my sister's cackles. "And cut it out with that dumb nickname."

Florence tagged along after I moved out of my mom's this evening—something I now regret.

Sitting on the water's edge, my little boathouse overlooks the bay, with the ocean breeze cutting through the air and whistling against the navy blue panels. My grandfather left it to my dad, who then passed it to me and my siblings, and we all decided it was a good place for me to live after college. It's a stone's throw away from the restaurant, rent-free, and personally, I think it has the best view in the whole town.

A "house" is being rather generous—it's basically one big room, with a kitchen and tiny bathroom. There's enough space for a king-size bed, sofa, and an eighty-five-inch TV. Rich mahogany floorboards and off-white paneled walls have spruced the small space up. The lower, outside level is full of old fishing gear and our family's fishing boat, while my level is elevated by reinforced stilts.

It's cold as balls this time of year, even with the extra insulation Dex installed. If the winters ever get too harsh, he lets me crash at one of his cabins or I stay with my family.

"Do you still wear your retainer?" Florence hollers from the bathroom.

"Get out of my things!"

She struts in, blonde bob bouncing with her steps.

"Ew." Florence shudders. "Please take off those vile shorts."

I glance down, frowning. "The ladies love it."

Like me and my brothers, Florence is tall. Once a gangly kid, she eventually grew into her long limbs. A septum piercing decorates her nose, along with an array of necklaces and rings around her neck and fingers.

I finish putting away the groceries my mom shoved in my arms before I left and pull out two beers, offering one to Flo. Twisting the caps off, we collapse onto the tan chesterfield.

"How long are you planning to stay with Mom?" I ask before taking a long pull of beer.

She blows over the lip of her bottle, creating a tuneless melody. "How long is a piece of string? Too long and we butt heads. I need a job, though..."

"We have some casual shifts going at the restaurant?"

She grimaces, making me laugh.

"Front of house, don't worry."

When Florence was thirteen, she convinced our dad to let

her do a shift as a dishwasher. Safe to say she isn't cut out for a culinary career. My sister is less involved with Our Place—she prefers it that way—but we still like to run stuff by her and keep her informed. She spent the last eighteen months traveling around South and Central America and wasn't due home until the spring. Mom's accident apparently cut her trip short, though I sense there's more to the story.

"A couple of shifts now and again won't help me get an apartment." Her hand swishes through the air. "Forget it. I'll work something out. Have you pissed off the new owner much lately?"

"Meh. I never know if they're actually angry because everything comes through Larry. I like to think they have a Voodoo doll of me by their bedside." I lean in close, lowering my voice as if we're not the only two people in my house, and whisper, "I'm changing the menu."

The liquid in her bottle sloshes as she dives forward, eyes wide. "Wait? What? How?"

"The *when* is next week." Florence's mouth opens to say something, but I cut her off. "I know what you're going to say. However, what they don't know won't kill them. It's my kitchen. Our restaurant. And I've had it up to here"—I hold two fingers to my forehead—"with them bossing me around. Plus, the menu has needed a face-lift for years. It's dated and I'm..."

Tired.

Bored.

Disheartened.

"...done with them thinking they have a say."

Her next words surprise me; mostly because Florence is the biggest troublemaker. "I don't know, Booth. Do you really want to do that? It's funny sending them sassy emails but going over their head? I don't want us to be in a position like we were in February."

Shit.

For my siblings and me, the restaurant is one of the last things we have left of our dad. From her distressed expression, she's worried. She wasn't here when we were told about the threat of being sold. I was. The constant worry that memories of Dad could be snatched out from under us kept me up at night because I felt like I'd failed him.

We weren't making money. Competitors were outselling us. Stock increased in price. And we remained stagnant.

It was the reason I pushed to change the menu for months prior; confident it would help get new customers in and attract tourists from the larger neighboring towns. Did anyone listen?

No. Because no one took me seriously.

"It'll be fine, Flo. Some harmless fun." I clink my bottle with hers. "The restaurant is safe, don't worry."

The sigh she lets out isn't reassuring. Her eyes stay trained on the label she's peeled to shreds. "Do you ever feel you don't know where life is heading?"

All the fucking time, I'm tempted to say. "You've only been back a week. Cut yourself some slack. It'll all fall into place."

She nods slowly, the weight on her shoulders lifting slightly.

After she leaves, I grab a quick shower, throw on some thermals, and step out onto the short balcony framing the house. There isn't a star in sight. Tiny snowflakes dance down from the sky to catch the light, glittering like fallen stars until they melt into the pitch-black waters.

Do you ever feel you don't know where life is heading?

Closing my eyes, I imagine myself standing at a fork in the road. The path on the left keeps my family's business safe. The other is one I forgot I'd mapped out, losing sight of it the day we lost Dad.

I'm proud of what I've accomplished, of the respect I've gained from my team, and the reputation I've built for myself. Was working in a small-town restaurant always my dream?

No.

The plan was to develop my skills, expand my knowledge, and push the limits of my capabilities. Once I felt confident enough, I'd apply for jobs outside of my hometown. I wasn't aiming high, like LA or New York, but somewhere customers' food palettes went beyond clam chowder and blueberry pie.

My dream was to curate taster menus, experiment with ingredients from all around the world, and shadow chefs who have worked in Europe, Asia, and Africa.

The number of people who know about this dream? One.

Me.

My reason for changing the menu isn't to piss the owner off —that's a bonus—but to find an output for the creativity threatening to burst out of me like a volcano. The last thing I want is to resent the place that was my first stepping-stone, where my feet have always landed safely, and laughter and happiness encompass me.

It's easier if everyone thinks the reason for my insubordination is to cause trouble.

All they see is me smiling and cracking jokes.

When really, my legs are kicking below the surface, waiting for a break in the current.

If I don't find it soon, I'm scared I'll drown.

CHAPTER SIX

alessandra

Where the hell is it?

I flip over the cushions of the sofa for the third time, searching for my little compact wallet.

I've already called the grocery store, they said they couldn't locate it. I remember having it after my store run three days ago. I hardly go anywhere, so where—

"Fuck." My eyes clamp shut as the cushion bounces off the floor in frustration.

Our Place is the last building I want to step foot in today, especially since I've been working before the sun rose. I'm not in the mood to speak to anyone, let alone have another run-in with Booth Sadler. Every interaction with him has been confusing. One second, I want to wipe his smug grin off his face, and the next, I want to...*not.*

I'm seriously debating ordering a new set of cards and driver's license when another email pings from my laptop. My head snaps in its direction, curls getting caught in my lashes. I swipe them away as I make my way over to the small dining table where I've been working all day.

Thanks to the time difference with our European offices, I

was bombarded with last-minute requests to review proposals in the middle of the night. I'd planned on giving them my feedback and responses until I got distracted by something I shouldn't have. Which seems to be the theme of this trip.

The time on the top right of the screen tells me it's past nine at night.

The restaurant closes soon, so maybe the chance of seeing Dimples is low. Weighing up the odds, I slip on my black boots, wrap a thick wool scarf around my neck to keep my hair contained, and throw on my coat.

Cold wind nips at my skin and I almost lose my footing on the slick sidewalk. There's been no fresh snow for days, and the ground is basically solid ice. Taking each step with caution, it doubles the time to walk down the incline of Robin Road and to reach my destination. The redbrick building stands out against the snow, and the navy blue paint glistens under the streetlamp, with its glossy white lobster sitting below the lettering.

I'll be in and out in five minutes, max.

A blast of warm air fights away the cold. Two sets of eyes dart my way. Patrick from the other day, and a blonde woman who rounds the bar to greet me.

"Hey, I'm so sorry, we're actually closing soon," she says softly, smiling politely.

My smile doesn't reach my eyes like hers. "I'm not here to eat. I think I left my wallet here last week."

"Oh, sure, lemme check. We keep a log of all lost-and-found." She returns to the bar, and I follow.

"It was on Thursday." Turning, I point toward the table along the exposed brick wall. "Right over there."

She pulls out a book and flips through the pages. "Hmm, I'm not seeing anything. Let me go check in the back. Wait here."

As the minutes pass, I get more antsy. The last table is

closing their bill when the blonde comes back, steps hurried and with a different smile on her face. This one is stiff, forced almost.

"Umm, would you mind coming to the office?" she asks. "I'm Johanna, by the way."

"To the office?" My head tilts in question.

"Yeah, it's, uh, policy. We have to verify it's you." She turns and shakes her head, muttering something under her breath.

It doesn't take a genius to guess what's happening, and despite my annoyance, I'm intrigued to see where this goes. Rather than question her, she leads the way to the back of the restaurant.

We stop outside what I presume is the office. Her hand hovers above the handle and she pins me with an apologetic look. "I really am sorry about this."

"That sounds really ominous, you know that, right?"

Sighing, her head drop forward. "Yeah. I know."

"Johanna"—I gently nudge her out of the way—"I'm pretty sure I know what's behind that door. Or *who*, for that matter."

She winces, but there's a quirk to her lips. "I'm not sure if that makes it better or worse."

"You know him well?" I unravel my scarf and unbutton my coat, handing them to her. I'm not wearing anything special, just a pair of black skinny jeans, heeled boots, and an off-the-shoulder knitted sweater.

"Unfortunately. Why?"

"Tell me something that'll put me at an advantage. What's his weakness?"

She chuckles. "I like you. What did you say your name was again?"

"I didn't." I don't mean for it to come out so bluntly. Luckily, she doesn't appear fazed.

"Touché. Well, he's always the one making the moves—so I suggest playing him at his own game." She winks at me.

"About time someone did. Use that big fat ego of his against him."

Without another word, I twist the handle and saunter into the small office with a confident stride.

As suspected, my eyes lock with a pair of blue ones, glittering with mischief.

Booth sits behind a large oak desk, hands tucked behind his head, wearing a lopsided grin.

He's a good-looking man. Very good looking. And he knows it.

Time to change tactics.

"Hello, *Alessandra*." The subtle purr in his voice should not send goose bumps rippling across my skin, nor have my tummy swooping low like I'm on a roller coaster.

Pushing the door shut with my butt, our gazes stay locked until we're trapped inside. My smile is sly, not wanting to give him the upper hand.

"I hadn't expected to see you tonight. What a surprise." My steps continue until I stand in front of the desk.

"A pleasant surprise or..." His arms drop to the desk and he leans forward.

"That's yet to be determined." I mirror his movement and place my palms on the cool, polished wood. My sweater gapes open, giving him a direct view of my cleavage, and I give myself one point when his eyes fall to my chest.

We're playing a reckless game of chess. He thinks the game is set. Little does he know the queen is the most powerful piece of them all. He can make whatever moves he wants. It won't be him saying checkmate at the end.

"You have something of mine?" My voice is low, and with the tip of my finger, I trace the sharp edge of the desk as I stalk around it, stopping when I'm less than a foot away from him.

I mark another tally under my name when his face flashes in surprise.

Today, he's in his chef uniform.

It's annoying how well he pulls it off.

The short sleeves of the crisp white chef jacket cling to his biceps, displaying his bronzed skin. The material around his torso and shoulders is baggy, but there's no hiding his broad chest and tapered waist. Somehow, the black and red bandanna keeping his chestnut brown locks back makes him even more attractive.

He digs into the front pocket of his pants, widening his legs as he does, and holds up my wallet between two fingers.

"This?" He reaches between us, offering it to me. Instead of taking it, I brush his hand aside and step between his open thighs, forcing him to look up at me. This is the closest we've been. From here, I see the muscles in his neck pulling taut as he swallows, the glistening of his lips when his tongue darts out, and the flare of desire across his features.

It's pointless denying I'm attracted to him. He's a distraction I can't tune out.

"Your license tells me you're thirty." He licks his lips. "Three years my senior. I happen to love older women."

I fight the urge to roll my eyes. Bending at the waist, my curls drop, surrounding us in a curtain of dark swirls. If I were to lean forward an inch, my lips would meet his. It would be dangerous for so many reasons, and he's none the wiser.

His chest rises and falls in quick succession, hot breath blowing through my hair.

This is becoming *too* fun. And it needs to end before it goes too far.

"Are you going to kiss me, Silver?" The hairs along my arms stand to attention at his cool, seductive tone.

"Do you want me to?" I whisper. "If you do, all you have to say is 'please.'"

He raises his chin, our mouths now a hair's breadth apart. "I don't beg, baby. But I bet you'd look fucking stunning doing it."

My body betrays me. Heat pools low and my nipples pucker.

But I still have the upper hand.

As if to taunt him one final time, my lips move to the right, ghosting over the spot I know his precious dimple hides. "If you expect me to get on my knees, you're more deluded than I thought, Booth Sadler. This is a game you will not win. Believe me."

I pluck the leather wallet from his grip and drag the corner down his smooth, defined jaw, triggering a shiver. There's an obvious bulge testing the confines of his pants.

My smile arches wickedly. "Better you give up now."

His dilated pupils eat up his icy irises. They draw me in, like a strong tide at midnight. Everyone knows not to go swimming once it goes dark, so before I can get swept away, I withdraw.

He doesn't move from his seat as I walk away. The burn of his gaze follows me across the room to the door.

With a brief glance over my shoulder, my tone less playful, I give him a final warning. "Don't underestimate me. I'm not some tourist you can pick up, play around with, and forget. There isn't a game I haven't won, and I have a feeling you won't like it when I show my true colors. Forfeit now while you're ahead. Please."

That final syllable slips out, shaking the black and white board we're playing on.

The pieces are tipping, dangerously close to resigning.

As I nod at Johanna on my way out of the restaurant after collecting my things, I can't tell if it's the king or the queen.

CHAPTER SEVEN

booth

"If my taste buds could orgasm, they would."

I grimace along with my brothers as my sister finishes her bite of tuna tartare, smacking her lips together with gusto.

"Never say that again while I'm alive." Patrick pretends to gag.

"Ditto," Graham mumbles.

Laid out along one of the two large wooden tables in the restaurant are half a dozen plates—empty and virtually licked clean. The menus are updated, ready to go out for tomorrow's lunch service. Today's team tasting allows for any final feedback on flavors and presentation, and is also a good excuse for us all to hang out.

We closed a couple of hours early for the occasion, and everyone—including my mom and Johanna's dad, George—was here. Most of the staff have headed over to the town's one and only bar, where we'll join them soon.

After that scene with Alessandra in the office, it's clear I need to get out of my head.

I'm not some tourist you can pick up, play around with, and forget.

Her proximity shouldn't have affected me the way it did. Neither should her rich scent; a little sweet and arousingly feminine. Fitting. She played me like a fiddle, and I walked right into her trap, handing her the bow.

But dammit, it was fun. A tiny glimpse of her perky tits had all blood rushing south. When she leaned in, and those curls I'm desperate to get my fingers tangled in crowded us and her plump lips grazed my cheek, I about died. By the time my brain rebooted, she was halfway across the room, leaving me with a warning and a raging hard-on.

I'm sadistic, because I thickened even more at her sassy threat.

Even thinking about her sultry voice turns me on.

"Booth!" a chorus of people holler.

My eyes dart up to find everyone staring at me.

"What?" My cheeks heat.

I really need to get laid.

"Your mom asked you a question," Johanna responds.

I turn to the petite woman at the opposite end of the table and gift her the smile that's been getting me out of trouble for years. "Yeah, Ma?"

The same color eyes as mine narrow at me, and the blonde-gray bob bounces as she shakes her head. "I said, what was the owner's response to the menu change?"

Ah, shit.

"Oooh, you're in trouble," Dex whispers next to me, earning him an elbow to the gut.

With a worried look at Johanna, I flare my eyes slightly, as if to say, *What do we do?* My gaze moves to Patrick, who's wearing a shit-eating grin. Florence is no help, too distracted by her phone, and Graham is too busy staring down at a cheerful Quinn tucked into his side. The possessive prick hasn't taken his hands off her all night.

With a tug on the waistband of my metaphorical big boy pants, I tell her the truth. Or half.

"They haven't shared their thoughts yet."

"Interesting," she murmurs. "When did you ask them?"

I swallow, noting how talk around the table has ceased. "Ask? Umm, it was more of a courtesy email." *That is yet to be drafted.*

"Booth." My mom's tone is serious. Not even her favorite smile is going to save me.

Admitting defeat, I throw down the dishrag that's been hanging from my shoulder. "The new dishes have a much better margin—ask Graham."

My brother glares at me from behind his glasses. "Do not drag me into your messes."

"Booth," she warns again.

"They don't know," I grit out, sulking like a schoolboy being punished.

My response doesn't surprise her. Claire Sadler is all-knowing, and very scary when you get on the wrong side of her. What's worse, however, is that she doesn't look mad or disappointed—which is arguably worse—she looks sympathetic.

I know turning down my ideas was hard for her, and right now I feel a fucking fool for going about it like this.

She glances down at the table, smiling softly. "These were some of the best dishes you've ever created. Delicious." Everyone echoes her praises. "I'm sure if you'd have told the owner, they would have considered."

"Doubtful." I fold my arms across my chest, feeling very exposed and self-conscious suddenly. "I'll pull the new menu and we can stick to what we know. Thanks anyway, I'm glad you liked them. "

"It's a bit late for that now." I stare at my mom in confusion. It's not too late whatsoever. "You've made your bed now, Booth. Best you make yourself comfortable and lie in it."

We all freeze, sharing a *what-the-fuck-is-she-on-about* look.

"Umm, okay?" I tread carefully, worried it's another trap. Women have been ensnaring me all week.

She turns from the table, grabbing her coat from the rack by the front door. "Okay. It's getting late. I'm excited to see what the customers think. See you all tomorrow."

"I know you'll do the right thing." George claps me on the back, making his exit too.

After a beat, I shake myself out of my confused daze. "What the fuck was that?"

Florence is the first to speak. "I don't know, but it was scary. I for sure thought she was going to hang you by the balls, Boothy."

"It sounded like she gave you permission to be disobedient," Graham replies. "Which you *shouldn't*. You piss off the owner too much, they could disown us at the drop of a hat."

My brother's words remind me of Flo's concerns the other day, who is currently gnawing at her lip. I know what she'd do.

Quinn's eyes widen when we direct our attention her way. "You want my opinion?" she squeaks.

"Duh, you're family," Flo responds and tugs a now teary-eyed Quinn into a hug.

"Oh. Um." She glances at Graham, who, to his credit, doesn't attempt to sway her. "I...don't like the pressure. Can I be Switzerland?"

Laughing, I look at Johanna, who doesn't need me to ask what she's thinking. "I saw how well the specials you came up with did earlier in the year. Everyone deservers to see what a talented chef you are."

Patrick is next, and he doesn't pull his punches. "There's a smarter way to go about this, and as much as I don't want to risk what we just saved...it feels like we need to take back a bit of ownership. We should have changed the menus in the spring. Do it." He nods once.

"We have a tie," I point out.

When a decision needed to be made on whether we should accept the current owner's offer, all the Sadler and Thomas kids had input, along with our parents. Which included Harriet, Johanna's younger sister.

"Jo, any chance you can get Harry on the phone?"

She shakes her head. "She's performing tonight."

We all turn to Dex, who blows out a breath. He fiddles with his hearing aid and winces when the feedback whistles in his ear. Since losing the hearing in one ear when he was a teenager, it's been a big transition for him. We all face him fully and speak clearly when we're together, which he always appreciates.

"No pressure then," he jokes as he scrubs a hand over his buzz cut. "I'm tired of not knowing who runs this place. The same place that's been like a second home to me, as it has for all of you."

A weight pushes down on my chest, stalling my breath. What started out as a bit of childish fun has turned into something more.

"I say we change the menu. I can't imagine they'd pull the plug over something so small." His words appear to ease the worry written on Florence and Graham's faces. He pauses, the dramatic bastard, then his lips curve deviously as we wait with bated breath. "Let's smoke him out."

AN HOUR LATER, WE'RE ALL PACKED AROUND TWO HIGH-TOP tables in Shirley's—the anonymous owner still the topic of conversation.

Shirley's has been around since before I was born and is the spot to go for a drink with friends after work or to celebrate a special milestone over a lukewarm beer. It's rough around the edges, the paint is peeling, the staff is unwelcoming, but it's an institution. It also wouldn't be what it is without Lenny, the owner, chasing us out of the building after the last call.

"You really think a couple of new menu items are going to have them revealing their identity?" Patrick challenges.

Jo peers up at him. "He's had it out for Booth the last couple of months. I'm confident they'll take the bait."

A palm slaps on the table, drawing all our attention to Florence. "Excuse me. All evening you've presumed it's a dude. What if it's a woman? This is the twenty-first century, fellas."

I hold up my hands in apology. "Very true. Regardless, I'm not sure this will lure them out."

"We could serve customers naked on rollerblades. That would get their attention." My sister chuckles to herself, oblivious to the straight faces staring back at her.

"One step at a time." Dex knocks his big shoulder into Florence. "Keep it in your pants for now, little Sadler."

She rolls her eyes. "Quit it with the nickname, you oaf. I'm bored with this now. Let's talk Christmas." Her face turns animated, and she rubs her hands together like a big kid.

"Christmas will be canceled if that storm rolls in like they're predicting," Graham throws in.

Like a bunch of retirees, we chat about the weather for longer than necessary. Dex goes to order in one more round, and Graham and Quinn take the opportunity to sneak out. Since reuniting, they've been inseparable. I peek a glance at Pat and Jo, who have been joined at the hip since they could walk.

While Graham's relationship is new, Jo and Pat have been dancing around each other for years. They were inevitable. After Jo left town unexpectedly, Patrick closed a part of himself off, until she returned earlier this year and they reunited.

Witnessing the way both my brothers found a new form of happiness, all because of the women in their lives, has me questioning things.

Am I really happy? When I've lost the passion for my job and have no one to share my life with?

On the outside, I'm the funny guy, always cracking jokes to lighten the mood. Easygoing and happy to go with the flow. Never one to cause a fuss. Or to be taken too seriously.

Only, since my family and friends have verbally backed my decision, I'm filled with nerves and regret. Nerves because what if they're blowing smoke up my ass, and customers hate the new dishes? Regret because what if this isn't what I want?

The cracking of pool balls colliding together pulls me from my thoughts, and I mentally shake myself.

I'm here, because it's what Dad would have wanted.

He's not around to do it anymore and I need to protect this place.

So, with a smile on my face, hoping no one sees the cracks I've been covering for way too long, I return to the conversation, poke fun at Patrick, and all feels right in the universe.

Hindsight is a wonderful thing, but foresight is better.

Sadly, I lack both.

CHAPTER EIGHT

alessandra

THE CANVAS LEERS AT ME. THE PATCHES OF WHITE PEEKING OUT between the layers of purple and blue taunt me.

Throw in the incessant notifications coming from my phone and my laptop, it feels like I'm about to be sucked into a thankless void.

I fling myself from the stool, frustrated, hungry, and tired.

I *love* my job. In my senior year of high school, I knew I wanted to work with my family. During my sophomore year at college, my penchant for business strategies and investments began. To this day, I can't imagine myself doing anything else.

My mom has always been proud of my brothers and me. From an early age she instilled the importance of having an ambition outside of academia and later our careers.

For me, that's painting.

It's my escape.

A silent, colorful way to release my emotions. A fantastic ruin of colors when I'm sad or angry and a beautiful landscape of tranquility when I'm happy.

Without it, I'd lose myself in the landslide of emails, the

conference calls filled to the brim with testosterone, and work trips that take me from east to west, then back again.

So long as I had a way to burn off energy when things got too stressful, all was fine. Since Thanksgiving, I haven't painted a single thing. Which means, when I'm not working, I'm thinking.

Thinking is dangerous.

The longer I sit here with my thoughts, the more confident I grow that this is a huge mistake.

I'm not someone to concede defeat. If I set my sights on something, that's that. No excuses. If there's a start, I'll find the finish.

Stepping foot in Sutton Bay wasn't even the start of my race. I'm way past the halfway point. It isn't a straight line to the finish either. There are unplanned hurdles. Bends in the road I'm scared to turn.

My shoe-box apartment is suddenly too small.

The people of this town alarm me, and there is no place to hide. No one knows me, because why should they? I've made no attempt to form friendships. Quinn from the bakery has tried to make small talk with me. Johanna waved at me from across the street the other day. The town's local chef is a relentless flirt with his sights set on me. The idea of getting to know them has my head swimming.

The four walls stifle me, and before I know it, I'm wrapped up in layers, and walking the streets, desperate for a sign.

After almost an hour, the only signs I have are frostbitten fingers as I wander the small park aimlessly. Most of the trees are bare, their naked branches twisting and curling up into the sky. The evergreen pines offer a splash of color to the bleak gray and white surroundings.

I still have no clue what I'm doing, but the cold air calms me.

I'm heading back up the hill toward my apartment when

my phone rings. Pulling off my gloves with my teeth, I dig into the deep pockets of my coat and see my mom's name. I swear the woman has a sixth sense because I could really do with her guidance.

"*Yassou*, Mama," I greet.

She's silent for a beat before saying, "I do not like your tone. What is wrong?"

I'd laugh at her impressive intuition if I wasn't about to unravel out of my skin. My voice comes out strained. "I think I'm in over my head."

Avoiding the happy couples and families as they pass me by in a blur, my footsteps slow as I near the restaurant.

"Alessandra, it's you who decided to be there. No one else." My mother isn't lecturing me, just pointing out the obvious. Coming to Sutton Bay was my idea. And what have I got to show for my time here so far?

Zilch.

"Your father says you've been working a lot. Maybe a break would be good?"

Annoyance flares.

"What else is there to do? I can't paint. I've spoken to no one. Work is the only thing keeping me sane." The volume of my voice gets the attention of a few passersby, and I tug my scarf up over my chin.

"Keeping you sane or keeping you from doing what you went there to do?"

I hate that she's always right.

"I'm going to be honest with you, thisavré mou," she continues. "Your decision to go there surprised me. Especially after what happened last year..." She doesn't need to go into detail. We both know what happened. I trusted a stranger with the most vulnerable parts of me and they tossed it aside without a second-guess. "Nobody would blame or judge you for not wanting to search further. But you did. Because you are determined, strong-willed, and wonderfully courageous. Sometimes I envy you for it."

My voice clogs with emotion. "But?"

"No buts. That is all." She's so matter of fact. "You like goals, targets, deadlines, yes?"

My brows scrunch. "Yeah..."

"One month. You make no progress, you come home. That is my final offer."

There's a huff in the background, letting me know my dad is a witness to my mother's negotiation, though I wouldn't be surprised if he had some involvement.

They were both weary of me coming here. This time however, my expectations are below ground level. I won't be making the mistake of giving out my trust blindly again.

One month gives me until the middle of January.

Is that enough time?

I come to an abrupt halt when I see Martin Willis step out of Our Place across the street. I haven't seen him since Thanksgiving evening.

In the light of day, I properly take him in. He's tall—well over six feet—and slender. His head is covered with an ushanka hat, hiding the thick, black hair peppered with gray I caught a glimpse of the other week. One word to describe him: distant. You can see it in the way he walks, in his eyes, how he talks. Purposefully, he keeps himself detached from everyone else. Not too much that he's completely aloof, considering he's a property manager and produce supplier, but enough that tells a story.

"Are you still there?" My mother's voice interrupts my thoughts.

"Yes. Sorry, sorry," I reply, but my mind wanders again.

Martin stares at something through the window for a long while, piquing my curiosity, before walking away. Once he disappears up the hill, I cross the street, wanting to know what caught his attention.

"So, you will leave if nothing happens by then?"

"Umm..." I'm not sure why I'm hesitant, when the idea of leaving was so appealing minutes ago. "Mama, let me call you back, okay?"

"Hmm. I will hold you to that. *S' agapó.*" *I love you.*

"Bye, Mama. S' agapó."

I hang up, stand in the spot Martin vacated, then snort when I see what he was looking at.

A menu.

Honestly, I must be bored if I was hoping for something more exciting. The white card sits nicely in the display case, pristine and bold.

Now, I'm hungry. The food I had the other week was delicious. I could definitely eat. My eyes scan the menu, contemplating what to have when something doesn't look right.

Tuna tartare?

That's one of my favorite meals. I wouldn't have turned that down for oysters.

The longer I scrutinize each item, realization sinks in.

This is not the same menu I was given during my first visit.

The doubt that sat heavy in the pit of my stomach earlier switches to rage.

I spent so long proving myself in my career, and while I'm swimming in new territory, I refuse to be trivialized here. Let alone by a smooth-talking, jokester of a man whose biggest concern is the dents in his cheeks.

With heated determination, I whip the restaurant door open and go on the hunt to prove why my true colors burn red, orange, and yellow.

I'm done being underestimated, especially by Booth Sadler.

CHAPTER NINE

booth

THE SHARP UNDERSIDE OF THE PASS DIGS INTO MY PALMS AS I clutch the edge of the stainless steel.

Gloria was the only chef I ever worked for, and for a woman who reminded me of my grandmother, she had a bite like a rottweiler if you didn't do what she said. When promoted, I promised myself I wouldn't be your typical jackass of a head chef who threw his weight around and demanded respect rather than earning it.

That's why, despite Kyle's tremendous fuckup, I remain calm.

Even though this is the third serving of crab cakes he's overcooked tonight.

"Kyle." My voice carries over the clatter of pans. "A word?"

From the other end of the kitchen, his resounding sigh has my jaw twitching in annoyance. The cracking noise isn't from my knuckles, but my molars grinding together as my last ounce of patience wears thin.

We're too slammed for you to lose your cool now, Booth.

"Today, please, Kyle." My words are pinched as I prompt him.

The sound of his shoes slapping against the linoleum floor lets me know he's taking his sweet-ass time. He sidles up next to me, bristling, his tone bored. "What?"

Breathe. Breathe. Breathe.

"Ten minutes ago I told you *this*"—I slide the entrée in front of him—"is not acceptable. The first time you said it was a mistake. The second you blamed the fryer. What's the excuse this time?"

We stare each other down. His white chef jacket is stained already. Has it been cleaned since his last shift?

An arrogant twitch of his lips leaves my calm exterior crumbling. "Maybe the crab cakes were made poorly, *Chef.*"

He knows I prepped those crab cakes this morning.

After he forgot to do it last night.

Service continues around us, and Simon covers me as I stand off with Kyle. My sous is equally as tired as I am with our line cook's attitude.

The sound of the door swinging on its hinges has Kyle's attention redirected, and his expression shifts to confusion.

I may not be a hotheaded boss who rules his kitchen by screaming and smashing plates in a tantrum, but I'm also not a pushover.

Stiffly, I say, "If you're not serious about being here, we can have a talk in my office."

"*Your* office?"

My mood instantly changes. That velvet-wrapped voice has the hairs on the back of my neck standing to attention. A grin spreads across my lips slowly as I turn to the woman whose gaze is ready to flambé me.

God, she's sexy when mad.

"Hello, Silver," I drawl. Kyle's mistake is quickly forgotten, along with the endless row of tickets we have.

Alessandra doesn't budge when a server walks in with an

armful of dirty dishes. Unlike me, they have some sense, because they retreat slowly when they see her expression.

"Who do you think you are?" she snaps, the ringlets resting over her chest vibrating with her quick breathing.

Laughing is not wise. "Is this a trap? It feels like a trap."

"I don't think it's a trap," Simon whispers behind me. "Maybe take this outside. And protect your family jewels."

"Nah. That's no fun." I nudge his shoulder, still partaking in a staring contest with Silver. "I won't be long. Don't forget, eighty-six on the tuna."

I can hear the smile in Simon's voice. "That was really flying out today. Good call. It's going to be a house favorite, for sure."

For whatever reason, that angers my little temptress even more.

I break eye contact long enough to look at my sous. "Keep me in your thoughts."

He signs the cross.

Alessandra storms out as soon as I round the pass, and I narrowly avoid getting my nose busted by the door swinging back at me. She walks toward the office confidently, like she owns the place.

Confused, I turn toward Jo and Pat, who look on at the scene with equal perplexity from behind the bar.

"Do either of you know what the hell is going on?" I ask.

"Nope. But I can't wait to find out." Johanna gently shoves Patrick. "Go and get some popcorn. This is gonna be good."

My older brother crosses his arms and narrows his eyes. "What did you do?"

"Nothing. I swear." I raise my hands, then catch the angry glare of Alessandra as she waits for me to follow. "Tell Mom I love her."

I follow my executioner, certain I'm walking toward my own funeral, and keep my eyes trained on the back of her head. Not daring to watch the amorous sway of her hips.

When we're both inside the office, I'm smirking like a madman, thinking about the last time we were in here. If she catches the look on my face, she may well murder me, so I keep my back to her as I close the door. "Did you want to finish what we started last week?"

"I want you to tell me why you find it so difficult to follow orders." The sound of the desk chair rolling over the hardwood floor follows her accusation, and now I'm really drawing a blank.

I turn, and frown when I find her perched behind the desk. With her arms folded on top of the other, she levels me with a look so cold, my balls shrivel.

"Umm, that's my desk."

"No. It isn't."

"You got me." I chuckle half-heartedly. "I share it with Patrick and Jo."

She leans forward, waves a hand over the room, and shakes her head. "You're misunderstanding me. Nothing in here is yours. It's mine."

Deciding to go along with this little game, I settle into the chair opposite her. "Okay, I'll play ball. *Everything* here is yours. Now what is it I've supposedly done that's got your panties in a twist?"

I regret the words as soon as they leave my mouth.

Smoke might as well be blowing out of her nostrils.

She rises gracefully, plucks a menu from the filing tray beside her, and slaps it down on the desk.

"This." She jabs at the paper. "Who said you could do this?"

"I did?" My eyes bounce between the menu and her fiery glare until I'm dizzy. "Listen, it's been a long week, but if you're pissed we changed the menu, leave a review on Yelp or email in your complaint."

"I didn't take you for an idiot, Booth Sadler." She sits behind the desk again, one leg crossing elegantly over the other. "I'm sorry you've had a hard week. Good news, though, it's ending before you can mark off Sunday in your calendar."

I raise my hand, because apparently I'm back in middle school. I'll admit, I was a little shit back in the day—always pulling pranks and messing around, but I usually knew what I was in trouble for.

Not today.

"Can I ask why my week is being cut short?" Concern trickles into my voice.

"You just did." Her eyes drill into mine as she points at the door. "You're fired."

CHAPTER TEN

booth

I'M A PRETTY GOOD JUDGE OF CHARACTER.

I can tell when someone is ingenuine or manipulative.

Then again, I get along with most people. Not to blow my own trumpet but I make friends easily, and most people like my low-maintenance, no-shits-to-give attitude.

Not Alessandra.

She has also proven that I'm a terrible judge of character and a moron.

I'm frozen in my seat, scouring my brain for any warning signs and come up empty handed.

The intense expression she wears never breaks. Not a single crack in her stony mask.

I blink slowly, hoping to make sense of everything, then a torrent of emotions hits me with each second that passes. Confusion. Disbelief. Denial.

And finally.

Anger.

Florence will never let us live this down when she finds out our mysterious benefactor is, in fact, a woman.

I'm never going to live this down because I've been flirting shamelessly with her, desperate for a morsel of attention, when behind closed doors, she's been making my life a living hell.

She never once led me to believe I stood a chance. But did I listen? No.

Fuck my *I-love-a-challenge* nonsense.

I hate them now.

Especially when they come in the form of a silver-eyed she-devil.

"You." It's not a question. More of a claim.

"Me," she replies casually.

"B-but, you've been here for weeks. How did no one know?" I've reverted to a state of confusion as I wrack my brain for any clues about her true identity.

Nothing. Then I remember the flare in her eyes when I introduced myself at the fair, the way they widened a fraction.

"That doesn't matter. I'm here now. I've got a very good memory, and I do not recall signing off on any menu changes. I could handle the obvious attitude via the emails Larry forwarded, but—"

"*My* attitude?" Interrupting her isn't smart. My mood bounces around the office like a ping-pong ball. Scratch that, a bowling ball. That's about to smash me in the face as my anger resurfaces.

"You're forgetting I'm your employer."

"I don't even know you." My tone is gritty, as if I've swallowed a mouthful of dirt. "How can you expect us to take you seriously when we have zero clue who you are or what your intentions are?"

"You say us, but I've had no issues with Patrick, Johanna, Graham, Claire, or George." She pins me with an accusatory look as she ticks each name off on her fingers. "Only you."

My dentist is going to lose her mind when I rock up with half my teeth shattered from clenching my jaw so hard. "Are you even surprised? We've been waiting around for months, anticipating the arrival of some corporate scumbag who probably hasn't stepped foot in a kitchen a day in his life."

"So you were expecting a man?" She motions down her torso. "Sorry to disappoint you. I'm very much a woman."

Yes, you fucking are.

One that I've been chasing for weeks and now despise myself for.

The reality of what's happening slowly sets in. One dreaded drop of truth at a time.

This is who owns my family's restaurant.

She's loathed me from day one.

My balls will not be intact by the end of this conversation.

I don't know when to keep my mouth shut.

I'd been skeptical the moment we all unanimously agreed to hand over the keys. I understood we needed the help, otherwise risk Our Place disappearing, but my agreement was given with a hell of a lot of cynicism.

The crack of my knuckles echoes between us as I grip the arms of the chair. "I wasn't expecting anything. That much has been clear since you took over. Why now? After months of throwing orders at us behind closed doors, why show up now? What's your end goal?"

If I wasn't staring at her so intensely, I'd miss it. Her severe exterior cracks. A hairline fracture she covers quickly. She straightens, her body language unreadable again.

Of all the eight billion people in the world, the owner had to be a raven-haired siren whose thick mane of curls I've been looking out for on every street corner.

"As an *ex*-employee, my end goal is no longer any of your concern. It's obvious I can't trust you—past or present. How do I know you haven't undermined me at every turn? I wasn't made aware of the restaurant working the Fall Fair. You changed bread suppliers without consulting with me. You didn't consult with me about the new menu. You just did it."

Shit, Quinn.

Graham will kill me if this screwed with her business.

Panic seeps into my veins. "Fine. Fine. Fire me. But leave the bakery out of it. Quinn has worked her ass off and she's relying on us as a customer."

Her silence is unnerving, but when she speaks, I miss it. "I didn't flat out reject changing suppliers—I simply asked we understand Ms. Jackson's business strategy before confirming anything. Had you asked about switching up the menu, I would have backed the changes and told you my favorite dish is tuna tartare. The same for the Fall Fair. I don't say no because I can, but you didn't respect my position or my rationale. The restaurant has only *just* made it out of the red—spending money thoughtlessly would be irresponsible." She barely takes a breath, and I can't seem to catch mine. "What else have you done behind my back?"

The door flies open, and I spin to find a concerned-looking Patrick and Johanna in the doorway.

"Hmm," Alessandra hums. "I was curious how long you were going to eavesdrop on us. May as well join the meeting."

Meeting my brother's stare, I shrug. "She says 'meeting,' but she means 'dismissal.'"

"Not happening." Patrick steps up behind me, with Jo on his heels. "You don't get to waltz in here and fire our staff. You may hold some power, but I draw the line there. You want to make those types of changes, that's a discussion you can have with my mother and George."

Patrick is a good guy; reliable, caring—but he will not see the people he cares about being stomped over.

The seconds tick by as we wait for Alessandra to rise to the challenge.

The only sound is the nervous tapping of Jo's foot and the blood pumping in my ears.

With an intimidating calmness, she nods. "Eight a.m.

Tomorrow. Here. We can discuss"—her gaze drags to mine—"disciplinary action then."

"I KNEW THIS WAS A BAD IDEA." JOHANNA GNAWS AT A HANGNAIL nervously. "This is all my fault. I should have talked you out of it. You're too pretty to make smart decisions."

Quinn floats over with a tray of drinks, joining my brothers, Johanna, and me. We're all squished around a table in Just Brew It, overflowing with anticipation over how the meeting between our parents and Alessandra is going.

And my fate.

"YoYo," I mutter, using the childhood nickname Patrick coined for her. "There's never talking me out of anything. You should know that by now."

"I still can't believe the owner has been living right above the bakery all this time." Quinn glances warily at the ceiling. "Am I supposed to hate her? What if she comes in for a coffee?"

Graham takes the tray from her hands, passing everyone their hot beverage and ushering Quinn to sit down. "Act normal. The last thing we need is her having more reason to be angry with us. Booth has done a stellar enough job as it is."

"You liked the new dishes!" I protest.

"I'm not talking about the menu," Graham grumbles. "I'm talking about you chasing her down like your next conquest. Now she not only thinks you're insolent but an insolent sleazeball."

"Hey, that's not fair. She brought as much fight to our face-offs as me." I don't mention that day in the office. Or how the air between us was one spark away from combusting.

He sighs, and Quinn rubs his shoulder. "Shit. Sorry. I know. I just hate that none of us are there. Within five minutes of making herself known, she was trying to kick you to the curb."

Graham is great for advice; a rational brain to bounce ideas off. Both my brother's opinions hold a lot of value to me, and as I turn to Patrick, who stews silently in his thoughts, my anxiety increases tenfold.

I appreciated him standing up for me yesterday. But the longer he remains quiet, the more I suspect he's pissed off at my antics.

The last thing I want to do is let people down.

"Shit." I wince, thinking back to how freaked out Florence was over my little stunt. "Has anyone told Flo about the meeting?"

"Nah, she's out of town until tomorrow. Why?" Patrick questions.

"She got upset thinking the menu change would stir trouble and was worried about us losing the restaurant." My head falls into my hands. "I've completely screwed this up. I'm sorry."

Someone slaps the bill of my cap, and when I tug it up, Graham is staring me down. "Enough of that. We all knew about it. Therefore, if she wants to fire you, she can fire us all."

Before I can respond, a chilly gust of wind blows through the bakery. It's not the below-freezing temperature from outside sending a chill down my spine.

It's the pair of gray eyes drilling holes into my skull.

"I think I have a girl crush," Quinn whispers as she watches Alessandra saunter into the bakery before shutting the door closed behind her. In a pair of black pants, a black blouse, and shiny black heels; she's dressed for a funeral. Mine.

We're all speechless. I'd expected my mom and George to show up. Not her.

She takes us all in. The odd thing about her is that she

doesn't look down her nose at us, just studies us closely, a sprinkling of curiosity there.

"I appreciate you all hanging back while the meeting took place. Claire and George are at the restaurant if you want to head over." Her interlocked hands rest in front of her as she stands there motionless.

After a beat, a stampede breaks out as we all rush to throw on our coats.

My arm is halfway through my parka when she speaks.

"Booth. A minute."

We all freeze, sharing glances to gauge the situation. Quinn, who was clearing our cups, swaps the tray for her coat and follows everyone else toward the door. She presses the keys to the bakery into my hand.

"I always liked you. I'll miss you." She's 100 percent serious.

Graham hooks an arm around her shoulders, leading her out into the street with Patrick and Jo. They all peer at me sympathetically through the frosted window.

Once we're alone, me with my hands stuffed into the pockets of my jeans and her still standing stoically, the trepidation deep in my gut builds and builds.

After what feels like an eternity, I blurt, "What did the jury say? Are you washing your hands of me?"

"Let's sit." She waves toward the abandoned table, and with gritted teeth, I lower into a seat. "Your mother and George put up quite the testimony on your behalf. It wasn't lost on me that they practically insinuated everyone would leave if I did indeed fire you."

There's no hiding my reaction. My shoulders collapse with relief. "You're not firing me?"

"Yet," she warns.

I inhale deeply, holding it while I wait for the ultimatum.

"Christmas is days away and it would be foolish of me to get rid of you now. This isn't how I planned my introduction to everyone. You might not know or like me, but I am in charge, Booth." She holds up a dainty finger. I notice it isn't tinged with paint like the first time we met. "One chance. That's it."

My breath sticks in my throat. If I let it out now, I'll spew all the ire I'm holding in.

"You're talented. Apparently, people enjoyed the additions to the menu, so they can stay. I won't have you break the contract with Quinn either."

I exhale loudly. Fuck my job if it means Quinn suffered.

"Thank you," I say curtly.

"Don't pull anything like that again." She pauses. "Your loyalty to your friends and family hasn't gone unnoticed, so at least I respect one thing about you."

"Now that you've stamped your authority and made yourself known, I guess you'll be on your merry way?"

Shut up, Booth.

She narrows her eyes. "*Au contraire*, pretty boy."

I can count on one hand the number of times we've interacted, and despite my better judgment, there aren't enough hands in this town to count the number of occasions I've wanted to see her smile.

The lift of her lips isn't what I imagined.

This isn't a warm, happy, or amused smile.

It's filled with promise.

"You'll be seeing a lot more of me." She rises, steely gaze dancing with dangerous amusement. "After what you said yesterday, I plan on making up for all the months I didn't *show my face.*"

The promise in her smile is an oath to make my life a living hell.

Challenge accepted, Silver.

alessandra

Like most teenagers, I went through a rebellious stage.

Much to my mom's heartbreak, I cut my curls, pierced my nose, and tried my first cigarette.

After almost coughing up a lung, that first smoke was quickly my last, but I remember going against everything my parents wanted me to do. Joining them for dinner. Tidying my room. Blasting my stereo at full volume. Staying out past curfew.

Nothing that got me into major trouble, just enough to make a statement.

To this day, I'm not sure what that statement was.

The same goes for my current stage of rebellion. Because that's what I'm calling this *thing* going on with Booth Sadler.

Only this time, I'm not rebelling against my parents, I'm rebelling against my sanity.

First, I allowed myself to get riled up and stormed into the restaurant, guns blazing.

Next, I'm vowing to actually manage him.

I'm not in control of my moods whenever I'm near him. My

limbs are being governed by a puppeteer, and my mind has been taken over by an invisible force.

Our Place is not the typical establishment Argiros Enterprises invests in. Restaurants, yes, but on a much larger, grander scale. Not in a town tucked away in a quiet corner of the country.

So why did we invest?

We didn't.

I did.

With my money and name.

It was a decision made in haste, and only by chance that I became aware of a family-run restaurant looking to sell. I saw my in, grabbed it by the horns, and was in contact with the escrow company Larry works for the following day.

By June, I was the proud owner of a quaint seafood restaurant in Maine.

The perfect reason to come to Sutton Bay.

I'd planned to reveal myself after Christmas, but my well-laid-out plans went out the window when I saw the menu. Booth has been a thorn in my side since day one, but that was the final straw.

And he didn't like that one bit.

When I made my identity known, it was time to face the music. I arranged a meeting with the previous owners, Claire Sadler and George Thomas, and prepared myself to be challenged, ridiculed, argued with. It was nothing like that.

George was serious, but respectful.

Claire, the matriarch of the Sadler family, was annoyingly delightful. Her plea for me to not fire her son was amusing, especially when she threatened to ground him. It was hard to not reciprocate her friendliness and even harder to decline her offer to show me around town.

They accepted my authority, assured me I wouldn't meet any blockers in the shape of a dimpled, six-foot-something chef, and didn't ask why I bought a restaurant hundreds of miles away from home.

Before we said goodbye, Claire informed me that their "kids" were at the bakery.

I knew I had to clear the air with the youngest Sadler son, and instead, we both stormed out of Just Brew It, seething and ready to draw blood.

Today, however, is a new day.

I started it by informing Larry his services were no longer required, and any further anonymity regarding ownership was unnecessary.

Next, I had a video call with Graham Sadler, which I found odd, considering he lives in town. Efficient, and to the point, I left the meeting satisfied that he had the finances under control as the restaurant's accountant.

Now, after a walk-through with Johanna, I'm standing at the end of the bar, observing her and the team.

I've ignored the murmured comments under people's breaths and disgruntled faces. I know what they think—that I don't belong here—but before I started working for my father, I paid my dues working in the service industry through college, not to mention the many bars and restaurants within our hotels.

I'm watching a young girl overpour a pint of porter when Johanna wanders over. "She's new. I've spoken to her twice about her pours. We'll get right on it."

"Everyone seems new." My eyes follow the gangly busboy zipping past us, who has smashed three plates since I arrived.

"We had a good team, but they graduated and left for college this summer. We're working on a training program, but with the holiday season in full swing, it's hard to find the time." Johanna nods to the tall brunette, running circles around everyone else. "Jules is our assistant manager. She's been here longer than me and is a huge asset."

Confused, I turn to her. "Your dad said you've been working here since you were a teenager. Jules looks no older than twenty-five."

Her lips twist in thought. "I had some time away..."

As if sensing her discomfort, Patrick stops shelving liquor bottles and slides in beside her, running a palm up her spine. "And ever since she came back, it's been a blessing." They share a smile; one only they know the meaning behind.

It really is a whole family affair in this joint.

"How are you getting on?" Patrick asks. He's not been as welcoming as his mom, but he's civil. Both he and Johanna have been eyeing me cautiously all day, like I'm going to fire everyone on the spot.

Nodding, I adjust my navy silk blouse, wishing I'd gone for something more casual. "You guys run a tight ship. I have no concerns—you know where improvements need to be made. I'm happy with how things are being managed."

They share another look, this one less intimate and more suspicious.

"So, Booth mentioned you were in town until..." Patrick trails off.

"I didn't confirm a date." *Thank god.*

"Gotcha. Well, I'm finishing up soon, I have to get my daughter from school. Is there anything else you need from me?" He folds his arms.

"Oh." My eyes dart between them. "I didn't know you had a child."

Johanna rolls her lips together. "Lottie is Pat's daughter..." There's nothing sharp in her tone, but from their expressions, it's information the owner should know.

"Sorry, I shouldn't have presumed." Needing to remove myself from their scrutinizing gazes, I change the subject. "Can I use the office to answer some emails? Then I'll be out of everyone's hair."

"Sure. You know where it is." He juts his chin toward the back of the restaurant and then walks off, leaving Johanna and me alone.

"Are you clocking off as well?"

"Umm." She twists her hands in front of her, and I inwardly sigh.

"I'm not docking points for you having a life outside of these four walls. Don't let me keep you. Have a good night." I attempt a smile that definitely resembles a grimace before turning to leave, but her words stop me.

"Booth's a really good guy," she rushes out. "He's a man-child, I won't deny that, but he's been the backbone of this place since before Ted passed. If I were going to own a restaurant, I'd want him on my roster."

"Ted?" I ask, head tilted.

This gets a reaction. Johanna's brows furrow deep, her eyes flaring. "Yeah. Ted Sadler. He opened this place with my dad." She shakes her head, the cautiousness toward me gone and a bite to her tone. "This probably isn't my place, but if you're going to buy a family-owned restaurant that's been open for almost thirty years, maybe do your homework. Perhaps we'd be a little more open to your sudden appearance."

She walks back behind the bar, not giving me the opportunity to respond. Which is good, because I'm not sure what to say.

I'm striding toward the office, not allowing my embarrassment to show until I'm sealed in the small room.

"Fuck," I curse loudly.

She's right. My family's business prides itself on integrity, as well as building strong relationships with our employees. And here I am, knowing nothing about these people.

With frustrated movements, I wrangle my hair on top of my head and go to secure it with the hair tie around my wrist.

The sound of the handle rattling has me spinning around to

find a surprised Booth. As if remembering who I am, deep creases line his forehead, and he sighs tiredly.

"I need the office," he says matter-of-factly.

With my hair out of the way, I go to drop my arms, but a sharp tug has my head jerking to the left thanks to my tennis bracelet getting caught. Not wanting to make a fuss, I wiggle my wrist, attempting to free myself.

His smug smile burns into the side of my face. "Need some help?"

"No," I snap.

I struggle some more, and my arm grows heavy.

After a minute, the smirk on his face expands, then he takes a step toward me. "Quit being stubborn."

Admitting defeat, my hand hangs limply against my ear, and I meet his amused gaze. "Patrick said I could use the office."

Booth's murmured "Fucker" is barely audible, and his hands fist at his side. "Will you be long? I have actual work to do."

"And I don't?" I throw back.

He crosses his arms. "I imagine your work comprises steamrolling over small businesses and making babies cry."

I forget my arm is attached to my hair, and I jerk my hand at him in frustration. "*Skatá.*"

Tutting, he ambles over. "Stop tugging or you'll make it worse. Here."

His large hand grips my elbow, while the other works its way into my mess of curls. My body goes rigid at his proximity. His smoky scent hits me. This time, I pick up notes of paprika, black pepper, and saffron. I stop breathing.

My eyes remain glued to the center of his chest as he works on freeing me.

"I've never seen a woman with so much hair." He's exasperated, and I suspect it has nothing to do with my locks. "You've got yourself in a mess here."

You can say that again.

"What language did you use before?"

Peering up, I find him staring down at me curiously. Since meeting Booth, I've only witnessed him flirting or pissed. Now, he seems meditative. Chocolate strands fall over his brow as his eyes dance around my face.

I finally exhale.

"Greek." My voice is hushed.

"You're Greek?"

"My mother is."

"I've never been to Greece. Or Europe. Have you?" His thumb brushes my jaw, causing me to jump. Which reminds me of where and who we are.

"Small talk? Don't tell me you're trying to butter me up now."

His head shakes, frustration marring his features, before he steps back. "There."

All the blood rushes back to my fingers as my arm falls to my side. "Thank you."

He drags a hand down his face, scrubbing at the hint of stubble decorating his jaw. "I want to apologize."

"Well, color me surprised. Though, I'd much rather have your cooperation."

Frowning, his head rears back. "No. I won't be sorry for fighting for my family's business. I'm sorry I pursued you so hard. It's clear now why you turned me down. I misread the signs. It won't happen again."

I ignore the need to tell him he didn't misread any signs and concentrate on what he's not saying.

"So you won't cooperate? Your words tell me you care, but your actions constantly jeopardize any alliance we could have. Why are you so dead set on making my time here difficult?"

"Jeopardize?" He spins around, hands clasped behind his head as he laughs. Despite the humor in his voice, his limbs are rigid. When he faces me again, he stares at me in disbelief. "Do you want me to be thankful for you saving this place? As if I didn't try for an entire year, only to be shot down and fail. We all tried, hoping to all that is mighty we wouldn't end up being ripped apart and turned into a chain restaurant. Then you show up, sniffing around for weeks, and rather than introduce yourself, get to know us, and what we're about, you fire me on the spot. You might see it as jeopardy, but I see it as clinging to the last shreds we have left of the man who built this restaurant from the ground up."

Blinking at him, I give him the space to slow his breathing. His outburst is unexpected, and while he's angry, there's passion and authenticity in his words. If his tirade hadn't been aimed at me, I'd be impressed.

"Do you even know the history of the restaurant? The town?" His arms drop.

"Why does that matter?" I run my palms down the front of my pants, resisting the urge to clench my fists. I don't enjoy being the stupidest person in the room, and if he quizzes me on who founded the town, that's what I'll become.

"I'm not here to change anything." I attempt to keep my voice soft. "Perhaps I went about it the wrong way, so *I* apologize."

His arms fly out to the side. "That's it? You're sorry?"

"You can't be annoyed at my lack of involvement one minute and be mad I'm here the next. Pick a lane, Booth." Irritation blooms. "What more do you want?"

"I want to know your plans. Where do you see us in three, five, ten years' time? Why did you buy us? What's your experience? Who are you?" He paces in front of me, each step adding to the tension in his muscles.

Who are you?

Great question. The answer?

I'm not so sure.

And I don't need Booth Sadler knowing that.

As for his other questions, I tell him the truth, even though I know it's going to ruffle his feathers further.

"I don't know what my plans are."

"Well, isn't that fucking perfect," he murmurs, before stomping out, the cracking of wood echoing around the room when the door slams shut.

CHAPTER TWELVE

booth

After my run-in with Alessandra, *again*, I storm to the front of the restaurant, eyes frantically scanning for Patrick. I spot his mop of sandy hair bent over a table of customers, nodding and smiling at whatever they're saying.

With my arms crossed, stance wide, I wait for him by the server's station. He catches my gaze, and from my body language, he knows we need to talk. Dubiously, he approaches me.

"Now, calm do—"

My hand swipes through the air, silencing him. "I refuse to work with her. She knows nothing. Cares about no one but herself. Plus, she admitted to having no future plan for us."

"You got all that in less than ten minutes?" He grabs a stack of menus and hands them to a passing server. Suddenly, I'm reminded of how Silver and I ended up in there together. He curses when I sucker punch him in the bicep. "The fuck! There are customers. What's your issue?"

I drag him to the back, where the ice machine and dishwasher are.

"My *issue* is with you feeding me to the wolves."

He looks guilty. "What happened?"

"She did," I spit.

"Booth..." His voice is impatient.

Clenching and unclenching my fists, I tell him about the conversation.

"I don't get it." Patrick sighs. "Earlier, she was fine with us. She highlighted some areas we were lacking, but we're already on top of it. I hate to break it to you, but she knows the industry."

"She doesn't belong here."

Patrick sighs, so I reign back my anger. Then my pacifist big brother goes and surprises me. "You're right."

My eyes bulge. Quickly, I grab my phone, slide up the camera icon, and click Record. "Can you repeat that?"

He slaps my hand away. "Be serious for once."

"Oh, I am. Seriously fucking confused about what to do. How are we supposed to operate during one of the busiest times of the year with her breathing down our necks? Tell me she hasn't had it out for me since day one?"

Tilting his head, he stares at me condescendingly. "You ask for it sometimes."

"You're not helping." I go to turn, but he clasps my elbow. "I really do agree with you. She doesn't belong here, but—"

"Not with the buts." My arms flop at my sides. "You love buts."

"My butt!" Johanna shouts from the front.

"*Butt* out," I call right as Patrick whistles his agreement.

Barf.

"As I was saying..." I roll my eyes at his patronizing tone. "Our plan worked. We smoked her out. This is what we wanted, so we need to deal with the repercussions. Let's use her surprise visit to our advantage. Convince her to funnel some more money into the overheads. Jo's been desperate to replace this lousy old thing." He kicks the dishwasher with the toe of his boot.

"And how are we going to do that, oh wise one?"

"By making her feel welcome. Involved. Part of the team."

I frown. "I'd rather stick my testicles into a blender."

"You talk about your balls too much."

"They're pretty."

"You're changing the subject." He flicks me between the eyes. "Don't be pigheaded because of a bad first impression. She thinks you're defiant. Prove to her that you're the dedicated, hands-on head chef we know you are. *Really* show her."

My mouth hangs open, ready to argue, when I pause. Seeing my reaction, Patrick nods, eyes widening slowly.

"Wait...are you giving me permission to be a pain in her ass?" I ask incredulously.

In a flash, his expression reverts to passive. "I have no idea what you're talking about."

He absolutely does. I'm stunned. Then, a lightbulb *dings* above my head.

"If anyone asks, this conversation didn't happen." I slap him on the shoulder. "Catch you later, I have to see a man about a lobster."

"That doesn't even make sense, you tool."

"Of course it does." I throw my arms up, gesturing to the brick walls of the tiny room we're hiding in. "This is Our Place."

Leaving him to bask in my witty words, I decide to catch up on work at home and head down toward the bay.

I left my beanie at my mom's, and the snappy winds nip at my ears, making them ache. With my head down, collar tucked up high, and sneakers slapping against the compact snow, I make it back in record time.

The internet around here is dire, and when my cell connects with the Wi-Fi, a weather warning notification flashes on my screen. The threat of a big snowstorm heading our way is the last thing I need. Hopefully, it'll pass before Christmas—which is one week away—but as a precaution, I drop Dex a text.

Booth: Please tell me The Nook is free? I don't fancy seeing out this storm in the boathouse.

Dex is one of the most talented carpenters I've ever met. A real master of the trade. After a summer job at the local lumberyard, he found his passion. Now, he owns several wood cabins across the state; all of which he built himself. The Nook was his first major project. It's mostly for family and friends, so he doesn't rent it out unless tourist season is at its peak. My house is well insulated, but with it sitting in the middle of the bay, there's always a risk of strong winds blowing out a window or losing power.

Dex: You're in luck. I've reserved it from the 20th through to Christmas Eve for you. No orgies.

Booth: That was one time.

Dex: Gross. How are things with Big Boss?

"Pfft, she wishes." My fingers stab furiously at the screen.

Booth: We're meeting for coffee tomorrow. A bit of bonding.

Dex: *sniff* I smell BS.

Booth: I'd never lie. Thanks for sorting the cabin.

I lock my phone and throw it on my rumpled sheets, strip out of my clothes, and stand under the scalding water in my shower until my skin turns pink. The entire time, I think about Alessandra. Not ideal when naked.

She might grate on my nerves, but she's still stunning to look at. Which angers me even more.

Once I'm dried off, I do a few hours of work, make dinner, then climb into bed. My mind runs through endless ways that I'm going to make Alessandra feel *welcome*.

It's obvious she knows nothing about the restaurant or the history of this town. Lucky for her, I'm very knowledgeable.

She wants to prove herself as worthy? I'll be the judge of that.

By the end of the year, she'll know so much, there'll be no point in her sticking around. I'll be so attentive and dedicated, she'll have no choice but to give me Employee of the Month. She might also want to serve my head on a platter.

I fall asleep, grinning like the Cheshire Cat at how clever I am.

The Einstein of Sutton Bay, if you will.

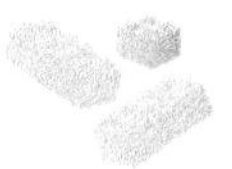

ARMED WITH TWO THERMOSES, I JAB AT THE BUZZER WITH MY elbow and wait.

It's rare I manage eight hours, but last night I went to sleep satisfied and smug.

Stage 1: teach her all there is to know about Maine fishing.

The thumping of footsteps sounds before a crack appears in the door. Illuminated by the streetlamp, offering some semblance of light on this dark, frigid morning, I just make out a pair of sleepy, suspecting eyes peeking through the gap.

"Morning, Boss. Ready to start the day?"

She winces at my overly perky voice. Not a morning person, it appears.

Bonus points.

"What's going on?" she croaks and widens the door.

My eyes sweep over her body, and I stifle a groan. She has to stop answering her door in nothing but silk and bare feet.

I bare my teeth in what I hope is a genuine smile. She doesn't deserve my dimples. "I've arranged a field trip. For educational reasons. I want to help you out. Teach you about the ways of the town and its people."

"Booth, I'm not in the mood. Go bother someone else."

I hold back my wince when the door slams against my foot. "Ah, so what you're saying is you're not interested in learning about the culture of this small town? Noted." I fold my arms and *tsk*. "Shame. I thought you really cared."

A puff of air escapes her lips and then she counts to ten under her breath. "Who said I didn't care?"

"Your attitude did." I raise an eyebrow in challenge; she raises one right back. *En garde.* "If you have better things to do than be an involved member of the management team..."

Goading Alessandra Argiros is fast becoming my favorite hobby. If she were a cat, her claws would be protracting.

She contemplates my invite. Like me, I suspect she loves a challenge, and she isn't about to back down when her commitment is being contested.

"Where are we going?" Her voice is tight with agitation, right where I want her.

"It's a surprise." I thrust a thermos toward her. "This is for you. You'll need layers for today's adventures. Thermals, if you have them. You've got ten minutes to get changed."

"This is a nightmare. I haven't woken up yet, right?"

"Oh, you're very much awake. Chop chop." The slapping of my hand on my thigh makes her jump. "Ol' Petey won't wait around all morning."

"Who the fuck is Ol' Petey?" she seethes.

I bend forward, our metal containers clanking as they collide, and I wink at her. "Our tour guide."

alessandra

Is it better to hide a body in the woods or feed it to the fishes?

The thought has popped into my head multiple times since Booth showed up at my apartment.

He's intentionally pushing my buttons; I'm not an idiot. Or maybe I am, because I've agreed to this stupid outing.

If I declined his invitation, I'd be forfeiting, and I refuse to have my integrity questioned.

I stomp down the stairs, swaddled in a pair of fleece-lined leggings, sweatpants, a sweatshirt, and a puffer jacket. The sun crests the horizon, a glow of orange warming the sky when I join Booth outside my apartment. He barely glances at me before striding down the hill.

My hiking boots slap against the snow as I jog to catch up. "Why aren't we driving?"

"Because our location is right there." He points toward the bay, but all I see is vast open water and rows of boats.

"You're going to drown me?"

"No." He rolls his eyes and sips his coffee. "I wouldn't want you to melt."

"Har-har." Desperate for caffeine myself, I take a large gulp. I'm surprised to find it's exactly how I like it. Black with a little sweetness.

We walk in silence the rest of the way, and a few minutes later, Booth steers us toward a long jetty, lined on either side with bobbing fishing boats. The sharp, briny smell of the ocean is stronger here, mixing with the scent of fish. Some boats are old and weathered, their paint peeling and barnacles clinging to the sides. It's clear which boats haven't been used this winter from the buildup of snow. The one we stop beside is well kept. It must be fifteen feet long, with a bright orange bow and white helm. In bold, white lettering reads *Sunrise* on the front of the bow, with a small orange and pink sunrise painted underneath.

Booth raps his knuckles on the side. "Petey, you here?"

A bang, curse, and grunt follow.

A head of white hair pops up from the cabin, and a smile with a few missing teeth greets us. "Mornin', bub." Ol' Petey, I presume, makes a hacking noise and spits into the water before nodding in my direction. "Sugar."

"This is Petey, the owner of this fine vessel, and our chauffeur today. Petey, this is Alessandra. She'll be joining us."

"Pretty name. Belongs on the side of a boat. Bit of a mouthful, though. Got a shorter name?" He has to be in his sixties. If someone were to ask what a typical New England angler looked like, you would find Petey's photograph in textbooks. His skin is wrinkled and tanned from long hours outside, and he wears a bright yellow rubber bib and boots.

I give him a kind smile. "Aly is fine. Nice to meet you, Petey."

"You too, sugar." He swivels around, the soles of his boots squeaking. "Don't be dubbin' around. Climb in."

Booth raises a leg, and just as he's about to swing it over, he pauses and pats his pockets in a panic. He catches me watching and quickly fixes his expression. *Weird.*

He climbs in effortlessly, and I think he's going to leave me to struggle my way onboard when a large, glove-encased hand pops into my vision.

I stare at it for a beat, contemplating what's worse: his help or the cold waters. Swallowing my stubbornness, I accept it. Once I'm safely onboard, he drops my hand like it's on fire.

"Ready for your first real taste of Maine living, Boss?" Booth asks slyly.

"Can we not with the nicknames. Silver is bad enough."

He goes to reply, but Petey shoves a life vest into his chest and gently passes me one. "Quit flirtin'. Go get us ready."

Booth doesn't argue with him.

While the cold breeze wakes me up, I watch them work in tandem. The low rumble of an engine sounds and the floor beneath my feet vibrates. We rock slightly before trundling forward.

"Take a seat behind me, sugar. Less wind," Petey shouts over his shoulder.

A small bench is bolted to the floor directly behind the helm. I fit the life vest on and sit down. Booth stands idly by, feet planted firmly, his stance strong as he rocks with the sway of the boat.

"Where are we going?" I call over the motor.

"Out to sea," Booth mutters sarcastically.

Petey throws something at his head. We're going to be good friends, he and I.

"Bugs. Gotta go a little farther out this time of year to catch 'em," Petey drawls, while steering us out of the mouth of the bay.

"Bugs?" My confused tone makes him chuckle.

"Lobstah'. Technically, we're outta season, but they're still around."

"Where are the traps?" I look around the boat.

"Already out. We'll be haulin' them up. Hope you've got ya sea legs about ya'."

Booth stifles his laughter into his fist, eyeing Petey, then me with a wayward look. Any idiot would have guessed there was a hidden agenda behind this "adventure."

The sun finally shows its face as we exit the shoehorn-shaped inlet, and the winds pick up without the protection of the steep cliffs. It's choppy, and my stomach dips each time we rise and fall with a large wave. Nothing I'm not used to. The salty ocean spray coats my face, the taste of it reminding me of summers in Greece.

"She's a beautiful boat. What inspired the name?" I ask Petey.

He gazes lovingly along the length of the vessel and pats the helm. "That she is. Just like my Moira. She was the one who painted the sunrise. Miss her every day."

My heart aches, but there's only love in his voice. "She's very talented. I paint a little myself."

"Huh, you don't say?" He looks me up and down, then smiles as if to say, *You're all right, kid.* "Where ya from, Aly?"

Here we go.

There's no point in lying now, considering Booth knows who I am, but disclosing personal information isn't something that's ever come easy to me.

"New York, born and bred."

"Ah, big city girl, I take it? Hope we ain't too simpleminded for ya." He throws a wink over his shoulder.

"Only one person comes to mind." I side-eye Booth, who scowls at me in return.

"What do ya do for work?" Petey turns to face me as the boat slows, leaving us rocking with the swell of the waves as we sit a few kilometers from shore.

"Investment. My family owns a private equity company, mostly managing hotels."

"And restaurants," Booth adds, voice tight. "*Aly* here is the new owner of Our Place."

Petey doesn't look surprised. "So you're the reason our boy here has his panties in a twist. Got to ask, why Sutton Bay? Seems a little far from New York's fancy joints."

"Don't bother asking. She won't te—"

"I saw an opportunity," I say, cutting Booth off. "You're right. It's not what we usually invest in, but I took a chance. Not many restaurants survive longer than five years. I was impressed to learn this one has been around for almost three decades." My gaze meets Booth's and I tilt my head a fraction.

"C minus for effort." He walks toward Petey. "Want me to drop the anchor?"

"Ayuh, here is good. Ready for some fun, Aly?"

I stand, just as the boat rolls and lose my footing. Both men reach out to steady me but I right myself.

"Easy there." Booth chuckles. "We can turn around if you're feeling a little queasy."

Dimples would be awful at poker. His scheming is written across his face, plain as day.

Two can play at this game.

My hand clutches my stomach dramatically as I exhale loudly. "I think I'm okay now that we've stopped."

He smirks triumphantly. I can't wait to wipe it off.

The men jump into action, quickly lowering the anchor and making room for the traps. When the engine is silenced, hungry gulls squawk overhead as they swoop through the air.

"Aly, switch ya gloves for these and come give me a hand." Petey holds out a pair of black rubber gloves. "Time to show us what ya made of."

For the next two hours I'm put to work.

It's grueling. Muscles I didn't know existed ache. My fingers cramp. The cold air numbs my nose and cheeks. I lose count of how many hauls we bring up. And most of all, it's the most fun I've had in weeks.

Petey takes the time to explain each step to me, how he measures each lobster to check the legal size, and even goes into describing the anatomy. He's a salt-of-the-earth man and a true connoisseur of his trade.

Booth, however, tests me. He does his fair share of work but doesn't attempt to help me or answer my questions when Petey is busy. A part of me doesn't blame him. The other part of me wants to dunk his head in the ocean. Clearly, he's done this before, probably grew up on a boat, but I can't help but notice his pallid complexion as we head back to shore.

"Looking a little green around the gills there, Sadler. Did you leave *your* sea legs at home?" That earns me a weak scowl.

Our captain scoffs. "Nonsense. Booth has been out with me plenty. Ain't that right, bub?"

"Yep." His head jerks up and down.

"Aly, I gotta say, you surprised me. Our boy here told me you couldn't hack it. Wanted me to ride again—"

"Why don't you concentrate on mooring us, old man?" Booth interjects, then closes his eyes and lets out a slow breath. "Hurry, too. I have somewhere to be."

This is pure gold and I'm going to enjoy every minute of it.

Petey either doesn't hear him or chooses not to.

The waterproof gloves Booth wears creak with the death grip he has on the side of the boat.

"Is there a scenic route, Petey? I'd love to see more of the bay." My gaze doesn't leave Booth's as I edge closer to him.

All color drains from his face, save for the rosy cheeks he's sporting from the cold. "Aly" is all he manages through clamped teeth.

"You want to get to know me?" He doesn't reply. "I spent summers on my grandfather's sailboat. I mastered the reef knot before I got my period. I warned you not to underestimate me, but you didn't listen."

He opens his mouth, but before he can speak, his eyes bulge and he throws his head overboard.

Booth 0–Aly 1.

alessandra

Weirdly, I'm not as smug as I thought I would be once Booth regains himself.

I'd only planned on proving to him I could handle the ocean. Not that he couldn't. Honestly, it shocked me. And Petey.

"Go, get." My newest friend flaps his hands at me and Booth—who's keeled over a mooring bollard. "My son is on his way down. He'll help get this all off boarded. Look after young skippy there. Ain't never seen him like that."

I'd much rather freeze my fingers off hauling the traps than take care of Booth.

As if hearing my thoughts, he moans weakly. "Aly. Call my mom."

"Good lord." I roll my eyes and attempt to pull him to standing. "Help me out here, you big baby. You're all muscle."

Apparently, a passing compliment is the cure, because he beams up at me, skin ashy and clammy. "You like my muscles?"

"I'd like you to weigh thirty pounds less."

"Liar."

With his arm slung over my shoulder, I drag him down the jetty. "Where do you live? I'll call you a cab."

"Don't bother." He raises a shaky finger to point at a teal-colored boathouse. "My humble abode awaits."

"That's your house?" I ask in surprise.

"Don't—" He breathes deeply, and I worry he's going to be sick again. "Don't be a snob. We can't all live in penthouses on the Upper East Side."

"That wasn't—never mind."

I steer us toward the little shack; the silence stretching between us with each step. Half of the house sits above the water, elevated by thick wooden stilts. A small wooden boat, covered in tarp, bobs in the water below.

He unhooks his arm and holds himself up against the door frame. I'm obviously not going to leave him to be pecked to death by the gulls. But this is awkward.

"Can you take it from here?" I ask.

He nods, still resting his head on the wood. "Lemme get my keys."

A few seconds pass. "You're not moving."

"Oh, believe me. *Everything* is moving. Just gimme a sec," he whispers.

Sighing, I move next to him and fish my hand into his pockets. There's no childish joke, proving how ill he is. With his keys located, I make quick work of the lock before shuffling him inside and shutting the door.

It's warmer than I expected, but still cold, and the wind whistles against the boarded sides. Imagine a bachelor pad meets a lobster fisherman's grotto. A bed, sofa, and plasma TV. That's it. His kitchen seems the most equipped. On the narrow counters sit a stack of cookbooks, two knife blocks filled with gleaming steel, a spotless gas top stove and oven, and a huge fridge much too large for one man.

What surprises me is the coffee table littered with LEGO. A half-built structure sitting in the center. Recalling he has a niece, I hold in my questions.

I forget where I am, until a deep groan sounds behind me, followed by squeaking springs. Turning, I find Booth facedown on the mattress.

Minus his coat and T-shirt.

The corded muscles on his back flex with his deep breaths, and I try, I really do, but my eyes follow the path of golden skin until it reaches the dimples in his lower back.

Motherfucker.

He's quadruple dimpled.

"Is this your first time being seasick?"

He shakes his head, and I just make out his muffled "No."

"Hold up." I walk over and stand next to the bed, nudging his ankle with the toe of my boot. "Petey said he's never seen you like this."

He twists his neck, drowsy blue eyes on me. "I forgot to take my anti-sickness medicine."

My lips curl around my teeth. "So your plan was to get me to puke my guts up. How did that go for you?"

Sighing, he hides his face again. "Terribly. Now, if you'll please leave me with some of my dignity intact, today's tour is over. Don't forget to leave a review."

Overlooking his failed ploy, I actually had fun today. I forget about his condescending comment regarding my knowledge of Sutton Bay because he wasn't wrong. Now, thanks to Petey, I know the history of this little fishing town, of the first families that moved here, and what's in season when.

Unintentionally, Booth gave me the best day I've had since arriving. I didn't worry about work or second-guess why I'm here.

Which is why I grab him some water, find a towel in the bathroom, and wet it before returning to his still form. I place the glass on his bedside table and lay the cool flannel across his nape. He sucks in a breath before melting into the comforter. Goose bumps raise the flesh of his back.

"You're being awfully nice. Do you treat all your victims like this before murdering them?" He sits up on his elbow and drains the glass in three large gulps.

"Don't be ridiculous. I'd pay someone to do my dirty work."

He chuckles. It's deep, masculine, and wraps around my body, stroking and caressing me all over.

"I've got to hand it to you, Silver. You surprised me today. Are you jacked underneath all those layers? You were hauling those traps up like it was your last mission on Earth."

I scoff and fold my arms. "Wouldn't you like to know?"

Jesus, Mary, and Joseph, Alessandra. Stop talking.

"Do not answer that, Booth. I can see it in your eyes. Bad boy."

Well, that pours gasoline on the fire.

His eyes light up and his angelic expression turns danger-ous. "Oh, but I can be such a good boy for you. Or not. Take your pick."

I ignore the shiver that runs down my spine. And I certainly don't envision him being good *or* bad. Because that would be stupid. Asking for trouble. Impulsive—which I'm not.

Or am I?

I'm here, in a random town with no plan. What's one more impulsive decision?

Nope. Nope. Nope.

There's no denying he lights a fire under me in so many ways. Nine times out of ten, he's infuriating, but there's some-thing about him that lures me in.

My phone dings, notifying me of a new email. Pulling it out of my coat, I read each word. Then again. I take a deep breath, that does nothing to calm me, and silently turn back to Booth.

Noticing the shift in mood, he frowns. "What's wrong?"

I'm an idiot.

It's bad enough I took the bait this morning and agreed to our outing, but there was a tiny part of me—minuscule—that thought he could be a grown-up about this all. That he would respect my position and me.

I flip the phone around, showing him the screen. "Perhaps it's the invoice I've received for a dual deck gas convection oven. Specifically, the one I explicitly told you not to buy."

"Fuck," he hisses and jolts up, only to sway backward. "Double fuck."

"You can't help yourself, can you?"

"It's not like that." Whatever truce we had moments ago dies.

"What's it like then?" I sweep a hand down my body. "You waited until now. Because you found out I was a woman—someone who's easier to undermine?"

That gets his attention. Nausea forgotten, he stands. "Your gender means nothing to me. Once again, if you knew anything about the restaurant, you'd know my predecessor is named Gloria. She taught me everything I know. My mother didn't hesitate to step up when my dad passed away, even though she hadn't worked in over twenty years. Johanna is one of the strongest women I know. Quinn built a successful business for herself from the ground up. My little sister could negotiate herself out of any situation. Heck, my niece is going places and she's only five. So no, Aly, my issue isn't that you're a woman. It's that you think just because your name is on the deed, you've earned our respect."

I quickly close the distance, our toes touching, heaving chests inches apart. "Then what? I made it crystal clear that purchases above two thousand dollars had to be signed off by me."

"How am I expected to manage a kitchen without working equipment?" His voice shakes, like he's ready to crack.

The feeling is mutual.

"One chance, Booth. I gave you one last chance." I raise my pointer and thumb between us, barely touching. "The ice is this thin. Stop making my job difficult and remind yourself that you wouldn't be here if it wasn't for me. I don't want to be here anymore than you want me to."

His nostrils flare.

Shit. I realize my slipup, but it's too late.

"Then why are you here?" His head tilts as he watches me closely, searching for answers.

"If you want me to trust you, then stop throwing tantrums."

He throws his head back in laughter. Nothing like the carefree rumble earlier. "For a moment, I saw a different side to you."

I straighten to my full height, ready for whatever he has to say. But he surprises me.

"Out on the water today, you actually looked content. Free. We don't know each other, and I won't lie, when we first met, I wanted to change that." A muscle ticks in his jaw. "Fuck, for some insane reason, I still do. You waltzed in here, without a clue how it's been the last few years. Nothing is easy about running a restaurant in the middle of nowhere, relying on tourist season, and hoping the weather doesn't sabotage your forecasted revenue."

Like a balloon, the fight hisses out of me and my shoulders deflate. Something tells me Booth doesn't lose his temper often, and from the tension in his body, he's struggling with it.

We're as stubborn as each other. Neither one of us wants to back down. The air crackles between us, popping and sparking with our animosity.

"You want me gone? Then prove I can trust *you.*" I poke a finger in the center of his chest. The thumping of his heart vibrates down my arm. "Prove to me you won't make rash decisions simply to get a rise out of me. I know you're talented, so don't throw it away because you're bullheaded. You want to be enemies? That's your call. But I promise you'll throw in the towel before the last round is over."

In the blink of an eye, his large hand encompasses my wrist, and I smash into his chest.

"Don't tease me with a good time." His heated stare evolves; the devious smirk morphing into a megawatt smile, dimples on full display when he finds me watching him. It's the blue flame eating up his irises that gets my attention, though.

I snatch my hand back and put some much-needed distance between us.

"Those dimples won't do much to save you. Lucky for you, you have a few days to get your act together." I spin and stride to the door. With a chaste glance over my shoulder, I say, "Merry Christmas, Booth. Don't make me regret giving you another chance."

Before he can respond, the door slams closed behind me.

A week with my family is exactly what I need. Far, far away from Booth Sadler.

Had I stayed another second, feeling the scorch of his eyes or the warmth of his touch, I would have said exactly what I was thinking.

Or worse.

I might have gone against all my rational instincts and kissed that stupid grin off his face.

CHAPTER FIFTEEN

booth

The storm arrives with a vendetta against Sutton Bay.

You can't see two feet in front of you thanks to the wall of white blasting through the streets. The town was prepared; coming together to help older residents stock up on food and essentials, and emergency kits and drinking water were handed out at the town hall.

Everyone was frustrated that it hit us three days before Christmas. Flights across the Northeast were canceled, leaving people stranded and unable to spend the holidays with their loved ones. The restaurant—like most businesses in town—is closed until it's safe to reopen. They're hoping it'll pass by Christmas Eve.

I knew I'd made a good call staying in The Nook. Mom wasn't too pleased, but she knew I'd be safe out here thanks to Dex's apocalyptic prepping skills. Last night, I drove to the cabin twenty minutes out of town. After getting the key from the drop box, I hustled inside, started a fire, and unboxed my Trevi Fountain LEGO set. With no TV, this was a quiet place of solitude to escape to.

Alessandra had been absent since she left my house. I refused to ask where she was, and didn't care.

Okay, so I cared a little. Blame suspicion. Nothing else.

The Nook, like my house, is open plan. But where I have a separate bathroom, Dex installed a bathtub out in the open overlooking the forest. The floor-to-ceiling window has no curtains, making you feel like you're bathing in the wild. Cedar covers the entire cabin, the reddish-brown wood creating a moody, rustic vibe.

There's a small room with a toilet and sink, and the little kitchenette doesn't have much space, but I make do.

Sautéed onions, garlic, and fennel fill the room with a mouthwatering scent. This is my sanctuary—where I cook freely, without boundaries or criticism. I own these flavors. This recipe. This kitchen.

I'm measuring out a cup of risotto, when a shuffling from outside makes me pause. Most of the lights are out, except the overhead in the kitchen, and the curtains are drawn. No one would dare venture out in this weather. Guessing it's a possum or raccoon seeking shelter on the porch, I ignore it.

The rice goes in, I add a splash of white wine, then cover with stock. The lid hovers above the pan when a thump vibrates through the house.

Bigger than a possum then.

Not wanting a moose to damage anything, I walk over to the front door and bang my fist against the wood, hoping to scare it off.

Instead, I'm met with a loud, feminine gasp.

I'm yanking the door open without thinking, and I meet the nozzle end of a pepper spray bottle. Forgetting all survival instincts, I raise my hands and screech like a banshee. The high-pitched noise sheds me of all masculinity points.

"Skatá! Booth!" Aly shouts and lowers her weapon. "I almost maced you!"

"Yep." I bend over, hands on my knees, heart racing uncontrollably. "Tell that to my blood pressure."

"What the fuck are you doing here?" she asks, less scared but equally confused.

"I might ask you the same thing?" It's pitch black outside, and I don't see any other vehicles next to my truck. "How did you get here?"

She dismisses my question, and strolls past me, which is when I notice the oversized suitcase dragging behind her as I close the door. "Um, going somewhere?"

"No. But you are. This is my rental." She turns to face me, hands on her hips.

"Nice try, but I'm serious. Why are you here? Did something happen at the restaurant?"

Her eyes narrow. "Are you following me?"

A bark of laughter erupts from me. "I was here first. Did you miss the turn for Hell?"

She pinches the bridge of her nose and mutters, "Give me strength," before looking back up at me. "I was due to fly home this morning, but all flights are grounded. I've hardly spent any time out of the town, and it seemed like a good opportunity to paint—" She stops herself, face turning wry. "It's just better than sitting home alone. I reserved five nights at the..." Pulling out her phone, she scans the screen.

Please don't say The Nook. Please don't say The Nook.

"The Nook."

Son of a sea biscuit.

She catches my reaction. "What? This isn't The Nook." She steps forward, eyes flaring. "Tell me I took a wrong turn."

"Did you happen to book through a guy called Dexter Moore?"

"Mm-hmm." Her eyes are pleading, but she knows what I'm going to say.

"Then welcome home." With a grimace, I raise my hands out to my sides. "I'll be your host."

"No. *No.* I'm going to book somewhere else." She taps away at her phone, mumbling something in Greek. "Where is the nearest motel?"

"Ten miles east of you're-not-driving-anywhere-in-this-storm." I have her beat, because my eyebrow is already raised. "You can argue with me about *literally* anything else, but not this."

"And you became my keeper when?"

"Believe me, you are not to be kept. But I take responsibility for your safety when you've never experienced the winters here. Let alone in the middle of nowhere, where it could take days to find your overturned car." I pause. "Where *is* your car?"

In lieu of a response, she raises her chin.

"Alessandra," I growl. "Where's your car?"

The stubborn thing just glowers at me.

That's when I spot her jeans, soaked through up to her knees with clumps of snow sticking to her shoes. Concern replaces my anger and I scan her over. "Is that what happened? Did your car go off the road? Are you okay?"

The fight ebbs out of her posture at my anxious tone. "I'm fine." Her gaze lowers and she chews her lip. "My tires got stuck in the snow. I didn't have to walk far, don't worry."

"Well, too late for that. I am." Gently, I grip her arm and steer her toward the fire. This close, I see her hair is dripping and cheeks are bright red from the cold. "Sit and warm up. Take those jeans off too."

"Nice try," she mumbles but doesn't pull away.

I move to the small chest of drawers, grab a pair of sweats, and toss them to her.

"I have my own clothes."

Sighing, I rub at my eyes with the heels of my hands. "Wear

them. Don't wear them. Just get out of those wet clothes." My head flops forward in defeat. "*Please.*"

Her frown melts away. She fiddles with the drawstring on the sweats and then does something really weird.

"Thank you, Booth."

Then surprise strikes twice when a soft smile graces her lips.

Gratitude and a smile. Am I in the twilight zone?

I don't like what the tilt of her rosy lips does to me. How smile lines crease the flawless skin on her cheeks. It's subtle and all in her eyes. They glisten with the embers of the fire, making everything else appear dull and lifeless in comparison.

I don't like *it* because it makes me want to *like* her. Makes me wish we met under different circumstances.

Throwing a thumb over my shoulder, I back up toward the kitchen. "I'll give you some privacy."

With her distracted, I quickly hide my LEGOs then stir the pot of risotto and pretend I don't hear the teeth of her zipper or the sound of wet jeans hitting the floor with a slap. I certainly don't imagine my sweats gliding up her long legs or kissing the dip of her waist either.

The pad of bare feet nears closer.

"It smells good. What are you making?" she asks softly.

"Fennel and lemon risotto. There's plenty to go around." I twist to look at her. And *shit.* This is not good. She's rolled up the waistband of the sweats and has stripped off all her layers to reveal a faded gray Princeton T-shirt.

She's a little less put together, with flushed cheeks, bright eyes, and wild hair. One word: breathtaking.

"You hungry?" My voice cracks and I cough into my fist to hide it.

Her nose twitches as she eyes the simmering pot. "I could eat."

"Wine?"

"Please."

I nod once.

Twenty minutes and some shaved Parmigiano Reggiano later, we settle in front of the fire, each with a hearty bowl of piping hot risotto.

We're silent, uncertain about how to navigate this.

Until she takes her first bite and moans around her spoon.

The sound goes straight to my dick.

I push it to the back of my brain.

But then she does it again.

Louder.

Then again.

I break the silence. If I don't, *I* will break. "Are you enjoying that?"

That much is fucking obvious, you idiot.

She nods enthusiastically. "It's melting in my mouth. I need more."

Did that sound dirty, or did I make it dirty?

Rather than responding, I opt for more silence. And pray for a pair of earplugs to block out her little moans of pleasure.

Once our dishes are empty, bellies full, and Aly has stopped making inappropriate noises around utensils, we stare at each other.

Before the tension can creep in between us again, I offer her an explanation about why I'm here.

"Dexter—Dex—is Patrick's best friend. Though, he's basically like a third brother. He owns a bunch of cabins all over, but this one is usually left unreserved for family and friends. It was safer for me to stay here during the storm than my house. I'm not sure how it happened, but he's obviously double booked it. I have texts to prove tha—"

"I believe you." She relaxes into the sofa. "Earlier I was hungry, tired, and cold. I know I'm not the only one, but I was... sad about not being able to spend the holidays with my family."

She sounds guilty for being sad.

"I get it. I'd be down if I couldn't spend it with mine too."

"So we're really stuck up here?" she asks.

I take a big gulp of Rioja, then raise my glass to her. "Until the storm passes, yes."

She returns the gesture. "Here's hoping there's plenty of wine. If all meals are like that, I won't complain. It was delicious."

"Careful. Someone might hear you and think you like me." I smirk.

She rolls her eyes.

As if sensing another argument, the vintage cuckoo clock on the wall whistles, scaring Aly, who almost drenches herself in wine. "Good god. That thing is hideous. Please tell me it doesn't do that all night?"

"It doesn't. Actually, it's broken, so no one knows when it's going to go off." I rise, stretching and bending side to side. When Aly's gaze falls to my exposed stomach, I'm not ashamed to say my movements become exaggerated. Before I can tease her, a yawn breaks free, and I decide we've both had enough for the day. "I'm beat. You take the bed."

She looks at the queen-size bed in the corner of the room and then the two-seater sofa. "Will you fit?"

"I always make it fit." She'd deny it, but when I wink at her, a redness creeps up her neck.

"You're an idiot."

While she gets ready for bed in the small bathroom, I grab a spare pillow and blanket to make up my bed. It will actually be a very tight fit, and I'm not looking forward to it, but hopefully we can escape our prison soon.

When Aly emerges, I thank my lucky stars she's not donning a little silk negligee. Her deep red pajamas cover most of her, and her curls are piled on top of her head. I use the bathroom, and when I return, she's peeling back the covers.

"Right, well, good night," she says softly.

"Sweet dreams, Silver. Don't let the bedbugs bite. Or do. See if I care."

She flashes me her middle finger before I switch off the lights and fold myself in half to fit on the sofa.

Fuck being a gentleman.

I blame the woman who raised me for offering up the bed.

My legs are numb, there's a spring shafting me in the ass, and my back will never be the same.

Groaning, I toss. Then turn. And for good measure, toss again. The wooden legs of the sofa creak with my movements.

"Booth, I swear to god, if you make another noise I will make you wish you never existed," a frustrated voice hisses at me.

"I'm already there. Go back to sleep," I whisper-shout.

"I *haven't* slept. Your moaning has kept me up."

"I've never had a woman complain before."

The rolling of her eyes might as well be audible.

Silence resumes until I hear rustling bedsheets, followed by a deep exhale. "Get in the bed."

She doesn't need to ask me twice.

It's a good thing the dark hides my delighted smile or she might maim me. "Aren't you going to buy me dinner first?" My joke falls flat, but I don't push it. I practically nosedive onto the mattress, huddle underneath the covers, and sigh happily. Rolling over, I find her viperous stare aimed my way. A streak of moonlight lights up her scrunched brow and pouty lips. I'm hit with the rich scent of her, picking up notes of sage and lavender.

"Hands and feet to yourself." She slashes an arm down the middle of the bed. "Do not cross this barrier. Not even a pinky."

I lie on my back, folding my hands behind my head, and shut my eyes. I still feel her glowering at me. "I know better than to go into shark-infested waters. Good night, Silver."

The mattress shifts as she *harrumphs* and gets comfortable.

It takes no time at all to fall asleep.

And the last thought that crosses my mind is that I can't choose which I like more. Her heated scowl because of my dumb jokes or the softer side she tries to hide that somehow makes her more beautiful.

alessandra

A SHIVER TICKLES THE LENGTH OF MY SPINE AS TWO STRONG hands glide up my calves. Rough fingertips add to the heady sensation.

Everywhere aches, and with every inch the hands move higher, my core clenches in anticipation. I've been wet from the second his heated skin brushed over me, featherlight but electrifying.

My breaths come in fast, increasing in staccato. When he reaches my thighs, he changes tactics, his touches becoming lazier. Rather than a straight line, he veers inward, stroking the soft skin and pushing my legs apart.

I'm bared to him now. Not a stitch of clothing to hide my soaked pussy. Without the sense of sight, I'm completely at his mercy. The blindfold he asked me to wear intensifies everything. I'd kill to see the glow in his eyes as he drinks me in. For now, his husky groans, smoky scent, and torturous touches are enough to push me over the edge.

He's a faceless, nameless seductor.

I jolt when his lips graze just below my navel. "Are you wet for me?"

His voice drips with lust, but it's the deep chuckle that follows when I shake my head that has desire pulling low in my belly.

"Stubborn thing, aren't you, Silver?" he whispers.

Wait!

Silver.

Smoky scent.

I rip off the blindfold and find the man who coined that nickname lying between my open thighs.

What's weird is the huge, white chef hat on his head.

And why is he wearing cycling shorts?!

"What the fu—"

As if dropped from a great height, I jerk upright and my eyes spring open.

I'm in bed.

The mattress is smooth, warm, and firm.

When I turn my head, mortification hits me with the force of a freight train.

I'm in bed, yes. But I'm not lying on a mattress.

My entire body is sprawled out over a sleeping Booth; leg hitched high over his hip and hand splayed across his solid chest. His hands are tucked behind his head like they were when he fell asleep. From the looks of it, he's barely moved an inch.

It's me that's crossed the barrier, crawled on top of him to cling to him like a baby koala.

Move too suddenly and I risk waking him, but I can't stay like this.

I raise my hand slowly off his pec.

My leg is the tricky part. Our legs are tangled together like twisting vines.

If I shift a little to the right and wig—

"Can you hurry so I can stop pretending to be asleep?" a gravelly voice grumbles.

Gasping, I push up to find his sleepy gaze staring at me in amusement. He yawns, not a drop of embarrassment to be seen. I'm the one drowning in it.

"How long have you been awake?" My voice pitches.

"When you jumped like you'd been electrocuted. Didn't take you for a cuddler." His lips twitch.

"I am not a cuddler," I argue.

His eyes drop to our intertwined limbs. "Could have fooled me."

I throw myself backward, immediately feeling cold. The fire went out hours ago and without it, the cabin is freezing. The drop in temperature has nothing to do with the loss of Booth's body heat.

"You should have woken me." I tug the comforter to my chest, even though I'm covered head to toe in red flannel. Booth, however, is naked from the waist up, the sheets draped over him to show the top of his blue pajama pants.

I was too pissed off at him the other day to admire him. Now, I can't tear my eyes away. Smooth, hard skin on full display. The divots of his abs shift slightly with his breathing, and a deep *V* cuts low on his abdomen. His chest is bare, but there's a smattering of hair below his belly button that disappears under his waistband. He's beautiful. All sharp lines and lean muscle.

"My eyes are up here, Silver." He purrs my name, exactly how he did in my dream.

Oh god, I had a sex dream about him.

He's not a mind reader, though the cocky grin he's flashing leaves me doubtful.

"You're adorable when you're asleep. Your nose scrunches up—just like this." He wiggles his nose.

"I am not adorable. Stop talking. Please. And wipe whatever happened from your memory."

He swallows, eyes sweeping over me. "Highly unlikely."

Frustrated with myself and his casual reaction, I throw back the covers and bolt from the bed. Stomping over to the large window in front of the bathtub, I ignore his laughter.

The view outside doesn't help my mood.

The storm has worsened. The tree line has been swallowed up by the thick wall of snow falling rapidly from the sky. It's so heavy, it creeps up the window, growing before my eyes.

We're not going anywhere today.

I sense him behind me. "Do you need to call anyone?"

"I spoke to my family yesterday. I should check in with them, though."

"Use my phone. The service is crap around here, but I get a couple of bars by the front door."

Thankfully, he's put on a sweatshirt.

"I won't be long." I force a smile when he hands me his phone. "Thank you."

Before I walk away, he says, "I'll make breakfast. Anything you don't like or allergies?"

"I'm not picky, but I can cook for my—"

"Aly, I'm cooking for you. Call your parents." He leaves me and starts throwing fresh logs into the wood-burning stove.

After speaking to my father and begging him to reassure my mom I'm safe, we say goodbye. I'm sad to not be with them, especially as I haven't seen my brothers in a couple of months, but we make plans to see each other soon. Christmas is always a mish-mash of American and Greek traditions. Instead of ham or turkey, we have *moschari lemonato*—a roast beef dish with lemon gravy. Out of everything, I'll miss my mom's *melomakarona* cookies the most.

Booth makes us the fluffiest scrambled eggs, which I devour. He doesn't stop me when I do the washing up and busies himself by stoking the fire.

We're quiet. Polite. Civil.

It's awkward.

I'm sifting through my bag, searching for a change of clothes while he lounges on the sofa, now in a pair of gray sweats. Every time his eyes drift toward me from the other side of the room, my body heats. I'm concentrating so hard to not think about him I don't see his duffel bag at the foot of the bed. Flailing, I reach for the closest thing to right myself, which is my suitcase, scattering the contents everywhere.

If I thought waking up curled into Booth was humiliating, my vibrator flying through the air and landing on the pillow with a *plop* is the pinnacle.

My head turns slowly, hoping to find an oblivious Booth.

He's staring right at the black silicone object with an impressed expression.

I prepare for his immature quip, suiting up in my armor, ready to call him out.

"Get it over with," I snap, hating my defensive tone.

He looks shocked at my outburst. "Is this another trap?"

"You're dying to make a joke." I gesture toward the vibrator. "Get it out of your system."

I fold my arms, hip jutting to the side as I wait. Daring him to say something with my eyes.

"I'm not one to miss the opportunity to make people laugh, but I don't find women's pleasure funny. Far from it." He doesn't budge. His posture is confident, legs spread wide, spine flush against the sofa as he observes me. "I take it *very* seriously."

He needs to stop talking.

"I don't think you're capable of being serious."

His head tilts. "When it counts, I can be."

My spine tingles with awareness; the hidden meaning clear.

Tempting him would be careless. The thing with Booth, though, is I can't seem to help myself.

My next words are smug, voice breathy. "My toy has never let me down like a man has."

Our gazes don't break, welded together by the sparks flickering between us.

His eyes blaze, burning bright and fierce. "Prove it."

He's the kindling with those two bold words. The lit match is held between my fingers.

"You think I won't?" I perch myself on the edge of the bed, ankles crossed, as I prop myself up on one arm.

"You haven't backed down so far. Why stop now?" His Adam's apple bobs as he tracks a fiery path over my body.

We both know why this isn't a good idea. One: we don't even like each other. Two: we work together.

But when he leans forward, elbows balanced on his knees with a yearning I can feel from across the room, all sense of reason evaporates. "You tell me no, and we forget this conversation ever happened."

"And if I say yes..." I don't blink. Don't dare move a muscle.

"Then you get that glorious body spread out on those sheets, stripped bare, and show me what you can do with that toy." He drags his thumb across his bottom lip lazily. "Prove to me I can't do it better."

All the air leaves my lungs. Because I want that. I'm actually certain he *could* do it better, but I'm not telling him that. The toy is a good six inches, and from the tenting in his sweats, Booth isn't lacking in the size category.

"Don't let your ego get too bruised when I prove you wrong." I shuffle toward the headboard.

"Yes or no. I want your explicit consent right now," his deep voice echoes.

"Yes." My response is instantaneous.

Those goddamn fucking dimples pop out. "Clothes off and lie back."

My heart pounds against my rib cage at his demanding words.

He rises, then prowls toward me. When he comes to the

edge of the bed, he doesn't sit. Just stands there, eating up every inch of me with a single look.

I've always been confident in the bedroom. I know what I like and when to ask for it. The only explanation for the slight tremble in my hands is the thrill of it all.

He's giving me the opportunity to say no; to not cross this line.

Right now, I want to feed the excitement coursing through my veins. To rise to his challenge. To surrender to this. Just once.

I get to work on the buttons of my pajamas, eyes on him the entire time. The lower I travel, the darker his irises get. When my shirt gapes open, scantily covering my peaked nipples, there's no blue left. Sky blue eaten up by midnight.

I'm like a human torch; hot from excitement. The cool air in the cabin kisses my skin while the heat of his admiration warms me from the inside out.

"I bet you're fucking soaked right now. Dripping down your thighs and aching to be filled." He jerks his chin. "Keep going. I want to see all of you."

I glance at the prominent bulge pressing against the front of his sweats, my voice teasing. "Eager, pretty boy?"

He shakes his head and chuckles.

With deliberate slowness, I slide my shirt from my shoulders and shimmy out of my pants, dropping them to the floor. I keep my knees tucked together as I recline against the downy pillow.

He raises a hand and, with two fingers, gestures to the side. "Open. Slowly."

"Bossy." Despite my sass, my legs drop open, exposing myself fully.

Booth sucks in a sharp breath as he scrubs a hand against the stubble on his jaw. He takes his time admiring me. "Fuck, if you're not the most stunning woman I've ever seen. You might have a sharp tongue, but you're all soft curves under there. You're in charge this time, baby. But next time—"

"No *next* time. This is a one-time-only occurrence. Right now, we're strangers. When we leave here, we go back to wanting to strangle each other. Deal?"

It's fleeting, but he looks disappointed.

"Deal." In two steps, he looms over me and plucks the toy off the pillow before dropping it between my open legs. "Get to work, Silver."

There's no turning back now.

He falls to his knees on the mattress, positioning himself at my feet. I grab the toy, and with one click, it comes to life. The low hum, our heavy breathing, and the crackling of wood disappear when I coast the silicone tip between my breasts, over my navel, and stop at the top of my pelvis. My eyes lower but snap up at his gruff tone.

"Eyes on me. I'll keep my hands to myself, but your eyes are mine, and it'll be my name on your lips when you come."

Not wanting to think he's totally in charge, I wink at him slyly and whisper, "Yes, *Chef*."

His laughter dies when the toy lowers. My skin tingles under the vibrations, and when it hits my clit, a gasp slips free. I drag it back and forth idly with the barest of touches. Torturing myself and Booth with the way his hands fist on top of the comforter.

"How does it feel?" he murmurs, eyes following the journey of my hand.

"So good," I husk.

"Tell me what you're going to do next." He pulls his bottom lip into his mouth when I moan.

"I like to start off slow, then I increase the speed." I click the button, the humming sound increasing.

"Look at you glistening. So pretty and pink." My eyebrow

rises in warning when he crawls forward. "I won't touch you. I just want to look."

The pleading in his voice makes me lightheaded, knowing he's turned on from simply watching me. It makes me feel sexy. Powerful.

I press down, pulsing it against my pussy as I shift my hips up and down. My arousal pools beneath me, desperate and greedy for more.

My control hangs by a thread, but if he touches me, this will all go up in an inferno.

Both wanton and deprived, I don't stop. My legs widen, my moans turn rough.

"Slower, Silver," he growls as I play with my entrance, pushing the tip in. "I want to see that beautiful cunt stretch around your toy."

I do as he says, too pleasure drunk to respond. It's not a thick vibrator, but it still has me gasping.

"What I wouldn't do for that to be my cock. I want you to imagine it's me. Filling you perfectly."

Stars burst in my vision, and when I regain focus, Booth is settled on his stomach, splayed out between my legs. The bed shifts, which is when I notice his hips lightly thrusting into the mattress.

This whole scene is lewd. Filthy. Hungry.

And it pushes me closer and closer to the edge.

"Don't stop. Fuck yourself with the toy," he grunts. "God, I've never been so fucking hard. Are you close?"

So close, it's overwhelming. All I manage is a jerk of my head and raspy "Yes" as my eyes flutter closed.

"Ah-ah," he chides. "Eyes. Be a good girl for me, Silver. Fall apart. Imagine it's me filling you up. Thrusting into you. Could you take my cock in that greedy pussy? I know you want that. I'd be so good to you."

Even in the heat of the moment, wordplay is our foreplay.

"Too bad this is a one-time thing. I should make it good for you then." I shift to my knees, hovering above my hand. The position causes the toy to hit me deeper, brushing my G-spot, as I gyrate my hips. Arousal coats my hand, dripping down my fingers and onto the bed.

Booth is right there, watching my every movement with apt fascination. Hips grinding in time with mine. He's laser focused on me, I'm not even sure he realizes what he's doing as he grunts softly with each thrust into the mattress.

He's losing control as he watches me unravel.

And that's all it takes.

"Oh god." Pleasure coils deep, pulling at my stomach muscles. "I'm gonna come."

"My name. I want to hear my name. Let go for me, beautiful."

Do I ever.

His name flies from my mouth, dancing with my cries. "Booth, fuck, right there." I bounce on the toy with each roll of my orgasm, my movements sloppy as I succumb to the blinding pleasure.

His hot breath blows across my sensitive skin as a deep groan rumbles from his throat. "There you go. Look at you. So good. *So good*, Alessandra."

It's my full name on his lips that sends a final jolt of electricity to my core.

His head thumps against the mattress. "Fuuuck."

We're both panting. My skin is slick with sweat, thighs sticky. As the fog lifts, I don't let myself question what we just did. Not now. I'll regret it later when we part ways.

I slump forward, legs collapsing beneath me, and watch Booth rise. His cheeks are flushed, and my eyes widen when they fall to the dark patch on the front of his sweats.

Did he...

He laughs and drags a hand through his messy hair. "Well, that's a first."

Oh. My. God.

Most men would be embarrassed, but I'm not sure Booth is capable of that.

Knowing that he came—without laying a finger on me, while fully clothed—reignites the heat between my legs.

I suddenly don't know where to look.

A touch to my face pulls me from my thoughts. With a hooked finger, he raises my chin. "You okay?"

The care in his voice and expression tug at something deep in my chest. It's a weird feeling. Foreign. He shouldn't be concerned about me after this, right? How can he go from despising me one second, to domineering the next, to *this*?

"I'm fine." My response is clipped, but he doesn't react.

"Good. That was—" He coughs into his fist, cutting himself off.

"We don't need to talk about it," I say, and grab my pajamas. "We actually shouldn't."

He frowns, eyes off to the side as I dress. "Right. Yeah. One time." When he looks at me again, his smile is watered down. "I'm gonna get some more wood and then I'll make us lunch. You like smoked salmon?"

"Sounds good."

He watches me for a second.

It's safer if I don't say anything.

When he opens the door, the blast of freezing air is a wake-up call.

I need to get out of here.

Because the look he flashes me before he steps over the threshold isn't filled with loathing or annoyance.

No, it's something much worse.

He wears the same infatuated expression I saw that day at the fair.

CHAPTER SEVENTEEN

booth

She's freaking out.

Or maybe I'm freaking out.

Either way, it's been tense since I walked back into the cabin with arms full of firewood. We both showered—separately. I made us lunch, and now thick, awkward silence hangs in the air.

I know little about Aly—she prefers it that way—but her internalized thoughts were written across her face. If there was one thing I've learned, it's not to push her.

She was a willing participant—so fucking willing and gorgeous. I gave her the opportunity to say no, and she made it very clear where we stood afterward. The error I made was diving headfirst into this complex pool of feelings, without a life preserver.

But my god, was she glorious.

She owned it. The room. Her body. Me. It was a struggle to get air in when I watched her take control of her pleasure. If I had died then, and the sight of her fucking herself on the toy was the last thing I saw, so be it.

Half of me was joking when I dared her to prove it. The other was ravenous.

So when she rose to the challenge, it shocked the hell out of me, knocked me on my ass, and left me stunned and speechless.

Well, almost.

I also couldn't help but spur her on and shower her with praise.

Because at that moment, we were strangers, like she'd said. Not Booth the chef or Aly the owner.

Then the bubble burst and we were back to reality.

Since then, she's avoided me, which is pretty hard in a small log cabin in the middle of nowhere. As much as I like to push her buttons, it wouldn't be wise today. We have lunch, she reads her book on the sofa, and I don't know what the fuck I'm supposed to do.

I'm restless. I want to bring out my LEGO, but I'm also not in the mood for her to tease me like my brothers do. Some might say it's childish, but there's something therapeutic about it.

The blizzard dies down, minutes tick by, and the silence becomes unbearable.

"We don't have to talk about this morning, but I'm going out of my mind right now," I blurt.

She peers at me over the pages curiously. "I'm not playing LEGO, but you're free to do so."

My brows slam down. "It's not *playing*. It's a collector's item."

She ignores my prickly tone. "Is it a hobby?"

"I'm not answering that if you're going to roast me." I pout.

My eyes fall to the table, feeling exposed. Her book thuds closed then her socked feet appear in front of me. "I saw it at your apartment after we went lobster fishing, and again last night. I thought it was for your niece at first. Lottie, right?"

I look up. "She wishes I'd let her play with my LEGO."

"You see how you're asking for me to poke fun at you, right?" She smirks, and perches on the sofa beside me. To my surprise, she opens up the ottoman I stowed the half-built monument in last night and studies it. "This looks familiar."

"Have you visited Italy?" I ask.

She nods, then her eyes light up. "Nicola Salvi is rolling in his grave knowing his architecture has been minimized to tiny plastic blocks."

"You know who Salvi is?"

"*You* know who Salvi is?" she retorts.

Ignoring her jab, I pull out the structure and bag of remaining pieces. "I'm not some dumb chef, you know."

"I—that's...that's not what I was implying, Booth."

"Could have fooled me," I mutter.

She sighs. "Booth, I really do—"

"I can't pretend it didn't happen. That makes it weirder. We need to air it out before we bury it."

The turn in conversation shocks her. "I thought we weren't going to talk about it?"

I flick a beige block. "Yeah, well, I lied."

She sighs and picks up a small black brick and studies the instructions I've laid out on the table. "We work together, that should make it obvious why it can't happen again. Plus, you don't even like me."

My head snaps to the right. "I never said that."

"You didn't have to. I'm not exactly your number one fan either." She laughs.

Like a goldfish, my mouth opens and closes, but what do I say? She's not wrong. Forty-eight hours ago, we were ready to declare war. Now, it's clouded with contradictions.

What I'm about to ask might sound desperate, but I'm genuinely curious. "If you weren't, you know—" I gesture at her.

"Your boss," she finishes.

"I was going to say 'Medusa,' but sure, that works too." I wink, and then I'm surprised for what feels like the hundredth time today.

Aly laughs. It's bubbly, bright, and coaxes out a smile that has her teeth gleaming and eyes crinkling. She looks quite cute. I don't tell her that, though, on account of me valuing my life.

"If you hadn't bought the restaurant, and you happened into town randomly..." I lean forward, hands linked between my spread knees as I watch the flames of the fire dance and flicker. "Would this be different?"

"What do you mean?" Her tone is cautious.

"Would you have given me a chance?"

There, it's out there now. I'm aware I sound like a crushing high schooler, but after this morning, who can blame me?

When I finally chance a look at her, her attention is on the fireplace, too, her sharp features cast in a warm glow. She's deep in thought, and the longer she leaves me hanging, the less I think I'm going to like the answer.

Above the crackling I barely hear her. "I meant what I said; I'm only here temporarily."

"And about me not being your type?"

I catch the corner of her mouth hitch up. "That might have been a fib, but I had good reason. You wouldn't take no for an answer."

I'm toeing the line. The need to get to know her is too strong to ignore, and inside these four walls, we've shed away the titles and disdain.

"When I asked what your plans were, you said you didn't know. Is that still the case?"

She doesn't flinch. It's her voice that gives away her wariness; a quality she rarely wears. "Bursting into the kitchen and announcing who I was might not have been my finest moment. I'd wanted to scope out the restaurant and the town first." She casts me a side glance. "I know the industry inside and out. You might all think I'm some money-grabbing investor, but my family's ethos isn't about that. We've backed up plenty of family-owned hotels in the past and merged them into our chain. While this isn't our typical investment, I wouldn't risk putting money down on something I didn't believe in."

The truth shines bright in her words, but also leaves me with more questions.

"If we're not a typical business for you to back, why did you?"

This question gets a reaction. Her lips flatten and hands fiddle with the hem of her sweater. A few errant curls escape, and before I know what I'm doing, I brush them away, the pads of my fingers lingering on the shell of her ear.

"Alessandra, why are you here?" I whisper. It's not accusatory, like the last time.

"Don't ask me that, Booth. Go back to wanting me gone."

My hand drops to rest on hers. "I'm not sure I can, unless you give me reason to. Do you not have an answer, or do you not want to share it with me?"

Give me something, you stubborn, stunning creature.

Maybe it's the confines of this tiny cabin and the proximity we've been forced into. Whatever it is, I want to crack her wide open to see all the beautiful, dangerous, secretive thoughts she keeps inside spill out. I imagine it would reveal bold colors and moody strokes, like the paintings she creates.

Her lack of response leaves the air between us void of color.

She slips her hand out from under mine, spine going taut and eyes narrowing. I curse myself for pushing her too far.

If I were to venture a guess, her reluctance to open up has nothing to do with me, but trust. Something I don't think she gives out freely.

And suddenly, I'm desperate to earn it.

She stands and returns to her book before I can change the subject. The pages flutter open as she cracks the spine.

With the snow having stopped, I escape and clear my truck before the sun sets. Aly's car is a short walk down the hill, and I clear it enough to drive it up to the cabin. For every second I sit in her car and breathe in her intoxicating perfume, the angrier I become that I didn't get a taste. *Fuck,* I'd witnessed her spread out delectably, watched her come undone, came in my pants, and we didn't even kiss.

Thank god it looks like we can leave soon, otherwise the temptation to press my lips to hers will drive me into a frenzy.

"Good news," I call as I enter the cabin and shake the snow from my boots. "We should be out of here by tomorrow evening."

Silence greets me.

My head snaps around, searching.

It doesn't take me long to find her.

Standing at the floor-to-ceiling window, Aly is wrapped in a white fluffy towel, hair hanging heavy as it drips onto the floor. Had I returned minutes earlier, would she have been hidden under a cascade of bubbles?

Pale skin flushed from the hot water, and face bare of makeup, she looks out at the wintery landscape. The white glare of the snow through the glass has her appearing gossamer. Like if I reached out and touched her, she'd float away.

All the more reason to hold her.

Jesus Christ, what is happening?

I need a stiff drink.

Or an intervention.

Coughing, I avert my gaze. "I can give you some space if you want," I say, louder this time.

She spins, lips parted as if she forgot she wasn't alone.

"Oh, no. It's fine. Sorry, thought I'd take advantage of the tub while you were out. Thanks for moving my car." She tugs at the towel. "So tomorrow?"

"As long as the storm doesn't return, the roads should be safe." I step closer until our shoulders are inches apart. "I'd feel better if I drove you back into town. I can bring you to get your car after Christmas or take you to the airport."

"I don't think I'll make it back in time." The sadness in her voice digs into my sternum.

Is she close to her family like I am with mine?

Not wanting to rub salt in the wound, I point to a tall conifer overshadowing the cabin. "See that tree? My brothers and I dared each other to climb it one year. I made it about fifteen feet before I fell, smack into the snow, and snapped my clavicle."

Her airy laugh bounces off the glass. "Your poor parents. How the heck did they handle three unruly boys?"

I puff out my chest. "Oh, this was three years ago. I was a big, brave boy. Didn't even cry."

"Oh my god." She's full on belly laughing now, bent at the waist as she tries to catch her breath.

It's a mesmerizing sound. Even lovelier to witness.

Leaning against the window, I drink her in. If today is all we get before it's back to reality, then I don't want to waste a second. "Hey, Silver?"

Swiping at her lashes, still grinning, she turns to me. "Yeah?"

"Will you have dinner with me tonight? Word on the street is the chef is quite talented. And handsome."

Her smile slowly retreats but doesn't completely disappear. It lingers on her blushing face and mixes with the indecisiveness swirling in her expression.

I pluck a damp curl off her shoulder and tap her on the nose with it, eliciting a scowl that holds zero malice. "We can split the bill at the end. Don't make it weird. I'm not your type, remember?"

With a parting wink, I saunter into the kitchen and pull out the ingredients for mac and cheese.

She doesn't respond, though I hear the rustling of clothes behind me as I mince the garlic. I deserve ten gold stars for not taking a peek over my shoulder.

A few minutes later, she joins me beside the stove and peers around my shoulder. She's in those goddamn pajamas again. The ones that are etched into my brain for an eternity. Well, second to the sight of her out of them.

"What's cooking?" Her tone is more relaxed compared to earlier.

My knife hovers above a clove as I look down at her, frowning. "You said it wrong."

"Huh?"

"It's 'What's cookin', good lookin'?' Pfft, you've got a way to go around these parts, Miss Argiros."

She flicks me on the ear before hopping onto the counter. "In your dreams."

You sure are.

Distracting myself—because my 180-degree feelings are making me woozy—I finish up the garlic and get started on the roux. "There's only one right answer to this question, so choose wisely." I lean in, voice low. "Do you like lobster?"

A dark brow arches. "Of course."

"Good girl. Maybe one day I'll cook you that tuna tartare you love so much. Now, pass me that stick of butter, and in that cabinet behind your head, you should find some all-purpose flour."

She passes me the ingredients from her spot, and we work in tandem, throwing digs and joking until the smell of gooey cheddar and nutty gruyère floats in the air.

Seated around the small dinner table, we eat in silence,

sharing fleeting looks between bites. It's nice, peaceful. And perhaps the most domesticated thing I've ever done.

Once the dishes are done, and our eyes grow heavy, we stare at the bed.

I hook a thumb over my shoulder. "I'll leave you to it. Wouldn't want you crossing the danger zone again."

She climbs in, then tosses a pillow at my head. "Get in, you goof. Spooning is PG after this morning's show."

I swear I try not to smile too wide as I slide in beside her.

"Sweet dreams, Silver."

"Good night, *Dimples*."

Sadly, no boundaries are crossed in the middle of the night.

Pretty hard when there's only one person in the bed.

I pretend to be asleep while she shuffles around. When the front door clicks shut and her engine starts, I stare up at the ceiling. A little disappointed, but mostly feeling like a fool.

Who knows how much time passes before I drag myself out of bed.

I'm half tempted to start a new fire and throw the note she left on the coffee table into the flames.

Booth,

The last few days were surprisingly the most fun I've had in a while.

Yesterday morning was...I'll let you fill in the blanks.

Thank you for distracting me when I couldn't be with my family.

I'm hoping it doesn't come as a surprise when I say yesterday shouldn't have happened.

There's no regret on my end, and you didn't pressure me into anything.

It's easier if I'm the boss you wish would disappear, and you're the employee who lives to irritate me.

Merry Christmas,

Silver

With the cabin locked up and my truck easing down the snowy road, I push all thoughts of her out of my head. I can't say I blame her. She forewarned me.

By the time I reach my house, I've done the complete opposite. My brain is flooded with her.

No life raft. No help.

No fucking clue what to do.

booth

"Lottie." I peer down at my niece lovingly. Quite the contrast to her sulky pout. "You have to eat your vegetables."

"They're yucky." She gags dramatically.

Lottie enjoys hanging out with me when I'm cooking. She's good company, even though she eats half the ingredients and asks a hundred questions per minute.

For the last couple of hours, I've been sweating my ass off in my mom's kitchen finishing Christmas dinner. With her leg still in a cast after her fall, I offered to cook again like I did at Thanksgiving.

"If you don't eat them, your dad won't let you have any of Aunty Quinn's apple pie."

Her head whips side to side until she gets dizzy, nearly toppling over.

"Okay, okay, you little toad." I kneel so we're eye level. "If you eat half your green beans and all your sweet potato casserole, we can sneak the rest to Curly."

"Will not!" calls a deep voice.

Lottie snickers behind her fingers. "Uncle Graham doesn't like us feeding Curly."

"What he doesn't know won't hurt him." I ruffle her hair.

"I'm literally right here. Listening to you both conspire." Graham walks in with his Dachshund, Curly, trotting behind him, tail wagging.

"Curly!" Lottie squeals and dives to her knees, rolling around with the dog, who eats up the attention.

"Stop teaching her bad habits!" He punches me in the shoulder.

"Um, ow. And no. I'm the fun uncle. It's my job. Right, toad?"

"Uh-huh." She nods, while avoiding Curly's sloppy kisses. "Last week, Uncle Boo showed me how to get chips from the vending machine. We got a dollar, some string, and then—"

I slap a hand over her mouth, silencing her. "And that's enough talking for today."

"Perfect. You're teaching my daughter how to be a klepto-maniac." Patrick walks in.

"Oh, come to join the party?" I turn to Lottie and blow a raspberry. "As the pooper!"

Her laughter is contagious. Even Patrick's scowl shifts to a smile as he watches her vibrate into a fit of giggles, wheezing, "Daddy poops."

When she calms down, he plucks her off the floor and slings her over his shoulder. "Let's leave Uncle Boo to it or we'll never eat."

I straighten and head back over to the stove, checking on the potatoes and cranberry sauce.

"Smells good in here," Graham says. "Thanks for doing this again."

"My pleasure. Your girlfriend helped on the dessert front." I point a wooden spoon at him. "Don't fuck it up."

He sits on a stool at the island, expression contemplative. "Never. Trust me. She's the best thing to ever happen to me."

His face goes all gooey, eyes hazing over. Usually his lovey-dovey show triggers nausea. Not today. Today it pulls at something deep in my chest...

He's not wrong, though. Quinn brought him back from the shadows after he dubbed himself unlovable thanks to his wench of an ex. Same for Johanna and Patrick. My oldest brother had given up on the idea of love, and buried himself in work, but he never forgot Jo after she up and left town suddenly. When she returned, she gave him a new lease on life; along with raising Lottie, she filled his heart.

My brothers haven't changed; they're the best versions of themselves. Because of a silly four-letter word?

"The water is boiling over!" Graham shouts.

I jump back, spinning the dial to kill the flame. "No need to shout."

"I said your name three times. You were miles away then." Deadpan, he asks, "Finally, find your brain?"

"Hilarious." Steam billows around me as I drain the potatoes and set them aside. "I was distracted. Still need to catch up on my sleep."

"Did you not get enough at The Nook?" His tone is suspicious.

Not nearly enough. Plus, last night, a certain woman infiltrated my dreams.

But I don't tell him that.

"Meh. The storm kept me up," I reply casually.

Then in walks Dex.

And boy, do I have a bone to pick with him. I gave him an earful yesterday about the double-booking situation and his response: my bad.

"What are we talking about?" Dex looks between us.

Graham jerks his head in my direction. "He's whiny because he didn't get enough sleep at the cabin."

"Hard to sleep when you're sharing a bed with the owner, you mean?" He smirks and knocks his shoulder into mine.

My eye twitches as I fight the urge to pummel him.

"New rule. Holidays are for family only," I grit out, right as Graham gapes at me and says much too loudly, "You slept with her!"

Pinching my nose, I sigh. "For over thirty years, you've been the quiet one. *Now* you decide to be a loudmouth?"

Graham shrugs. "I'm not the one sleeping with the enemy."

"Jesus." I turn to Dex, making sure he can read my lips. "Isn't there some confidentiality rule you're breaking by disclosing your guest's identity?"

"Sue me. Now spill." Fingers steepled under his chin, he beams at me.

"Oooh, tea." My sister strolls in with a pair of reindeer antlers on her head.

"No. *No.* One hundred percent no." I point at each of them, ending on Florence. "There is no tea. The cup is dry. Go about your lives, stop interfering in mine, and let me finish dinner."

They're all silent for a beat before they bark with laughter.

Graham is the first to speak. "Rich coming from the guy who makes it his life's mission to stick his nose into *our* business."

I ignore him, spoon a knob of butter into the potatoes, then angrily mash them.

"So who's going to tell me what's going on?" Florence chirps.

Dex is the one to respond. "Booth appears to have changed alliances and has *finally* charmed Alessandra into bed with him."

"You fucked the boss?!" Harriet—who I didn't even hear come in—shrieks.

Harriet is Johanna's younger sister and my high school girlfriend. We gave each other our virginities and then promptly realized we were better off as friends. Even though she lives in Tennessee, we've remained close.

Right now, however, she's the straw breaking the camel's back.

"Everyone out! A kitchen is no place for gossiping." I throw a handful of uncooked cranberries at them. "For the record. I didn't sleep with her. Yes, we both got stuck in the cabin together, but we were forced into that situation. She left, then probably jumped on the next flight out of here. End of story. Now, leave me in peace or I'll throw the food in the trash."

To my relief, a chorus of sighs and one "You're no fun" meet my ears before they reluctantly traipse into the dining room.

With a deep breath, I shut my eyes, collecting myself.

Dex is getting laxatives in his serving.

I finish the potatoes, glaze the ham, plate up the sides, and forget all about Alessandra.

Twenty minutes later, the table is crammed full of food, and we're all fighting for a seat.

"Mom, what's with the extra place settings?" Patrick points at two empty chairs.

"Did I not tell you? I invited a couple of friends who are alone this Christmas because of the storm." She glances down at her watch. "They're running late."

As if on cue, the doorbell chimes. My siblings and I exchange curious looks. It's not unusual for my mom to invite people over. For the last two years, Martin Willis has joined us.

"Booth, sweetheart, would you answer that, seeing as you're up?" my mom says.

"Sure, Ma." I set the gravy dish down and head to the front door.

To no surprise, Martin stands on the other side of the threshold.

Only, he isn't alone.

Shoulders back, face impassive, and chin held high, Aly stares at me, completely unbothered. The only giveaway to her discomfort is the white-knuckling of her hand around the paper bag she's holding.

Me? My heart is ready to punch out of my chest while my brain simultaneously tells me to slam the door shut.

Neither of us speaks. The silence drags as the cold air claws at my face. I grip the door so hard, the wood creaks.

"You okay there, Booth?" Martin's eyes dart between Aly and me.

I lose the staring contest and gesture inside. "Yeah, sorry. Come in."

"Ladies first," Martin says to Aly, who barely glances at him as she hurries through the door.

I take three seconds to calm myself before turning to our new guests, a smile plastered on so tightly, my cheeks ache. "Martin. Merry Christmas. Good to have you again this year. Everyone is in the dining room. Why don't you head in, I need to speak to Alessandra."

Martin doesn't question me and ambles away.

"There's nothing to discuss," she snaps once he's out of earshot.

Folding my arms, I give her a once-over. Which is a mistake. Her beige duster coat is unbuttoned, giving me the perfect view of the forest green dress molded to her body. My teeth clench as I'm transported back to the cabin. With her. Sans dress. Lean legs spread. Dusty pink nipples rising and falling with her moans. Taut tummy contracting as she comes. Only this time there is no toy. Because she's riding me to the finish.

Huffing, she storms away, but I snatch her by the wrist to gently tug her back.

"There's plenty to discuss." I drop her hand, our glares inches apart. "I've asked this of you plenty—but why are you here?"

She sucks in a long breath, like the answer keeps getting

stuck in her throat. "Your mom is the sweetest manipulator I've ever come across."

"Sorry, my mom?" Then it hits me. Her guests. "*She* invited you?"

A throat clears, and we spin to find Mother dearest at the end of the hallway. Throwing daggers in my direction. "*She* did, Booth Elias."

"Elias," Aly titters.

I don't look at her.

"Alessandra, so lovely of you to join us. I'm sure my youngest son was offering to take your coat."

Because I value my life, I do just that.

My gaze sticks to the back of her head as she shrugs out of her coat, letting it drop into my arms without a backward glance. With the paper bag in hand again, she pulls out a Tupperware and a bottle of wine.

"It's really kind of you to have me. It's not much, but I had time to make some *melomakarona*—a family recipe. It's a traditional Greek dessert."

"Oh, how lovely. Let me take you through." Baked goods are the way to my mom's heart. She loops her arm through Aly's and escorts her away, chatting happily.

What the fuck is my fucking life?

CHAPTER NINETEEN

alessandra

I'LL COME TO REGRET THIS DECISION TOMORROW.

It had been one day since I escaped the cabin, when I bumped into Claire yesterday afternoon in the grocery store. I was on the hunt for an easy, one-person dinner and hadn't expected an invitation to Christmas at the Sadler household, let alone that I'd accept. She's good, I'll give her that. After politely declining for five times, she came out victorious. Her only request: a dish for the table.

After leaving the store—armed with the ingredients needed to make my grandmother's *melomakarona*—I spent the day baking and mentally preparing to see Booth again. The Greek spicy honey cookies are a crowd-pleaser when my mom does them. But just in case, I bought a bottle of wine to wash it down with.

The disappointment of not spending the holidays with my family is the only explanation for why I said yes.

Nothing else.

Claire is nice.

Her son is...complicated.

Regardless, he didn't play any part in my decision-making.

Nada.

So why does my skin still tingle from where his fingertips brushed my shoulders?

"Everyone, I think you've all met Alessandra by now," Claire announces to the room, and I'm met with a mixture of greetings. Some friendly. Most cautious.

I avoid Martin's gaze, but it proves difficult when I'm seated next to him at the table. Fortunately for me, he's deep in conversation with George.

To my left is a new face and one of the cautious greeters. "Hi, I'm Harriet, Johanna's sister."

"Ah." I take her outstretched hand. "Nice to meet you. Alessandra."

Nodding slowly, she releases me. "I know who you are."

Okayyy.

"Not a fan, then?" My question catches her off guard, and the attention of half a dozen sets of eyes around the room.

"I'm impartial." She takes a sip of water before relaxing into her chair. "On one hand, you saved my family's business, so some would argue I should be eternally grateful."

"And on the other?"

"I think you went about it the wrong way. Plus, you clearly have it out for Booth."

"You don't hold back, do you? Not even sixty seconds in my seat." I sling an arm over the back of my chair to face her fully. Something about my tone or posture has her shedding a little animosity. She's blunt, but I can tell from the way she's fiddling with her napkin it's not natural.

"Shit, I'm so—"

She clamps her mouth shut when I clink my glass with hers. "Don't apologize. Stand by your words."

Everyone decides a catfight isn't going to break out and returns to their conversations.

Ignoring the strange tension, I ask, "You and Booth talk a lot?"

"You could say that. Not about you, though. Don't let it get to your head." Maybe Booth put her up to this. Like her sister, she says what's on her mind, and I can't fault her for it, but this act seems forced.

"No ego will ever be bigger than his." I nod toward the man on the opposite end of the table, who averts his intent gaze in a panic.

Harriet tries to hide her amusement. "Oh, believe me, I know. When he visited me during the summer, I thought it would be too big to fit into my apartment."

Who knows why, but my grin slips and a weight drops in my stomach. "Does he stay with you a lot?"

"No. My sister lived with me until February, so I didn't have the space. We've always kept in touch since high school. It's been nice to reconnect more this past year." She finishes with a smile aimed at the other end of the room. I don't need to follow her gaze to know who is likely smiling back, dimples popping.

"You're close then?" *Shut up, Aly.*

"Yeah, he's a great guy. I'm lucky to have him." Someone shouts her name and our conversation ends.

With my spine flush to the chair, I take a large gulp of water and push down the brainless green-eyed monster trying to make an appearance.

Before I overthink it, the food is served, and we dig in. I feel out of place at first, but I'm made to feel welcome. With each bite of the mouthwatering food, with each joke, my tension fades.

Once the table is cleared, I dab at my mouth with my napkin when a low voice murmurs, "I'm sorry to hear you couldn't visit your family."

I'd almost forgotten Martin sat beside me. *Almost.* He's wearing a dark gray dress shirt with a tie, and slacks. They're a little tired looking—like him—but something pulls in my chest at the effort he's put in.

With a steady gaze, and hopefully steadier voice, I say, "I appreciate that. Can't imagine I'm the only one stranded in town." My next question is pushing it and my conscience screams at me. "I hope the storm didn't ruin plans with your family?"

His gaze drops, a forlorn expression pinching his lips. "No. It's mostly quiet. Claire has been kind enough to invite me the last couple of years."

My throat clogs with emotion. So many, it's a struggle to swallow. "I—uh...No family at all?"

His reaction is unreadable, and before he responds Claire grabs everyone's attention.

With all eyes on her, no one notices the way mine stray to Booth as he towers above her. His hand hovers behind her, ready to keep her steady if she wobbles on her broken leg. A warm, happy air surrounds them both as she thanks him for making dinner and for their guests.

When Claire gets choked up talking about her late husband, he swoops in, tucking her under his arm and asking everyone to raise a glass for his dad, and Johanna and Harriet's mother.

Robotically, I mirror everyone's movements.

Dessert is passed around and Quinn gasps around a mouthful of melomakarona. "Boh, ma gob. Deez are delish." She swallows and gapes at me. "You have to share the recipe with me. I'll serve them at the bakery. Oh! Oh! I'll call them"— she flourishes her hands above her head—"Alessandra's Cookies."

Dex, who I've met today, coughs into his fist. "Booth would love a bite of them."

I take a sip of wine, brushing off the comment, and mentally planning Booth's demise.

The chef of the hour has the humility to cower and slumps down in his seat.

My smile is aimed in Quinn's direction. "Thank you. My cookies always go over well. People love them so much, they get overexcited. Some might say..." I flick my wrist in the air. "Prematurely."

Water sprays across the table like a geyser.

"What the fuck, Booth?" Florence cries as she wipes her face.

"Florence, language. Booth, behave," Claire scolds.

It's like a tennis match. Everyone's eyes bounce back and forth between Booth and me. Maybe coming today wasn't such a bad idea.

But alas, I speak too soon.

"My son," Martin whispers, carrying on our conversation like it didn't end almost an hour ago, "hasn't visited in a while. He wouldn't recognize the town if he did."

The sight of my grandmother's dessert turns my stomach.

"How old is he?"

Stop, Aly.

He thinks for a few seconds. "He'll be forty-seven in April."

A buzzing drowns out all other voices.

"Do you visit him?"

Shaking his head, he sighs, the sound heavy with contrition. "He wouldn't want to see me."

Don't push it. Now isn't the time.

"I'm sure he misses you." There's a slight hitch in the last word, but I push through. It's not easy. More like running head-first through a brick wall, only to face another. "Does he have a family?"

I watch his shoulders slump with the weight of his guilt. It's written plain as day across his face. Why? That's a question I can't bring myself to ask.

I've gone too far.

"I wouldn't know."

And I don't want to.

Like a record jumping, the sound of my chair scraping across the hardwood floor silences everyone.

"Excuse me." I'm already halfway around the table. "Where's the bathroom?"

"There's one at the end of the hallway." I barely catch Johanna's response as I speed out of the room.

My skin is tight. Throat tight. Everything is tight.

Worst of all, my stomach constricts as my dinner threatens to make an appearance.

I bypass the small door leading to the bathroom and make a beeline to the back of the house. When the cold air slaps me in the face, I finally take a breath, and reality comes crashing down.

Linking my fingers together behind my head, I open up my chest and slow my heart rate. The stars twinkle high above, winking and sparkling against the midnight black. It looks different here. Clearer. Brighter. Like I'm looking at a newly discovered night sky.

As my mind clears, frustration at my stupidity creeps in. There was a plan. One I didn't follow.

"I've always loved the skies here. The Milky Way is so bright during the summer."

My heart stutters as a deep voice ripples through the air. I don't turn at the crunching of shoes over the snow.

"When I was little, my dad told me it was a runway in the sky where dreams went to land while we were sleeping. The brighter the band of the light, the happier the dreams."

It's only when the heat from Booth's body warms my right side that I realize how cold I am.

He speaks carefully, like I'm a skittish animal about to break loose. "I doubt you'll answer, but what happened in there?"

I should tell him it's none of his business. To demand he go back inside. Ask why he even cares.

But really. Deep down. I don't want to do any of that. He's right that I won't answer his question, though. "I like that."

I risk a glimpse at him. His head is tipped back, the muscles in his neck stretching as his eyes glitter under the tapestry of stars.

"When did you lose him?" I ask.

His breath plumes in front of him with his heavy sigh. "It'll be seven years in May. Sounds insane to say that out loud. Still feels like yesterday."

"Everyone I've spoken to speaks highly of him. His legacy is stamped everywhere you look when you step into the restaurant." Booth twists toward me. "I wish I'd met him."

His brows jump. "Don't take this the wrong way, but if he were still here today, you wouldn't be in town. That's not to say he wouldn't enjoy meeting the woman who turns my brain into soup and boils my blood at the same time."

Huffing, I tug at the sleeves of my dress. "That's the most descriptive compliment slash insult I've ever received. Unless turning your brain into minestrone is also an insult?"

"I'll let you be the judge of that." He winks.

Damn him and his winks.

"Did you want to come back inside? We're exchanging gifts." He laughs when my eyes go wide. "You weren't required to bring anything. It's mostly for Lottie. I can drive you home if you want to leave."

Ten minutes earlier, leaving sounded like the best solution. Since Booth stepped outside, staying doesn't seem so bad now; plus, I remember what else I brought.

"Oh, I have a present for Lottie." Spinning on my heel, I take a step toward the house, only to be jolted back with a firm grip on my hand. My head snaps down to where Booth's fingers lock around mine, then up. "I know I haven't met her properly, but I didn't want to come empty handed. Is it weird?"

A short burst of laughter bubbles from him, eyes gleaming in a mix of surprise and amazement. "You're the most complex woman I've ever met. Do you come with instructions? If you do, they're probably written in a foreign language because I've been trying to work you out for weeks with no luck."

I move to free myself, but he tugs me forward, the tips of our shoes touching. "I don't want you to *work* me out," I say flatly.

"Yeah, that much is clear, all right." He scans my face. "You fire me. Rehire me. Drive me insane. Then drive me more insane with that unforgettable performance in the cabin. You act sweet one second, then ghost me the next. You tell me we're better off hating each other, yet you turn up on Christmas Day with a present for my niece and baked goods for my mom. I can't work out if I want to solve the beautiful riddle that you are, or continue wandering around aimlessly with no answers, so long as it means I can spend time with you. So, yeah, you're complex. Turns out my feelings toward you are too. Want to know why?"

The shiver that runs through me vibrates up his arms. Finally, he drops my hand, only to grip me by my shoulders. His touch is firm. I stop breathing. The lack of oxygen is the only explanation for why I step forward. My heavy breasts brush against his chest, and I stifle a gasp when I feel the hard length of him press against my hip. "If I say no, you're going to tell me, anyway."

Nodding, that smirk stretches wide across his face. "See, you're catching on." He bends, nose brushing the edge of my jaw. "My feelings for you are complex because when you scowl at me, it gets my blood pumping. Makes me want to bend you over the nearest flat surface so I can hear those sweet little moans of yours again. The same noises I jerked off to this morning."

My body ignites into an inferno at his filthy words.

"But?" I tilt my head a fraction, baring my throat to him, and closing my eyes as his hot breath tickles the sensitive skin below my ear.

"No buts." Gently—so fucking gently—his lips coast along the column of my neck. "I light up like a bonfire when you look at me like you want to kiss me."

I do want to, I'm tempted to scream. If I open my mouth, whatever comes out will be unpredictable and break whatever spell he's cast on me. I want to savor this moment for a while longer and remain enchanted under the moonlight with him.

So I stay silent and let my body do the talking.

Pushing my hips forward, his hands fall to my waist, rocking me against him. The movements are subtle yet turn my legs to rubber.

Then the conversation with Harriet booms in my head and the spell breaks.

Noticing the change in my body language, he pauses.

"You've only looked at me like that once. And I'm burning, Aly. When you looked at me just then, you wanted my lips on yours," he murmurs against my pulse point. "What changed?"

I refuse to verbalize my misplaced jealousy. "Our lips will not be meeting."

The heat cocooning me disappears as he gently pushes me away.

His eyes glitter with promise, fueling my silent rage. "They will. But only when *you* know exactly what you want."

And then, he walks away.

CHAPTER TWENTY

booth

When I return, my family has relocated into the living room, where no one bats an eyelash.

I left Aly five minutes ago, but before I joined in with the wholesome festivities, I tucked my painful erection into the waistband of my briefs, fighting the need to fist myself as I replayed her breathy sounds in my head.

Had I gone too far? At first, I presumed yes.

Until she pushed as much as I pulled. Back and forth.

She was asking me to take, and fuck, if I didn't want to right there and then in the snow. To melt it and have the steam rise above us as we scorched the ground.

She wanted me.

Or I thought she did until I sensed a hint of hesitation.

Forty-eight hours earlier, she told me she didn't. Or couldn't. Either way, I needed her to be sure about what she wanted. If it's one night or ten, fine. But I wouldn't have her pretend it didn't happen.

It was torture to feel the thump of her pulse against my lips. Even now, as I smile at my family crowded around the fire, her scent lingers on my skin and clothes.

"Hey, where did you go?" Harriet squishes in next to me on the sofa.

"Had to take a call."

"On Christmas Day?" Her face says I'm full of shit.

Collapsing into the cushions, I keep my voice low. "I was checking on Aly."

"Ah, yes. I also go and check on the welfare of my sworn enemy." She smirks.

"I never said that." I shove her shoulder.

"Um, you absolutely did, and I quote"—she whips out her phone and scans through our texts—"'This woman's second job is being the bane of my existence.'"

"Doesn't sound like me," I brush her off. "Anyway, what does it matter? Can't I be nice to a guest?"

She looks at me pointedly. "Do you want to get into the panties of all your mom's dinner guests?"

We glance at Martin Willis, sitting silently in the corner.

"Yeah, I didn't think so." Wiggling her shoulders, she settles back. "She wasn't what I was expecting."

"How so?"

"Well, she wasn't a dragon-witch, like you described. She seemed nice, in an intimidating, big sister way. I was ready to give her an earful, until she acted like she enjoyed it." She leans in, whispering, "She scared me, and yet I wanted to make friendship bracelets with her. She's full of surprises."

Snorting, I snatch Harry's glass of eggnog out of her hand and take a large swig.

"That's one way to describe her," I mumble.

I'm still aching from the last round of whiplash Aly inflicted.

Whenever we're together, she surprises me. Is she going to be sweet, where she laughs freely and smiles openly? Or will she be sharp and commandeering with her explosive confidence?

The guessing game is rousing.

What I know is that she's probably halfway home by now after that display in the yard.

Bringing the rim of the glass to my lips, I slowly sip the smooth nutmeg beverage, muscles relaxing.

Then Aly materializes, and every nerve ending goes on high alert.

When she spots me, she winks.

Winking is *my* thing.

Good lord, she's Uno reversed me.

With swaying hips, bouncing curls, and a killer smile, she saunters into the room.

"Do you want me to say something at your funeral?" Harry snickers. "Because you are toast, my friend."

Gulping, I watch Aly's face soften. She gracefully lowers to her knees next to Lottie playing with her dolls, and offers out a hand.

My niece pauses, eyeing the manicured hand before slipping her smaller one into it.

Everyone grows quiet.

"Lottie, right?" Aly's voice is gentle and kind.

"Uh-huh." Lottie nods. "And you're the Scary Boss Lady. That's what JoJo calls you."

"Oh, kill me now," Jo hisses and buries her face in Patrick's shoulder.

Aly smirks in amusement, then pulls out a neatly wrapped gift from the bag in her other hand.

"According to everyone around Our Place, *you're* the Boss Lady." Sliding the gift across the rug, she smiles. "Merry Christmas, Lottie."

Lottie gasps, then ravages at the paper with the force of ten hungry hyenas. She squeals and runs over to Patrick and Jo. "Look! Look! I can boss Uncle Boo around in the kitchen."

My head swivels. "Come again?"

Grinning proudly, Lottie skips my way and shoves her gift in my face.

Black and white checked pants, crisp white jacket, and a matching hat. Not forgetting the plastic spatula and knife set.

I'm silent before hooting with laughter. "A chef's outfit?"

Lottie's face turns serious and she whips a finger into the air. "Gimme twelve lobster rolls. Stat." Giggling, she hugs the costume tightly. "I love it. Now we can be chefs together."

Well, shit, my heart is gonna burst at the seams—a normal occurrence when Lottie acts adorable. Only this time, there's a new ache to the organ, tingling deep inside. I almost don't want to look at the culprit. When I do, her eyes are trained on her hands tucked between her knees, a shy, contented smile on her lips.

She certainly is full of surprises.

"Spud, what do you say to Alessandra?" Patrick stands behind Lottie and turns her to face Aly.

"Thank you *soooo* much. I'm never taking it off. When I'm older, I'm gonna be just like Uncle Chef Booth." My niece spins to beam at me, but at her declaration, my heart drops. Why would she want to be *me*? A twenty-seven-year-old coward, clueless of where his career is headed.

I don't voice my thoughts. With a forced smile, I grab the chef hat and tug it over her head. "No toads in the kitchen."

Lottie does a quick wardrobe change, and everyone fusses over her as she struts around the room, shouting out, "Eighty-six" and "Drop the fries!"

Out of the corner of my eye, I watch Aly. She sits next to my mom, their chatter barely audible.

"...believe me, he's always been like this." My mom laughs under her breath, and my ears perk up. *Are they talking about me?*

"It's fine. We've come to an...agreement. Things are a lot more professional now."

If professional means me watching her fuck herself on a black vibrator, then yeah, *professional.*

Patting Aly's hand, my mom gestures to Lottie, playing. "You really didn't have to bring anything. I'm glad you joined us, though. I bet you can't wait to have a family of your own one day."

Aly is never one to slump, her posture always poised and proper, but I watch a ripple of discomfort run through her body. "Oh, no kids for me. By choice," she quickly adds.

Mom does a poor job at hiding her surprise. "You're young. Plenty of time to change your mind."

I sit straighter, wishing someone would distract my mother so she'd stop jabbering.

There's a stiffness to Aly's smile, but she's still polite. "Nope. Not for me. It's not something I see in my future."

"But having children is so—"

"Hey, Ma?" I interrupt loudly, feet already carrying me across the room. "George was asking for your hot toddy recipe."

The woman loves to share her recipes. I make sure she's steady on her feet, escort her over to an unknowing George, then slide in next to Aly. She narrows her eyes, but the playful bite of her bottom lip gives way to her amusement.

"You heard that?" she asks.

Nodding, I run my fingers through my hair. "Yeah, sorry. My mom has a knack for poking her nose in people's business."

Swatting the air, she relaxes back into the chair. "Nothing I haven't heard a million times over. I've learned to live with it, but I won't change my mind. About kids, that is..." Her tone suggests she's waiting for *me* to persuade her otherwise.

"I'm well versed with the 'but when you find the right person, you'll want your own' argument."

Her head whips to the side. "You don't want kids?"

"Nope." She looks ready to say something, so I place a

finger over her lips. "Don't tell me *you're* going to give me the talk."

She huffs, pushing my hand away. "God, no. It's…" With a quick glance at Lottie, she quietly says, "You're great with kids. I'm shocked, that's all."

"I love kids. Lottie is one of a kind, but having my own?" I shiver. "Doesn't interest me. I like my time and freedom. And knowing I can return them."

That makes her laugh. "It makes sense. With you being a man-child and all."

She squeaks when I lightly pinch her side. "Smart-ass."

The laughter of my family, crackling of the fire, and classic Christmas songs playing through the radio surround us. We sit in silence, enjoying the evening as it unfolds, when a thought pops into my head.

"When are you flying to New York?"

Her mouth twists to the side. "I probably won't now. They're forecasting another storm, and I don't want to get stuck there."

Elbows balanced on my knees, I keep my voice casual. "The restaurant is hosting a New Year's Eve party. We've done it since the first year we opened. You should come. Everyone is. And by everyone, I mean the whole town."

If you blink, you'd miss it, but her eyes flit toward Martin in the corner.

Then I'm reminded of her tense body language and nervous disposition as I watched her across the table earlier. Lowering my voice, I ask, "Has something happened between you and Martin?"

Eyes wide, she shakes her head. "No. Why would you ask that?"

I'd be shocked if she said yes. Martin is harmless, and while he's always been a loner, he's slowly become more present in the community.

"When you rushed outside…" My words trail off when I sense Aly closing herself off.

I'm witnessing the bricks being laid down, one by one. Humor is replaced with a cool stoicism, her go-to defense mechanism.

I don't want to battle tonight, but it doesn't mean I'm not planning to smash through her walls eventually. If she'll let me, and god, I hope she does.

It's insane to want someone that might not want you. To yearn for a person you were so intent on disliking that the switch in feelings knocks you on your ass. There's no telling how this is going to end, and it's likely she'll turn me away, do what she needs to do, and leave.

The question is: Do I risk having no part of her at all, or do I try to soak up as much as she's willing to give?

My answer is clear with my next words.

"Say yes, Silver. I promise you'll have fun." I lower my voice so only she can hear. "Maybe I'll let you kiss me at midnight."

The scowl she tosses my way lights me up. "I haven't signed off on a party."

She's teasing, so I go along with it. "Tradition. It'll be bad luck if you don't come."

Eyebrow raised, her gaze lowers to my crotch. Her lips brush the shell of my ear and a shiver wracks through me. "We know *you* do."

"Hey, now that's no—"

Aly stands abruptly, facing my mom. "Claire, thank you so much for having me. Everyone." She looks around the room. "I really appreciate the hospitality."

A chorus of farewells follows, and without a glance in my direction, she disappears, leaving me speechless.

Something pokes me in the ribs. Lottie looks up at me, eyes innocent. She places the chef's hat in my hands. "Sorry, Uncle Boo. When I grow up, I wanna be Scary Boss Lady."

That's when I look at my family, all eyes on me.

"Oh, Booth," Quinn sings cheerfully and claps her hands. "She's going to eat you up and spit you back out."

I look back at the doorway Aly disappeared through and murmur, "That's what I'm betting on."

CHAPTER TWENTY-ONE

alessandra

NEXT YEAR'S RESOLUTION: DON'T ALLOW ATTRACTIVE CHEFS TO lure you to parties.

Booth wasn't kidding. The whole town is here. With the tables pushed aside, people laugh, dance, and drink around the restaurant floor. A makeshift DJ booth sits in the corner, blasting '90s music as the lights from a small strobe burst over the dance floor.

I'm used to fancy galas, so when I slipped on my little black dress, I didn't stop to think the attendees at Our Place's New Year's Eve party would be in jeans and sweaters. Standing at the entrance, the room's attention is on me.

Marvelous.

Midnight is an hour away. After video calling with my parents and brothers, I picked up my paintbrush, only to stare at the canvas blankly again. Nothing. I gave up and rushed to get ready and hightailed it over here, not wanting people to assume I was going to be a no-show. That would not work in my favor, especially as I slowly gain the trust of my employees.

Ignoring the peculiar stares, I head over to the bar, desperate for a drink, and find Johanna prepping what looks to be a Tom Collins. Since Christmas Day, her smiles are more relaxed, genuine. The same for Patrick, who waves at me from the other side of the bar.

"Aly, hey," she shouts over "Wannabe" by the Spice Girls. "What's your poison?"

I nod at the drink in her hand. "I'll take one of those, please."

She slides the glass toward me. "Take this one. It's Booth's but he's disappeared..." She scans the room before her eyes flare in amusement. "Never mind. Found him."

Following her gaze, it shouldn't surprise me what I see.

Jazz hands, floppy chocolate hair, and an ear-to-ear grin.

He'd look ridiculous if it weren't for the shirt molded to his chest and arms, the sleeves rolled up to display corded, bronzed skin. A sheen of sweat covers his skin, making him glow under the flashing lights.

Any other man, the gyrating of his hips and lip-syncing, would give me the ick, but of course, Booth does the complete opposite.

"Are you joining them?" Johanna's question has me pausing.

Them. Which is when I see Harriet beside him, matching his moves as he serenades her passionately.

Shaking my head, I snatch up my drink. "I'd hate to interrupt them."

Jo's eyes flit between me and the dance partners. "It's not what it looks like," she says as Booth grabs Harriet by the hip and dips her.

"It can look however it wants. Why would I care?" Hopefully, she can't hear the tightness in my voice over the bass.

Shrugging, she finishes pouring a beer and passes it to another patron. "I think he'd care if he was standing where you are. They're just friends. Trust me."

"With a history?" Now I sound like I care. Before I left the Sadler household, I spotted a wall filled with prom photos. Front and center sat Booth and Harriet, looking cozy.

"You could say that." She contemplates her next words before saying, "I'm going to pretend you're not my boss for a second. We all saw the chemistry between you two at Christmas. Booth isn't one to chase, yet somehow..."

My nose wrinkles. "Somehow...?"

She bites her lip. "His eyes follow wherever you go. I swear he looks for you in the mornings when he comes into the restaurant."

I take a large gulp of my drink. "Let's pretend this conversation never happened?"

Laughing lightly, she nods. "Deal."

Pulling out a twenty, I slap it on the bar but she slides it back. "I'm not charging the boss."

"You mean Scary Boss Lady?"

Her cheeks turn scarlet under the fluorescent lights. "That child is a menace."

I wave her off. "If she ever wants to work for me, let me know."

She laughs. "You'll regret that during her first week."

We chat until a crowd forms around the bar, and I leave her to it. While scanning the room, I touch up my lipstick, admiring how the ruby red matches my nails. Spotting a quiet corner, I make my way over but come to a halt when I spy Martin. Yeah, not tonight. Turning in the opposite direction, I scan the room and find Graham, Quinn, Dex, and Florence. Accepting it's my safest bet, I join the group.

Their welcome is a huge contrast to a few weeks ago, and I relax as I fall into their conversation easily.

"Have you decided how long you're in town for?" Quinn asks.

Fighting the urge to glance in Martin's direction, I shake my head. "I have a few more things to do first, but probably at the end of January."

"Are we privy to these *things*?" Graham, while quiet, is direct and transparent.

I'm choosing my words carefully when Florence's cheerful voice saves the day. "Oh, but if you leave before then you'll miss the Valentine's Fair!"

"Is there a month this town doesn't host a fair?" My question has everyone laughing.

It wasn't a joke.

Dex leans down, a smirk playing on his lips. "So...How was your stay at The Nook?"

I suck my teeth. "It would have been five stars had I not had an infestation."

He barks with laughter. "That's one way to describe him. But seriously, I'm happy to fully comp your stay. I swear I didn't realize The Nook was live on my online booking system. Probably a sign I need to hire some help."

"Not necessary." I clink my glass with his. "It's a beautiful place. Have you ever considered expan—"

"No business tonight, Silver. Just pleasure," a voice purrs behind me, sending a shockwave of goose bumps along my spine. Despite my thumping heart, heated veins, and coiling stomach, I don't show how he affects me.

"Welcome to the party, Baby Spice." With a look over my shoulder, I slowly sip my drink.

"Did you call me baby?" His chest brushes my shoulder as he joins the circle, our hands inches apart.

"Of course that's your takeaway."

Cheeks flushed, and messy locks flopping over his eyes, he flips his head back and swipes a hand through his hair. A move I didn't know could be sexy.

Out of nowhere, another tall frame crowds me, and I look up to find the restaurant's line cook leering down at me. A strong aroma of liquor hits me when he opens his mouth. "Fancy seeing you here."

I'm usually good with names, but his escapes me.

"At the party being hosted at the business I own?" I respond with a pinch of sarcasm that goes right over his head.

"Do you really own it if you bought it with Daddy's money?" He chuckles. No one else joins him.

I pull back my shoulders. "*My* money."

Something in my tone draws Booth's attention away from the conversation he's having with his brother, and he frowns at us. "Kyle, you all right?"

Kyle. That's it.

"All good, Chef. I'm about to buy Alessandra here a drink. C'mon, baby, it's on me." He wraps his sweaty hand around my wrist and goes to tug me away. The word *baby* makes me nauseous.

I glare at where he grips me.

Booth spots my discomfort and steps forward. "Easy. You've had enough to drink. Let go of her, Kyle."

"Psht, I know when enough is enough." He peers down at me and licks his lips. "I know somewhere quiet. I saw you looking at me the other day."

Booth closes the distance between him and his line chef, but before he has a chance to react, I'm pressing the heel of my pump on Kyle's foot until he hisses.

"If you don't drop your hand, I'll make it impossible for you to find employment across the whole of New England." My voice is even, gaze steady as my words sink into his thick skull.

When he doesn't budge, I lean my weight forward, and his teeth grit.

"Five. Four. Three."

He stumbles back, ticking in anger as he grips his glass tight. His mouth drops open, probably ready to throw a slew of insults my way, but Dex steps in and calmly drags Kyle toward the front door.

I let out a breath and rub at my tender wrist.

"Are you okay?" Booth whispers as he cradles my arm gently and inspects the skin. "I'm going to fucking ki—"

"No, you're not. No business tonight, remember? Let him cool off and give him a warning on his next shift."

"Aly, he put his hands on you," he seethes.

"And I'll add him to the long list of boys intimidated by women in high positions. Nothing I haven't handled before." I flip my hand over and squeeze his forearm. "But thank you."

He relaxes under my touch and shuffles forward until his hip presses into me. "You really are scary. Is it weird I like it?"

"Yes. You're very weird. Especially after watching your choreographed dance routine." I collect my hair into one hand and lay it over my shoulder.

Booth's eyes flare, and I feel the trickle of heat as his gaze traces along my collarbone, over my breasts, then lower. Like a line of powdered dynamite being lit, a spark ignites, the fire flowing straight to my core.

The restaurant opened up two days after Christmas, and things between us have shifted considerably. We still enjoy giving each other a hard time, but rather than him storming off or me losing my patience, there's a playfulness to it. Each snarky comment or ridiculous joke shared is laced with temptation.

It's a game of who will break first.

And I refuse to bend. Ever since he declared we wouldn't kiss unless I begged, I've had to dial up my willpower. Every fleeting look and chaste brush of our hands is a dare.

There's a hunger in his gaze. He's pushing me. Waiting for me to snap. Rather than bow to the deep-seated desire brewing in my veins, I step back.

"Oh! Everyone!" Quinn shouts and bounces on her toes.

"Midnight strikes in two minutes. Grab your partners." She's so overcome with excitement, cozying into Graham, that she isn't aware they're the only couple present. She spots Dex and Florence's rigid postures and giggles. "Hey, I didn't say you had to kiss." Then her eyes slide to me and Booth. "Or do."

My protest dies on the tip of my tongue when Harriet bounds over and loops her arm through Booth's.

"I've asked the DJ to play B*witched next," she says breathlessly.

To his credit, he takes a few seconds to break our staring contest, but when he looks down at his "friend," a smile erupts on his face. "Sounds good, Harry."

There's that stupid pinprick in my chest again. A silly, naïve sensation that shouldn't exist between me and him.

Which is why when the crowd starts to countdown, I knock back my drink and face the dance floor. Preferring to look anywhere else but at them.

Ten. Nine. Eight.

A large hand grazes my waist as I keep my eyes trained on the partygoers.

Seven. Six.

"Alessandra." A deep voice tickles my ear. "Look at me."

Five. Four.

"That's not a good idea." At my refusal, the heat of his body disappears.

And so do I.

I blame the alcohol for my tantrum as my heels clack against the parquet floor on my journey to the kitchen. When the door stops swinging, I grip the edge of the stainless steel table, head pounding as the cheers from outside vibrate in my skull.

Dumb. Dumb. Dumb.

This man is killing off my brain cells.

Never, and I mean *never*, have I reacted this way over someone. Had I turned around and witnessed him pressing his lips to Harriet's, I would have blown a gasket.

Which is why I need to go. Now.

I'm about to unlock the fire exit when the door hinges creak behind me. The music gets louder, and then muffles as the door swings shut.

There's no need to check who it is. "Go back to the party."

"No," Booth responds immediately, voice tense.

"No?" I laugh, and hang my head in exasperation, my back to him. "I'm sure Harriet is looking for you. Don't make her wait."

His returning chuckle is humorless. "You're unbelievable."

"I beg your pardon?" I whip my head over my shoulder.

"You heard me." He takes one long stride forward, hand running along the shiny worktops. "Jealously is a new look for you, huh? How does it feel?"

"You're deluded." I bristle. Facing him fully, I ignore his smug expression. "I'm in no mood, Booth."

Another step.

"What are you going to do, fire me? Tried that once, and you went back on your word so fast, I got motion sickness."

My hands twitch with the need to wipe that smile off his face.

"You're pushing your luck. Now get out of my way." My anger simmers below the surface.

He holds his hands out to the side. "I'm not stopping you. You're free to go. But answer me this first."

Slowly, he eats up the space between us, until the tips of my Manolos brush his boots.

"Spit it out." I hate that he sees right through me. It makes me feel weak. Predictable. Out of control.

"If I'd kissed you at midnight, what would you have done?"

Spontaneously combusted. Melted into his embrace. Never wanted it to stop.

"I wouldn't have let it go that far," I lie.

His lips turn down and head cocks to the side. "Liar."

"Imbecile."

"Beg me."

"Bite me."

"Only if you ask nicely."

The insults bounce back and forth, each pass filling the room with an electric energy.

Worried my next words will push us past the brink of no return, I snap my mouth shut. Averting my gaze, I lock eyes with the kitchen door and march past him.

I'm a foot away from freedom when strong hands encompass my waist and pull me flush to a firm chest.

I feel every hard plane of his body. The beating of his heart pulses all the way down to my toes. A little fight leaves me when he arranges my hair in his fist to coast his lips down the side of my throat.

"You want *me* to beg, is that it? Say the word and I'll drop to my knees right here." When his teeth skim my wild pulse, my legs threaten to buckle. "I know what I want, Alessandra, and it's you. I'll take anything. Once, twice, a hundred times —whatever you'll give me. Deny it all you want, but knowing an ounce of you was jealous is a high I can't come down from."

My hips push back, all sense lost when his cock nestles against my ass. Hissing, he buries his face in my neck, hands skimming up my rib cage until his thumbs brush the underside of my breasts.

"Should I have reason to be jealous?" The remaining rational part of my brain asks.

"If you had asked, you would know Harry is one of my best friends. We dated in high school, swapped virginities, and that was it. Nothing close to romantic since we were seventeen." His candor is obvious, and I flush at my overreaction.

"I don't know what I have to give or how much I want to. It's difficult for me, Booth, and I'm not here permanently—"

"When I say anything, I mean *anything*. You give me a minute; I'll cherish it like a lifetime." He sighs when I thrust my chest out, filling his hands with my supple flesh.

My decision sits on the tip of a pendulum. Swaying left to right. One side is sensible, not leading me astray. The other has a fever erupting through me with an unquenchable thirst.

A taste. A sip. That's all I need.

"Tonight. One night."

The words are barely out of my mouth before I'm spinning around, dizzy from the rapid movement, but no comparison to the head rush when Booth smashes his mouth to mine.

There's no getting acquainted. It's all lips, tongue, and teeth as we unite ferociously. Clawing at one another. He pushes. I pull. He bites. I suck. The taste of him floods my senses, over-whelming me.

I gasp when he pushes me against the table, the sharp edge biting into my back as his hips pin me in place. A desperate noise leaves me when he breaks the kiss, only for his lips to lead a hot trail along my jaw and down my neck, mumbling words of satisfaction into my sensitive skin.

"You feel exactly like I knew you would."

Arching into the warm hand gliding up my spine, my eyes flutter closed. "And what's that?"

"Like the cause and cure of all my torment." My eyes ping open when he fists my curls and presses our foreheads together. "I'll take your one night, Aly. But don't be surprised when you come pleading for more."

I shove him away, then tug him back. A perfect summary of our relationship. "You're so full of yourself."

"And you fucking love it." His grin is short-lived before his lips are on mine again, hands cupping the backs of my thighs to hoist me up on the cool metal surface. His hips settle between my spread legs, and my short dress rides up. I bite back a groan when his thick cock, hidden only by his jeans, presses against my core.

He's in full control of this kiss. Molding and moving me to his will. His fervent touch softens me, until I'm pliant in his hands, but I'm as power hungry as he is.

Shock colors his face when he stumbles back. The pointed toe of my heel rests on his sternum. My other leg dangles off the table, hands planted behind me.

"Take them off," I command.

His eyes glitter when they drop to my red silk thong.

One large finger travels from my knee to ankle. That playful, crooked smile is on full display as his gaze rises. "Red panties. Red nails. Red lips. Which will look prettier wrapped around my cock?"

"Only one way to find out." I widen my legs. "Now, be a good boy and do as you're told."

He chuckles darkly.

Gripping my ankle, he lowers my leg, giving him the space to step closer. The thumping music is no match for my rampant heart when he slips his hands underneath my bottom and drags my thong down my thighs. All dominance dissolves when he balls the material in his fist and brings it to his face to inhale deeply.

"Fuck, if you don't smell divine. I'm dying for a taste." His gravelly voice vibrates over me. "Would you like that? Me tongue fucking your tight cunt?"

I'm completely bared to him, the cool air from the overhead fans kissing the wet, heated flesh between my legs. He tilts his head, admiring my aching pussy with his lip trapped between his teeth.

"But I can't do it here." He shakes his head in disappointment.

"Not up for the challenge," I rally.

Growling, he holds up my panties. "Don't make me gag you with these. I am very much up for this, however, I take food hygiene seriously."

He scans the kitchen as if it's his most prized possession.

It's a fair point.

"So where are we going?" Disentangling myself from his grasp, I drop to the floor and adjust my dress. "There are cameras in every room."

Booth thinks carefully for a beat, and then satisfaction blooms over his face. "Trust me?"

"No." It's a half truth.

He intertwines our fingers and guides us toward the door. Glancing over his shoulder, he says, "We'll work on that."

The blaring music drowns out my argument as we step back into the throng of people. *We don't have time to gain each other's trust,* is what I want to say.

It takes a minute to maneuver our way through the bodies, and when we reach a door, a set of keys materializes in Booth's hands. I don't have time to ask what we're doing before I'm pushed inside a darkened supply closet, and the snick of the lock echoes in my ears.

My pleasure might as well have been lying dormant until this very second. Years of being sexually active are nothing compared to the heat that's coiling deep in my veins as Booth's eyes assault me.

There's no joking. No coy smirk. His features darken—not from the lack of light, but carnal desire.

"Now be a good girl for me. Face the shelf and bend over." He tucks my panties into his shirt pocket. "I want your ass on display as I fuck you into forgetting all about that little black toy of yours."

CHAPTER TWENTY-TWO

alessandra

The air in this tiny supply closet pulsates.

A cataclysmic force standing in wait as I contemplate my next move.

It's alive; feeding off my racing heart and overstimulated senses.

Everything about Booth has me finely tuned. His touch, smell, look, sound, taste. Wanting him would be like taking your first hit. The thrill and excitement draw you in. Damn the consequences.

Saying no doesn't feel like an option. Or maybe I don't want to.

If I don't give in to it now, my cravings will worsen.

His deep voice cuts through the roaring in my ears. It's softer now. "You're in control, Aly. Always. We can go back out to the party and prete—"

I silence him with a firm press of my lips, my tongue strokes his as my decision settles over me like a cool breeze. My moment of hesitancy is blown away when he sighs into my mouth, his large hands squeezing my waist.

I pull away an inch, our noses brushing. "Do you ever shut up?"

A streak of moonlight from the narrow window is our only source of light, highlighting the menacing smile on his face. "Never, baby. And I happen to know you love my dirty mouth."

"Is that so?"

He nods, and my stomach muscles contract when his fingertips ghost up the inside of my leg, not stopping until he glides through my wet folds.

"Fucking soaked," he coos. "So needy for my cock, aren't you?"

My limbs slacken. He's so vocal as he plays with me, whispering filthy words as he works a finger into me. "Fucking perfect. Do you want another?"

I nod, my walls tighten when he adds a second finger. He toys with me, stroking and petting me deliberately.

As quickly as he starts, he retreats, and I'm left swaying from the loss of his touch.

He eyes the row of liquor bottles behind me. "Do I need to show you how to be a good girl?"

His cocky tone stokes a fire in me, riling me up.

But I want this. Want *him.*

So with my chin held high, gaze hard, I twist away, grip the middle shelf, and arch my back in offering.

"*Fuuuck.* Look at that." Booth's words roll off his tongue like gravel, thick with lust. "Lift your dress, Silver."

The slide of soft velvet over my backside feels like tiny pricks across my skin.

The clear and amber liquids glitter under the dull lighting. I steady my breathing, but at the sound of his belt buckle, it hitches. My eyes stay forward. I want to look, but love not knowing all the same.

His calloused palm runs over my exposed cheek, squeezing

and lifting as he groans in appreciation. Suddenly, the hot, blunt tip of him rests between the globes of my ass.

"You really are something," he whispers hoarsely with shallow thrusts of hips. He doesn't enter me, just saws back and forth through the cleft of my bottom.

I'm done being teased. A hiss escapes him when I tilt my hips up slightly, causing the head of his cock to press into my entrance.

"Fuck. No condom." He sighs.

Dangerous. This is so dangerous, my voice of reason whispers.

I ignore it. Too pent up and impatient for any alternative.

"Bare," I rasp. "Fuck me bare. I've been tested and my tubes are tied."

I know the moment my desperation flips a switch in him. His grip becomes bruising and his breathing grows heavier. One hand falls to my neck, fingers curling around my nape to twist my head.

My core clenches from his intense, passionate gaze as he peers down at me. "Are you sure?"

"Yes. If you are too." Tucking my chin over my shoulder, I ensure he sees the resolution in my eyes. "I want all of you, Booth."

That's his green light.

"I've been waiting to hear you say that."

He shucks his jeans halfway down his ass, shoves up the hem of his shirt, leaving me to salivate at the view. Of course he's beautiful. His cock is thick, long, with a vein running along the underside that I want to trace with the tip of my tongue. Slices of muscle frame a trail of dark hair at the base. Wrapping his hand around his shaft, he fists himself with firm tugs.

"It's not going to be gentle, Aly. I can't. I've waited too long." His voice pitches with each pull of his hand.

"I don't want gentle. Fuck me like you need it." I dangle the bait with my next words. "Unless you're not up to it."

"You're the devil." His palm lands in the center of my spine, pushing me forward. "But don't forget to scream my name when you see god. Now hold on tight."

I grip the metal legs, my breath halting as he notches himself at my soaked entrance.

Like our kisses, there's no warming up.

We both cry out as he slams home, one hand clutching my hip while the other tugs on my hair. His pelvis meets my ass roughly. Not a second later, he draws back before pistoning forward. That's the pace he sets, rutting into me with abandonment, grunting and groaning each time he slides in so deep, I see stars.

Nothing compares to the sensation.

And I lose myself to him with each punishing thrust.

His voice pulls me out of the thick haze I'm sinking into. "God fucking dammit, Alessandra. You're so fucking tight. Watching you take my cock like this is a dream."

The music drowns out my cries and the lyrics blur as pleasure seeps into my veins. "Shit. Oh—Oh, that feels so good. You feel so good. So deep."

"I know, baby. I know. And you're taking each inch so beautifully."

His hand leaves my hair to tug down the neckline of my dress. My breasts spill out, and Booth immediately tugs and tweaks my diamond-hard nipples.

I'm close already. On the precipice of detonation. But my body craves a fraction more.

"Strangle my cock, Aly. I'm not finishing until you come around me with this needy cunt."

Every time he speaks, my body temperature rises.

"Fuck, you're doing it now. Squeezing me so tight." His grip hardens, and my back bows. "You love when I talk dirty to you?"

His teasing tone lights a fire under me that only he's capable of; built of desire and witty remarks.

"I'd *love* it if you actually fucked me," I say breathlessly.

"Oh, Silver." I gasp when he pinches my nipple. "I can't wait to shut you up with my cock."

He holds nothing back. Glass rattles. The shelves bang against the stone wall. Our skin slaps together.

"Oh god. I'm going to come. Booth, fuck. Booth!" I scream.

His voice is tight; movements hurried. "Just me and you, baby. Let me feel it, Alessandra."

Every inch of my skin, every fiber of my being, every nerve ending sings when he drives into me. My toes curl. My voice grows hoarse. My body loses sense as I careen toward mind-bending euphoria.

I break completely as my orgasm takes a hold of me. Nothing—*nothing*—has felt like this before.

Before I fall into a heap of sated bones, Booth keeps me upright with a firm grip on my hips. He isn't tender, and I grow crazed for his masculine sounds as he continues to pound into me.

Completely at his mercy, another orgasm tingles low in my belly.

"Fuck, Aly. *Aly. Aly. Aly.*" He chants my name like a prayer, taking what he wants.

And then we both see the light in synchrony.

My second orgasm barrels toward me.

I'm narrowly aware of Booth pulling out of me, then hot stripes paint my bottom and lower back. The slick sound of his hand against his hard flesh mixing with our panting has me keening through the aftershocks.

He loosens his hold, and I wait for him to retreat. Instead, he drops to his haunches.

My breath stutters when he grabs my ass cheeks and

massages his cum into my scorching skin. "What are you doing?"

"Shhh," he says softly. Such a contrast to his harsh tone from earlier. "You create art. So let an artist admire his work."

Filthy. So fucking filthy.

"What a beautiful mess." I'm not sure if he's speaking to me or himself. "Fuck, I don't want to forget this."

His eyes meet mine, flickering with the afterglow. I know what he's about to ask, and my response is reason number one I never should have stepped foot into dangerous territory with him.

His jeans hang open, his half-hard cock shining under the dull lighting of the closet. Digging into his back pocket, he holds up his phone.

"One picture." And because I enjoy playing with fire, I bow my spine seductively and sway my ass in his face. "Make it worthwhile."

He shakes his head and chuckles, and a flash illuminates the space.

Something in the bright white light has my brain rebooting.

I just fucked Booth—my employee—in a supply closet, while a hundred people stand outside.

This is the second time I've found myself in this situation with him, and I have to question if my sanity dissolved since landing in this town.

"Aly," he warns. "I can hear your big brain from here. Don't overthink it. One night, remember?"

I ignore the trickle of disappointment that seeps into my chest at his reminder.

"You're hearing things." I wiggle my hips. "I can't go back out there like this."

He looks sad at the idea of cleaning me up. Booth glances around, then leans over me to tear off a piece of paper towel. With careful swipes, he cleans up his mess, then fixes my dress.

When I face him, I'm not surprised to find him looking smug as he scrubs a hand down his jaw. His smirk grows when my eyes narrow.

"Don't say it."

"I don't have to. The way you came around my cock is confirmation enough." He leans in, nose skimming down my cheek. "Twice. You didn't scream like that with your toy."

"You're fired," I mumble, though my satisfied tone contradicts me.

"Nah. I'm your favorite employee." Before I can blink, he lays a chaste kiss to the edge of my mouth, tucks himself away, and steps toward the door. "See you at work, boss. What a way to bring in the new year."

His parting wink is the last thing I see before he disappears.

Despite knowing there's only one outcome, I can't find a modicum of regret over what we just did. Well, there is some. I'd never admit this to Booth, but I'm quickly wishing I hadn't declared this a one-time occurrence.

That is until I realize he still has my panties.

Motherfucker.

CHAPTER TWENTY-THREE

booth

Two days.

That's how long it's been since I last saw Aly.

In those forty-eight hours, I've fucked my fist three times, with the picture of Aly painted in my cum as my muse.

I wish the restaurant had been open on New Year's Day, as it would have stopped me from overanalyzing my feelings. Sadly, we were closed, and I lost myself in an ocean of what-ifs.

What if it happened again?

What if we met under different circumstances?

What if we weren't worlds apart?

I've never done this with a fling before.

But that's the issue. She doesn't feel like a fling.

Today, I'm grateful to be back at work; the sizzling of food and clanging of pans drowns out my thoughts. It's oddly busy for early January, but rather than question it, the team works tirelessly through a grueling service.

The shift wouldn't be as bad had Kyle shown up.

The bone I had to pick with my line cook after his drunken state at the party was a big one.

Red mist blurred my vision when he snatched Aly's arm up

roughly. To no surprise, she handled the situation. Doesn't mean I didn't want to deck the prick.

His shift started four hours ago, which makes firing his ass that much easier. It's not only his borderline harassment toward his employer and a female, but his piss-poor work ethic, tardiness, and lacking skills. His resume was obviously fluffed up, but I gave him the benefit of the doubt and was willing to train him.

A mistake I won't make again.

Simon slides two entrées in front of me, and I thank my lucky stars I can rely on him.

"Good work, Chef," I tell him as he gets to work on the next ticket dangling in front of us.

"Wasn't prepared to get slammed like this today." He blows out a breath. "Why aren't people vegging out on the sofa recovering from the holidays?"

"Beats me." I give the edges of the plates a quick wipe, then press the bell to notify the servers.

Ten seconds later, the door swings open, but instead of Theresa, a wary Patrick stands in the door frame.

"I don't like your face." I press the bell again, and Theresa quickly scoots past Patrick to collect the order.

"I don't like yours either." His voice lacks its usual wit. "But there's something more pressing to discuss than your ugly mug."

"Charming." I grab a fresh container of cilantro. "What do you need?"

"Umm." His hesitation irks me.

"Pat, spit it out or get out. Respectfully."

He glances behind him. "You need to come to the office."

That doesn't sound good.

Simon is already shoving me out of the way to trade places, taking over the pass without question. After scrubbing my hands and removing my apron, I meet my brother outside the kitchen doors.

"You're worrying me," I hiss and follow him toward the back of the restaurant.

He doesn't have time to respond, because my missing line cook appears from the office and barges past us.

Spinning around, I shout after him. "Kyle, where the hell have you been?"

His angry steps pause, and he fixes me with a furious stare over his shoulder. "Why don't you ask that bitch, Alessandra? Get a tighter leash for her." His eyes narrow. "Unless you put her up to this?"

Rage takes over my limbs as I stride toward him before I'm jerked backward.

"Now is not the time," Patrick whispers as he gestures subtly to the crowded tables. "Let him go."

We watch Kyle storm away. Once he's out of sight, I pivot on my heel, Patrick right behind me, and crash into the office.

Seething, I take in the scene.

Cool, calm, collected. That's how Aly appears as her red fingernails clack against the keyboard. Images flash in my head of those fingers curled around the edge of the shelves as I rutted into her.

Not the time or the place for those thoughts.

Her eyes dart up. "Booth? What's going on?"

Patrick is silent as he closes the door.

"I'm hoping you can tell me." My voice rises. "I ran into one of my employees, and he looked ready to commit murder. Something tells me you're involved." I withhold the fact he called her a bitch, a detail that still has my blood boiling.

"*Ex*-employee," she corrects nonchalantly.

"You fired him?" My feet stay rooted to the spot. I'm motionless, apart from the muscle ticking in my jaw. "Who was with you?"

Well, that does it. Silver flames swallow up her irises as lethal anger creeps into her posture. A python ready to attack. "I can dismiss someone without assistance. Last I checked, I was in charge."

Patrick's discomfort radiates off him, but I'm ready for her.

I love her fire. How she doesn't hesitate to stand up and speak out when she's been wronged. The thing is, *she's* wrong, and has completely misunderstood my concern.

"Hey, Pat, give us a minute, would you?" I don't break eye contact with Aly.

"My pleasure." He hurries out of the room.

The second the door clicks, she jumps to her feet and slams a palm down on the desk. "What the fuck, Booth? I thought we were past all this? Now you're humiliating me in front of your brother?"

With careful steps and mouth sealed shut, I round the desk. She tracks my movement like a predator. A few weeks ago, I would have matched her heat with a dumb joke. Today, I try a new tactic.

When she's in touching distance, I gently take her shoulders and turn her toward me.

"At no point was I questioning your capabilities. You saved me from firing him—something I hate doing. I'm sure you did a stellar job and I hope you made his balls shrivel." Her brows furrow. "I'm pissed at you, Alessandra, because you did it alone. He's a dick and a creep. And after his behavior at the party, I don't want him near you."

Her mouth twists as she studies me. I see the moment she believes me and her shoulders lose their tension. "I don't need a bodyguard."

Laughing, I press my lips to her forehead without thinking. "No, you need a throne. And maybe some chill pills."

She smacks my chest, lips pursed as she fights a smile.

"Poor Patrick almost pissed himself. You'll have to apologize." I smirk.

"Kiss my ass."

"Gladly."

While we bicker, the space between us disappears, until my hand rests on her hip, thumb moving in lazy circles beneath the hem of her sweater.

"What are you doing later?" I blurt. She looks shocked, and before she can say no, I hold up my palm. "Not a date. Get over yourself, jeez. Drinks with the team."

"I don't know..." She steps away, fiddling with the diamond bracelet on her wrist.

"It's tradition," I quickly add. "Uh, after the first shift of the year, we all go out and celebrate. C'mon, it'll be fun."

After some hesitancy, she agrees. "Fine. One drink."

"Sounds good. Now, I have a job ad to put out and a few hours left until I clock out." I throw her a salute. "Wear something pretty, yeah?"

"Goodbye, Booth." Her eyes roll as she sits down, trying her hardest not to react.

"Don't miss me too much," I shout over my shoulder.

When I'm a few feet from the office, I scurry to pull out my phone and bring up the group text.

Booth: Celebratory drinks at Shirley's tonight

Graham: That's not a question.

Booth: Clever boy. This isn't an invitation, it's a demand.

Patrick: I'm surprised you're still breathing.

Flo: Oh, has Booth been told off again?

Quinn: What are we celebrating?

Dex: Booth finally getting laid.

Booth: *middle finger emoji*

Booth: I never ask for anything. Do this for me.

Jo: You asked me to scratch your back this morning. Literally, not metaphorically.

Booth: I couldn't reach and you have long nails.

Graham: You asked me for a LEGO set the other week.

Booth: That was a Christmas gift, you heartless prick!

Booth has left the chat
Quinn added Booth to the chat

Quinn: Hi, Booth, :) Graham and I would love to join you tonight.

I picture Graham scowling at Quinn's upbeat response and chuckle.

Booth: Thanks, Quinn. You were always my favorite.

Jo: Hey!

Booth: I promise you won't regret this ;)

"This is my biggest regret of the year," Dex grumbles around the rim of his glass.

"It's January second." Johanna laughs.

"Exactly. And nothing will top this."

I kick his shin under the table. "Shut up. How is this any different from any other night we meet for drinks?"

Patrick and Florence return to the table and divvy out a round of drinks.

"So tell me again," Florence starts, tapping her finger on her chin. "You told Alessandra that we do this *every* year so you could hang out with her?"

My cheeks heat. "When you put it like that, I sound pathetic."

"Because you are," Graham kindly adds.

Standing abruptly, I slam my gin and tonic down. "I'm leaving."

Johanna clears her throat, Dex lets out a low whistle, and Quinn's eyes go wide.

"What?" I ask in confusion.

Florence is the one to respond. "I wouldn't go yet, big bro." She grips my chin and twists my head toward the door.

My heart tumbles out of my chest. Everything becomes irrelevant, other than *her*.

I told her to wear something pretty. In typical fashion, she did the opposite. This isn't pretty. It's downright sexy.

It's still below zero outside, and with her coat slung over her arm, her entire outfit is visible. High-waisted, navy and white striped pants hug her hips and ass before flaring out at the bottom. A low-cut silky top showcases the pillowy tops of her perky breasts. What has my pulse going berserk is her hair piled high on her head. Inky ringlets frame her oval-shaped face, giving me an unobscured view of her slender neck.

She's a sensual masterpiece. A collector's item that refuses to be hidden away. Because what a pity it would be to hide the breathtaking beauty that people write sonnets about.

The world was never prepared for a woman like Alessandra Argiros. And neither am I.

I lose track of the minutes spent staring at her, and when we lock eyes, that secret smile paints her cherry lips. I'm positive she chose that shade to torture me.

She holds up a finger and grabs the attention of the bartender. With a glass of red in hand, she sashays over. Confident and bold.

"Evening," she greets everyone, squeezing in between Dex and Quinn.

"Oh, yay, Aly!" Quinn cheers. The other girls smile and say hello, and something sparkles in Aly's eyes at their friendly welcome.

"Fancy seeing you here." My voice breaks at the end like a prepubescent teenager.

"Jesus fucking Christ." Graham sighs. "And I thought I had no game."

Aly ignores me and jumps right into conversation with Dex. *Now, hang on for a fucking minute. She's with me.*

I turn to my sister, hoping she can distract me with her blabbering, and find her gaze set on Aly and Dex, too, a tiny frown on her face. Poking her in the cheek, I draw her attention my way. "What's up with you?"

Her eyes flare. "Nothing. What's up with you?" She glances back at Aly. "Oh, is Booth pouting because his girlfriend isn't interested?"

I palm her face and shove her away. "When are you leaving the country again?"

She flaps her hands. "Never if I can't find a job!"

Patrick quirks a brow. "I offered you shifts at the restaurant."

Flo's cheeks redden at his condescending tone. "I don't know if I can hack working there. There's too much going on."

Aly's gaze *finally* falls in my direction. "What was your favorite destination on your travels?"

"Huh?" I call over the music.

"Booth," Flo whispers. "She's talking to me."

Nope. I can't do this.

Who invited her? This is torture.

I stand abruptly. "I'm going to the restroom."

"Thanks for letting us know." Dex winks at me over Aly's shoulder.

I'm going to put ants in his bed.

Throwing back my drink, I escape the awkward tension. After relieving myself, I take a few minutes to breathe.

I need to get my shit together. Aly likes me. I think. Well, she liked me the other night. Or did she?

My head spins and I press the heels of my palms into my eyes until my vision goes white.

She's making me lose my mojo and mind with each second she pretends I don't exist. Does she want one night? Does she want two? Does she want to watch me suffer?

With some semblance of sanity, I head back out but stop short when I spy the scrawny figure lurking next to our table.

"Motherfucker," I hiss as my feet carry me over.

"I think you've had enough to drink." I catch Johanna saying, her voice even.

Kyle ignores her and snatches up Aly's wine, downing it in one.

Aly eyes the glass in disgust when he clumsily places it on the table.

"Oh, I'm sorry, Your Highness. Were you not done with that?" he slurs.

She doesn't budge as she gives him a disinterested side

glance. "Please, help yourself. But I'd listen to Johanna; she's a smart woman."

"Pfft, I'm not listening to anyone, let alone you." He crowds her, sneering, and everyone stiffens. Not Aly, though. "You prance in here, thinking you're better than all of us."

He doesn't notice me standing behind him, a good four inches taller, chest heaving. Aly spies me and subtly shakes her head. I stay quiet but don't back away.

She's got this, but like heck is she leaving my sight.

Aly coolly retrieves her lipstick from her purse and applies a fresh layer of killer red. I understand why she's good at what she does. Brilliant, actually. It's also the reason she floored me the moment she got on my radar.

Nothing fazes her. An unflappable force of nature. I could spend an eternity watching her rule the world.

But not today.

Because I want this piece of shit gone.

"Kyle." She sounds bored. "You're not the first, and certainly won't be the last, man to try to intimidate me. I don't think I'm better than these people"—she gestures to everyone around the table—"or you." She caps the tube of lipstick and finally looks at him. "Because I don't think about you at all. So thanks for stopping by, but I think it's time you left."

Her expression is flat, apart from her eyes. They glitter in warning; one he doesn't heed.

Scoffing, he stumbles forward, his hand landing roughly on her shoulder. "You'd be a lot prettier if you smiled more. Too bad you're a fucking stuck-up little bitch who needs to be put in her place."

Someone gasps. My brothers and Dex rise from their seats. And I do something I've never done in my life.

Tapping Kyle on the shoulder, I look him dead in the eyes.

My knuckles crack.

His nose crunches.

And he crumples to the floor.
"Her smiles are for me, asshole."

alessandra

"Stop looking at me like that," I snap.

Booth's puppy dog expression intensifies. "Don't shout at me. I'm injured." He hisses when the ice pack shifts across his swollen knuckles.

"Because you punched somebody!"

I blinked, and Kyle was on his ass, clutching his nose as Booth stared at his clenched fist in shock. He isn't a violent man and a sliver of regret laced his features when blood gushed from Kyle's nose. Before he could kick up a fuss, Dex and Patrick hauled Kyle out of Shirley's and Graham drove everyone else home.

I've been pacing the length of Booth's boathouse since then.

"Aly, sit down. You're making me dizzy," Booth says softly from the sofa.

My hands fly up in the air. "You *punched* him, Booth. You could get arrested."

He laughs but clamps his mouth shut when I scowl at him. "Sorry, it's not funny. Well…it is. The sheriff went to school with my parents. Plus, Kyle is a dick who deserved it."

He's not wrong. I won't tell him that, though. For one, I can't work out why I'm mad.

"I had it handled."

"Oh, I'm sure. Kyle should thank me. If I left him to you, he'd need a lifetime of therapy."

His grin widens at my sneer. "Come here." He crooks a finger at me and my stomach dips at his heated gaze.

My pacing stops in front of him. "That's not a good idea. I might hurt you."

His head cocks to the side. "So what you're saying is if I wasn't injured, you'd consider it?"

An *oomph* leaves him when a pillow hits him in the face.

"You won't be able to work. What's the restaurant supposed to do?" I drop to my knees and gently lift his hand. Eyes trained on his mottled red knuckles. "You didn't need to do that for me."

With his good hand, he hooks a finger under my chin. "I know. I wanted to. *Had* to, actually."

Booth doesn't think; he does.

At first, I put it down to him being impulsive and immature, but the more time I spend with him, the more I understand. He's loyal to the core, headstrong, and puts his all into everything he does. And he's found me worthy of falling into that bracket.

An odd sensation seizes me as I catalog his bruised hand, sincere expression, and, well, him.

After placing a gentle kiss to his knuckles, I surge upward and seal my lips to his.

A weightlessness accompanies the feel of his mouth against mine. I could float into the atmosphere, disappear into the Milky Way, if it weren't for the unstoppable magnetism grounding me.

Since New Year's Eve, my defenses have weakened considerably.

Ignoring the meaning behind it all, I deepen the kiss, weave my fingers through his messy hair, and wordlessly ask him to follow my lead.

His grip is harsh as he cups the back of my neck, tongue exploring my mouth lazily. Our touches roam, and a deep rumble vibrates in his chest when my fingers curl around the waistband of his sweats.

When they trace over his smooth, hard skin, my desire skyrockets.

Groaning in frustration against my lips, he pulls away. He plucks my hand out of his pants and holds it against his cheek, smiling at me carefully.

"I don't think that's a good idea." His words negate his torn expression.

Mortification drips over me. His rejection is a punch in the chest.

I shoot to my feet, snatch up my coat, and make it two steps before a strong forearm anchors me to his chest. "Fuck, no. You're misreading this. I *want* you." His hard length presses into my lower back in confirmation.

"You said this isn't a good idea." I despise the dejection in my voice.

"Silver, you said one night. And that was after you left me high and dry in the cabin, swearing to pretend that morning never happened. Then the supply closet happened... Forgive me for being a teensy bit confused right now."

Twisting in his hold, my eyes fix on the divot at the base of his neck. "I'm not good at"—I point between us—"*This*. I've already told you I'll be leaving soon."

His shoulders deflate. "Will you look at me?"

I raise my gaze, and he tucks a lock of hair behind my ear. "I'm not asking for your hand in marriage." He exhales a slow breath. "We're attracted to each other, you excite me, and I'd like to spend time with you until you leave."

His honesty is refreshing. Reading between the lines, he's suggesting a no strings agreement. Could I do that? For one, it would make my remaining time in town more entertaining and hopefully be a good distraction.

Most of my relationships have been casual. But no one has roused me like him. And that's the scariest part.

My decision is obvious or stupid.

"We have to keep things professional at work. And no telling your family." After Dex and Jo's comments recently, that's likely impossible.

His smile slips. "Oh, um, so about that."

Point proven.

I cock my head. "Gossip much?"

"Hey, it wasn't me. They have no boundaries." His expression tells me he's full of crap. "I swear it stays between us. I'm nothing if not professional."

He's a goof, but in the kitchen, he's a master.

"Okay then, it's settled." I poke him in the chest. "But if you refer to us as fuck buddies, I'm pulling the plug. When it's time for me to leave, we go our separate ways. After that, I'm simply the woman that signs your paychecks."

The corner of his mouth picks up. "Deal."

He holds out his hand, and the second I slide my palm into his, he's crushing his lips to mine. That small contact sends pleasure zipping through my body, as if he's everywhere at once.

Breaking the kiss, he whispers against my lips. "But tonight, we're going to talk, then sleep."

I frown. "That sounds very domesticated. And any sleeping shall occur under different roofs."

He ignores me and steers me into the small bathroom. "There's a spare toothbrush under the sink. Help yourself to anything."

"This is classed as kidnap—" The door shuts in my face.

The wood muffles his voice. "Quit fighting it, baby. Until you cross town lines, I'm making the most of our time together."

I raise my middle finger.

"Don't flip me off either. Or there'll be trouble."

I throw my hands up in frustration but ultimately give in.

Not even two minutes later, I'm livid.

Flinging open the bedroom door, I stomp to where he's lounging on the bed, an arm slung behind his head.

My furiousness, for whatever reason, ignites a fire in his gaze. "What have I done this time?" he drawls.

"Well, I helped myself to *anything,* and came across your collection of cleansers and toners." I thrust my hands on my hips. "You're deluded if you think I'm using leftover products from your last one-night stand."

He's silent for a millisecond before bursting into laughter.

"Aly, Aly, Aly," he sings playfully as he sits up. "Where've you been my whole life?" We both falter at his sentimental question. He recovers and attempts to keep a straight face. "The products are mine."

I blink once. Twice. "Come again?"

"They're mine. Can't a guy have a ten-step skincare routine without being judged?" He dips his head. "Now, for someone so intent on reminding me how misogynistic the world is, that's very sexist of you to presume they weren't mine."

"I'm already regretting this agreement." I huff, and stomp back into the bathroom to finish getting ready, ignoring his snickering.

When I reemerge, he uses the bathroom—forgoing his nightly routine considering how quick he is—and returns in just a pair of black briefs.

I'm standing at the foot of the bed, and avert my gaze when he ambles over. He comes up behind me, minty breath coasting over my neck. "Question: Do you like being jealous?"

I don't dignify him with a response and watch him slide back into bed with a smug expression on his face. As he's about to crack another joke, I slip my silk cami up and over my head, letting it drop to the floor.

That shuts him up.

His eyes trail down my torso, gaze tickling my skin like featherlight touches. I flick the buttons on my pants and slide them down my legs to reveal black lace panties that match my strapless bra.

Gulping, he shakes his head vigorously. "I deserve a Nobel Peace Prize for saying no to sex tonight."

"Which side is mine?" My voice is light, sweet almost, and I bend at the waist, giving him an eyeful as I unbuckle my heels. When I straighten, a T-shirt hits me in the face.

"Put that on, you siren. Before I go back on my word and fuck you into this mattress until the sun comes up." Each word is forced through gritted teeth.

With a quick scan of his bare chest, I unclasp my bra and slip on the white T-shirt, the threadbare cotton doing little to hide my perky nipples.

Booth groans dramatically and rolls onto his stomach. The springs bounce as he punches the mattress. "How? *How* are you sexier in my clothes than in your underwear?"

"Behave, or you'll have both hands out of action," I reprimand. Pulling back the sheets, I climb in beside him and fluff up my pillows.

Booth pauses his tantrum to flip a switch by his head, leaving the bedside lamp to cast the room in a warm orange glow. When he twists toward me, my stomach clenches at the intimacy of it all.

"So, sleep?" I ask abruptly.

He shakes his head and shuffles closer until his pelvis brushes my hip. "Lie with me."

I inhale deeply, then roll to my side. Butterflies erupt in my belly, the stupid little insects fluttering around even more when he cups my cheek and flashes me a crooked grin.

"Tell me something no one else knows?" he says in a hushed tone.

Alarm bells go off. Not even one hour in and he's already pushing the boundaries of this arrangement. I can't understand his need to get to know me. He's no longer the enemy, but sharing parts of myself I carefully keep under lock and key doesn't come easily.

He senses my trepidation. "I'll go first then." His hand slinks to my nape, thumb running in circles below my ear. "I was a baby when George and my dad opened the restaurant. According to my mom, Florence, Harriet, and I took our first steps right next to the driftwood bar our fathers spent a week building. We did our homework in the office, had family dinners after hours, and took prom photos on the restaurant floor. So it's no wonder I decided on a career in hospitality."

I listen closely, at the way his voice rasps slightly at the mention of his father. My hand drifts to his chest, and I mindlessly trace shapes over his smooth skin.

"When I was thirteen, Gloria, our previous head chef, let me shadow her on a slow Monday afternoon. From that day forward, I was hooked. I begged for cookbooks that Christmas, started working as a dishwasher when I was old enough, and tried my hand at anything and everything. If it was edible, I wanted to cook with it. To me, being a chef wasn't a career, it was my passion, something I spent my youth fantasizing over..."

"But?"

Remorse sweeps over his face like a dark shadow at my question.

"My fantasies didn't involve me working in my family's restaurant. I wanted to travel. To use ingredients from all corners of the world. To shoot my shot in Michelin star restaurants so I could say I tried. Our Place was always going to be a stepping-stone in my career, but it wasn't supposed to be permanent."

"What's stopping you from pursuing those dreams?"

He smiles sadly. "My dad passed unexpectedly. Freak accident. His death left a crater-size hole in my family and as the grief lessened, I realized I couldn't abandon his legacy. He always told me how proud he was to see me behind the pass he helped install and to hear the gushing reviews from customers when they tried my food. Turning my back on the restaurant would have meant turning my back on his memory."

My fingers splay over his heart, eyes not wavering as I stare at him. "What did your dad think of your dreams?"

His heartbeat stutters under my palm. Regret etches deep in his face, lining his mouth and forehead. "He didn't know. No one does. Not even my siblings."

"Booth," I start. "You can't believe he wouldn't have supported you. No matter where you worked or moved to."

His thumb shifts, grazing my bottom lip. "That's nice of you to say, but you don't know that, Aly."

I'm speechless. Underneath the cocky smiles and cunning wit, torment sits below the surface, waiting in the shallows for the tide to change. He does a good job at concealing it.

Something we have in common.

"I love my job. I feel I should end with that, considering you're keeping me employed and all," he jokes, and at the flip of a switch his pain is gone.

His ability to lay it all out stuns me. It makes me want to peel back my veil and share what keeps me up at night. But if I verbalize it, I'll have to follow through with my plan, and I'm not sure I have the guts for that just yet. Or ever.

The sound of his laughter fades when he takes in my expression. "Hey, what's wrong?"

My hand falls, and I study him closely, searching for the

ulterior motive behind his candor. "Why did you share that with me?"

Surprise morphs his features. "Well, that's a good question." His tongue clicks against the roof of his mouth as he thinks before he lifts a shoulder. "I guess I trust you."

If anything from this whole evening petrifies me the most, it's that. Why would he put his trust in me? There's too much weight and pressure held within those words. A responsibility I don't want to take on.

"You shouldn't," I declare. "You don't know me. Five minutes ago, you hated me."

He recoils. "I've never *hated* you. I regret how we went about things initially, but you've surprised all of us. You're also right. I don't know you, and I'm trying to change that." With the grip he has on my neck, he tugs me close. "I want to know what goes on in that beautiful, stubborn head of yours. To know what makes you tick. Your favorite foods. Maybe one day you'll let me cook for you. I'm not looking for anything serious, Aly—we can both agree on that. But that doesn't mean I don't want to soak up every minute we have. Because after you're gone, I can say, 'I met this incredible woman and for a little while, she was mine.'"

"I want you to know me," I exclaim, my face turning into a furnace at my outburst.

Rather than ask how he can gain it, he brushes his lips over mine tenderly. "I know, Silv. And whatever pieces of yourself you give to me, I'll treasure them like the gifts they are."

Speechless, my mouth parts. Booth takes advantage. His tongue strokes mine softly, lips moving languidly. He rolls us, pinning me to the mattress with his bulky frame and settling his weight on top of me.

Groaning and sighing, we tangle, giving ourselves over to the kiss. My fingers trace the ridges of his spine before cupping his firm ass, encouraging him to press harder into my aching center.

"Stop trying to seduce me, woman," he growls against my lips.

I giggle. *Fucking giggle.* This man has transformed me into a horny, giddy mess with his sweet declarations and all-consuming kisses.

I roll my pelvis, earning a throaty groan when the underside of his cock drags over my clit. "*You* kissed me."

The world turns upside down as he flips us, with me plastered to his front.

"And now I'm going to cuddle you. Sleep well, my little witch." He tucks my head under his chin and sighs.

"I don't cuddle, Dimples." I attempt to wriggle from his clutches with no luck. "Free me."

"Shhh, I'm sleeping." His drowsy words blow through my hair.

Not even three minutes later, he's snoring, arms locked around my lower back like a straitjacket.

Giggling. Cuddling.

I don't dare ask what's next.

Because what if I like it?

CHAPTER TWENTY-FIVE

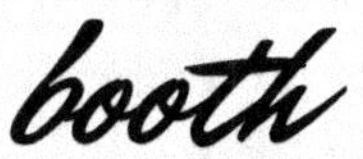

THIS.

I could get used to *this.*

Onyx curls tickle my nose as her head rests on my chest. Every inch of my skin tingles as her soft breathing caresses my neck. For such a non-cuddler, she's clinging to me like her life depends on it.

I like this.

This won't last.

It's hard to comprehend that reality when all I want to do is ignore it. As cliché as it sounds, it's never been like this before.

The funny thing is, what I thought would terrify me, doesn't. And maybe that's more terrifying. Rather than over-think it, I enjoy the feel of her body molded to mine.

The fight glimmered in her eyes when I asked her to share a secret. They say the eyes are the window to the soul. In Aly's, I saw a chaos of emotions swirling in those stormy depths. It took all my strength not to beg her to tell me why panic seized her; a reaction so ill-fitted for someone that wears their strength and confidence like silver-plated armor.

Today is my day off, and I'm not sure of her schedule. I

decide on more sleep, not wanting this to end. But the second my eyelids close, her deadweight shifts. Her breasts crush into my chest as she stretches, yawning quietly, before blinking up at me. Behind the sleepy haze, a ripple of shock appears, like she forgot where she was, before serenity washes it away.

Deep satisfaction swells behind my rib cage when her head drops to my neck, a low hum vibrating from her throat as she presses her nose to my pulse point.

"You smell like smoked chicory," she murmurs.

She shakes with my rumble of laughter. "Is that a good thing?"

"Mm-hmm." She lifts her head again. "I have to go. Jo invited me to meet with the wine rep this afternoon."

I tighten my arms. "Jo is a cock block."

She wrangles out of my hold to straddle my hips. The barrier of our underwear needs eradicating.

"Are you working today?" She peers down at me coyly.

Lifting a hand, I twirl a strand of hair around my finger, then let is spring free. "Nah. I'm going to meet up with Harriet for lunch before taking Lottie ice-skating."

Her lips tilt up, voice sickly sweet. "That's nice."

"There is *nothing* going on there. She's like a sister to me."

She grimaces. "A sister you gave your virginity to?"

My stomach turns. "Gross. Harry would tell you I'm too young for her anyway. She has a thing for older men." A shiver runs through her when I glide my hand down her back, cupping her tight ass and grinding her into me. "I like you all hot and bothered over me."

"Oh, you bother me all right," she deadpans, then lowers her top half, aligning our fronts.

We lie together, watching the pink sky paint the snowy bluffs. The headboard sits flush against the large window spanning the back of my house. I have blinds but prefer nature's alarm. Gulls swoop and dive into the water, circling the trawlers bobbing across the bay. Like the icicles hanging from the roof, warming under the sun's rays, she melts into me, soft and pliant in my arms.

"I'm curious. The paintings you were selling. Was it all a ruse to spy on us?"

Her eyes narrow, chin balanced between my pecs. "Yes, and no. I do paint, but I rarely sell my art. Or at all, really."

My chest expands at this tidbit of information. She gives me a crumb that might as well be a banquet.

"Will you show me?"

Her brows hike up.

"Your art. If that's okay?" I brush a lock of hair off her shoulder.

Aly is clandestine to her core. So when a smile erupts, outshining the sunrise behind us, and says, "I'd like that." It's as if I've won the lottery. No. Better. So much better.

"I have something for you," I rush out and lean over to my bedside table. "Close your eyes and hold out your hand."

She stares at me skeptically before obeying.

Rummaging around, I find what I'm looking for and drop it in her palm. Suddenly, I feel stupid, but it's too late.

Aly's mouth drops open and she raises the tiny plastic flower. "Is this...LEGO?"

My face heats. "Yeah. Um, now you can't say I never gave you flowers." I scratch my jaw. "You don't have to keep it, it's more of a joke." I go to reach for it, but she snatches her arm away.

"Hey, mitts off." She smiles thoughtfully at the little red rose.

Our gazes clash and my heart jumps wildly. The tension between us evolves. If we speak, it'll vanish. So we stay silent, our breathing shallow as something unknown and tempting ripples. It's always been there, only now there's no fighting it. If

I were to reach out and touch it, sparks would fly, colors would burst, and I'm certain there'd be no turning back.

The chime of her phone pops our tranquil bubble.

I protest when she plants a chaste kiss to my cheek and jumps off me.

The little vixen licks her lips when her eyes drop to my morning wood. "Do me a favor…"

"I'm listening." I sit upright, tracking her movements as she slips out of my T-shirt and into her clothes.

"Do nothing about that little problem, okay?" Her gaze drops again. Dark amusement flickers with her devious smile.

"Little?!" I shout and scramble to the end of the bed as she saunters to the door. "Come back here and say that to my face, Alessandra Argiros."

She kisses the tips of her fingers and blows me a kiss. "No touching, *Chef.*"

When she disappears into the bitter January morning, I bring the discarded T-shirt to my nose, inhaling her lavender and sage scent, triggering a wild obsession that refuses to be reined in.

Collapsing back into my seat, I pat my belly, filled to the brim with ten slices of cheesy goodness.

Harry eyes my empty pizza box and her half-eaten pie. "Where do you put all that food? It's not normal."

I blot my mouth with a napkin and shrug. "I'm a growing boy."

"Idiot." She laughs.

Dough is a small pizzeria in town, with only a handful of tables. Harriet and I have been coming here since we were teens. It's actually where we went on our first date. Thinking back to those two gangly teenagers, awkwardly sharing a pepperoni slice, makes me chuckle.

Closing the lid, she leans forward, her voice just above a murmur. "So...how's it going with Aly?"

My lips quiver, a smile threatening to emerge at the mention of her name. "Hmm, I presume she's good. Why do you ask?"

A wad of napkins hits me in the face. "Don't play coy with me. I saw you two sneak into the supply closet. Now spill."

"There's nothing to say."

"You're telling me nothing is happening?" She stares at me dubiously.

I beckon her closer and keep my voice low. "I swore to her I'd keep it quiet. It's casual, so don't get ex—"

"Ah-ha!" she shouts and slaps a palm to the table, gaining the attention of the staff behind the counter. "I knew it!"

"—cited," I finish flatly. "Seriously, Harry, don't tell anyone. Our siblings have some clue, but it's only while she's in town. After that we're...ending things."

Aly has just begun opening up, so the mention of *the end* sits heavy and sour in my stomach.

Then a wayward thought assaults me. It feels like betrayal talking about Aly behind her back, but something has been niggling in my head since Christmas. Against my better judgment, I look to Harriet to fill in the blanks.

"Hey, I have a question," I begin.

She points at me. "Don't think we're not looping back to your friends-with-benefits arrangement. Shoot."

"On Christmas Day, did you hear what Aly and Martin were discussing before she left the room?"

She blinks in surprise. "Oh. Yeah. It was a little awkward between them." Her mouth twists. "Aly was asking about his family. Or his son, specifically."

"His son?" I search my brain for any recollection of him having a family. "Was Martin married?"

Nodding, she sips her soda. "Yeah, but it ended before we were born. His son is closer to our parents' age. I think he married and had a kid young, but I remember my dad talking about him once. He said Martin was a different person before his wife and kid left Sutton Bay. From what I gather, he saw little of them after that."

"Wow. I never knew." I tilt my head. "But why was their conversation awkward?"

"Maybe not awkward, but Aly seemed really adamant on knowing whether he visited his son. Then suddenly, she was excusing herself and disappeared. I hadn't thought about it much until now. Why do you ask?"

Debating how to word this, I drag a hand through my hair before responding. "She seemed...spooked. Which isn't like her." I take in Harriet's smug face. "Shut up."

Harriet waves down our server for the bill while I replay every interaction I've witnessed between Aly and Martin. Her stiff posture, pinched face, tense words.

Martin seemed unaffected. Which is his usual look. His relationship with his estranged family could explain his somber temperament and sad eyes.

A chill runs through me.

Martin's sad, *gray* eyes.

So pale, they're almost silver.

"Don't forget to stomp your feet," I holler up the driveway to Lottie.

Patrick and Johanna are at the restaurant today, and Lottie's mom was called into work last minute. I'd never turn down a day out with my niece. I'm not proud of it, but in the past, she's been the perfect babe magnet. Patrick never took advantage of the "single daddy" persona—so someone had to. Today, however, when the women's hockey coach skated over to me on the lake, I was quick to declare Lottie as my niece and myself *unavailable.*

Lottie halts outside the front door and pounds her little snow boots on the ground, leaving splatters of white around her. When she's satisfied, she pushes open the door and bounds into the house.

"Grandma! It's me!" she shouts.

I'm close behind, mirroring her as I stomp my feet before stepping inside.

My mom greets us in the hallway.

"Did you two have fun?" she asks while helping Lottie out of her snow pants.

"Yep." Lottie grins from ear to ear while spinning in a circle. "I did a pillow-et."

Laughing, I flick her pigtail. "It's *pirouette.* But you nailed it. Very impressive."

That little ounce of praise has her preening—she's a lot like me in that sense. Probably why she's such a cool kid.

"Are we eating dinner here?" Lottie's eyes ping-pong between my mom and me.

"Meatballs are cooking as we speak. Why don't you get cleaned up and then play in the den?"

Lottie nods at my mom's instructions and zips up the stairs.

I glare at my mother, who swats me away, already knowing why I'm mad. "The doctor said I could put weight on it now. Quit your fussing."

"Light duties. Standing at the stove for hours doesn't fall into that category. You're a menace."

She ignores me and hobbles into the kitchen.

"I would have cooked," I continue.

"Sweetheart, I know that, but you're always working such long hours. I thought you'd like a break." To my relief, she settles on a stool and elevates her injured leg.

"I love it, Ma." I shrug while stirring the bright red marinara, garlic and rich tomato wafting through the air.

"Do you?"

The wooden spoon crashes to the counter, sending sauce flying and staining my T-shirt.

"Of course." I don't face her, worried my expression holds the truth.

She's silent for a beat, making me nervous. "I've been thinking a lot lately about you kids and how your dad would have handled all these changes and milestones. We never spoke to you about your future in the restaurant…"

A sweat breaks out on the back of my neck.

I'm exposed and slightly panicked over how to respond. If I reveal the truth, it will break her heart, knowing my dreams don't involve staying in Maine.

Chuckling nervously, I say, "Well, I don't exactly have any transferable skills to land myself another job." I pout at her over my shoulder. "Aly's already fired me once. Don't tell me you're giving me the boot too?"

My humor does the trick in deflecting my mother's inquisition, and I relax when she rolls her eyes.

"Speaking of Aly…" she starts. "She's a surprising young woman, isn't she? Very successful. As is her family's business. It makes me wonder what their interest in Our Place is."

Yeah, you and me both.

"Maybe they're trying out a new business venture. Small-town restaurants can be very appealing." Unease furls in the pit of my stomach, but I can't ignore the question sitting on the tip of my tongue. "Hey, do you know if Martin Willis had any other kids?"

Mom looks puzzled at my sudden change in conversation. "What do you mean?"

"I know he has a son from his previous marriage, but is that it?"

Her head tilts in thought before shaking it. "Gosh, he's so private, but I doubt it. Since his wife left, he's kept to himself. She was sweet and taught third grade at the school. I don't know what happened between them, but one day she was gone, taking their son with her. I remember him. Spitting image of Martin."

Matching gray eyes, perhaps.

"Why do you want to know?" she presses.

"No reason," I reply way too quickly. Giving her my back, I rummage through the pantry. "Do you have any *pappardelle*? It will go nicely with this sauce."

"You should ask Alessandra out."

Oh, for fuck's sake.

My siblings say I'm a busybody, but my mother is a connoisseur of meddling.

"Ooooh, like a date? Do people make kissy faces on dates?" And enters chief meddler: Lottie Sadler.

"There will be no dating," I declare.

Lottie gasps. "Who are you marrying?"

My hands fly to my sides. "How the heck did you come to that conclusion, you toad?"

The little devil *tsks* and uncurls her hand toward me. "That's a swear. Dollar please."

"Is not," I mumble but quickly pull out my wallet and slap a dollar in her hand, hoping it ends this conversation.

It doesn't.

"We're talking about Alessandra. I'm telling your Uncle Boo he should take her out for a nice dinner," my mom declares casually.

My mouth gapes. "What the fu—" Lottie looks at me with dollar signs in her eyes. "—dge, Ma? When did matchmaking become your side hustle?"

She huffs. "Can't a mother want to see her son happy?"

"Sure. Visit Pat and Graham. Leave me out of it." I point at the two troublemakers. "Now, both of you sit at the table. Dinner is almost ready."

Thankfully, they leave me alone after that, and we chat about Lottie's friends at school and what she wants from Santa *next* Christmas. Shortly after we finish eating, Patrick arrives to collect Lottie. I help my mom with a few chores, say goodbye, and leave armed with a Tupperware full of meatballs.

When I pull up outside my house, I find a text from Aly.

> She-Devil: I hope you've kept your hands to yourself.

> Booth: You're a wicked, wicked woman.

> She-Devil: If you behave, I'll make it worth your while tomorrow night…

I make eight typos before I string a coherent text together.

> Booth: I'm listening. No touching whatsoever.

> She-Devil: My place at 7.

I'm grinning maniacally. Lust surges through my veins at a million miles per hour at the idea of being with her again.

Then I remember the conversations with Harriet and my mom.

How do I forget the crazy theory that's taken root?

My head spins with all the different explanations, but it's one in particular that won't stop popping to the surface.

Is Aly Martin's daughter?

alessandra

MY footsteps falter as I stare at the overflowing cart in the middle of the aisle. Chewing my lip, I take in the spices, chicken thighs, lemons, orzo, and tomatoes, along with a bunch of other items.

Am I overstepping?

The small grocery store in Sutton Bay stocks most essential items, but I drove to Jacob's Bluff, the larger neighboring town, in search of specific ingredients.

Something twinges in my chest. Booth is due to arrive at my apartment in an hour. Yet here I am, about to spend over one hundred dollars on groceries because of the guilt I've felt since he revealed his deepest, darkest secret and I gave him nothing.

Pushing down my doubt, I steer the cart toward the checkout, and almost collide with a willowy woman.

"Florence?" I exclaim, swerving so I don't crush her toes.

Her white-blonde bob swishes when her head whips in my direction. "Oh, Alessandra. Hi. What are you doing here?" She crumples up the papers she's holding and shoves them in her tote as red creeps up her neck.

I pretend I didn't see *resume* typed in bold lettering along the top.

Glancing at the food, my lips flatten. "Stocking up on groceries."

"Yeah, same," she rushes out, though she shows no evidence of shopping. "That's a lot of food for one person."

"Who knows when another storm is going to hit?" I shrug, hoping she doesn't press me further.

She nods slowly. "Good point. Well, have fun tonight. Tell Booth I sa—" Her mouth snaps shut.

I sigh in defeat. "Your brother is a blabbermouth."

Apology laces her features, but she has the same vexatious glint in her eyes like Booth. "Sorry. I caught him styling his hair when I popped around earlier. When I quizzed him on it, he got so worked up I thought he was going to pop a blood vessel."

Waving her off, I keep my tone light. "I'd appreciate it if you didn't tell anyone else. It's, umm…"

What the hell is it we're doing?

Florence mimics zipping her mouth shut, then throws an invisible key over her shoulder. "Booth? Who's Booth? Sounds like a douche."

I FINISH ASSEMBLING THE ITEMS ALONG MY NARROW KITCHEN countertop when the buzzer to my apartment goes off.

Steeling a breath, I don't overthink it. Friends do nice things for each other all the time. Though none of my friends back home have texted me since I moved here. Which says a lot.

I cringe, realizing I'm thirty years old, with surface-level relationships, and one bad decision away from having an identity crisis.

The buzzer sounds again.

Unable to contain my smile, I press the intercom. "What's the password?"

His amused voice crackles through the speaker. "Booth Sadler has a gigantic co—"

I cut him off and buzz him in.

Not thirty seconds later, a heavy hand pounds on the door. In no rush—mostly to taunt him—I pad over and crack it open. "Can I help you?"

He looks up from where he's casually leaning against the wall, donning a worn navy backward cap. His crooked smile is filled with filthy vows and my skin breaks out in goose bumps as I drink him in from head to toe.

His cockiness—while annoying—isn't misplaced. He really is beautiful, with a masculine edge.

A deep hum rumbles from his throat. "You can start by letting me inside and then giving me those lips, Silver. I'm fucking starved."

Since our rendezvous in the supply closet, my vibrator hasn't gotten close to satiating me like he did. Likely his plan all along.

Needing him to fill the void, I abandon my teasing. As soon as he steps over the threshold, I'm hoisted into his arms, leaving no choice but to wrap my legs around his waist.

He thrusts his tongue into my mouth, and groans when I loop my arms around his neck. We stumble into the apartment, my heart racing with each lick and nip. Somewhere along the way, he loses his coat and cap, and I take advantage by running my hands over the corded muscles on his shoulders and arms.

I lose myself in the kiss, to the point I don't realize we've moved into the kitchen. The fridge rattles as he presses me up against it, his hot mouth trailing down my neck and over my collarbone as I feel him thicken beneath me.

My head lolls to the side, and a high-pitched gasp leaves me when he draws my hardened nipple into his mouth over my tank.

"Oh fuck," I call out when he clamps down with his teeth before flicking it with the tip of his tongue.

"Aly?" he rasps between my breasts, not stopping his delicious torture.

"Yes. Whatever it is, *yes*." Desperation seeps from my voice.

"I love the enthusiasm, baby. But would you mind telling me why there's an entire grocery store in your kitchen?"

I freeze.

Fuck, fuck, fuck.

"Let me down." He drops me lightly on my feet. I slide out of his hold, hoping he doesn't pick up on my embarrassment. "Okay, so don't look into this too much, but I thought we could cook together. Whatever. If you don't want to, I'm sure I can give it to a food bank."

I keep my gaze on the faucet, the *drip drip drip* of water taunting me as the silence ticks by. An unfamiliar discomfort makes it impossible to face him.

"Like I said"—I throw a hand toward all the food—"it's no big deal."

"Alessandra," he says sternly. "Look at me."

Bracing myself, I take a calming breath before glancing at him.

"Wipe that frown off your beautiful face first. And then come here." He crooks a finger at me, and I bite back my retort.

Each slap of my feet against the tiled floor sounds like a drum in my ears.

When I'm less than a foot away, he crouches to my level, eyes burning into me. "Why are you freaking out?"

"I'm not," I say stiffly. Some of my resolve dissolves when he cups my cheeks gently.

"Okay, you're not. Do you know what you are?"

I shake my head.

"You're the most impressive woman I've ever met. Being in your presence does something to me I can't put into words. I could go on about how breathtakingly beautiful you are until I'm blue in the face. Your brain is astounding—so smart and perceptive. Yet somehow you've refused to see the shit-eating grin I've been wearing since you said you wanted to cook together."

My breath catches. All my fight falls away at the conviction in his voice. I curl my lips over my teeth. "It's not weird?"

He laughs and plants a kiss between my brows before striding to the other side of the kitchen. "You're weird for thinking it's weird. Now get your ass over here and tell me what we're making."

All worries demolished, I join him. His eyes light up when I tell him we're making a traditional Greek dish, my *giagiá's* recipe, making my heart swell. He listens intently as I go through the steps for *youvetsi* with chicken.

Twenty minutes later, Booth is "helping" me prep the chicken before it roasts in the oven. His version of help is standing behind me, chin perched on my shoulder, arms looped around my waist.

It was cute at first. Until he started backseat cooking.

Use this pan instead.

Sauté it some more.

Here, let me show you.

I slam the knife down when he murmurs, "Try dicing it like this," in my ear.

"Did you want to do this?" I snap.

His breathy laughter tickles my nape. "Sorry, sorry. You can take the chef out of the kitchen..."

I twist my upper body. "Really? I wish I knew how."

"Look at you taking charge." He presses his hips forward, hard cock settling at the base of my spine through his jeans. "What's the next step?"

An internal fuse must blow, because the recipe I was raised with is, *poof*, gone.

"What's the matter, Aly? Something distracting you?" With a flick of his finger, the strap of my tank falls off my shoulder. My hands tremble when he scrapes his teeth over my skin. "Maybe you *do* need my help."

I shake my head, searching for a single brain cell so we can finish this recipe. "Shh. Um, we need to..." I spy the tomatoes. "Right, we need to cover the chicken in water, olive oil, and tomato sauce. Then sprinkle it with cinnamon."

"Cinnamon? Nice." His words barely register as he steps up beside me, the loss of his touch immediate. I watch him, entranced, as his large hands work methodically. His presence is large, but in the kitchen his movements are graceful and fluid.

I've never questioned his skills or his commitment. Since the night he revealed his dream to work elsewhere, it was clear he'd put that to rest. I can't stop thinking about it, though. Any kitchen would be lucky to have a talent like his, and my mind keeps wandering to the restaurants in our hotels, each specializing in a range of cuisines from around the world.

It's easy to picture Booth conquering those spaces like he is a small corner of my heart.

"Earth to Aly." His voice pulls me back into the room. While my mind wandered, he whipped up a pan of tomato sauce that now simmers over the stove.

"Perfect. Once that's done we combine and bake for forty-five minutes, uncovered."

Almost robotically, I open the preheated oven. The wave of

heat that blasts me in the face is nothing compared to the red-hot fire roaring inside me.

Before my next move, he leans over and switches off the flame, the fingers of his left hand splaying across my hip.

"What are you doing?" I whisper.

"We can come back to this." The words vibrate from his chest, fingers edging over my belly. "But you're too fucking distracting standing in the kitchen like this. I can't keep my hands off you for another second."

I'm spinning around before he finishes speaking.

There's nothing soft about us when we're together. It's harsh, passionate, deliberate. His touch is confident, like my body is a recipe he's been perfecting for years, not weeks.

I scramble to get his shirt off, reveling in the way his muscles quiver under the scrape of my nails. My hands move south, fumbling with his zipper.

"You want my cock again, Silver?" He presses my palm against his throbbing length.

Without speaking, I lower to my knees, but in the blink of an eye, the air is knocked from my lungs when Booth pins me against the wall.

"Me first. It's a fucking crime I haven't tasted you yet." A burst of pain comes from my lip when he slowly drops to *his* knees.

His fingers curl around the waistband of my lounge pants, slides them down my legs, then throws them haphazardly across the kitchen. His breath catches when he finds me bare. Through hooded eyes, he stares up at me, fingertips skimming above the dark strip of hair on my pelvis. "I should be disappointed there isn't any lace for me to peel off you. But I guess it means I can do this without any interruptions."

My question dies on my lips when he hooks a leg over his shoulder and buries his face into my pussy.

His tongue lashes over my center. No gentle caresses or

teasing touches. He devours me like a man starved, lavishing me as I slump against the wall, his hands being the only thing to stop me from collapsing.

"*Gamoto.*" *Fuck.* "Yes, Booth." My hands wind into his messy hair, anchoring his mouth to me as my orgasm crests. "I need your fingers. Fuck me with your fingers."

"God, I love it when you tell me what to do." He flicks the tip of his tongue against my clit before plunging two thick digits into my pussy and pumping into me in rhythm with his wicked mouth. "Come for me, Aly. Then I'll give you my cock, you greedy fucking girl."

In no time at all, I'm catapulting over the edge.

Stars blind me.

Booth doesn't let up. He relentlessly licks, sucks, and kisses me through each ripple of pleasure. The forearm he has pressed to my stomach keeps me in place as he tortures me.

Minutes? Hours? Who knows how much time passes, but when he finally concedes, he grins up at me, tongue running over his glistening lips.

"Who knew Alessandra Argiros could be so sweet and submissive."

His teasing wink and cocky words have the right effect.

On wobbly legs, I set the half-cooked ingredients in the fridge.

When I face him, I'm the one smiling suggestively as I run my hand down his jaw.

"How about we switch it up?"

CHAPTER TWENTY-SEVEN

booth

Aly's bedroom is feminine and minimalistic.

As she herded me to her room, I spied her easel and a pile of blank canvases in the corner of the living room. Before I could ask her for a tour, she had my zipper down and her soft warm hand was fisting my cock.

It could wait.

Now, Aly watches me from the doorway. Each sweep of her eyes heightens my senses. I hold out my hand for her, but she backs away.

"I'm going to use the bathroom. Make yourself comfortable." Her gaze trails to where my jeans are shoved halfway down my thighs. "With fewer clothes."

My blood turns molten at the sensual sway of her hips as she drifts out of the room. I press my palm into my erection, willing it to calm the fuck down.

I'd rather not finish in my pants again.

Her cream bedsheets look expensive—probably with an infinite thread count. It's no secret she's here temporarily, yet seeing her unpacked suitcase leaves a fist-sized hole in my chest. My eyes home in on her dresser. Among her perfume bottles and jewelry, a row of frames line the back.

When I stepped foot in her apartment, the question surrounding her parentage disappeared. Without her here to distract me, my mind wanders. I pick up a photo of five people; Aly stands in the center, surrounded by two taller men with olive skin, brown eyes, and light brown hair. An older woman with matching features stands on one end while a bald man of similar age stands on the other.

Her brothers and parents, I presume.

I can't help but notice Aly shares no similarities with either parent or her brothers.

Not everyone looks like their parents.

That has to be it. Because the alternative is too far-fetched.

Right?

"You're not very good at following instructions, are you?" a sultry voice says behind me.

When I spin around, the frame clatters to the wooden surface, eyes popping out of my head.

Sheer black lace decorates her porcelain skin, the intricate detailing drawing my eyes to her breasts and the flare of her hips. The sheer material does nothing to cover her dusky pink nipples and the landing strip I want to nuzzle my face into over and over again. Her stomach is taut, but thighs and chest are delectably soft.

Untamed curls spill over her shoulders, perfectly tousled from my hands.

No artist—past, present, or future—could capture the bewitching beauty before me.

A vision in ebony; carved for my eyes only.

She doesn't flinch when I bang my fist on the dresser and groan. She smirks, my torment entertaining her.

"Have I died?" I rasp.

"Not yet. Now lose the clothes and put this on." Something black and flimsy hits me in the chest.

I hold it up between my thumb and forefinger. "A blindfold?"

Her lips press together, eyes sliding to the bed in silent command.

Who am I to question the woman?

She laughs softly as I shed my clothes lightning fast.

My gray briefs drop to my feet, and my stiff cock juts out proudly. Needing to ease some pressure, I stroke myself before she wags a finger at me.

"Ah-ah. No touching, remember? On the bed and cover your eyes," she commands. "Be a good boy."

Fuuuuck, that shouldn't make me harder, but it does. It really fucking does.

Obeying her, I settle against the pillows and slide the blindfold on to rest over my brow. "This isn't some kinky payback for all the times I've annoyed you, is it?"

She circles the bed with a predatory gaze.

"Do you trust me?" she asks as the tip of her finger draws a path up my abdomen.

Do you *trust me?* I want to return, but bite my tongue.

"Always," I say instead and plunge myself in darkness.

As the seconds tick by, my heart beats more rapidly. I jolt when she takes hold of my wrists, lips grazing the shell of my ear. "Raise them above your head."

Doing as she says, something soft loops around my hands as she secures me to the wooden slats of her headboard.

Her touch disappears again, and I listen intently. A drawer opens, rustling, and then it closes.

The lack of sight and touch amplifies everything. So when her hand returns to my skin, it feels like one hundred.

"Where do you want me, Booth?" Her touch drifts to my thigh, millimeters away from my aching cock.

"*Fuck.* You know where, Aly. Touch it for me. Please." There's a desperate urgency to my voice.

"Oh, but the games have only just begun," she murmurs in mock disappointment.

Her journey stops inches from my balls, then disappears. My hips thrust up, searching for her touch.

"Tsk, tsk. Such an eager boy."

"You know I'm not a boy, Aly. Let me show you," I beg, mind spinning.

She's silent. Then something tickles my left nipple. It's soft, hardly noticeable. It trails over my sternum, then circles my other nipple at a torturous pace. *A feather*? To add to the suffering, she blows along my stomach, leaving a trail of goose bumps in her wake.

"You wicked thing. You're going to pay for this." I strain against my restraints when she moves south. "You're going to feel me for days when I'm done with you, beautiful."

I whimper. Fucking *whimper* when her lips land on my nipple, swirling it with the tip of her tongue.

"That's what I'm counting on," she croons.

Her touch leaves me again, and I'm about to lose my goddamn mind.

As if I've touched a live wire, my hips rise off the mattress as the feather brushes over the head of my cock, dragging from tip to root. She does this for an eternity, back and forth, while I unravel under her touch.

"You've been so good. Do you want your reward?" At some point, she's shifted, her voice farther.

"I want free so I can fuck your sweet cunt again," I growl.

Cool air kisses my throbbing length, and the bed dips as she maneuvers herself between my thighs. Anticipation drives me insane, then finally—*fucking finally*—she puts me out of my misery when her hot mouth encompasses the tip of my cock, tongue swirling leisurely.

"Ah, fuck, shit." My head thumps into the pillow as I resist the urge to thrust up. "Take me deeper. Show me what that sinful mouth can do."

She pulls away with a pop. "Don't forget who's in charge."

"God, you. Always you." I am a man undone.

My response pleases her, and her mouth returns, no holding back. She takes me to the back of her throat with ease, tongue gliding over the underside of my cock as she bobs up and down.

"Aly, take the blindfold off. Please, baby. I wanna watch."

Without removing her mouth, she reaches up and plucks the blindfold off. Thanks to the dim lighting, it only takes a second for my vision to refocus. When it does, I want this image burned into my brain until the end of time.

Hair tied back, eyes glassy, straddling my thigh.

A seductress on a mission.

What fucking does it, is the smudges of red lipstick around her mouth and the base of my cock. Lipstick she wasn't wearing before.

"You're such a goddamn tease."

Her smile is evil and then she lowers her head. Her tongue plays with the tip, gaze set on mine as I tug at my bindings. "Look at you. I bet you'd look even prettier choking on it. Show me how deep you can take it. Make it sloppy, beautiful. Mess those lips up a little more."

Role forgotten, she follows my instructions enthusiastically.

This time when I reach the back of her throat, she swallows around me and holds. Over and over she does this until the telltale sign of heat brewing low in my spine starts.

I'd love nothing more than to shoot down her throat and watch her swallow every last drop, but I'm ravenous to feel her come around me again.

"Untie me," I order.

She hums around me, the sensation shooting straight to my balls as she shakes her head.

"Aly. I *need* to fuck you, baby. I've been so good. C'mon."

She knows I could have broken out of these restraints at any moment. When she ignores me, eyes flaring in challenge, I snap.

With a sharp tug, my wrists slip free, and I'm diving forward.

She squeals in delight, pushing at my chest while her legs wrap around my waist as I pin her to the bed.

"Games over, Silver. You've had your fun." The head of my cock nudges her pussy through the lace. "Soaked through again, you messy girl."

I swallow her whimpers as I continue to thrust shallowly, bumping her clit with each pass. I tug down the cup of her bodysuit and suck a tight bud into my mouth, licking and biting.

"You're fucking weeping for me," I rasp against the curve of her breast. "Are you done playing now?"

Her head jerks from left to right, but there's a fire burning in her half-lidded stare. She's torn. Fighting with dominance and submission.

She chooses sides when she spreads her thighs, inviting me in.

All joking ends when my fingers hook into the thin material wedged between her pussy to snap it, leaving the garment in tatters. "This is going to be quick, but we've got all night."

My little temptress raises her brow. "Very presumptuous of you to assume I won't kick you out after this."

My head falls back in laughter. "Remember, Aly"—I notch myself at her entrance and ease in an inch—"you're mine until you leave."

And then I plunge all the way.

"Booth!" she screams, sharp nails clawing at my back as she

gasps for air. "Fuck, that feels—you're so deep like this. My god, I need you to move right this second."

"As you wish." I slowly retreat, wink, then snap my hips forward.

Her cries. My moans. The slapping of skin. A symphony of sounds orchestrated by us.

I slide my hands under her ass, raising her to rest on my thighs as I angle myself deeper, watching as I disappear inside her. The sight erotic.

Our bodies sheen with sweat as I maintain a steady rhythm. I bend, suckling a rosy peak, toying and biting as her hips undulate in time with mine. Her body sings, but the melody of her cries is the sweetest noise.

My balls draw up and I slow the pace. "Where do you want me to finish?"

She doesn't hesitate. "In me. I want your cum. Fill me."

Fuck, her mouth.

Her eyes widen as I lean back, dragging her with me as I thrust harder. The pad of my thumb circles the tight bundle of nerves, and that does it.

"Booth. I'm coming. Shit, shit. I'm coming."

Her walls clamp around me, fingers scratching at my thighs, head thrown back.

Watching her fall apart has me following closely behind. It takes two pumps then I'm spilling deep inside of her, voice hoarse as I shout through my orgasm and collapse on top of her.

It's pure bliss. Her wrapped around me, panting against my shoulder as I bury my face in her neck. It makes me want to slow down time.

As our breathing evens out, hearts calming, I soak up the moment.

Euphoric. Fulfilling. Thrilling.

That's how each second spent with her is.

I tease my brothers tirelessly when I witness them pining after their partners. To me, it was ridiculous.

Now here I am, lying in the bed of a woman who I'm certain is my perfect match.

It's a cruel joke that we're worlds apart. That she has to leave and I can't go.

The killing blow to it all is that I've handed my trust over to Aly with ease. While I don't know what secrets she's hiding, I know I haven't gained hers.

And I don't think I will before our time is up.

CHAPTER TWENTY-EIGHT

alessandra

"So...a blindfold?" Booth mumbles sleepily between my boobs. After he fucked me into oblivion, we cleaned up and dragged ourselves back to bed. I didn't have the energy to get angry about my shredded lace body suit. Because who could get mad about that? "Care to share with the class where that idea came from?"

I bite down on my lip.

His ego couldn't handle the knowledge that I used the blindfold because of the sordid dream I had about him in the cabin.

I pretend to be asleep, which doesn't last long when he dives under the covers and nibbles a path from my hip to my belly button.

"Booth! Cut it!" I squeal as I attempt to pry myself from his clutches.

"Don't lie to me, Silv." He sucks at the skin above my navel. My only view is his mop of chocolate waves as he lies between my legs, teasing me. "But if you tell me you've done that with another man, I can't be held accountable for my actions."

Snorting, I shove at his head. "And what if I have?"

His head snaps up, eyes blazing.

I poke my index fingers into his cheeks, forcing his dimples out. "And you accuse me of being jealous."

He growls before pressing his face to my stomach again. "You're mean."

"I know," I quip.

"I like it," he mumbles.

"I know that too."

He looks back up, his envy gone as he studies me carefully, fingers absently tracing the dip of my waist. It's at that moment my hunger decides to make itself known.

His eyes light up. Stark naked, he runs out of my bedroom, shouting, "Don't move!" over his shoulder.

My question about what the heck he's doing is answered when I hear the refrigerator opening and the beep of the oven.

"Combine *everything* you say?" he hollers through my apartment.

There's no containing my delighted smile. "Yes! Sprinkle it with cinnamon and then add the orzo after forty-five minutes. Then bake for another ten."

Despite the clatter coming from my kitchen, I doze off. The smell of my mother's home cooking rouses me, and I wake to find an overjoyed Booth beaming down at me, a hearty bowl of youvetsi in his hand with two spoons.

"Time to eat, beautiful." His gentle voice, along with his gentler touch, keeps me locked in a sleepy haze. Still naked, I tuck the comforter around my chest as he helps me into a sitting position. I reach for the bowl, but he shakes his head. "Let me." I'm about to argue when he reaches out and presses his fingers to my furrowed brow. "C'mon, let me look after you."

Drip, drip, drip, with each sweet and thoughtful gesture, my resolve melts away.

His whole body glows with happiness when he sees I'm not going to fight him. With assured movements, he scoops up some orzo and chicken and guides the steaming food into my mouth. He watches me intensely. As I wrap my lips around the spoon, as I slowly chew and swallow, and especially when my moan of indulgence echoes through the room.

The act of it all is oddly erotic, comforting, and intimate. Silently, he feeds me, stealing himself a bite every so often until the bowl is empty.

"Well..." he says coyly, breaking the silence as he places the dish on my bedside table. "How was it?"

Reaching out, I swipe a smudge of red from the corner of his mouth. Lipstick or tomato sauce, who knows. "It was delicious." His cheeks darken at my compliment.

He doesn't make a bold joke. Instead, he shuffles under the covers with me and resumes his position, hard, warm body splayed out on top of mine with his chin resting on my stomach.

That's where we stay, chatting and napping. The past few hours has left me feeling full, not of food, but feelings. Some confusing, but most satisfying.

The light stubble on his chin scratches my skin and the fullness remains. But as I watch him, watching me, determination takes root.

Determination to do what I came here to do. Determination to accept whatever outcome unfolds from my time in Sutton Bay. Determination to open up to him.

"What are you thinking, beautiful?" My insides light up at his husky voice, weighted in sleep.

"That I'm sad we have to leave this bed," I say honestly.

"Hmm. Wanna play hooky with me tomorrow?"

I'd do anything to burrow into these sheets, getting lost in them with him.

But for the first time since stepping foot in town, the nauseating nervousness isn't that bad.

"What's the scariest thing you've ever done?" I ask quietly.

"Oh, umm..." Something flickers in his eyes before he blinks it away. "I'm not sure I've done it yet. Or if I ever will. I guess that doesn't count." I give him a pointed look and he chuckles before his gaze turns somber. "Saying goodbye to my dad was pretty scary; knowing that was it. I wouldn't catch him stealing food from the kitchen when Mom wasn't looking or be blinded by the flash of his ancient Polaroid camera as he captured family moments." Sadness laces his smile. "I'd like to be braver. What about you?"

My head flops against the pillow and I stare at the cracks in the ceiling. "I'm trying to be brave too."

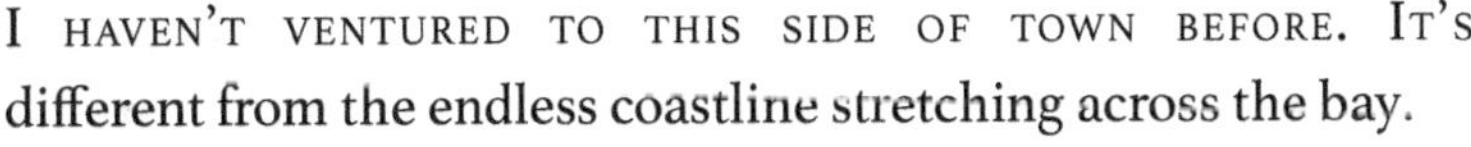

I HAVEN'T VENTURED TO THIS SIDE OF TOWN BEFORE. IT'S different from the endless coastline stretching across the bay.

Rolling hills, vast pine forests, and snowy mountain peaks. During the warmer months, I imagine tall grass and wildflowers adorn the horizon. Now, it's blanketed in white. A chill sets in my bones, that has nothing to do with the weather and more to do with the building at the end of the drive.

Camouflaged into its surroundings with its off-white batten siding and shutters, sits a farmhouse. Patches of red peek out under the snow-covered roof. Not a lot of farming happens this time of year, but as I take in the fields surrounding the house, I picture blueberry fields and cornfields.

It's huge; once a family home.

Much too big for one person.

Gravel kicks against the underside of my car until I come to a stop next to a dark blue pickup.

A part of me hoped he wouldn't be home.

But as the front door opens, revealing the one person I've spent weeks avoiding, I cling onto the determination from last night like a lifeline.

I reach into the pockets of my coat, searching for my gloves, when my fingertips brush against something hard. I remove my left hand to reveal a plastic red rose. Booth has no idea why I'm here—in this town or sitting outside Martin Willis's house. This tiny gesture from him gives me the final shove I need.

My boots crunch on the ground as I step out. The thick parka and hat I'm wearing suffocate me as Martin watches me curiously.

"Alessandra, everything okay? Did you call?" he asks worriedly.

I shake my head, hands fisted in my pockets as I stop a few feet away. "No. Sorry, maybe I should have. If now isn't a good time, I can come back."

Please say you're busy.

"It's fine. Please, please, come in and out of the cold." He gestures inside, and with a heavy exhale, my fingers white-knuckling around the rose, I step through the doorway.

It's fine.

This isn't like *last* time.

I can do this. I can do this. I can do this.

CHAPTER TWENTY-NINE

booth

"Behind!" I shout.

My chefs make room for me as I stomp toward the sink and slap on the faucet. A sigh of relief escapes when the cold water soothes the burned skin on my palm. It's going to blister like a bitch. I watched Simon remove the cast-iron skillet from the oven moments earlier, but my thoughts have been elsewhere all afternoon.

"You all right, Chef?" Simon calls.

Nodding, I untie my apron with my free hand and fling it over my shoulder. "I'm gonna take a break while I get this wrapped up. You good?"

He throws me a salute. "We've got it handled."

Thank fuck I have Simon to help, especially since we've been down a line cook.

I grab the first aid kit from above the sink and force a smile to the customers enjoying their lunch as I make my way to the office. When inside, I inspect the damage. It's not the worst burn I've had, and I'm more annoyed that it will be a hindrance for the next few days until it heals. It's bad enough my knuckles are still bruised and sore from punching Kyle.

Once I've applied burn cream and slipped on a food preparation glove, I collapse onto the sofa and shut my eyes.

Last night was...*fuck,* it was magical. Cooking, fucking, eating, and sleeping. Simple acts turned vibrant with Aly as my partner. Since we said goodbye outside her apartment this morning, I've been distracted. When I asked what her plans were today, she grew elusive.

I didn't push her to explain, but now, a small part of me wishes I had.

Five minutes of shut-eye will restore my depleted energy. Just as my brain switches off, my phone buzzes in my pocket.

A frown wrinkles my brow when I see Martin's name flashing on the screen.

"Hey, Martin. How are things?" I greet.

"Hi, Booth. Um, they're okay. Listen, something odd happened, and I wasn't sure who to call." There's an edge to his tone.

My stomach turns. "What is it?"

He hesitates, adding to my anxiety. "It's Alessandra."

"WHAT DO YOU MEAN, SHE WALKED OUT?" I WINCE AT MY HARSH tone. "Sorry, I'm struggling to understand."

Martin looks at me sympathetically. After we hung up, I drove out to his property.

"I'm really not sure what else to say. She came inside, I went to get us some coffee, and when I returned, she was climbing into her car and driving away."

My hands hang between my open knees, fingers flexing as I

attempt to keep the tension at bay. "And you said she seemed 'off'?"

His eyes slide to the window overlooking the drive leading up to his farmhouse. He appears as antsy as me. "Her turning up out of the blue was a little surprising and when she came inside, I couldn't get a straight answer out of her regarding why she was there. When I asked if it was something to do with the apartment, she said no. It was only when…"

"When what?" I straighten in my seat.

He stares at his feet. "At Christmas, she asked about my son. No one has ever asked me about him before. Then today, she brought him up again."

I lean forward. "What did she want to know?"

He releases a breath, like the world has been resting on his shoulders until this point. "If he lived in town. Why don't I keep in touch? Do I know where he lives?" His eyes lift to mine. "I've tried calling her several times, but after a few rings, it goes to voice mail. I called you because I was, um, worried about her. And I presumed you were close."

"She didn't say where she was going?" I ask.

He shakes his head.

When Martin first called, I dropped by Aly's apartment before driving here. Like him, all my calls went to voice mail too.

My brain screams at me. The question that's been brewing for days refuses to be pushed down any longer, but I can't. I simply can't let it break through the surface until I speak to Aly.

"I appreciate you calling me." I stand and grab my coat from the sofa. "I'll let you know when I find her. I'm sure she's fine; she's been busy with the restaurant. You know how it is?"

He stands, shoulders slumped as he fiddles with the cuff of his shirt. "She seems very accomplished. A real firecracker like my Judy."

My movements stop. "Judy?"

Grief taints his expression. "My wife. A formidable woman who—well, let's say deserved a lot better."

I stand there awkwardly as I witness a reel of emotions play in Martin's eyes—*his gray eyes.*

"I've known you my whole life, and I never knew you had a son or wife."

He waves me off. "It's not like I've been the warmest of people over the years. I hear what they say."

I grimace, knowing exactly what they say.

Aloof. Recluse. Outcast.

For such a pillar in the community, so many have dubbed him as companionless. I'm regretfully guilty of that.

"I was ashamed for a long time. It was easier to not talk about them." He stares longingly out the window. "I missed out on so much, and now I can't help but wonder what else I've missed out on."

I follow his gaze, and just make out the tire tracks cutting through the snow. One set belonging to a woman I desperately need to find.

IT TOOK MARTIN SOME CONVINCING TO LET ME INTO ALY'S apartment. My heart sank when I saw her easel and paints gone, but on closer inspection, her other belongings remained. Quinn hadn't seen her. She hadn't visited Our Place. Shirley's was closed, and after driving around for almost an hour, I was losing hope I'd find her before night fell.

My knee bounces as I call her one more time. When it goes to voice mail after two rings, *again,* I slump back into my sofa and stare out the window. Ocean spray coats the glass, and I watch the water rivulets chase each other.

I pull up the text I sent her hours ago.

> Booth: Martin called. Can you let me know you're safe?

I blink, worried I'm imagining it when three bubbles pop up and disappear on the screen. Then it vibrates.

> She-Devil: I'm safe. Sorry for worrying you. I'll call when I'm back in town.

I deflate in relief.

And then I'm shooting to my feet.

She *isn't* in Sutton Bay.

Aly wouldn't dare set foot in a motel. There's only one place I can picture her; wrapped in a fluffy white towel, hair dripping wet, and skin flushed as she stares out at the frosty scenery.

It's a long shot, but I'm grabbing my coat and keys, hauling ass to my truck. I stop at the grocery store before heading north to my destination.

Twilight stains the sky a dark violet as I drive along the dirt path, my bones shaking as my wheels hit the large potholes concealed by the snow. Dex is out of town, building a new cabin up by the Canadian border, with zero service. When I see the soft amber glow of lights through the small window of The Nook, I really hope I'm about to get pepper sprayed by a silver-eyed vixen and not some unsuspecting vacationer.

My heart races as I jog up the front steps. I plant my hands on my knees, collecting myself before I knock. I'm not given the chance.

The door's yanked open, and the scowl I adore greets me.

Hidden behind her steely gaze, solace cracks through.

She can deny it all she wants, but Alessandra is happy to see me.

My hands twitch at my sides, desperate to touch her, but I have to tread carefully.

Before she can invite me in—or slam the door in my face—I'm stepping inside.

CHAPTER THIRTY

alessandra

Instant relief.

That's the only sensation to describe finding Booth on the cabin porch.

There was no smugness or wisecrack. His arrival is a balm to my soul. Warm, comforting, and familiar. Weeks ago, he was everywhere I didn't want him to be. Now he's exactly where I need him.

A revelation I wasn't prepared for.

He removes his beanie and coat, shakes out his hair, and toes off his boots. It's then I notice the brown paper bag at his feet.

"I'm gonna make us some dinner." I don't utter a word as he strolls toward the kitchen before calling over his shoulder. "Get the table set, beautiful. Then when we're done, you can decide what we talk about or I can leave. Whatever you want, but I'm feeding you before anything."

His tone is final, face serious, and it's only when goose bumps tickle my arms that I see the door is still wide open.

"C'mon, Silver," he hollers, propelling me into action.

With the cold sealed out and table set, I watch him go through the motions as I sit on the kitchen counter.

Something smoky and sweet fills the air, tickling my nose. The grumble of my stomach is a reminder I haven't eaten since this morning.

Booth doesn't demand an explanation about why I disappeared. He doesn't ask why I was with Martin. Instead, he glances at me, knife pausing mid-chop as he smiles.

I've never been an overly emotional person. But the crinkling of his eyes and those goddamn dimples make me want to burst into tears with gratitude.

Twenty minutes later, he drops two bowls on the table, ushers me to sit, and drags our chairs so close together I'm practically sitting in his lap. He nudges me with his elbow and winks. "It's a smoky sweet potato chili. Eat or you'll offend me."

So I eat.

When we're done, he leads me to the sofa, drapes the fur blanket over my shoulders, and feeds the fire. My poor, confused heart can't understand why he's taking care of me. Still, he doesn't ask questions, just pulls me into his safe, strong arms.

We startle when that hideous cuckoo clock whistles behind us. It jump-starts my vocal chords, because when I open my mouth, I don't stop.

"I'm adopted."

He doesn't react to my outburst.

"I've always known. It was never a secret. My parents— adoptive parents, but I've never called them that—brought me home when I was four days old. My brothers are their biological children, but my mom had an emergency hysterectomy after a complicated birth with my second brother. The fact I look nothing like them would have clued me in, but when I was old enough, they sat me down and explained what adoption was, and while I hadn't become theirs the same way my brothers had, it changed nothing." I tuck a wayward curl behind my ear and take a deep breath before continuing.

"I want to preface this by saying I've never once felt like I didn't belong. Love, security, and happiness are all I've known, childhood through to adulthood. It's cliché, but the idea of turning thirty and not knowing about my beginning triggered something. Who were my birth parents? Why did they put me up for adoption? Where are they now? I've never resented them, I just grew curious. Outside of that, simply having a gap in my medical history started to worry me." I take a gulp of air. "It was an open adoption, but when I turned six, my birth mom asked my parents to stop sending photos and updates. We never found out why."

The steady beating of Booth's heart against my back encourages me.

"When I was twenty-eight, I started looking for answers. It took me six months to build up the courage to request my adoption records. All I knew about my mom was that she was sixteen when she had me and didn't know how to raise a baby."

Booth shifts me until my legs lie sideways over his, my head resting on his shoulder. "And your birth father?" he asks cautiously.

My shoulders lift. "He wasn't listed on the original birth certificate."

His arm twitches from where it's banded over my stomach.

"But I had my birth mother's name. I contacted the adoption agency and asked them to reach out to her—to see if she'd be willing to meet. When I heard nothing for weeks, I figured she wasn't interested. Then, after almost two months, they contacted me. She still lived in New York. How insane is that? She was *one hour* away that entire time." My laughter is flat, and Booth senses the mood change. "We arranged to meet in the city. Three hours I waited in the restaurant for her," I whisper, voice wobbly.

"Aly," Booth breathes against my neck and squeezes me tighter.

"It took her two days to email me and explain it was a mistake. That's all it said, 'This was a mistake. I'm sorry.' For the first time in my life, I felt like I didn't belong, and I hated myself for it. She owed me nothing, yet I arrived at our meeting spot with my hopes held tightly to my chest. I wasn't looking to fill a void, but after that day, I think I lost a little piece of myself. Maybe she saw me through the window and decided I wasn't worth the trouble."

A rough hand cups my cheek until blue eyes gaze down at me. "You're worth everything."

My heart can't cope. Not with his words, his sincere expression, or the way his lips caress mine. There's nothing romantic or sexual about it. Wordlessly he tells me he's here.

"I'm sorry you didn't get the outcome you'd hoped for. I can't speak on her behalf, but I can say with confidence that she's missing out on getting to know an amazing woman." He pecks me on the nose before settling us against the cushions.

"It still left me questioning the identity of my birth father. I couldn't ask her and you'd think I would have learned my lesson." Craning my neck to face him, I give him a knowing look. "You know as well as I do, I don't give up easily."

His soft chuckle tickles my face.

"My brother suggested I try one of those genetic testing sites. My expectations were pretty low at this point. When the results came back, I wasn't sure how to feel when I found out I had relatives in a small fishing town in New England," I say matter-of-factly.

Five minutes I was in Martin's living room before the fear of being rejected again became unbearable. When I twist in Booth's hold, he isn't stunned. His expression is neutral, almost prepared.

"You knew?" I whisper.

Apology is written across his face. "I had suspicions." He intercepts my question. "Just small things. The way you'd act around Martin, the questions you asked him, and then…"

"My eyes," I finish.

He nods. "They're identical."

Groaning, I rest my head on his chest. "I royally freaked out. The poor man was making us coffee. He probably came back and thought I'd disappeared into thin air. I felt ready to face him, but as each second ticked by and I was alone, my mind replayed those hours in the restaurant."

Sturdy fingers weave into my hair, coaxing my head to tilt up. "Hey, it's going to be okay. He was a little…confused, but when he called, he was worried more than anything. Worried about you."

My lips twist. "Do you think he knows?"

Booth sucks in a breath. "I think he suspects something…"

"God, I don't even know where to begin."

"Be upfront. Martin's a good guy. He won't turn his daughter away, especially one he never knew existed."

I rear back. "Sorry, what?"

His confused expression mirrors mine. "You think he always knew?"

"No, that I'm his daughter." Wiggling out of his hold, I massage my temples. "Booth, Martin isn't my birth father. He's my paternal grandfather."

His brows jump to his hairline. "Wow, okay. I wasn't expecting that."

"Yeah, it's a head fuck. There were two hits on the ancestry search. Martin's was the only name listed alongside an unnamed male, who I presumed was his son. I tracked down birth and marriage certificates. At the time I was born, his son would have also been sixteen. His name is Harvey. There wasn't much else about him after graduation, so I started researching the town he was born in."

Like a penny in a well, I see the moment it sinks in. "That's why you're here."

I jerk my head once. "At the time, it seemed smart. I gained access to my inheritance when I turned thirty, and the first thing I spent it on was a—"

"Restaurant," he interrupts, dumbfounded. "Shit, Aly, I gave you such a hard time about being here. I'm sorry."

I can't help it, I laugh. "And so you should have. I bit off more than I could chew, but I'm also not the type of person to commit to something and then drop it. You and your family deserved more than that. In my head, I needed an excuse to be here so I could scope out the town and people before revealing my identity. I didn't think it would take me this long to do it."

He mulls over the information I've dumped on him. He's not angry or accusatory, but the longer he stays silent, the antsier I become. "Can you say something? You're never quiet for this long. Tell me what I should do."

My yelp of surprise bounces off the walls when he abruptly stands, holding me bridal style. "I say bed."

"What?" I huff as I hook my arm around his neck.

His gait is steady as he strides toward the bed. "Sleep. You don't need to decide tonight, and you're tired. Plus, we both know you never listen to me, anyway. Tomorrow, we can come up with a plan."

"We?"

He chuckles, and smooths away the divot on my forehead. "Yeah, Aly. *We.* It sounds like you've been facing this alone for long enough."

With the gentlest of care, he lays me down on the bed and stretches out beside me.

I've always felt loved and accepted by my parents. The blood we share is irrelevant. But there's a small chapter missing in my story. They couldn't understand my need to find those missing pages, even after the disappointment with my birth mother.

Of all the sweet things he's said to me recently, his next words take the cake.

"You're the most driven person I've ever met. Sometimes, though"—he sweeps my hair off my face and stares at me fondly—"it's okay to let others take the wheel. Let me take the driver's seat for a while. And when you're ready, I'll be right by your side when you want to take over again."

With him, I'm understood. He challenges me without questioning my character. My temper doesn't faze him; it fuels him. He's matched me every step of the way.

As blue meets silver, it dawns on me.

Booth doesn't just stare at me; he *sees* me.

So I take my foot off the pedal and relax into his embrace.

I don't trust easily, but with him, I could. Maybe I already am. Before I drift to sleep, I imagine it's easy to do a lot of things with Booth.

CHAPTER THIRTY-ONE

booth

"C'mon, my little ice queen," I holler over my shoulder.

Not one second later, a flurry of cold white powder explodes in my face.

"Oops," a sweet voice says.

Blinking away the snow from my eyes, I turn to look at Aly, twenty yards down the trail, with the prettiest death stare aimed my way.

"There's my girl. Now hurry. The sun is gonna set soon."

Powering ahead, I smile to myself when the crunch of her snow boots nears closer.

Aly was...well, *Aly* when we woke this morning.

Her story astonished me. The hurt in her words was obvious, no matter how hard she tried to mask it. It's unfathomable that someone wouldn't want to know her. To witness her opening up like she did last night was monumental. There was a beauty in her vulnerability.

Aly's strength is a castle. A fortress never weathered by the elements. Brick by pristine brick, she dropped her walls and let me inside.

Martin was her grandfather. *Not* her father.

She took a huge step visiting him yesterday. Today, however, her walls are up again, and underneath her stoic expression, she's frustrated.

So when we rolled out of bed, coddling her was not an option. I welcomed her fire and let her do what she needed to do. I understand why she guards her heart with ferocity, and last night I got a glimpse inside before she sealed it shut again.

"Where are we going?" she asks breathlessly, her legs finally catching up to me. She blends in with the snowy landscape in her beige suede coat and cream knitted scarf and gloves.

"There's a spot close by. The storm stopped me from showing you around last time." I heft the large backpack over my shoulder and she eyes it suspiciously.

"And you're not going to tell me what's in there?"

"Nope." I flash her a grin.

"I'm not helping you bury a body." She blows a curl off her face.

"Unless it's mine?" I bump shoulders with her.

She cuts me a side glance. "I'm still on the fence about that."

Her sharp wit and banter are a good sign; it's her silence that's unsettling.

After breakfast, I wanted to distract her before we headed back to reality. When she wasn't looking, I stuffed what I needed in a bag, told her to dress comfortably with plenty of layers, and steered her out of the cabin.

Now, we're surrounded by towering evergreens, their branches bowing with the weight of the snow. There isn't a single cloud hanging in the crystal blue sky. Under the afternoon sun, the forest sparkles as the rays catch on the white canopies. It's whimsical, like something out of a fairy tale.

A flash of red catches my eye and I pull us to a stop, pointing to a hundred-foot pine. "See that?"

Aly squints, leaning in close to follow my finger before gasping softly. "What is it?"

"A woodpecker. Listen." My arm snakes around her waist, sealing our bodies together as we wait.

After a minute, the bird lets out a *tchur* as its red head jolts forward. Drumming echoes through the trees and bounces off the bark.

"Wow," she whispers. "Days like today remind me how different this place is to the city."

Chuckling, I nod. "It's pretty great. Some people say seeing a woodpecker pecking can symbolize resilience and perseverance?"

Aly swallows, shaking her head. "I didn't."

I glance down at her. "I think there's a reason we're witnessing it today."

Her brow wrinkles a little but she doesn't say anything more, lost in her own thoughts again. Smacking a kiss to her rosy cheek, I link our gloved hands together and lead her the rest of the way until we reach a familiar break in the tree line.

A large chunk of my childhood took place here. Summers splashing in the shallow waters. Springs spent fishing with friends. Fall campfires and spiced cider. Winters racing on fresh blades.

I dump the bag on the floor while Aly gapes at the frozen landscape stretching past the frosty horizon.

"This place is...*Wow*." Her marvel strikes me with pride. "A lake?"

"Yeah." I dust off the snow and reveal the sign sitting on the shore, veiled slightly by pale reeds. Rosewick Waters. "A little hidden gem."

"It's like we've stepped foot into Narnia," she whispers.

"It's pretty magical. You should paint it."

While she takes it all in, I rummage around in my bag.

"Now, I checked your shoes—not in a fetish kinda way. Unless you're into that." I dangle the skates between us by the laces. "Turns out you're the same size as Florence."

She drags her gaze away, a dreamy look on her face until she spies the footwear. "Absolutely not."

"Okay, okay." I lower to a knee and hold out my hands. "It's a no to the foot pics, but there's zero negotiation on the ice-skating."

With pursed lips and slightly furrowed brow, she says, "I don't know how. I'll be like a baby giraffe taking its first steps. I've humiliated myself enough in the last twenty-four hours."

Well, that certainly won't do.

The skates thud at my feet. In a heartbeat, I'm towering over her, fingers clasped behind her neck. "No," I state firmly. "No, you don't get to do that. I'll take your hardheadedness, insults, and cold shoulders, but I will not allow you to say that what you did yesterday was anything short of remarkable. *You* are remarkable, so don't you forget that. But if you do, I'll be here to remind you."

Moisture clings to her lashes as she shakes her head. Then her words cut me right down the middle. "You won't always be here. Or I won't. Remember?"

I'd forgotten.

My smile is weak. "Then I'll have to double down on my efforts. Starting now."

Fire and ice battle it out as I press my mouth to hers. My tongue demands entrance, and I ignite when her taste hits me. No amount of time is enough with her.

Maybe ignoring the end date and my rapidly increasing feelings is careless.

Maybe I'll live with the most amazing memories. Of moments just like this.

Maybe. Maybe. Maybe.

"In case that wasn't clear," I mumble against her lips before stealing another kiss. "That was me telling you that you're incredible and you can do anything you put your mind to."

She doesn't fight her smile or me. "You're not too bad your-self, Dimples."

I SPOKE PREMATURELY.

Either Aly isn't putting her mind to it, or she really is terrible.

I'm not complaining, because I've had her lithe body pressed against mine for the last hour. Her frustrated little huffs and grunts are adorable.

More importantly, she's switched off.

"One last try on your own," I say encouragingly.

Her knees are bent, ass nestled into my lap as she grips my wrists hovering at her sides.

"Okay." She puffs out her chest, hands shaking. "But tell me when you're going to push me."

"You got it. On my count. Five, four, three—Go!"

"Booth!" she screeches as I nudge her forward and she glides away, arms flailing in the air.

Cupping my hands around my mouth, I instruct her. "Keep your knees bent! Eyes up! Stop looking down! Now turn!"

"You didn't teach me how to turn!"

"It's easy. All in your hips." She's really picking up speed. Her hair whips behind her as she races toward a huge bank of snow. "Aly, turn! Now!"

"You are the worst instructor! I hat—" Her tirade is cut off when she body slams into a drift, a plume of snow dancing up into the air.

"Shit. Shit. Shit." I glide across the ice, pumping my arms

and legs before skidding to a stop. "That was impressive. Ten out of ten."

Two menacing eyes, with lashes weighed down with flecks of white, track my movements. A gloved hand shoots up. I should have seen it coming. The moment our fingers make contact, she's hauling me down. I not so gracefully land on top of her, and then I'm the one screeching.

A sharp bite zaps down my spine when a handful of snow is dumped down my clothes. "Fuck, you little witch! I was helping you."

"You sabotaged me! Now eat snow too." And I literally do when she shoves a handful in my face.

We roll around, wrestling each other in the snow until we're wheezing with laughter, faces flushed, clothing soaked through. Frost bitten and shivering, we eventually stop and catch our breaths.

Birds chirp around us as we settle on our backs, staring up at the sky.

"Thank you," she murmurs softly.

I glance at her side profile. "For what?"

"For being you. Shamelessly, without any walls or falseness. You don't treat me like something about to crack under the pressure. I needed this." She meets my gaze. "I'll never forget this or my time in Sutton Bay."

My heart jackhammers in my chest. "I won't forget this either." *I won't forget you.* "Now, let's get back and warm up. There's a bathtub waiting with our names on it."

CHAPTER THIRTY-TWO

alessandra

I'M IN TROUBLE.

My time here was supposed to be fleeting. In and out. I'd try to connect with my blood relatives once, and if they weren't interested, farewell Sutton Bay. The restaurant wasn't a mindless investment, but an opportunity to be here. Meaning, the relationships I built with the employees would be surface level. That's not to say I'd neglect my responsibilities as the owner, but since being here, it's clear they don't need me.

If all fails with Martin and my birth father, at least I was able to save a family-owned business.

Watching Booth's muscular, naked body climb into the steaming bathtub is also a win. Our situationship definitely isn't surface level. The most unnerving part? I'm not drowning below the surface. I float effortlessly with him.

I hate that this can't be permanent.

His deep groans pull me from my inner turmoil. My blood heats as his tight ass, perfectly round, disappears into the bubbles and he settles against the tub.

With his eyes closed, he blindly reaches for me. "Get in here, beautiful."

My towel drops to the floor, and I pad over to where he waits. He cracks one eye, that single pupil blowing wide when he takes me in.

The hot water stings my cold skin as I step into the tub and situate myself between his open legs.

"Much better." He wraps his arms around my tummy, fingers tracing over an old scar on my abdomen. "What's this?"

"I had my appendix removed when I was fourteen." Raising his hand from the water, I count the small white welts along his skin. "I bet you've lost track of where you got all these from?"

He huffs. "Comes with the territory."

That's how we stay, losing track of time, our hands wandering over each other's slick skin. The touches aren't sexual, but comforting. Like we're memorizing the contours of the other.

The view outside the floor-to-ceiling window is spectacular. A light dusting of snow floats from the sky, glittering against the deep orange sky as the sun descends.

I'd happily stay here, hiding from reality and responsibilities, but that's not us.

As if reading my mind, Booth murmurs, "I have to head back into town tomorrow. Simon's been covering my shifts, but he's burned out since we fired Kyle."

He massages my biceps as they bunch up with tension. "I should too. God, I need to message Martin so he kno—"

"I've already told him you're okay," Booth interrupts. "That was all."

I twist in his hold. "Thank you." Resting my forehead on his chin, I inhale his smoky scent lingering with the calming eucalyptus aroma of the bath.

"He, um, asked if he could meet with you."

My head snaps up. "He did?"

"Did you want me to tell him it's too soon or...?"

"You don't have to do that." My voice grows tight, and I wince at my defensiveness.

Booth peels my dripping hair off my shoulder. "When are you going to get it into your head that I'm not here to take charge? You lead; I follow."

I wind my arms around him, pressing my face into his neck. My body is bare, but my next request leaves me most exposed. "Will you come with me?"

His fingers drift up and down my spine. "You don't even need to ask."

My heart sings, the trust in his words strikes a chord deep in my chest. His own heart strums against mine, both beating in harmony as I lay open-mouth kisses down the column of his neck.

"What about what's important to you?" My question comes out senselessly.

He stills.

"What do you mean?" he asks warily. When I raise my head, he blinks down at me rapidly.

"About working somewhere else. The dreams you told me about. I've seen you work, Booth. Your talent knows no bounds. Have you ever thought about researching other oppor—"

"They're dreams. That's all. Ones I put to rest a long time ago." I blanch in surprise. His tone and face are harsh. A stark contrast to the gleam in his eyes when he shared his aspirations with me.

"But why?"

"I don't want to talk about this, Aly."

Water sloshes over the sides of the tub as he spins me; back to chest again. His thickening cock nudges my bottom.

He's avoiding the subject, tactfully diverting my attention. I want to be mad, to draw the truth from him. Which is unfair. He's been nothing but patient with me, so I'll do the same until he's ready.

I push back into his erection, drawing a hiss from him.

"I'm going to do filthy things to you tonight, Silver."

"Promises, promises."

Arousal curls my toes as he palms my breasts. The cool air pebbles my skin, eyes fluttering closed as I drift into ecstasy under his touch. He pinches and rolls my nipples. I widen my legs and succumb to his skillful hands, right there in the bubbles.

Our conversation temporarily forgotten.

MY YOUNGER SELF SAW NERVOUSNESS AS A WEAKNESS.

Dance recitals. Volleyball competitions. First dates. Anytime my hands became clammy or stomach somersaulted, I'd talk myself out of it. I didn't get the jitters.

That ideology still holds true today.

The idea of seeing Martin again has my temples pulsing and legs bouncing, leaving me delicate and feeble.

My solace? Booth.

But he's not here to talk me off this cliff. And he probably wouldn't. He'd tell me it's not that high up, and if and when I jump, he'll be there at the bottom to soften my fall. He's not far, about a hundred yards away working the lunch service, but tell that to my brain.

I'm about to crawl out of my skin when my phone vibrates on the desk.

"How's my favorite daughter?"

A smile pulls at my lips, my father's voice always filling me with happiness.

"Your *only* daughter is fine. How are you?" I manage to laugh, though it's weak.

"Uh-oh. I've been married long enough not to accept 'fine.' What's wrong?" Concern laces his words.

There's no fooling him or my mom. Which is why I don't mince my words.

"I finally met with Martin and let's just say it didn't go to plan." I grimace at the reminder.

My dad lets out a slow breath. "Oh, Aly. What happened?"

His defeated tone is telling. My parents begged me to reconsider when I told them my reasons for buying Our Place, not wanting me to relive the meeting with my birth mother. I understood their worries, but listening to others' advice was never my forte.

"It was me, not him. He still doesn't know. Or at least I don't think he does. I turned up at his house, with no warning, and after five minutes, left without saying goodbye." My head thumps against the back of the rolling chair. "We are meeting him again this afternoon."

"*We?*" my dad asks in surprise.

Oh shoot. For obvious reasons, my parents don't know about Booth. Well, they do, but as the head chef.

"A friend is coming with me. He knows Martin, so it'll be less awkward." The lie rolls off my tongue easily.

"Well, okay. You'll call us when you've spoken to him? No matter the outcome?"

No matter the outcome.

If Martin turns me away, he means.

"I will, Papa. I'm sorry I haven't called much." Guilt sits heavy in my stomach.

"It's fine. I just wanted to check in and..." He trails off, piquing my interest.

"And?"

"It's fine. Forget about it."

His vagueness frustrates me. "Papa?"

A deep sigh echoes down the line. "We have an issue in Berlin. William quit without notice and it's left us in quite the pickle."

Quite the pickle is an understatement. William is a senior investor based in Europe and for the last nine months, he's been working hard to nail down a deal with a small chain of boutique hotels in Germany. It's a huge investment, something that would really put us on the map in a region we've barely scratched the surface of.

Without saying it, I know what he's insinuating.

I sit up in the chair. "When do you need me there?"

"Aly, there are more important things. You have a lot on your plate."

He's not wrong, but I can't stay here forever. He knows that. I know that. Everyone here knows that.

"Give me until the end of February. I can send someone from my team out there in the interim and familiarize myself with the project remotely," I insist, voice even despite the pang of disappointment.

So that's that. It's more time than I originally planned to have with Booth—and in town—yet somehow, it doesn't feel like enough.

And because the universe loves to rub salt in the wound, the man himself walks in, smiling wide, a dishrag tucked into his apron and red bandanna tied around his head. It's unfair he's the perfect specimen of a man. It's even crueler he's turned out to be one of the most incredible too.

"Hey, beau—*Oh,* my bad." The last of his sentence drops to a whisper when he sees the phone pressed to my ear.

Holding up a finger, I swivel in the chair. "Send me the details, Papa. I'm sorry I have to go, but I'll call tonight. Give my love to Mama. I love you."

"Was that your *special* friend?" he asks coyly.

The tips of my ears burn. "Goodbye, Father," I reply flatly, and his deep laughter is heard until I hang up.

When I spin back around, my face shows no signs of the news my dad shared as I give Booth a small smile. It's ironic, because it wasn't long ago he was praying for my mysterious disappearance. Now the idea of telling him has a sour taste lingering in my mouth.

"Your dad?" He settles into the chair opposite.

"Mm-hmm." A small divot forms between his eyes at my brusqueness. My face might be under control, but my voice isn't. "Sorry. Just lots going on. Are you finished for the day?"

"Yeah. Clocked off, Boss." He salutes me.

I roll my eyes. "Don't call me that."

He saunters over, perching himself on the corner of the desk beside me and ducks his head. A shiver runs through me as Booth's smoky scent assaults my senses. "What, am I only to call you that in the bedroom, *Boss?*"

"You're ridiculous." I laugh and push his face away.

We share a smile, the air between us buzzing, our greedy gazes never quite getting their fill. His eyes dart left, breaking the connection, and I follow. The clock reads five p.m., but it may as well scream it.

We're meeting Martin at 5:30.

"You can change your mind, you know?" Booth's deep timbre cuts through the haze. God, it's incredible how well he can read me.

I continue to follow the hands of the clock.

Tick. Tock. Tick. Tock.

Could I change my mind? Should I?

"No." I shake my head vigorously. "No, I don't want to do that. I've waited long enough."

"Okay," he whispers and shuffles closer until his knees touch my thigh. "I'll be there every step of the way. If it becomes too much, you give me a sign and we can leave. Tap me on the thigh or something. But, Aly?"

"Yeah?" I turn to look at him.

"I'm really proud of you, whatever you decide."

This. Man. This perfect, caring, beautiful man.

CHAPTER THIRTY-THREE

alessandra

WHEN BOOTH SHARED THAT SAYING GOODBYE TO HIS FATHER WAS the scariest thing he'd done, I felt pathetic.

Booth's constant assurances and pep talks have diluted that view. Sharing my biggest fears with him was unnerving, but I'm almost confident I wouldn't be sitting in Martin's living room this second if it wasn't for him.

I'm more emotionally prepared this time around, and knowing a light tap on his leg is all it'll take to shut this down is a huge reassurance. Booth sits next to me on the sofa, his denim-clad thigh pressed to mine, my hand firmly clasped in his.

His presence anchors me. Holding me steady to endure whatever storm I'm about to face.

I allow myself to take in Martin's home properly now. Despite its size and being filled with random clutter, it feels empty. There are no photographs, no signs a family lived here. Worn oak floorboards are the only tell. They've endured years of traffic, perhaps even played on by a young boy once upon a time. The floral upholstered furniture and drapes are drab but give a hint to a woman's touch.

The rattling of china draws closer until an uneasy-looking Martin appears. His tall, wiry frame curves in on itself, shoulders sagging. Thick hair, more gray than black is combed neatly to the side. Like on Christmas Day, he seems overdressed for the occasion. His eyes flit between us and the large bay window, his discomfort evident.

The air grows tense as he sets the coffee and cookies on the table.

Between his unease and my chagrin, the atmosphere here is stifling.

"I'm sorry abo—" I start, just as Martin asks, "Cream or sugar?"

He cringes, and my grip on Booth tightens.

"Aly will have one sugar, black—because she isn't sweet enough. I'll take a splash of cream, please. Thanks, Martin." Booth's lighthearted joke does the trick. My muscles relax and the thick fog clinging to my brain lifts.

I wait for Martin to serve our drinks, and once he's settled in the pale green wingback, I dive in.

If my voice wobbles or I lose my cool, it'll be okay.

I can do this, but it's easier with Booth here.

As if sensing I'm about to speak, he flashes me a reassuring look and strokes his thumb over the back of my hand.

"I'm sorry about turning up unannounced the other day." When Martin looks up, I hold back my flinch at the silver eyes staring back at me. "I suppose you have some idea why I'm here?"

He remains stoic, no reaction to my bluntness. "I'm not sure how I didn't see it before. You..." His gaze drops, fingers twisting so tight his knuckles turn white. "You look just like Harvey. The eyes. The hair. You even have the same nose."

I stiffen and Booth shifts beside me.

"I'm not going to ask if you knew, because it's clear you didn't," I say. "Harvey's name wasn't on my original birth certificate, so I can only assume he didn't either. Unless he wasn't interested."

Martin's expression is torn. "He, um, I haven't seen him for..." He clears his throat. "We haven't spoken in a long time. He must have been quite young when you were born. How old are you?"

"I'll be thirty-one in May."

After some quick math, he nods. "Sixteen. He would have been sixteen."

I nod. "The same age as my birth mother. I don't blame her for the choice she made—or either of them. I'm just looking for answers. To understand my heritage and medical history. I don't expect anything, if that's your concern. I'm not on the hunt for some hidden inheritance."

I want to protest when Booth lets go of my hand until he rubs my back in reassuring circles.

Martin's silence irritates me, which I know is unfair—which irritates me further.

"Harvey's mom, do you speak to her?"

"Not in over thirty years," he replies solemnly.

My heart drops.

"Do you know the best way to contact Harvey?"

His regret simmers and I already know his response. "It's been so long. I'm sorry." The last two words are barely above a whisper.

"There's no record of a Harvey Willis after his graduation from a high school in Wisconsin. Is that where they live?"

Again, nothing.

My skin grows flushed. "Do you know if he's married? Has other children?"

He shakes his head and he slumps further into himself. With each question and no answer, we both grow more irate.

Realization hits me in the chest like a sledgehammer.

He doesn't know where they live. He knows nothing about his ex-wife or son. He knows *nothing*.

All of this, for nothing?

I up and left my apartment, my job, bought a restaurant on a whim, and spent weeks in a small town in the middle of nowhere. And for what? This is nothing like the meetup with my birth mother. Somehow it's worse. I gave up nothing then. Now, so much is on the line.

Subtly, Booth taps the side of his leg with his index finger. My eyes follow that tiny movement. My emotions don't control me. *I* am in control. If this were a meeting with a prospective investment and it wasn't going smoothly, I would shut it down.

Which is what I need to do here.

"Obviously, this was a waste of time. I apologize for bothering you." My voice is sharp enough to cut a diamond.

"Aly," Booth whispers softly as I wipe my sweaty palms down my pants.

Monotone words halt me.

"He might have taken his mother's maiden name." Martin scrubs a thin hand down his face. "The reason I don't know his or his mother's whereabouts is because I never looked for them, as per her request, and I wanted to respect her wishes."

My stomach churns. What reason would his wife have for never wanting to see him again? Thankfully, he stops my mind from going to the worst places.

"I was absent. Work obsessed." This is the most I've gotten all evening, and it doesn't come easily. His jaw is tight, eyes hard. "She asked me to spend more time with her and Harvey, and I ignored her. Providing my family with a big house"—he gestures around us—"toys, nice clothes was more important. When she slowly withdrew, I didn't fight. I worked longer hours and buried my head in the sand. I realized too late that her threat about leaving me wasn't empty."

Indignation tickles my throat.

The remorse etched in Martin's face tells me he's punished himself enough over the years. If I thought he was uncomfortable before, it's nothing compared to his rigid posture and distraught expression now.

His candor doesn't change the outcome.

"I'll try." His eyelids close, heavy with emotion before opening again. "I'll try to reach them. Please...please give me some time. It's the least I can do."

Time isn't something I have much of. That's not to say my search ends when I leave Sutton Bay, but can I do this without the safe, supportive arms of the man next to me?

For some unknown reason, that question bothers me.

I did well alone. Long before Booth came along.

A soft touch stalls my inner conflict. I turn to find a set of calming, blue eyes watching me carefully.

Give him a chance, his face says.

So I do.

I twist to face Martin, shoulders pulled back. "Okay. But if they don't want to know me, just say it. Don't indulge me or try to protect my feelings."

He nods once.

Expecting this interaction to be over, I make for my escape just as he murmurs behind me. "I'd like to know you, Alessandra. If that's okay."

With a single glance over my shoulder, my dying hope clutched close to my chest, I catch his shoulders collapse. Only to lift at my response.

"Friday morning, at ten o'clock. We can meet at the bakery before I head to the restaurant."

I don't wait for his reply. I'm aware of my unpleasant, surly attitude, and he's likely second-guessing his request to know me. That's his choice.

Mine is to get out of this room. This house.

The second I step outside, I finally breathe, gulping down the blistering cold air until solid arms encompass me.

"You did it. You did so good. I'm so proud of you." Booth's warm breath coasts over my cheek.

I don't trust myself to talk. The tight hold he has on me keeps me upright.

But it shouldn't.

Relying on him is foolish. Our time is almost up. He won't be there to pick up the pieces when it ultimately falls apart; fractured by more disappointment. That's my job. No one else's.

It's about time I remember that.

CHAPTER THIRTY-FOUR

booth

Still waters run deep.

To most, Alessandra Argiros is calm, controlled, composed. Her waters glassy and undisturbed. But I see her. The raging river that she is. White waters crash along the banks as she carves out a path in the world. She's powerful, her inner strength running deeper than she knows.

Small ripples in her composed demeanor reveal themselves. Hardly noticeable unless you look close enough. I'm overly aware of everything to do with her. The way her lips pinch tight when she's concentrating. The slow lift of her right brow when I say something amusing—or stupid. The small curls framing her face that refuse to be tamed after a long, tiring day.

And the way she stares into space, distracted by her thoughts when she thinks no one is looking.

It's been three days since the tense meeting with Martin. She hasn't brought it up, but I know it sits heavily on her mind.

Do either of them realize how similar they are? How the towering walls they've built over the years can't hide their obstinate nature. Martin's stubbornness is subtle through his silence and pride, whereas Aly's is more obvious through her smart mouth and immoveable opinions.

I want to ask how I can help, but then I risk unraveling everything we've overcome. So instead, we throw ourselves into our work. Aly's has demanded her attention for the last two days, and the restaurant has been surprisingly busy for mid-January. I'm exhausted after my shifts, and while I don't believe she's avoiding me, we haven't seen one another outside of Our Place since the meeting with Martin.

Our time should be spent entangled in her bedsheets or making out on my sofa like two horny teenagers. But instead, I'm drafting up new prices for the menu as per Aly's request.

"You almost finished here?" Patrick calls from the other side of the restaurant. He flips over the last of the chairs before walking to where I'm trying and failing to concentrate. Sometimes when we're working a late shift together, I finish up on the restaurant floor rather than the office. I'm quickly regretting my choice today.

"No," I groan as my head thuds against the large wooden table.

The chair creaks beneath his weight as he sits opposite me. "Lady trouble?"

"Fuck off."

"I'll take that as a yes then." He chuckles. "Seriously, though, I thought you and Aly were past being at each other's necks. So what's got your panties in a twist today?"

Sitting up, I frown at him. "My panties aren't in a twist."

He scoffs and jabs a finger toward the kitchen. "You bit my head off earlier when a server accidentally put through a clam chowder."

"I eighty-sixed it not five minutes earlier!" I protest.

"Yeah, and mistakes happen. You're the last person I expect to be a prick about it."

My posture collapses. He's right. I've been irritable all day.

"Sorry," I grumble, raise my head, and force a smile. "There's just been a lot going on. I didn't mean to take it out on you."

Stacking his arms on top of each other, he leans forward, concern scoring his face. "You wanna talk about it?"

Yes! I want to shout. My siblings and I don't keep secrets from one another. Since our dad passed, and with him being the eldest, Pat's taken it upon himself to fill that role as best as he can.

The issue eating away at my brain isn't mine to share, though, and I won't betray Aly's trust. "Nah. Nothing to tell. Ignore me."

He stares at me thoughtfully, not convinced. "You like working here, right?"

I'm so blindsided that the room spins.

Why would he ask that? Did Aly say something?

No. She wouldn't. We share that mutual understanding.

"What kind of question is that?" My voice pitches.

His eyes narrow. "Something you said a couple of months ago. Before the fair. It stuck with me."

The scrutinizing look he's giving me makes my skin itch. I fiddle with the stack of papers on the table. "You're over-thinking it. I can't even remember what I said."

"You said, 'I'm not sure how much longer I can continue doing this.' It's not the first time you've said something like that either."

Goddamn him and his elephant memory. "Yeah, and I was talking about the new owner. Seriously, Pat, drop it."

The little white lie doesn't pacify him, and his resounding exhale makes me feel like shit.

Just tell him.

"Sometimes it feels like your heart isn't in it anymore. Don't get me wrong, you're still fantastic at your job, but something's missing. I was always so jealous of your passion, but these days, you seem eager for your day to end." Patrick is our dad, through and through, with their wise words and logical thinking. It might as well be my father speaking. "Do you want to be here?"

I almost choke on the anguish suffocating my airways.

Rationally, there's nothing to be ashamed about. We all fantasize. About picking the winning scratch card or owning a vintage sports car. I imagine a career outside of these four walls —but that's all it will ever be. A fantasy.

I would never abandon my family to chase after a dream fated to crash and burn.

The real kicker? I've fooled no one. Just myself. And in doing so, I've failed to see the spark I've lost.

My insides twist. A corkscrew of emotions.

It would gut Patrick to know the truth, so the easiest thing to do—the thing I've been doing for years—is put on a happy face.

My cheeks stretch, teeth flash, and lips pull tight. "I *want* to be a millionaire, but I'll settle for you cooking me dinner next week while I hang out with my niece." Snatching up the papers, I stand, face aching. "It's all good, Pat. Don't worry about it."

Patrick rises, eyeing me carefully before nodding slowly. "Okay. I'll drop it. But you know I'm always here, right?"

"Yes, yes." I round the table and slap him on the back. "My very own Dear Abby. I'm gonna use the restroom. I'll meet you out front."

Seemingly persuaded, he resumes his duties.

The second I'm alone, a shaky breath leaves me.

I've got to get my head straight. My dad might not be around anymore, but there are still other people relying on me.

Pulling out my phone, I type out a text and wait.

Booth: Do you want to come over tonight?

My fingers tap against the side of my cell impatiently until her reply comes through.

> She-Devil: I'm snowed under with work. Rain check?

Dejection settles deep in my bones. Which is ridiculous considering we've been clear about the lack of strings in this arrangement. Yet something deep in my heart tugs sharply at the idea of not seeing her tonight.

I delete several responses before settling.

> Booth: I'm holding you to that, beautiful.

> Booth: Good luck with Martin tomorrow. Call if you need me.

Her reply doesn't come through until hours later, when my eyelids fight to stay open.

> She-Devil: Thanks

Maybe it's the lack of sleep stirring my judgment.

Thanks. One Word. That's not Aly. She'd usually reply with something sarcastic about not needing my protection. If she's mad at me, she makes damn sure I'm aware. This text is passive and short.

I dismiss the irrational thought and put it down to the late hour.

Easier said than done. I toss and turn in bed, overthinking everything I've said and done the last few days. This is where it becomes tricky with Aly. She's quick to close up when she feels cornered, but she's had the space to unpack the last few days. She didn't push me away when I turned up at the cabin, so why would she now?

Then my thoughts turn dangerous. I imagine an alternative universe where this isn't temporary. I picture her in my kitchen —no, *our* kitchen. We'd argue about who does the dishes, she'd moan sinfully over whatever she's eating, and then I'd worship her all night long.

The life we could have together is crystal clear in my head. Except for one detail. Here or there?

My dream girl versus my father's legacy.

That's now two dreams that will never come true.

CHAPTER THIRTY-FIVE

alessandra

BUBBLES POP ON THE FOAM OF MY UNTOUCHED CAPPUCCINO.

A blinding headache pulses in my head, nothing to do with the lack of caffeine.

It's 10:11 a.m. and Martin's a no-show.

No call or text.

I could call, and perhaps I'm being petty, but I need him to prove he wants to be here.

Which he isn't.

As I'm about to get up and leave, Quinn skips over with a lot of pep in her step. Her bright smile wilts when she spies my drink. "Oh, is something wrong with your coffee?"

"No, no. Sorry, I got distracted and forgot about it. Your cappuccinos are always perfect," I reassure her.

"I'd be happy to make you another. On the house. It's nice to see you sitting in with your coffee more these days. Not that you can't take it to go." She slaps a palm to her forehead before looking at me hopefully, and now I feel bad. "Sorry, I'm a blabbermouth. You do whatever you want."

I'm usually too busy to sit in with my morning coffee, but coming to Just Brew It has become part of my daily routine since Christmas. Quinn's chipper personality is oddly contagious and she makes the most mouthwatering pastries.

Her sunny attitude makes the idea of leaving less appealing suddenly. I relax into my chair and give her a genuine smile. "I'm okay for coffee, but I'd love one of your almond croissants."

She beams at me, claps her hands, and jogs behind the counter. Rainbows might as well shoot out of her ass she's so adorable.

Not one minute later, a flaky, buttery croissant appears in front of me. To my shock, Quinn slides her own steaming cup down and sits across from me.

"I hope this is okay. I haven't had a break yet, and you looked like you could use some company."

Laughing lightly, I sip my lukewarm coffee. "I really looked that miserable?"

Her eyes grow comically wide. "Not miserable. Um, more, faraway?"

She's not wrong, and I don't know what response that warrants.

"Did you want to talk about it?" she says warily, as if talking to a skittish animal. "A new set of ears can be helpful."

"It's a long story. And I doubt your break is long enough to hear it all."

She nods in understanding. "That's fair. Plus, I'm basically a stranger." Her shoulders perk up, and I see the lightbulb pop up above her head. "Oh, but let's change that. Johanna, Florence, and I are having a Galentine's dinner next month. You should join us."

Quinn finds my bewildered expression hilarious.

"Layman's terms: wine, cheese, and pajamas," she clarifies. "Florence mentioned strippers, but she's the only single one in attendance."

My brows shoot up and Quinn realizes her slipup.

"You're like fifty percent single." She shrugs innocently. "So maybe half a lap dance?"

It's difficult not to laugh at her serious expression considering the topic at hand. "I appreciate the invitation, but I wouldn't want to intrude." The last thing I want is a pity invite because she spotted me looking pathetic in her bakery.

This might be the first time I've ever witnessed her frown. "I wouldn't have invited you if I didn't want you there. Jo mentioned it yesterday." Her response comes in fast. "It'll be nice getting to know Booth's..." With knitted brows, she asks, "Sorry, what are you two? It's tiring pretending we don't know you guys are—" She makes a circle with her thumb and index finger, then slides her opposite one through the hole.

My coffee almost sprays out of my nose.

She smirks and hands me a wad of napkins. "Complicated, got it."

I ignore the suggestive raise of her eyebrow and laugh, only it dies when I remember the last conversation I had with him.

I'm a broken faucet. The poor guy doesn't know if he's going to be scalded or given the cold shoulder. It's anyone's guess why he remains interested.

Before I can dwell on it any further, I smile at Quinn. "Count me in."

She opens her mouth, but the chime of bells over the front door distracts her. "Mr. Willis. Fancy seeing you on a Friday."

I still. My reason for being here was momentarily forgotten.

Not wanting to give anything away, I twist to face the newcomer and gasp.

Face red as a tomato, shoulders heaving up and down as he steadies his breathing, hand clutched to his chest with a pained expression. Quinn and I jump to our feet and run to where he's keeled over.

"Martin, are you okay?" I rush out.

He wheezes in lieu of speaking.

"Could you get some water? I'll help him sit," I say to Quinn, who disappears as I guide Martin to the nearest chair.

He pants for air and, after a few deep breaths, finally talks. "I'm s-so sorry, Ales—" Quinn returns, and he downs half the glass before resuming. "The ignition on my truck blew and I forgot to charge my cell overnight." He shakes his head in annoyance. "I'm so sorry."

Quinn might be a chatterbox, but something about Martin's pitiful expression has her creeping away quietly.

I encourage him to drink more, and then it hits me.

He didn't blow me off.

"Wait," I gasp. "Did you walk here?"

Sheepishly, he nods. "If I could run, I would have been here sooner." He cups his knee. "Not as good as it used to be."

Martin's farmhouse is on the outskirts of town, a fifteen-minute drive away. Meaning he walked the entire way, as fast as he could, just to get here.

To meet me.

He wanted to be here.

My brain struggles to compute this information.

"If you need to go, I'll understand. Maybe another time," he says softly.

I'm due at the restaurant in—I glance at my watch—five minutes.

I'd accepted his absence and now that he's here, I don't know how to respond. As I study Martin's rueful expression, that kernel of hope regrows.

Sutton Bay isn't permanent, and when I first arrived, it seemed pointless to make any connections. I'm still cautious, but less skeptical, so like I did with Quinn, I lower my guard. "I have time for another coffee."

His eyes flare before he schools his features.

Quinn's takes his order, and five minutes later we both have our hands cupped around steaming mugs. The silence that stretches between us is delicate; one wrong move and it will collapse. If this were an investment pitch, my voice would dominate. I'm not pitching anything now—or maybe I am. Either way, I speak with conviction. "I know it's only been a few days since we last spoke, but have you found out any information about your ex-wife and son?"

"Wife," he corrects solemnly. "We never divorced."

I don't react.

"You must think I'm an awful man for not knowing of their whereabouts, but when Judy left and took Harvey with her, I tried to maintain contact. Harvey visited occasionally, but when he started high school, the visits stopped. Resentment had me working myself to the bone, and eventually she asked me to give it my all or stop altogether." I'm stunned at the sudden vat of information he reveals. "To this day, it's my biggest regret. After you left my house, I reached out to an old friend who, let's just say, knows how to find people. He's tracked them both down."

Tremors vibrate through my body, the five-second pause feeling like a lifetime.

"Judy lives in Milwaukee, and Harvey..." My fingers squeeze the handle of my cup. "He lives in Green Bay with his wife and owns a construction company with his son."

I have another brother.

There's a lot of information to unpack and the weight of it all immobilizes me, leaving only my vocal chords intact. "Did you speak to him?"

His gaze flicks over my face, searching for emotion. He won't find any. I've desensitized myself for this moment. The odd sense of grief of losing something I never truly had.

"Please don't drag this out," I whisper harshly. "If he doesn't want to know me, that's fine. I've been here before."

Sympathy and regret carves deep lines into his. "When I called, he hung up as soon as he knew who it was."

A switch flips. This day is ten steps forward, one thousand back. All hope slides away, pooling at my feet.

"When was the last time you spoke to him?" He catches the sudden change in my tone.

"Thirty-three years ago."

What a mess.

I could ask for Harvey's contact details, but the idea of Martin being a buffer made this a lot simpler. It's anything but.

As if sensing my doubt, he quickly says, "I'm going to write to him. Do you want...do you want me to tell him who you are?"

My eyes drift to the window. People walk past, paying us no mind, oblivious to the two strangers whose lives have crashed together. One in denial. One close to quitting. Water droplets fall from an icicle hanging from the streetlamp, and after five drips and five steadying breaths, I face forward. "It wouldn't make sense to lie. My biological mother's name is Rebecca Timmons. I was born in a small town in New York called Ringwood on May twenty-fourth, 1993." I recite each detail like items off a grocery list.

He nods. "Okay. Is there anything else?"

"It would be helpful to know of any medical problems that run in the family."

Tick. Tick. Tick. Just like a business transaction.

In front of me sits my grandfather. Inside, I'm numb.

Maybe I'm broken.

Would a human who isn't emotionally stunted react this way to finding a blood relative? There's no how-to guide on how to navigate this. So I do what I know best.

Martin watches me silently as I grab my purse and coat before standing. He mirrors me, hands hanging limply at his sides.

"I appreciate you taking the time to meet with me."

"Of course," he says carefully. "Would you like to—"

The bell chimes, cutting him off. I don't want to know what

he was about to ask. My heart and brain are warring against each other. I'm one depressing fact away from crumbling.

He blinks at the ground. "I'll update you when I hear from Harvey."

If. If you hear from Harvey, I want to correct.

I wave goodbye to Quinn, who has done a terrible job at pretending she wasn't watching our awkward interaction unfold. Not having the courage to say anything more, I make a beeline for the door.

Martin's words stop me in my tracks. "Could we do this again? I have some old photos of Harvey you might like to see."

Ever since I started this journey, I've staggered through a network of passages. My life has turned into a labyrinth. The more I wander, the farther away the exit.

I can't rely on the man who hasn't spoken to his son in over thirty years. I can't rely on the people of this town to not gossip about my sorry start in life. I can't rely on myself to say anything nice. Relying on people is a mistake.

"I don't think that's a good idea," I say rigidly before making my escape.

Feigning ignorance is easier. Which is exactly what I do as I storm down Robin Road. Shoulders back, chin high, expectations low.

Patrick and Johanna watch me carefully as I enter the restaurant. I ignore the full house of customers as I stalk to the office, ready to bury myself in work calls and emails. Anything to distract me.

Reliance is a weakness I can't afford.

Which is why when the biggest threat to the stronghold I've meticulously built strolls into the room hours later, a carefree smile pulling at his lips, my shields go sky high.

booth

THE CORNERS OF MY MOUTH SPLIT AS I PLASTER ON A CHEESY grin.

It's that time of the week when Mrs. Stewart demands she talk to the chef so she can complain about something ridiculous. According to my mom, it's been going on since our first week of opening.

Her whining is part of my routine. If she didn't show up, I'd be calling the cops to carry out a welfare check.

With beady eyes, she tuts at the tiny stain on my chef coat, while her husband eats his hamburger silently.

Poor guy. She probably removed his voice box for talking back.

"Mrs. Stewart, I promise you that today's catch of the day was, in fact, caught today." My palms press together in front of me in a prayer.

I'm praying that Patrick will finally let me ban her.

She turns her nose up at the *empty* plate in front of her. "It didn't smell fresh. An awful fishy odor was coming from it."

Lord, give me strength.

I'd rather chop off my own hands than serve bad fish. Not to mention the health hazard it would cause.

I glance down at her plate. "Did it taste fishy?"

She balks. "What are you implying?"

"Nothing." My grin stretches so wide my eyes water. "I'd be happy to send out a complimentary blueberry cobbler."

Her head jerks with a huff. "I suppose that will suffice. I'd suggest you throw out the rest of that trout before someone else orders it."

Salmon. She had salmon.

"Absolutely. I'll get right on that." I look between her and her husband. *Blink twice if you're in danger.* "Enjoy the rest of your evening. See you next week."

"We shall not be dining here ever again," she shouts after me.

"We shall not miss you," I grumble for my ears only.

I poke my head into the kitchen. "Simon, two blueb—"

"I know the drill." He chuckles and slides two desserts across the pass. "This isn't my first rodeo."

If I don't laugh, I'll cry. "You're a champ. I need to talk to Jo. You got this?"

"Do what you gotta do." He nods before tearing off a new ticket from the printer and reading it out.

The bar staff are zipping back and forth as they fulfill drink orders. Even amid the dinner rush chaos, my brother and Johanna take advantage of any spare second to catch each other's eye.

Here I am, incapable of holding Aly's attention even if my life depended on it.

I spent all morning thinking about her, wondering how it went with Martin. My phone battery suffered thanks to the amount of times I refreshed our text thread. Nothing. It took all my self-restraint not to call or message her.

Johanna spots me waiting at the end of the bar, and holds up a finger. She stabs at the portable point-of-sale tablet, entering in an order, then heads my way.

She props her hands on her hips and exhales. "Tonight is a busy one. How are you all doing in there?"

"Feeling the pressure. I've never seen a January like it." I take in the full tables, not an empty seat in the house.

"You're telling me. Maybe you can convince Aly to stop hiding in the office and to come and give us a hand."

My head whips to the side. "Aly's *here*?"

"Um, yeah. She came in about seven hours ago." Suspicion creases her brow. "Something going on between you two?"

"Your guess is as good as mine." I regret the words as soon as they leave my mouth. "Fuck, pretend I didn't say that."

"Okay, let's pretend I didn't tell you this." She glances around, like Aly is about to jump out. "She looked pretty pissed when she walked in. Quinn texted to say that she and Martin were having coffee this morning at the bakery and it appeared...tense. I'm not trying to gossip. I just thought you should know."

I squeeze her shoulder. "No, thanks for telling me." My eyes drift to the back of the restaurant as I weigh up my options.

"She's still here. Maybe seeing you will cheer her up." Jo shoots me an encouraging smile until she reads my mood. "Is it serious between you?"

"That's the million-dollar question." Suddenly feeling drained, I prop my elbows on the bar and drop my head into my hands. "She's leaving."

"When?" Jo asks.

I shrug. "That's it, I don't know when, and we agreed this was casual. I know you don't like her, but there's a lot more to her than meets the eye."

"Hey." A bony elbow jabs me in the ribs. "I never said I didn't like her. I don't *know* her. Apparently, she accepted Quinn's invitation to our Galentine's dinner, so hopefully that'll change. It means she's here for another few weeks too."

Johanna's optimism confuses me further.

"Booth?" she whispers. I peek through my fingers and find her staring at me in delight. "It's not a bad thing that you like her. So what if she's leaving? New York isn't far. I've seen how you are with her—you couldn't be more obvious. But I've also seen how she looks at you when she thinks no one's watching."

"Yeah, and how's that?" I ask sarcastically.

She smiles at me gently. "Like she can finally stop searching. When her eyes land on you, she's found it."

Invisible strings stand me to attention. I'm hyperaware of my heart thumping in my chest, threatening to break free.

"None of us have ever seen a woman that puts up with your shit either. The way you two argue is bizarre, but who am I to judge?"

I chuckle. "It's our foreplay."

She shudders before grabbing me by the shoulders and shoving me away. "Don't *make* me judge you. Go find her, you charmer."

My legs need little encouragement. Those strings propel me toward the office. Outside, I pause, hand hovering above the door handle before I slowly twist it. A low hum buzzes beneath my skin, increasing in intensity when I spot Alessandra behind the desk.

Fuck, if I haven't missed her.

She's deep in concentration, eyes darting left and right as she reads the screen of her laptop. Her gaze cuts to me at the creak of the old door hinges. Focused to frustrated.

"What are you doing?" Her abrupt tone is my first warning sign.

I dismiss it.

"Well, hello to you, too, beautiful." Hoping to lighten the mood, I wink at her. *Nothing.*

Jo wasn't wrong, she's pissed, and I bet it has to do with this morning's meeting. This version of Aly isn't new to me, nor does it scare me off.

I round the desk and crouch in front of her. With the tip of my finger, I move to tuck a glossy curl behind her ear, but when I brush her cheek, she wheels out of reach.

"I asked what you're doing, Booth?" she asks impatiently.

Something is *very* wrong. Aly can be abrasive and snappy, but this is different. On closer inspection, dark shadows line under her eyes. The desk is littered with papers and documents. A coffee stain marks her otherwise pristine blouse.

She's unsettled.

"I'm checking in on you," I reply calmly. Sitting on my haunches, I rest my hand on the arm of the chair—mostly to stop her from putting more distance between us. "Talk to me."

Behind the frustrated glow in her eyes, there's a fragile softness.

"I'm busy. And you should be too." She goes to spin away but fails. "Let go."

"Talk to me," I repeat and tighten my grip on the chair.

"What are you, a parrot? Stop trying to get under my skin. I don't have time." Panic accompanies the anger in her voice, her face a complexity of emotions.

My shoes scuff across the floor as I shuffle closer. "That doesn't work on me anymore. Pushing me away is only going to make me try harder. Did he not show up?"

She stiffens.

Anger pools in my stomach at the thought of Martin standing her up. I find it hard to believe, considering his reaction earlier in the week.

I raise my hand to cup her cheek, voice tender. "Jo says you've been here for hours. Let's call it a day."

For a second, her muscles slacken, and she leans into the touch.

"You can trust me, Silver," I whisper.

Like she's stepped on a live wire, her eyes ping open and she jumps to her feet. "Don't call me that."

Taken aback, I choose my next words carefully. "Did something happen?"

"Yes. No. It's..." She releases a tense breath. "This was a mistake. We should have stuck to one night."

My head snaps back at the abrupt change in direction.

I'm used to her sharp words, but these hit differently. These are tipped with venom, made to harm. And they strike me square in the chest.

My knees scream in pain. I'm at her feet, because when am I not? I've fallen without warning. There's no time to gauge how close the ground is until I'm meeting the concrete face-first.

Smack.

When Aly draws arms, backing down isn't the solution. You've got to fight fire with fire.

Rising to my full height, I brush off my pants. "I didn't take you as a liar."

With eyes wide—in shock or anger, who knows—she points at the door.

"Get out and go do your job," she spits.

I lean forward, eyes narrowing. "Is that what you want? Because not five days ago, you were singing a different tune. Crying out my name and falling asleep in my arms. Sure didn't seem like a mistake then."

"People do stupid things when they need to get laid. You've fulfilled your duties. Well done." She crosses her arms, stance wide as she prepares for war. "You're dismissed."

I'm not surrendering. If this is how she wants to get out her frustrations, then so be it. I'll be her punching bag. I'll take each hit gladly if it means she quits hiding.

"Is that all you've got, *Silver*?" I dig. "Or are you ready to be honest?"

Sage and lavender stuns me when she steps into my space, and I bite back a groan.

"How's this for honesty?" she barbs. "You use humor and

stupidity to stop people from looking too closely. If you dropped the act, they'd all see what I see."

"And what's that?" I press closer, our fronts flush.

"You're not scared of letting your family down, but of going after what you want. It's an excuse." She jabs me in the chest. "You're scared of failing."

I'm not sure what response she was hoping for, but I doubt it was this.

I snatch up her wrist and smash our lips together.

However this ends, we're going out fighting.

She gasps as I bite down on her plump bottom lip before sucking it into my mouth. Her hands grip my shirt to push me away, but I fist the back of her hair, sealing our fate. She meets me with fervor.

Pain, anger, and raw desire fuel this kiss.

I'm mad. Mad at her for trying to go at this alone. Mad at her for pushing me away. Mad at her for calling me out.

She's mad. Mad at me. Mad at life. Mad at the world.

We are madness. A beautiful carnage.

This can't last forever, so I give her my all in sixty seconds before breaking the kiss. She's left panting and clutching at my clothes. Dazed, until the coolness in her gaze freezes over.

"Why did you do that?" Her fingertips brush along her swollen lips.

"If you really want me out of your hair, then consider me gone. I'll be cordial and well behaved until you jet back to New York." I grasp her jaw with one hand and tilt her head back. "At least I got one last taste. But on the off chance you're bluffing" —I graze my lips over her temple, breathing her in—"you know where to find me. Hide all you want, Alessandra."

Her hands float in the air as I retreat, eyes never leaving hers.

"But I see you. All of you. And it doesn't scare me."

alessandra

Humans hate making mistakes.

Thousands of centuries of being wrong and we're still incapable of accepting it.

Thanks to my ancestors, I'm flawed. Fortunately, my mistake won't go down in the history books, but it still festers in my head.

After coffee with Martin, I began spiraling. I locked myself away in the office, stewing in my thoughts, and when Booth appeared, eager to help, I lashed out.

He isn't unfamiliar to my bite, but I saw the flash of pain when I threw his fears in his face, hoping to deflect from my own.

I realized my mistake as soon as he punished me with that kiss. It seared through me, hot enough to weld us together. When he tore our lips apart, I felt the connection pull taut, on the precipice of snapping.

Hide all you want, Alessandra. But I see you. All of you. And it doesn't scare me.

Why? After I was so awful to him?

When he disappeared, I wanted to chase after him to apologize. But my stubborn nature, so strongly ingrained, cemented my feet to the floorboards.

I've never felt so exposed as I have with Booth. It terrifies me. What scares me the most is how badly I wanted to shed the armor, let him comfort and take care of me again, like he did at The Nook. He was who I wanted to turn to when the stress of everything became too much.

Rather than embrace what my heart screamed for, I neglected it. Booth might not have left angry, but now that he's had two days to mull it over, he's probably grateful.

It's for the best. Better now than later when we're in way over our heads.

My obstinance keeps me from reaching out, and like a coward, I've worked from home and evaded the restaurant like the plague. My fridge is barren and I've resorted to takeout for tonight. That or starve.

I'm about to check for an update on my pizza order when the buzzer sounds and my stomach grumbles in celebration.

"I'll be right down," I say quickly, and release the intercom button before the delivery driver can reply. I slide on my slippers, open my door, and jog down the stairs to collect my food.

"I'm sorry, do you have change for a fifty?" Without looking up, I rummage in my purse for something smaller. "Actually, just keep the change."

"Oh, darling, look, she's tipping us."

That is not the voice of a teenage pizza delivery boy.

My neck cracks with how quickly it snaps up. I blink, convinced I'm hallucinating, because why else would my parents be standing outside my apartment? It's late, the streets dark. Perhaps a trick of the shadows?

It's only when my mother taps my chin with her slender finger that I accept this is reality. "Alessandra, do not gape like a fish. It is very unflattering," she scolds, though there's warmth in her chocolate brown eyes.

I look at my dad, his gray eyebrows knitted in fatherly concern. He drags a small suitcase in front of him and smiles softly. "We'd check into a hotel, but we thought maybe our lovely daughter could put us up for a few nights."

I'm overcome with emotions and after weeks of holding them in, the dam breaks. Tears spring from my eyes and a muffled sob escapes me as my dad wraps me in a bear hug.

"What are you doing here?" My voice cracks.

"One of your friends called us," my dad murmurs into my hair.

"My friend?"

He nods against the top of my head. "Your special friend, I believe."

And now I want to cry for an entirely different reason.

"A charming young man." My mom lets out a low whistle. "A chef too."

Booth.

Booth, who overlooks my spite and prickly personality.

Booth, who shows up time and time again.

Booth, who has somehow invaded my heart and brain.

They're usually at odds with one another, but for once, they agree on one thing.

Booth Sadler is the man I don't deserve but want anyway.

Once upstairs, my parents listen attentively as I update them on everything that's happened since meeting with Martin. Shame sticks to my voice like tar as I tell them how I acted in the bakery and the unfair things I said to Booth— leaving out our friends-with-benefits agreement.

They don't judge or berate me for my behavior, though I deserve it.

When the food arrives, my appetite flees.

My parents are happy to steal a few slices of my veggie pizza while I digest the fact that A: they're in Sutton Bay, and B: Booth called them.

A glass of water appears in front of me. I take it from my dad with a weak smile. He settles himself on my right, while my mother strokes my hair lovingly on my left. Sandwiched between two people who don't need to ask how I'm feeling. With them, there's no hiding.

Hide all you want, Alessandra.

"I'd like to meet Martin," my dad announces, and my mom hums her agreement.

"And this Booth," she adds.

Perfect. They would want to befriend the two people I'm actively avoiding.

The cold liquid caresses my throat as I take a long sip. "Martin isn't the most sociable of people. And Booth is...busy."

"He didn't sound busy when he rang your father two days ago." My mom levels me with a look, calling me out on my bullshit.

"What did he say exactly?" I ask hesitantly.

Dad glances at my mom before answering. "He was worried about you and wasn't sure how to help. He assured us you were well, but that the last week would be a lot for any person, even someone as strong as you."

I look at him in disbelief. "He did not say that?"

My dad nods, beaming proudly. "It was more along the lines of, 'Sir, your daughter is the most extraordinary woman I've ever met. I hope I'm not overstepping, but I think a visit from you and your wife is exactly what she needs right now.' Does that sound accurate, Lydia?"

The room spins.

"Yes, darling. And he invited us for dinner at Our Place." My mother has hearts in her eyes.

I'm still in shock as I imagine Booth flirting with my mom. He'd say all the right things, making her blush and calling her my older sister. He'd charm the socks of my dad with his work ethic and strong leadership skills.

It's too much.

"Did he say anything else?"

They both lean forward, trying to catch my gaze as I avoid eye contact.

"Should he have?" my mom presses.

"No. Just curious."

There's no fooling them. "Is he your boyfriend?"

My head swings around to gawk at my mom. "No, *Mother.* He's a friend. An employee of the restaurant." *One I occasionally get naked with.*

"Hmm." She inspects her nails. "I've never known an *employee* to speak so ardently about their boss. Wouldn't you agree, Daniel?"

"Yes, my love," Dad replies.

What on earth is happening?

"Okay, enough of that." I vault from my seat. "Let me make up the bed for you."

"And where will you sleep?" my mom quizzes as she follows me into the bedroom.

"On the sofa."

She perches herself on the edge of the mattress. Her eyes follow me as I gather fresh bedsheets. At sixty-two, she's still the epitome of Mediterranean beauty. Wavy, mocha-colored hair, piercing brown eyes, and olive skin. My dad's family is Irish, with fair skin, fair hair, and green eyes. Because of my dark hair, it's easy to assume I favor her.

The diamond engagement ring she's worn for the last forty years glistens as she pats the bed. "Come sit."

"Let me finish this, Mama." I give her my back and close my eyes. Not ready for a one-on-one conversation.

"Now, Alessandra. We need to talk." Her serious tone has the same effect it did when I was younger.

I play the obedient daughter and join her. She snatches my hand up and kisses the back, her nude lipstick smudging across my knuckles.

"I love your brothers unconditionally, but in my dreams, I saw a third child. I've always believed dreams to be our future, should we play our cards right. After I had Alexis, and they told me I couldn't have any more children, I was heartbroken. I asked your father every night, 'What did I do? Why am I being punished?'" Her expression turns thankful. "Your father was wonderful during those dark days, reassuring me I did nothing wrong. And do you know what happened five years later?"

My vision blurs. I know what happened, but she tells me anyway.

"My beautiful, fierce, inspiring daughter was born. And our family was complete." The fine lines around her eyes deepen as she smiles nostalgically. "You might not be my blood, but you are my heart."

I mirror her smile as my chest aches. "I've never doubted that. I think I ended up with the family I was supposed to."

Her fingers caress my cheek as she regards me carefully. "But you doubt your heart? You keep it locked away and only share it with a select few."

Dropping my gaze, I trace the polished gold bands adorning her finger.

"Look at me, thisavré mou," she whispers.

When I do, her eyes sparkle with sadness and my lip stings as I try to stave off the tears.

"That heart of yours deserves to be loved. Stop thinking it doesn't. Nothing that happened when you were born or when you met your birth mother is any reflection of the woman you are. This Martin is trying. And from what you have told us, he is a lot like you. Guarded and wary of opening up. Please do not hide the marvelous years you've gifted me as your mother from the people who want to know you."

In the company of my mom, I don't have to be strong. She does it for me. I fall into her arms and let go. Anger, sadness, regret, gratitude. Each tear represents a different emotion. Every heave of my chest as I sob in her embrace alleviates the crushing pressure I've been walking around with.

"What about Harvey?" I whisper brokenly.

She smooths my mess of curls off my wet cheeks. "One day at a time. Give Martin a chance. If not for me, for yourself."

I hiccup, then nod. "Okay."

A pointed nail prods me in the chest. "And who knows... maybe you have room in your heart for someone else. Perhaps a chef?"

I've got to hand it to her. The woman is smooth.

"We really are friends." I roll my eyes when she pouts. "Or were. I said some horrible things to him...It doesn't matter anyway. He's here and I leave for New York soon."

"Long distance can work. Look at your father and me." She pinches my cheek when I deadpan. "Leave the sheets. We can do it. You have other things to do."

I'm yanked to my feet. "I do?"

With surprising strength, my mom leads me toward the front door before shoving my coat and scarf in my hands. She's lost it.

"Say goodbye to your daughter, Daniel," she shouts through the apartment.

"Goodbye, Daughter," my dad hollers, not questioning his wife's motives.

"Are you kicking me out?" I ask, baffled.

"For the night. I think you owe someone an apology."

I curse the rickety planks as I creep up the front steps.

I'm swaddled from head to toe like a woolly mammoth thanks to my mom. It was already late when my parents arrived. It's only now, standing on his doorstep, I check the time.

11:37 p.m.

No lights on. Not a peep from inside. A hooded figure outside the window.

If I were the owner of this house, I'd call the cops on myself.

What am I doing?

He's going to take one look at me and slam the door in my face.

With careful footsteps, I abandon my mission.

I make it four steps.

The rattling of the door handle has me freezing like a deer in headlights. Then a gravelly voice rolls into the pitch-black evening. "I've been listening to you march across my porch for the last ten minutes. I'm tired. Are you coming or going, Silver?"

I slowly pivot on my heel and face him. "I'm not sure."

Booth flicks on the porch light, illuminating his handsome face. His hair sticks up in all directions and he rubs a hand over his bare stomach. Heavy with sleep, his eyes track over my body. "Did your folks show?"

Pitter-patter goes my pathetic heart. "Yeah. Yeah, they did. Thank you for calling them."

"What's it going to be? It's cold," he mutters gruffly.

The scratchy scarf around my neck is too tight suddenly. I quickly unravel it and let out a breath before saying, "I came to apologize."

There isn't a trace of emotion on his usually jovial face. "I don't want your apology."

"Oh. Yeah, of course." I retreat another step. "Go back to sleep. Sorry for disturbing you."

He palms the door, opening it wider. "I don't want your apology because there's nothing to apologize for. What I want is you in my bed. I'll be angry at you for taking two days to come here in the morning."

Before I can respond, the dark room behind him swallows his silhouette. I hesitate for a nanosecond before my legs guide me up the steps and over the threshold.

"Lock up, would you?" he calls from the bed, where he's sprawled out like Adonis, the moonlight painting him in a blueish hue.

I don't question what's happening. The sound of the lock turning is barely audible over the blood pounding in my ears. I shed my clothes, leaving a trail of wool and cotton behind me until I'm left in only my bra and panties.

The cool bedsheets soothe my heated skin. A canyon separates us, reminding me of that first evening at the cabin.

Only this time, I want the distance eradicated. A hair's width is too far.

Rising to my hands and knees, I crawl across the mattress before climbing into his lap, slowly lowering myself. Every muscle, tendon, and nerve ending unwinds as I wrap my arms around his torso, cheek pressed to his chest.

Heavy arms surround me, better than any blanket. Strong legs lock me in place.

"That's better." His voice loses its tension. "That's much better."

The steadfast beating of his heart quells my nerves, and I say what I've wanted to tell him since he walked out of the office.

"You didn't deserve the horrible things I said. You might not want my apology, but you deserve one. So, I'm sorry," I mumble. "I find it hard to trust. Even before this journey to find my birth family, I've been wary of others. When I realized I'd grown reliant on you, I freaked out. This isn't your burden to carry, yet you've somehow shouldered the weight since I told you about my past. Would I have gotten this far without your help?"

His breath stutters. "If you don't want my help, I can step back."

I prop my chin on his chest. "Doing things alone has always been easier. I was so deep in my head about trusting you that I hadn't realized I already did. Inexplicably." My index finger follows the outline of his bottom lip. "I'm not reliant on you; I'm stronger with you."

"Nah, Silver. It's all you. Your strength is your own." He bends forward, locking our gazes. "I'm not going anywhere if you need a break, though. I'm here because I want to be. Okay?"

A small smile lifts my cheeks. "Okay."

He sighs, fingers running over my back in soothing motions. "Your dad told me about Germany. It sounds exciting. Big opportunity."

My breath catches. He discusses it like you would the weather.

"If I only have you until the end of February, do me a favor?"

I pinch my eyes closed and nod, clutching him tighter.

"Give me all your days, hours, minutes until that date. If things don't go as planned with Martin or Harvey, talk to me. Call your parents. Get mad and upset, but don't do it alone. Let me in." The cadence in his voice cracks me open.

My lip trembles, so I press them to his skin, hiding my emotions. "I can do that."

"Don't think about the goodbye. All we need is today; forget about tomorrow." He presses a kiss to my crown, reaches into his bedside drawer, and produces a little plastic rose. Like the petals on the tiny, red flower, my heart flourishes and blooms.

"Sleep now, beautiful."

Today.

As I stare at the flower, I count how many *todays* we have left.

Thirty-eight.

And then they end.

I'll deal with the misery of our farewell when the time comes.

For the next thirty-eight days I'm going to pretend tomorrow doesn't exist.

CHAPTER THIRTY-EIGHT

booth

I raise a three-finger salute. "Scout's honor, sir. I'm missing the tip of my pinky to prove it."

Aly's dad slaps the table, his deep laughter drawing the attention of the other diners. Lydia rolls her eyes at his outburst, but it's full of amusement. Below the table, Aly squeezes my thigh.

She peers down at my left hand curled around my water glass. "Oh my god, you're not lying."

"Nope." I hold up the digit. "First time I was asked to prepare a lobster, I got my finger caught in its pincer. It took two years before I could look them in their beady eyes again."

The women join Daniel in his amusement, all cackling at my crustacean-related sob story.

It's odd being served food that I usually prepare. Most chefs hate eating where they work; I'm one of them. This evening has been surprisingly relaxing, however. I haven't worried about how long the food takes or the presentation. Maybe I should, but my attention has been on the woman to my right and her parents.

They're not what I expected. After Aly revealed her identity,

I looked up Argiros Enterprises and my eyes almost fell out of my head when I saw its net worth. Their wardrobe suggests they have money, but it ends there. They're down to earth, with dry senses of humor and nurturing demeanors. I picture them sitting in a Michelin star exactly as they are now in my family's restaurant. The love they have for Aly—and each other—is clear as day.

When I left Aly after our argument, I didn't hesitate in picking up the phone to dial the number on Argiros Enterprise's website. She needed support; the type I couldn't provide. It was easier than expected. The moment Daniel's secretary mentioned there was an incoming call regarding his daughter, he dropped everything and rang me back five minutes later. Concern laced his voice, and he thanked me endlessly.

He assured me he and his wife would fly out as soon as possible. Rather than end the call, however, we found ourselves discussing Aly. His fatherly praise shone through the phone and nothing was stopping me from applauding her.

What silenced me was hearing him confirm Aly was leaving. It was inevitable and hollowing. A fact I had to face.

She took her sweet time turning up at my door, and I *was* furious with her. Not over what she said, but that she robbed us of two days. I refused to waste any more when a big red *X* marked her departure.

You're not scared of letting your family down, but of going after what you want. It's an excuse.

Her words, though hurtful, left a lasting impression. The *truth* hurts.

I wasn't ready to admit it to Aly, or my brothers. Plus, we only had time for one epiphany and Aly's took priority. Mine wasn't worth the trouble, and I'd made peace with that. Dwelling on it would only open up old wounds.

Daniel dabs at his mouth before dropping his napkin on his

plate. "God, that was exactly like the home-cooked meals I had as a kid." He admires the whitewash walls and fishing equipment. "There's something welcoming about it all. I just can't put my finger on it."

There's no containing my smile at his compliment. "That was what my father and George aimed for. Home away from home. I'm glad you can see it too."

"Everything you've learned has been here?" Aly and her mom continue their own conversation, but the hand on my leg flexes at the question.

"Yes, sir."

His head dips. "Daniel, please."

I finish the last bite of my lobster roll. "I started off cleaning dishes and slowly worked my way up. I worked part time while I attended culinary classes at the local college. I was a cocky little shit as a teenager and thought I'd become head chef in no time."

"That wasn't the case?"

My head shakes with laughter. "If you knew my father, you'd know the answer. He wasn't a ball buster by any means, but it was important to him we knew life wasn't always easy and that hard work paid off." My gaze falls to the framed picture of him and Johanna's mother above the bar. "I owe him everything for where I am today. He was my biggest cheerleader."

"That's admirable. Sounds like a great man. I'm sorry for your loss." He gestures across the table with a curious smile. "And this is the end goal? Or have you considered branching out with your talents?"

"Darling," Lydia warns. "No work talk at dinner."

Her interruption is a blessing. Daniel doesn't pick up on my stricken expression before I push it away. But Aly does.

"Sorry, sorry." He raises his hands in surrender. "Got to listen to the ladies, Booth. They're in charge."

"And you will do well not to forget it." Lydia casts him a

loving glance before turning her attention to me. "Booth, you must come visit us in New York. We will put you up in one of our hotels. It has a wonderful restaurant. The Silver Goddess will be much to your liking. That's Alessandra's favorite. We will introduce you to the head chef, Pedro."

"Silver Goddess, hey?" My lips twitch as I hook an arm around Aly's chair and whisper, "Maybe I'll start calling you that."

She pinches my bicep. "Stop it."

Lydia, with her keen ears, beams at us excitedly. "What's funny?"

"I call Aly 'Silver,' though she didn't like it at first."

"Silly girl. She has never been good at taking compliments," her mom teases and winks at her daughter. "Alessandra *is* the Silver Goddess. *Argiros* means 'silver' in ancient Greek—the hotel opened the same year she completed our family." She studies how close we're sitting before nodding eloquently. "A lovely coincidence."

"You don't say." When I divert my gaze to the woman beside me, she chews her lip, gaze trained on her empty plate. My hand finds hers under the table, and when those silver eyes stare at me, all the noise and people around us fall away. "A perfect coincidence."

We walk Aly's parents back to her apartment. They have an early flight tomorrow and her mom was more than happy to suggest Aly stay with me again. I think she and my mom would get on like a house on fire.

Aly and her dad are busy chatting about an upcoming

project when I'm wrestled into the surprisingly strong arms of Lydia.

"Thank you for seeing her heart." She cups my chin, smiling at me warmly. "*I agápi íne san ton ánemo; den borís na ti dis, alá borís na ti niósis.*"

I laugh when she releases me. "I'm sorry, I don't speak Greek, Mrs. Argiros."

"Lydia, sweet boy." With a pat on my cheek, she whispers, "You will know what it means soon enough."

Too stumped to reply, I step back, giving Aly space to say farewell to her parents. When they disappear into her apartment, she wilts. In a flash, I'm there, caging her in my arms.

"I have a little surprise for you."

She shivers against me. "Is it in your pants?" Her hips push back. "If so, it really isn't a surprise. Or little."

Groaning, I bite the soft flesh below her ear, drawing a squeal from her. "Make that *two* surprises."

Twisting her upper body, she peers up at me. "Are you going to tell me what my mom said?"

Chuckling, I lead her down the street, back still pressed to my front, waddling together like penguins. "I wish I could. Something in Greek."

"Oh god. She's insufferable."

"Aren't they all?"

Left. Right. Left. Right.

Our legs work in tandem. Aly giggles as we make our way down Robin Road. Once inside my house, I flick the lights on and jerk my head toward the coffee table. "Go look."

She narrows her eyes before wandering over. Bending at the hips, she inspects the contents of the table I laid out earlier. "Paint by numbers?"

My cheeks flame as I stand next to her. "Okay, so your mom mentioned you haven't done much painting since you got here and…" I squint at the ceiling. "It's no grisaille, but it could be fun."

She watches me, eyes glowing in the dim lighting before she says sardonically, "Oh, sweetie, you said it right." She fakes wiping away a tear.

"Har. Har." I grip the back of my neck and grimace. "It's dumb, isn't it? I'll give it to Lottie."

Delicate fingers walk up my front, slink over my chest, then curl around my jaw. "Don't do that." She glances at the paint kit. "I love it."

Her smile is too powerful. The happiness that erupts over her face has my white flag waving. I am *done*. You win, Aly. Now give me all of you.

"So you'll paint for me?"

Her gaze roams my face.

In this moment, I feel Aly's trust. She's shared details I know she doesn't give freely and being trusted with them is major. Something about the lightness in her voice, the freeness in her touch, and the secret smile that isn't so secretive anymore is pivotal. *This.* This is trust.

It's tangible. Heavy like granite and delicate as silk. To have it is to cherish it.

The tip of her nail sends a shiver through my bones as she traces the contours of my face. "How about I paint you?"

My voice is raspy. "Like one of your French girls?"

alessandra

"Quit squirming!"

A pillow muffles Booth's girlish giggle but does nothing to stop the shaking of his shoulders. "It tickles."

My legs bracket his hips as I straddle his butt while he lies facedown on his bed. Shirtless, with smooth, golden skin on full display, his muscles twitch as I run a damp washcloth over his back. Maybe the lack of sleep is to blame for this absurd idea. Booth is a willing participant, albeit the most unusual canvas I've ever painted on.

"I'd still consider this painting with numbers." His chuckle vibrates through me.

I pause. "How so?"

He twists his neck and waggles his eyebrows. "Because I'm a ten."

The squeal he lets out when I splash cold water on his face doesn't do much to deter the crazy surge of hormones running through my body. He's so cocksure. With any other man, it would be off-putting. Booth owns it, makes it attractive and endearing, like with a lot of things he does. Pair that with his delicious body, it's hard to not be lured in.

"You really are an idiot," I say with faux annoyance. The cloth splats on the floor as I drop it over the edge of the bed and dry him off with a paper towel. "Okay, are you ready?"

"Ready as I'll ever be." He blinds me with a dazzling smile before tucking his face back into the downy pillow.

We've lined up the tiny pots of paint the kit came with on a tray. The brushes are cheap, the paint may never wash off, but a thrill of excitement runs through me as I dab the brush into hot pink.

I slap a hand over my mouth to stop my snort when I think how ridiculous we must look.

"Hey, what are you doing up there? No penis drawings!" he protests.

"Shh. Let me concentrate."

The streak of pink stands out against his tanned skin. Following each ridge of his spine, I drag the brush down and stop between the two dimples above the waistband of his shorts. Dip, paint. Dip, paint. Dip, paint.

With each stroke, he softens into the mattress, sighing peacefully. My tongue peeks out between my teeth as I layer on the colors. There's no pattern to follow, design to recreate. This is unrefined, imperfect, and messy.

Tires squeal internally, and I freeze.

I'm painting.

The thoughtful gift, followed by my silly suggestion, has me feeling airy. No creative block or obsessing over tiny details.

He's chipped away at me, one patient, effortless step at a time. My flaws don't stop him. There are quite literally no strings keeping him here; he wants to be here with me.

A splash of water lands on his back and that's when I realize I'm crying. Crying because I'm happy and free and grateful and loved. Crying because I haven't felt like this in a long, long time.

Booth detects the change in mood, and turns his head. I

don't hide the evidence of my emotions streaking down my face.

"Alessandra, baby," he breathes. "What's wrong?"

My skin heats. I *hate* crying with a passion. Twice in twenty-four hours is unheard of.

Trust, Aly. We trust him. He trusts us.

I give in completely. The tears fall to frame my watery smile. "I'm happy. And painting." My laugh is more like a blubber. "I'm just really happy and I don't know what to do with it."

He's thrown for a beat before the corner of his mouth picks up, eyes softening. "I like how it looks on you, Silv. I really fucking like it. Thanks for letting me witness it."

"Witness?" My paint-smeared fingers drag through his locks, not caring about the mess I'm making. "You're the cause." I bend down and press a gentle kiss to his cheek. "Thank you."

His swallow is audible and shock flashes across his face. Does he seriously think the cause of my happiness is anything else?

He's still twisted at an odd angle when he reaches back and squeezes my thigh. "This today is a good one, huh? I bet the next one is better."

Not tomorrow. Today.

Our gazes lock. Then, I'm bouncing off the springs with an *oomph* as he flips us over. His unruly hair flops over his brow, making him look rakish.

"Are we done painting?" I ask breathlessly.

"So fucking done," he growls.

I feel the kiss all the way to my toes. My fingertips tingle. My insides explode. It awakens a craving so acute, nothing will ever please it. Only he feeds the hunger.

Booth's hands cradle my face softly, so at odds with the punishing rhythm of his tongue as it plunders into my mouth.

The paint is forgotten. The sheets are destroyed. A rainbow of ruin encircles us and we lose ourselves to it. To each other.

I slide off his shorts, legs hooked high on his hips, finding him bare. Stitches tear due to his eager state to rid me of my clothes. When there's nothing between us, only then do we pause our hurried hands.

"My turn." His voice is playful, gaze fiery. I'm so distracted by the hot, thick length of his cock throbbing against my inner thigh, I miss him reaching over to the pots of paint.

Red fingers dangle above me; his lips curve menacingly as he snatches up my wrists and slams them above my head.

"Don't you dare." I gasp when his hips shift. Then, with his paint-smeared hand, he wraps his fingers around my throat. Not too hard, but enough to slow the flow of oxygen.

"Okay?" he asks softly.

I nod, and shimmy my hips until the head of his cock slides over my soaked entrance.

"You're so sexy like this, Aly." He pushes in. I'm so slick, it takes no time at all for him to fill me completely. "So goddamn beautiful painted with my handprint and filled with my cock."

"God, Booth," I moan.

Tonight, I give myself over. Behind the fire and lust, understanding shines. He has my body, my mind, and my trust.

He stills and releases my wrists and throat. Hands glide down my arms, over my breasts, and stop at my waist. Vivid red decorates my body and somehow, vibrant blue coats his chest. "I want you on top. I need to watch you."

Without removing himself, he rolls us again, until I'm straddling him. His cock hits me so deep like this, I have to wiggle my hips to adjust.

"Lean back, put your hands on my knees." I obey him and groan at the angle. "That's it. Good girl. Now move. Fuck yourself on my cock."

My head falls forward, both our gazes hazy as I slowly start to rock my hips.

He hisses, hands flying to my waist. "Fuck, yes. Like that. Look at you."

We work together, him directing my pelvis exactly where he wants it as I undulate above him. The pace is slow, but there's a feral need inside of me, clawing for more.

"Booth." That single word is a plea. One he's happy to oblige.

"I know, Silver. I'm there with you." His hands slide around to firmly grip my bottom, fingers flexing into the soft flesh as he increases the tempo.

It's still not enough.

"What is it? What do you need? Let me give it to you." His voice is harsh, like he's holding back.

"Fuck me," I moan with a slow roll of my hips. "Fuck me like you hate me."

"I could never hate you." His smile is devilish. "But I can fuck you like I do."

My voice isn't my own when he thrusts upward and his hand returns to my throat. I cry out, stars lining my vision. His other hand guides my movements, taking over my body and what he needs.

"God, I'll never." *Thrust.* "Tire." *Thrust.* "Of." *Thrust.* "This. You were made for me. Look how this gorgeous cunt of yours weeps for every inch of my cock. Who does this pussy belong to, Aly?"

"You," I cry. "It's yours."

He slows, and I curse in protest.

Our chests smash together as he bolts upright, voice taunting against my lips. "Work for that cum, Aly. Ride me hard and work for it."

I want to lash out. Scream at him for torturing me. But I've drifted into another universe where I cave to his demands. Only ever his.

My hands slap against his paint-smeared shoulders. I rise

on my knees then drop down roughly, drawing out a deep moan from our throats. My breasts sway every time our thighs slap together.

"Fuck, Aly. Fuck, yes. Keep doing that." He grunts as I repeat the motion, fingers flexing along my jaw. "You're squeezing my cock so tight."

"I'm c-close," I stutter as pleasure coils deep.

My movements become frenzied as I chase what we both want.

I let go.

He lets go.

We let go.

Together.

His roar of pleasure mixes with my throaty cries. My body shakes as his cock pulses inside of me.

We come down from the abstract high. The proof of our union is smudged over my flushed skin and embedded deep within my soul.

Inside and out, he's marked me. A permanent reminder.

One I'll never forget.

***

"You're hovering," I hiss.

Booth's lips turn down as he pushes off the back of the sofa. He's not working today and all morning since we woke up, he's been lurking around me like I'm a ticking time bomb.

He's usually good at not overstepping. It probably has something to do with my parents leaving and the fact I've been staring at Martin's contact in my phone for over ten minutes.

"You don't need to make the call today. Give yourself some

grace." He rounds the sofa to join me. In only my underwear and one of Booth's oversized T-shirts, I tuck my toes under his thigh to warm them.

I take a deep breath through my nose. "If I don't do it today, I'll keep finding an excuse. He deserves an apology."

His hand works into my hair, fingers scraping against the base of my skull. "Martin will understand."

My eyes flutter closed at his lulling touch. "Today," I whisper. "I want to do it today."

"Today it is." Warm lips brush my cheek and the sofa shifts as he stands.

Cracking an eye open, I watch him stroll into the bathroom. Reminders of last night come catapulting back when he grips the back of his T-shirt and tugs it off in one go. His skin is still tinged from the paint; a lot like my breasts and thighs, both of which ache deliciously.

When the door shuts behind him, my eyes drop to my phone again.

I don't think as I click the Call button next to Martin's name.

A small part of me hopes he doesn't answer. I'm embarrassed over my behavior at the bakery, but since talking with my mom and Booth, this entire trip would be a waste if I didn't try.

I can handle meeting him for coffee occasionally and getting to know him. Seeing pictures of Harvey as a child would be strange, but he's only doing what I'd asked for. Giving me answers.

The phone rings twice before his monotone voice greets me. "Hello?"

"Hi, Martin. It's Alessandra."

He sucks in a breath. "Oh. How are you?"

My fingers tap a nervous beat against my thigh. "I'm good. And you?"

"Yes. Good."

God, this is painful. It shouldn't be this painful. My brash exit at the bakery probably didn't help, and considering Martin's subdued character, it might be down to me to salvage this.

Booth would know how to handle this.

You've got this, Aly.

"I'm sorry. About the other day. The thing is...I've spent so much time preparing myself for all the potential outcomes of connecting with my birth family that I hadn't considered what the hell I was supposed to do if I actually met them. Everything went from zero to sixty faster than I'd planned." I wince at my frantic tone.

One Mississippi. Two Mississippi. Three Mississippi.

"I'm probably not what you were expecting either." The misery in his voice tugs at my heartstrings.

"No, Martin, it wasn't you, but the situation..." How do I explain this to a man who carries a lot of deep regret and whose home holds no memories of a family he lost?

I glance at the bathroom door and practically hear Booth say, *Give it to him straight, Silv.*

So I do.

"I didn't have any expectations of coming to Sutton Bay. The experience with my birth mom cut me deeper than I let on, but already you've surpassed her. Harvey's decision about whether he wants to meet me is his call." I take a steadying breath. "I guess what I'm trying to say is that even if nothing comes from that, and if you're still willing, I'd like to get to know you while I'm in town. And maybe to stay in touch once I leave?"

Four Mississippi. Five Miss—

"I'd really like that." My shoulders relax at his optimistic tone. "I guess we're both pretty new to this."

"I'm sure there's a tutorial somewhere online." We share a

nervous laugh. "My schedule is pretty flexible. How about another coffee? And maybe you could bring those photos of Harvey?"

"Coffee sounds good. Is tomorrow too soon?"

My smile is genuine, voice sincere. "Tomorrow is perfect. I'm looking forward to it."

We hang up, a wave of relief crashes into me. When it retreats, I'm left feeling content. Like I've accomplished something. *Finally.* After spending so much time wanting to prove to others I can face this alone, it's surprisingly refreshing to know I did this with the support of people who care for me.

With that over with, the nervous heat clawing up my neck is replaced with a chill. I pad over to Booth's dresser, desperate to cover up my blue toes. "Hey, which drawer do you keep your socks in?"

"Huh?" he shouts over the spray of water.

"Socks. Where are they?"

"Baby, I can't tell if you're saying socks or cocks. I hope it's the latter."

"You're useless!" Accepting he's no help, I rifle through the dresser but pause at the contents of the bottom drawer. *What the fuck.* Pulling the questionable amounts of spandex out and arranging it on his bed, I wait for him to finish in the shower.

A couple of minutes later, with a towel wrapped low around his waist, he emerges. And freezes. "What are—*Oh.* So I can explain that."

I gesture to the bed, completely dumbfounded. "You can explain why you have seventeen pairs of cycling shorts? *Seventeen.*"

He has the gall to look amused.

"Do you own a bike?"

The smell of his body wash momentarily stuns me as he breezes past. "It's around here somewhere."

"So you're not going to explain?"

He's suspiciously evasive, his silence a clear *no*.

"Well, I guess it's a good thing I texted your brothers while you were in the shower." That gets his attention. Unlocking my phone, I spin it around to show him the photo Graham kindly shared.

His jaw drops, eyes growing comically wide before he dives for me. I'm quick, dashing out of his way to put the bed between us. Feeling like I finally have the upper hand, I wave the screen in his direction. "Aww, look. You can see Little Booth. Was it cold that day?"

"Alessandra, I swear to god, I will take you over my knee. Delete that photo."

My smile is menacing as I admire my new wallpaper.

Dressed in a pair of bright blue spandex shorts, three sizes too small, Booth stands triumphantly outside Our Place, his leg propped up on a fire hydrant. According to Patrick and Graham, Booth would dress in cycling shorts during the warmer months and strut around town looking to pick up women. If it wasn't so ludicrous, I'd be impressed.

"I heard these made quite the impression with the ladies," I taunt.

That costs me, and before I know it, I'm being flipped into the air and carried into the bathroom. The sound of water jetting against the tiled walls hits my ears. "No, Booth! My hair. It's not hair-wash day. It'll get frizzy."

"Too bad, Silv. You should have thought about that before poking the bear." He chuckles as cold water pelts down on us.

I'm screaming so loud, I'm surprised the neighbors don't call 911.

At some point, Booth loses the towel, but I'm still fully clothed. Eventually the water warms.

Whispering softly against my lips, he says, "I don't need those shorts anymore."

Wrapping my arms around his middle, I stretch up to kiss the underside of his jaw. "And why's that?"

His face lights up. "I've got the girl."

CHAPTER FORTY

booth

I'VE BEEN FLOATING ON CLOUD NINE FOR THE LAST THREE WEEKS.

Not a lot has changed about my routine; I work, see my family, relax at home. If anything, I've upgraded.

Silver eyes scowl at me over the pass. A warm hand rests on my thigh at the dinner table. While I build LEGO, she paints beside me.

My mundane life is now splashed with colors.

The main color: Aly.

She's fiery red. Frosty blue. Raven black. Candescent silver.

She drifted effortlessly into my day-to-day, as if we've been doing this dance for years. The restaurant keeps us busy during the day, but in the evenings, she's all mine. We never sleep alone. We've gone to dinner in Jacob's Bluff. I've driven her out to see Puffin Point Lighthouse, and we've even visited Petey as he returns from a haul. She's no longer the notorious owner. She's just Aly.

My silver goddess.

Not only does she fit in with my family and friends with ease, but her relationship with Martin has taken a surprising turn. In the past three weeks, they've met up for coffee five times. Nervous at first, there was no denying the lightness to her after their first meeting.

Last week, she came to my house, with a guarded smile and a handful of old pictures of Harvey. I gave her the space to process as she laid them out on the coffee table and we looked over them together. The resemblance between Aly and her birth father is uncanny. Raven curls, silver eyes, fair skin, sharp features.

She was silent as her fingers traced the outline of a thirteen-year-old Harvey. I waited for her shutters to come down or a dismissive comment. It never came.

The only downside? There's still been no word from Harvey, who refuses to take Martin's calls and hasn't responded to his letters.

We take each day, enjoy the other's company, and ensure the next day is better than the last.

"Evenin', gentlemen." I swivel on my stool toward the gruff voice.

Dex towers above Graham and me as we sit at the bar in Shirley's.

My brother looks around Dex's wide shoulders. "Is he with you?"

"Nah. He'll be here soon," Dex replies and glances at our empty glasses. "I'll get another round."

"Would it kill him to be on time?" Graham whines as Dex walks to the other side of the bar to greet Lenny.

Patrick sent us all a very ominous text this afternoon, asking to meet at Shirley's for a drink. He and Johanna spent the weekend at one of Dex's other cabins. Considering the debauchery Aly and I got up to in The Nook, they should be grateful it wasn't available.

Chuckling, I butt shoulders with him. "We're *early*, you martian. Can't you be away from Quinn for a few hours?"

His lips twitch. That's a no then.

Suddenly looking very smug, he swipes his glasses off his face and cleans them on his sweater. "Hello, pot. Meet kettle."

I gawk and jab at my chest. "Me?"

"Yes, you. You're attached to Alessandra like a bad rash. Poor girl is going to need treatment for life."

From across the bar, Dex watches us, reading our lips and chuckling to himself before returning. "Oh good. We're already discussing Booth and Aly's excessive PDA?"

"The fuck?" My gaze dances between the two of them. "We do not partake in PDA, thank you very much."

Considering our labelless relationship, we keep our physical interactions to a minimum. Behind closed doors, however, my hands are glued to her. Or my lips. Or tongue. Or co—

"You're doing it right now!" Graham protests with a look of disgust.

I throw my hands up in question. "Doing what?"

"Making the same face you use when you're looking at Aly."

Dex slaps me on the shoulder with his beefy hand, probably bruising me. "What Graham's trying to say is that you eye fuck each other. All. The. Time." He settles on the stool to my left. "Face it. You're whipped."

I turn my snarl to Graham when he mimics the crack of a whip.

"Oh, you think you're funny?"

He takes a slow sip of his club soda, smirking at me over the rim. "Hilarious, actually."

My head swings left to right. "We do not *eye fuck*. I'm not whipped. We're just...we're just..."

Ah, fuck. I'm stumped.

"You, my friend, are well and truly fucked." Dex's smile widens at something over my shoulder. "Looks like all the Sadler brothers are. Here comes lovesick fool number one."

We follow his line of sight to find Patrick bouncing in, with the same size grin he wore the day Lottie was born. I straighten, heart pounding in excitement. "He did it?" I whisper to Graham, who shrugs.

"That, or Lottie is going to be a big sister." Even his stoic ass is incapable of hiding his joy as Patrick joins us.

"Hey, sorry I'm late." My big brother only smiles wider before letting out a breath.

"Something you want to share, Pat?" Dex teases.

"Shit, is it that obvious?" Patrick chuckles and sits on Graham's right. The four of us line the bar like a misfit boy band.

"She said yes?" I bring my fist to my mouth.

It does nothing to hide the almighty *hoot* I let out when he nods vigorously, eyes shining. "She said *yes*."

Graham hooks an arm around Patrick's neck, tugging him in for a hug while Dex slaps his palm on the bar top and shouts, "Fucking finally!"

Balancing on the footrail, I stand tall and wave at our grouchy barman. "Lenny! Ring the bell! Jo and Pat are getting married!"

AFTER JOHANNA AND PATRICK'S ENGAGEMENT ANNOUNCEMENT, my mom called for a celebratory family dinner. We all found cover at the restaurant for the evening so we could celebrate the happy couple. Everyone saw it coming—Pat bought the ring months ago and was just waiting for the perfect timing. With Valentine's Day two days away, love is well and truly in the air.

"Stick a fork in me. That was delicious." I lean back in my chair, rubbing my belly.

"Uncle Boo." Lottie giggles next to me. "You made the food. Of course it's delicious."

"Ah, you're good for my ego. Never change, you little toad."

Aly rolls her eyes and chuckles. "It was okay. Did anyone think it needed more salt?" She glances around the table and is met with a chorus of *yeses*.

"You're all a bunch of traitors! Even my own mother," I call. "Lottie, let's go."

My niece giggles as I chuck her over my shoulder and make a break toward the door. Her infectious laughter triggers everyone else as she bangs her little fists against my back.

"I'm gonna barf!" she squeals.

"Lottie," Patrick cautions, though there's no hiding his amusement.

"Sorry, Daddy," Lottie chirps over my shoulder. "I'm gonna toss my cookies."

Everyone erupts into more laughter.

At that, I deposit her on the ground the right way up and shove a finger in Aly's direction. "You're a bad influence."

She shrugs. "You should learn how to accept constructive criticism."

Graham snorts next to her. "Aly, where've you been hiding? We've waited almost thirty years for someone to put him in his place."

"Cheers to that," Patrick adds before raising his glass from the opposite end of the table.

I sidle up next to my mom, pouting. She snickers but strokes my hair like she did when I was younger. "My poor boy."

She had her cast removed a couple of weeks ago and has been taking advantage of the freedom. "Coffee, anyone? Cake? Quinn made some lovely cupcakes for the occasion."

Quinn stands and begins collecting the empty dishes. "Let me help, Claire."

"Pssht." My mom flaps her hands in Quinn's direction. "Nonsense. You kids go and enjoy yourselves in the den. George and I will tidy up."

George, who has no choice in the matter, kisses Johanna on the head and follows my mom into the kitchen. We all move to the den and demolish the sweet treats Quinn brought.

It's like middle school prom with the way we're all seated. The girls sit on one side and the guys on the other. Dex chats everyone's head off about something wood related, but I'm too busy eavesdropping on the girls.

"So you'll come?" Florence squeals, clapping her hands.

Laughing lightly, a small smile appears on Aly's face. "If that's still okay? I can bring wine and cheese. I'm not sure what the norm is for Galentine's Day."

A ringing sound fills the room as Jo clinks her glass with Aly's. "You had me at cheese. Wear something comfy and if you want, you can stay the night."

Quinn's eyes bulge. "I've never had a sleepover, but something tells me it's not going to be like it is in the movies."

Florence shrugs. "I dunno. I still plan on getting drunk and talking about penises. Sounds a lot like the sleepovers I went to as a teen."

Delete. Delete. Delete.

"You realize I'm marrying your brother?" Jo grimaces.

"Rule number one of Adult Sleepover Club," my sister whispers—poorly. "Never name the penis."

It's hard to fully regret eavesdropping when I take in Aly's serene expression. I like seeing her with my people, laughing and enjoying herself.

She fits in perfectly, but also doesn't. It's like jamming the incorrect piece into the puzzle. You can make it fit, but it'll never look right. She shines doing what she loves, as she jets around the world making grown men cry while negotiating deals.

I'm saved from my brooding when my phone rings.

When the area code reads *New York*, my curiosity piques. Aly's parents?

I excuse myself from the room before answering. "This is Booth."

"Just the man," an animated voice greets. "This is Pedro from the Silver Goddess in New York. Daniel passed me your number. Are you free to talk?"

alessandra

I'm used to leaving a boardroom full of men stunned speechless. It usually follows me shutting down one of their misogynistic comments or proving that I *actually* know what I'm talking about. Shock horror.

Honestly, it's my favorite pastime.

Having three slightly inebriated women with love-heart headbands bouncing on their heads gawking at me is a first.

"Wow," Quinn whispers. "That's...sorry, I'm at a loss for words."

Johanna sniffles, looking guilty. "I feel awful for being so rude to you when you first arrived."

Laughter erupts from me, causing them all to stare at me like I've lost my mind. "Sorry. It's just when you berated me, it made me like you even more."

"Oh." Johanna shimmies her shoulders. "Well, happy to do it again."

Florence squints at me with one eye. "I think I fell in love with you when you fired my brother. I wish we got it on film."

I finish raise my glass of wine. "To women taking charge."

"To women taking charge," they all cheer.

There's a slight flutter in my chest.

When I first arrived in town, my mission was to keep my head down. Johanna was an employee, so there were certain appearances to uphold there, but with Quinn and Florence, what was the point in getting to know them? For all intents and purposes, they were no one to me.

But as we sit in front of the roaring fire in Johanna's living room, wearing our pajamas and Galentine's Day headwear, I wish we'd done this sooner.

They're important to Booth, and he's important to me. Outside of that, they're wonderful women. Each with their own hardships they've openly shared, which led to me sharing my own story.

"Unlike these two townies"—Quinn jerks a thumb at Jo and Florence—"I'm new to town, but I've gotten to know Martin pretty well over the last year and there's definitely a change in him. He's always ten minutes early for your coffee meetups, and I swear he sits a little taller when you walk in."

My gaze drops, unsure of how to respond.

"God, sorry, me and my big mouth," Quinn mutters and picks at a slice of brie on the charcuterie board.

"No. It's not you," I quickly interject. "I just can't work out why he didn't fight for his wife and child. I've only heard one side, but it still doesn't make sense."

Florence tilts her head. "Maybe he was scared. Still is. Sometimes people only fight when they have a chance of winning."

"You think he knew his wife was always going to leave?" Jo asks.

"Yeah. And when he didn't fight, it solidified her decision. From a young age, I always thought he looked sad. Remorseful. It makes sense now." She offers me an encouraging smile. "Perhaps this is his redemption. Not just to get to know you, but potentially reconnect with his son."

Florence's theory adds up.

"What will you do if Harvey doesn't make contact before you leave?" Quinn asks quietly. "And what about the restaurant?"

The room falls silent.

I hate the answer to this question. Especially when it was first given to Booth.

"I have to leave for Germany." The invisible hand wrapped around my heart clenches harder. "The plan was never to be here longer than three months. Martin and I have agreed to keep in touch." I pick at a broken cracker on my paper plate, pushing it around. "Also, let's face it, the restaurant coped fine before I marched into town. I'll be around should you guys need anything."

The room pulses with the unspoken. Quinn looks to Jo, who worries her lip before glancing at Florence, who breaks the silence. "And what about you and Booth?"

My chest constricts and the cracker turns to dust between my fingers. It's useless lying to them. "We've agreed to keep things casual while I'm here. I'm sure we'll keep in touch, too, but it wouldn't work with me being in New York and him here. I hardly have time for friends because of my job, let alone a relationship."

The words taste ashy.

Quinn's bottom lip curls while Jo shakes her head subtly.

"Respectfully, that's a load of bull." Florence ignores our reactions to her abrupt tone and rises to her knees. "We all know my brother is a fool, but I thought you were smarter."

I choke on air and splutter while staring at her in shock.

"Jeez, Flo, don't hold back," Jo grumbles under her breath.

Frustrated, she throws her hands up. "It's true. Aly, you like my brother, correct? And he clearly likes you. We've never seen him like this with anyone and we've only just gotten to know you, but something tells me you've never been like this with anyone either." Florence's brows rise in challenge.

My mouth opens, ready to state my case, but it's lost.

"Seems like a waste of something good." She shrugs. "That's all I'm saying."

Theoretically, long distance is doable, but flights and FaceTimes would only work for so long. Eventually, we'd want more. More than either of us can give. I'm needed in New York, and Booth's already paved his future in Sutton Bay. He's made it explicitly clear his life starts and ends here. There's no convincing him otherwise, no matter how badly I want that *more*.

Drawing in a breath, I pluck the wine bottle up and top up everyone's glasses. "Booth has been incredible over the last few weeks—I don't know how I can repay him for what he's done for me. He's an amazing man, with so much potential, I just can't see it working." I give them each an apologetic look, lingering on Florence the longest. "I'm sorry."

Booth's sister goes to speak again, but Jo stuffs a bread roll in her mouth. "That's enough from you, missy. Leave her alone."

With the interrogation over, we continue the evening. Once the wine is gone, Quinn makes us hot cocoa while we watch '90s rom-coms. My soul is happy when we all say good night, but also a little sad this might be the last time we all hang out.

I've finished in the bathroom, heading toward the guest room, when Jo rounds the corner.

"Oh, this is for you in case you get cold." She hands me a spare blanket.

"Perfect. Thanks for letting me stay tonight. It was a lot of fun." We share a smile, but before I can take a step, her words stop me.

"What did you mean when you said Booth had potential?"

Shit. I'd hoped no one caught that. Blowing out a breath, I shake my head. "It was just a figure of speech."

She frowns. "Or like me, you think he's too big for this town."

"What do you mean?" I ask hesitantly, voice low so the others don't hear.

Jo peers down the hallway, grabs my wrist to drag me into the bedroom, then closes the door behind us. "I won't be as blunt as Flo, but she's right, you don't suit playing dumb."

I cross my arms. "Was Galentine's dinner just a ploy to lure me here?"

She huffs. "It's a real thing. And we've genuinely loved having you here." Her head tilts and eyes narrow. "Booth is like a little brother to me, and for as long as I've known him, being a chef was all he spoke about. When I returned to town, I was shocked to find he was still working here, because I'd always envisioned him in some high-end restaurant in the city."

Face like granite, I don't react, not wanting to betray Booth's trust.

"His siblings have seen it. I've seen it. Even his mom. It's only him who hasn't."

"See what?"

She smiles sadly, her words heavy. "He doesn't belong here. He's trying so hard to be what he thinks we all want him to be, he's forgotten about his dreams." Her eyes drop, hands twisting. "Grief can be manipulative like that, but if his dad was here today, he'd be so disappointed Booth gave up."

"Have you ever told him this?"

She sighs. "Patrick tried the other week, but he shot him down."

Exhaustion hits me like a freight train and I rub at my temple.

"I'm sorry. This was unfair. It's just you're close with him, and we all want him to be happy with his decisions." Suddenly,

I'm pulled into a tight embrace. "I want you to be happy, too, but if this is what you both need, then I'd like it if we stayed in touch after you leave. Not just as colleagues, but friends?"

I hesitate for two seconds before I loop my arms around her. "I'll hold you to that."

After Jo leaves, sleep is impossible. A myriad of thoughts attacks my brain from all angles.

I'll miss these women—my friends.

I'll miss the unspoiled winters.

I'll miss sparring with the local chef.

I'll miss plastic red roses.

I'll miss his dimples.

I'll miss him.

Kissing Booth.

I stare at the hand-painted red sign hanging above an unattended wooden stand.

Voices and laughter fill the town hall as families and couples zip back and forth between the different vendors. Handmade soaps. Local beers. Soy wax candles. Pin the wings on the cupid. Face painting. The small parking lot even has a miniature fairground for the kids.

"Does this town throw a fair for every occasion?" I ask Quinn.

Her stall is situated opposite the Kissing Booth and my tummy rumbles at the delectable cakes lining her table.

Laughing, she dusts icing sugar from her sleeves. "I'm afraid so. They've gone all out this year to make up for the Winter Fair being canceled due to the storm." She eyes the gaudy pink and red love-heart decorations overhead. "It's so cute."

"You and I have very different tastes."

She giggles before her eyes flare at something behind me. "Well, not all things. We have Sadler men in common."

I follow her heated stare to find Graham and Booth walking our way. The former has his eyes trained solely on the tiny baker. I'm surprised his glasses don't fog over from his intense gaze. Graham is quiet, but good lord, his love for Quinn speaks volumes.

When Booth's gaze meets mine, the happy couple is quickly forgotten.

Blue denim hugs his thighs and a cream sweatshirt shows off his wide shoulders and thick biceps. His damp hair clings to his forehead, like he's just stepped out of the shower. There's something so masculine about his arms, revealed when he casually rolls his sleeves up. Corded muscles run up them, and the small white welts of healed burns simply add to his ruggedness. I know exactly how those rough hands feel on my skin.

"Silver." His teasing tone interrupts my thoughts. "Don't look at me like that, or I'll be dragging you into the nearest supply closet."

I bite my lip, pulling a throaty groan from him. "I'm open to that."

He chucks an arm over my shoulder and smacks a kiss to my cheek. "No can do. My shift's about to start."

"I thought Simon was covering Our Place's stall today?"

Like two unruly caterpillars, his eyebrows dance. "He is."

"Jesus Christ, not this again," Graham grumbles as he gestures toward the abandoned stall across from us. "You promised you wouldn't do this again."

Booth vibrates with laughter. "Yeah, but Aly hasn't seen me in action."

"I'm confused..." My words trail off when I read the sign again.

Kissing Booth.

Booth.

"Oh my god. This isn't real." I spin out of his hold. "You're manning a kissing booth?"

He gestures dramatically down his body. "Duh. I *am* Booth."

My palms muffle my words as my head drops into my hands. "You were a lot more tolerable when seasick."

For the next hour, I'm forced to watch Booth flash his blinding smile to almost every female in Sutton Bay as they line up at his stall—plus a few men. He drinks it up, chatting and laughing with each person as they hand over their ticket. At first, the idea of him kissing strangers repulsed me, but to my surprise, he places a chaste kiss on their cheek or hands them a Hershey's Kiss if they prefer.

His entire family has turned up, laughing at his cheesy pickup lines and over-the-top character. At ten dollars a ticket, he's making a killing.

I turn to Jo, who's been wolf whistling the entire time. "What does he do with the money?"

A wave of sadness washes over her, but it's quickly replaced with adoration. "He donates it all to a charity that raises awareness about brain aneurysms and treatment. I lost my mom to one when I was sixteen."

My hand quickly finds hers, squeezing tightly. "I never knew. I'm so sorry."

She shakes her head. "Thank you. It was a long time ago. He's been doing this for years—even when I wasn't living here."

My attention drifts back to Booth to find him already watching me. He raises his hand and crooks a finger in my direction. *Come here*, he mouths.

I fold my arms, pop a hip, and stare him down.

Someone nudges me in the back, and I turn to find Graham smirking at me. "C'mon, Aly, it's for charity."

Mortification has my body overheating when everyone chants my name.

Aly. Aly. Aly.

Now I really hate small towns.

I scowl at Graham. "I like you better quiet."

Not wanting to drag this out, I stomp over toward the stall. Booth's smile widens with each step until I'm standing a foot away. "Let's get this over with."

"Jealous, Silver?" he purrs.

"Hardly," I grit out.

"You can't be mad at me. I didn't even flash them my moneymakers."

My eyebrow rises. "What on earth are moneymakers?"

Déjà vu assaults me when he circles his face and two divots form on his cheeks. "These."

He leans in close, blue eyes dazzling, and before I know it, the crowd's cheering as he presses his lips to mine lightly. The kiss is short and sweet, not our usual, but it has the same effect. Mind bending. Intense. Powerful.

He pulls back an inch, leaving me breathless for more.

"You're an idiot." My lips ache as I try to hold back my smile.

"Yeah, I know." He strokes a thumb over my cheek. "You love it."

Yeah. Yeah, I do.

CHAPTER FORTY-TWO

booth

The calendar hanging on the noticeboard in the kitchen is a big slap in the face.

Every time a new ticket prints out, I'm forced to look at it.

I want to tear that calendar to fucking shreds.

Working together like a well-oiled machine, my chefs scrub down each surface and stock up, ready for a new day tomorrow.

Simon is filling up one of the stations to my left while I jot down what items need ordering tonight. Since we fired Kyle, he's really stepped up his game. Which I didn't think was possible.

"Hey," I catch his attention. "You ever thought of being a head chef?"

He turns to me, surprised. "Here?"

"Um, I guess, in general?"

His brows pull together as he thinks. "I mean, yeah...I love working here, but I suppose if the opportunity ever came for me to run my own kitchen, I'd be open to it. Why do you ask?"

Not wanting to rouse suspicions, I resume my task. "No reason, just curious."

"Oh, right." He studies me closely.

Dumb. Dumb. Dumb.

That was a stupid question to ask.

Ever since the call from Pedro at the Silver Goddess, my mind has been working overtime.

Aly doesn't know, and the more time that passes, the less chance I'll tell her. At first, I was pissed, thinking she'd put him up to it after I confided in her. According to Pedro, it was in fact Daniel, Aly's dad, who passed my name and contact info to the executive chef. Turns out, Pedro has been looking to open a seafood restaurant in Manhattan and, after hearing about my experience, wanted to chat.

Face-to-face.

In New York.

Next month.

He wants someone who has years of experience handling seafood to help curate the menu and to oversee the first few months after opening. *Me.* He was interested in me.

Stunned speechless, it took me a few minutes to collect myself before I asked him for some time to think it over. That was a week ago.

Obviously, I have to turn it down.

So why haven't you?

It's at my fingertips. The untouchable dream I'd laid to rest long ago. If I close my eyes, I can see it. Full creative freedom. Patrons who aren't intimidated by fancy-sounding dishes. In a city where people from all around the world could walk in and try my food.

Behind my eyelids, it's a yes.

But when my eyes open to see the kitchen my dad helped install, it's a no.

I make a promise to myself to call Pedro tomorrow.

After I send the team home, I head out front to find Johanna is the only front-of-house staff still here. She's tidying up the server station when there's a knock on the window. We both turn to find a couple standing out in the snow.

"Oh, Booth, will you get that? I've got my hands full." She holds up the empty ketchup bottles.

"Got it." I'm already walking over to unlock the door and greet the couple with a warm smile. "Evening folks, you okay?"

A light dusting of snow coats the sidewalk. The streetlamp outside the restaurant flickers, so it's hard to make out their faces. The woman speaks first, her voice cheerful but tired. "Please tell us you're still serving food?"

Their shoulders deflate at my apologetic expression.

"I'm sorry. We closed the kitchen an hour ago. Are you just passing through?"

"We're staying in Jacob's Bluff, but my husband suggested we try here." She gestures to the man behind her. "Clearly he forgot to check the closing times."

He chuckles. "I didn't have my readers. It's been a while since I've had Maine clam chowder, can you blame a guy?"

"The only place I can recommend that would be open at this time is two towns over." I scratch my jaw, feeling bad. "Why don't you come in from the cold while you make a decision?"

They murmur their thanks, stomping their feet before coming inside.

Johanna looks over at us curiously.

Under the restaurant's lighting, I can make them out. She has dark skin and cropped, straight brown hair, a similar shade to her eyes. When I turn to her husband, an odd sense of déjà vu hits me.

He notes my curious expression and smiles timidly.

"Sorry, have we met..." My words trail off when he tugs his hat off.

Black hair. The color of coal. Curling tightly around his ears.

Pale skin flushed pink from the cold.

A sharp chin and nose.

But it's the eyes that hold me captive.

I've only met two people with eyes like them.

If someone asked me to guess his age, I could say with the utmost confidence he's forty-six. Forty-seven next month.

I know what he looks like as a baby, crying in his mother's arms.

I laughed at his disgusted expression as he held a wriggling trout in his arms.

He doesn't need to respond. We haven't met. But from the handful of photos Aly has shared, standing in front of me is Harvey Willis.

alessandra

It's late when an abrupt *bzzzt* noise interrupts the silence in my apartment. I jump from my spot on the sofa, and without checking, I let him in—because who else would it be?

Through my hazy state, giddy excitement takes root at the thud of his boots from the stairwell.

His knuckles barely touch the door before I'm swinging it open and throwing myself into his body. He's late and I'm greedy for him as I seal my lips over his and drag him inside. But when my face nuzzles into his neck and hands slide over his shoulders, they're tense. I attempt to make some space to look at him, but he squeezes me harder.

"Hey. Is everything okay?" My voice is muffled against the collar of his coat.

The curls around my hairline flutter as he exhales deeply. "Can we talk?"

My heart drops. "What happened?"

When he finally releases me, his expression is pensive. "Let's sit."

He tugs me toward the sofa, but my feet dig into the floor.

"Let's not. Something is wrong, and I need to know. Spit it out, Booth."

He doesn't coddle me; he's direct, and speaks the next three words calmly. "Harvey is here."

However delivered, this news was bound to tilt my world on its axis. But I have Booth, who keeps me standing. After processing his words, I blink once, then the hunt for answers becomes a priority.

"How do you know? Did you see him? Does he know about me?" My voice is surprisingly level.

It's been weeks since Martin first reached out to his son. Day by day, the hope I held onto dwindled. I'm aware I could have reached out to Harvey without Martin's input, but gradually, I've wanted this more for Martin than myself. We've grown close, our weekly meetups something I look forward to.

Booth's gaze tracks my face slowly. I'm an open book to him. He's studied my pages, familiarized himself with my words, and accepted my hard exterior. He knows me, and because of that, he doesn't waver.

"He and his wife showed up at Our Place after we closed looking for somewhere to eat. They're staying in Jacob's Bluff. I...I don't know if he knows about you. I came here as soon as I could. Martin doesn't know. I thought you should tell him." He sucks in a breath after rattling off each detail. Then he waits. Patient. Steadfast.

"How did you know it was him?"

"The eyes. Hair. I just knew." He drags a hand through his hair. "To be sure, I offered to make them a reservation for tomorrow night and he confirmed his name. Martin was right, he took his mom's maiden name. He goes by Harvey Campbell."

My head thumps against his chest as I plan my next steps.

A calloused palm curves around my throat, tilting my head up. "What do you need?"

"You." My chest deflates with the breath I didn't know I was holding. "I need you."

"You've got me, Silv." His fingers skim my jaw, the soothing touch lulling me to sleep. "Do you want me there?"

"I want you there." The knowledge that he'll be by my side quells the bubbling anxiety.

"Then that's where I'll be." He tucks my head under his chin. "It's where I always want to be."

THE SCENT OF FRESHLY GROUND COFFEE FILLS THE AIR. A FIRM hand rests at the base of my spine. The sun shines through the window, highlighting the dust mites as Martin settles into his chair.

Those are the things most people would pay attention to.

My eyes remain glued to the row of framed photographs sitting on the mantelpiece above his fireplace. Four photos that were not there during our last visit to the farmhouse, all of his son at different stages of his childhood.

"He really hasn't called?" I ask for the second time and finally drag my gaze away.

Martin stares into his cup, the steam slowly ebbing as it cools in his hands. "I thought maybe my answering machine broke or I missed the call, but nothing."

We arrived at the farmhouse first thing and explained how Harvey turned up at Our Place last night. Considering he refused to answer Martin's calls or respond to his letters, we're all a little shell-shocked and unprepared for this development. Martin especially.

"This is good," Booth says. "Maybe he's willing to talk. I doubt he's here on vacation."

Martin nods solemnly but doesn't look convinced. "How did he seem?"

"Happy. He and his wife were friendly. We chatted a little about his construction business."

This gives Martin some relief and he looks at me with a gentle smile. "If he calls, do you want me to tell him about you?"

As we've gotten to know each other, I've learned that Martin is very intuitive and mindful. Our coffee mornings always start with him asking how I am and, once assured, he relaxes. It's no longer awkward or tense.

"There's no use in waiting." I lean forward. "If you get the opportunity, take the time to get to know him again. He's your son above everything else. I'll understand and respect his decision if he doesn't want to meet me. I simply ask that you talk to him. Be honest. If I've learned anything in the last year, it's that taking the jump is the hardest part, anything that comes after is easier when you have people who you trust surrounding you." My eyes drift to Booth, who's already watching me intently.

Like me, Martin isn't overly emotional. So when he reaches over the coffee table to clasp my hand, that single touch tells me how much this means to him. "If he's as lucky as I am in getting to know you, he'll be in awe of the wonderful woman you are."

I squeeze his hand, breath seizing in my throat. "Thank you."

He glances at the clock and straightens. "Now, I'm sure you two have better things to do than keep an old man company. I'll call if there's an update."

Bundled in our coats, Martin waves at us from the doorway as we walk to Booth's truck. We're about to climb in when the sound of tires rolling on gravel has us pausing, and we look down the driveway to find a red pickup trundling toward the house. Martin frowns at the vehicle in confusion, clearly not expecting any more visitors.

When it parks up, a woman with dark skin and chocolate brown hair steps out. She looks shocked to see us, but she's quick to smile when she spots Booth. "Oh, it's you! Twice in twenty-four hours."

Usually keen to chat with anyone, Booth is eerily quiet. He stares at me through the open door, mouth screwed tight.

The sound of another door opening has my attention drawn to the truck again. The driver's side swings open, revealing a tall gentleman with dark hair. His shoulders drop as he slowly scans the snowy fields. With his gaze locked on the farmhouse, the air fogs in front of him as he releases a loud exhale.

Martin's cheery smile evaporates, and his hand hovers midair.

I'm confused until the man turns our way and it all makes sense.

He raises a hand in Booth's direction, then smiles politely at me. Maybe I imagine it, but I swear his gaze flashes with recognition. Which is impossible. I'm a stranger to this man.

A stranger to my biological father.

CHAPTER FORTY-FOUR

alessandra

My hands shake uncontrollably as we speed off the property and the farmhouse disappears in the rearview mirror. After a few minutes, a stuttered breath escapes me and Booth reaches across the console, weaving our fingers together. Corkscrew trees and vast, snowy fields flash by as we return to town.

"Talk to me." The deep timbre of his voice calms me.

"He didn't know who I was, did he?"

Booth briefly takes his eyes off the road to glance at me, brows furrowed. "No. I don't think he did." His fingers stroke over my racing pulse. "How are you doing?"

My cheek rests against the seat as I twist toward him. "I'm okay, I swear. Harvey didn't look angry. Maybe a little shaken. It was like his entire childhood flashed before him. And Martin's face...my god, he was frozen."

We couldn't stick around. Martin had just laid eyes on his son for the first time in over thirty years, plus, he had some pretty life-altering news to share.

"Martin's strong, he'll know what to say, and hopefully

Harvey will listen. What do we do now?" Booth slows the truck as we approach a stop sign.

"I need a distraction. I need work. There's nothing I can do until Martin calls." My gaze drops to our intertwined hands. "I need to finish prepping for my trip."

His fingers flex against mine, giving away his dislike. *Trip* implies I'll be returning, but it's easier than speaking the truth. His sadness is hidden behind a wide grin and twinkling blue eyes. "To the restaurant it is, then."

He flicks on the radio and sings out of tune the entire way back. His over-the-top performance is exactly what I need, allowing me to switch off and pretend, if only for a moment.

Right as we pull up outside Our Place, his phone rings with a call from the restaurant's meat supplier. After listening in for a couple of minutes, it's clear there's an issue with this weekend's delivery. I can tell he doesn't want to leave me, but he can't ignore his responsibilities—neither of us can.

"Go." I shoo him with my hands. "I'll be fine."

He frowns and presses the phone to his shoulder. "I don't have to go. Not if you do—"

I silence him with a kiss and unbuckle my seat belt. "You do have to go. I'll call if there's any news."

His eyes narrow before he huffs a breath. "Okay." Then he triggers a stampede in my chest with his next words. "I'm proud of you, Silv. Really fucking proud of you."

Oh, stop that, I chastise my rampant heart.

Beeping his horn obnoxiously, I wave at him as he drives away.

Without him, the rest of the morning drags into early afternoon.

I'm scanning through the performance reports of a potential investment when my ringtone blares through the office. I've kept it facedown on the desk all day.

It rings three times before I suck in a breath and answer.

"Hey, Martin." My voice wobbles, but mentally, I'm poised for whatever's coming. My skin is thick, toughened from past disappointment. The worst is that Harvey doesn't want to know me. *No.* That's the second. Him not giving Martin a chance might strike me harder.

"Alessandra, hi." His tone gives nothing away.

"How did it go?" My laptop snaps shut and I push back from the desk to pace the room.

Years and years of regret and self-resentment are felt through the phone when he sighs heavily. "He listened."

My lip trembles at the joy in his words.

"And?"

"He stayed. We spoke. It got emotional at times. It's not all water under the bridge, but I'm just grateful he stayed and listened..." He pauses. "He's still here."

I cup a hand over my mouth. "That's wonderful. God, that's just so wonderful, Martin."

"He and Sandra—that's his wife—are staying for lunch."

I suddenly don't want to make this about me. Martin's lost so much, and after just hours with his estranged son, there's a lightness to his voice. I don't want to taint it with the question screaming to be asked. It rattles against my skull. Fists banging so loudly, it drowns everything out.

Blood roars in my ears and my knuckles crack as I grip my phone. "Did..."

The words get caught in my throat.

Martin's intuition shines through.

"I told him about you." It sounds like he's smiling. "He'd really like to meet you, Aly. Maybe you could join us for lunch?"

CHAPTER FORTY-FIVE

booth

"Roy, you've saved the day once again, my fine fellow."

My upbeat tone is lost on the red-faced, surly man snarling at me. If you didn't know him, you'd think he was about to swing at you with one of his meaty fists, but this frown is his happy one.

"Get gone, Sadler. You're too cheerful," he grumbles and reties his white butcher's apron.

"All from seeing your handsome face." I give him a two-finger salute. "Thanks for sorting everything out so quickly. Catch you next time."

Roy has been providing fresh, high-quality meat to the restaurant since I was a kid. Not one to mince his words, he gruffly explained over the phone that the sirloin steaks due for delivery tomorrow were contaminated. He suggested it was easier if I came in person to resolve the problem—probably because of his aversion to technology.

I was ready to deliver every excuse under the sun to not come out here, but Aly was adamant. My girl was holding strong, but I wanted to be on hand should she need anything. A joke. A hug. A kiss. I'd give her the world if it put her at ease until Martin touched base. So far, she hasn't texted or called.

Waving in his direction, I head toward my truck at the back exit of the butcher house. The building is large, covered in corrugated steel, an hour away from town. It's only when I step outside that the incessant beeping coming from my pocket reminds me what shitty cell service it has.

And I've been here for almost two hours.

"Fuck. Fuck. Fuck." I scramble to pull my phone out. A string of texts and missed calls from Aly stare up at me. My growl of frustration echoes around the small parking lot.

> She-Devil: Hey, can you call me back?
>
> She-Devil: Martin called. Harvey knows and wants to meet.
>
> She-Devil: Heading over now. I'll be fine. I'll call once I'm done :)
>
> She-Devil: I'm sitting in my car outside the farmhouse. I don't know if I can do this.
>
> She-Devil: I know you're not ignoring me and maybe I'm freaking out a little. I'll regret sending this later, but I could really do with one of your stupid innuendos right about now.
>
> She-Devil: It's snowing, and it made me think about The Nook. Can we go one last time before my trip?
>
> She-Devil: Okay. I'm going in.

My chest splits in two. An array of emotions ransacks me. Panic. Distress. Anger. Misery. Pride.

Her trip. That's what she's been calling her departure and I haven't had the stomach to correct her.

There's another four-letter word I can't bring myself to acknowledge. It'll do us no good. Not with her *trip* coming up.

Her last text was over an hour ago, meaning she's either still at Martin's or gone home.

The journey back to town is a blur; my hands work on autopilot as I take the back roads in my urgency to get to her. The farmhouse is nearest, so that's my first stop.

My tires skid to a stop, kicking up stones and dirt, when I see Aly's car in the driveway.

I'm diving out of the truck when the front door creaks open, lighting up the path.

Illuminated in the entrance stands Aly. Even her silhouette has my pulse racing. The need to kiss her, check how she is, and to hold her engulfs me.

I make it one step before she's flinging herself at me, clutching at my clothes as she hugs me tightly. All feels right in the world with her in my arms. Wild curls hide her face, and I weave my fingers through them to get a proper look at her.

I'd prepared myself for almost every outcome.

When a smile breaks out on her face, the corners of her eyes creasing, this is the one I was willing to sell my soul for.

Aly can handle anything. She's a turbulent force of nature. *The Silver Goddess.* We mere mortals are lucky to coexist with her.

"Hey, beautiful," I murmur against her cheek. "I'm so sorry. There was no service at the butcher house. I got he—"

Her lush lips silence me. The kiss is brief, perfect, but brief. "It's fine. You have nothing to apologize for." When she pulls away to link our fingers together, all worry disappears. "Do you want to come in and officially meet Harvey?"

"I'd really like that."

And in we go.

She leads.

I follow.

CHAPTER FORTY-SIX
alessandra

There are moments in life that stay with you until your heart stops beating.

For some, it might be the birth of their children or the day they marry their soul mate.

Not all moments are happy, and it could be the loss of a loved one or being told your days are being cut short.

Every moment teaches us something and builds resilience.

I learned two things today.

The first is that depending on others fortifies you.

By simply having one or one hundred people to turn toward during your time of need is a gift. A single word or lengthy talk with one of those people makes you feel invincible. What's more powerful is they don't need to be present to bring you solace. Existing is enough.

When my calls to Booth went straight to voice mail, that old insecurity tried to creep its way in.

Relying on people is more hassle than it's worth.

You don't need to involve him in this.

This time, my walls went up for a different reason: to keep those thoughts away. I didn't *need* to involve him; I *wanted* him there. Depending on Booth draws out an inner strength I didn't know was possible.

He hasn't let me down once, and would have been here in a heartbeat. As I sat in my car, staring at the red truck parked next to me, imagining what Booth would say and do gave me the courage to step outside and tap my knuckles against the solid oak door.

The second thing I learned is that Harvey wanted to be here.

To meet me.

The daughter he never knew existed until today.

"He's in here," Martin says as we stand outside the living room door. "I'll give you two some space."

I blink at the door handle. Then, before I overthink it, I'm wrapping my arms around Martin's middle and squeezing. "Thank you. For everything you've done to make this happen."

He doesn't move at first, then after a second, he relaxes and returns my hug. "It's you I should be thanking, Aly. Had you not come to Sutton Bay..." His voice catches. "I'm not sure I would have ever seen my son again. I've not only reunited with him, but I've gained a granddaughter."

My body stills.

Martin quickly pulls away, head jerking side to side as he mutters, "Sorry. I didn't mean to imply we were family or any—"

"We are family." My smile wobbles, hands tremble, but a new warmth seeps into my chest. "You might not be the family that raised me, but you're the family I've been lucky enough to gain."

His distress melts, and the lines in his face deepen with a smile I've never witnessed before. That alone gives me the final dose of courage to walk through the door.

I inhale deeply, close my fingers around the handle, and step inside.

Harvey flies to his feet the second I enter, almost knocking over a glass of water in his flurry to stand. Familiar eyes I've only seen in photos blink back at me as he wipes his shaking hands on his jeans. He's tall, black curly hair disheveled like he's been pulling at it.

We both stand stock still, studying one another silently. My mouth is so dry, I worry sand will pour to the floor when I speak.

Thankfully, he speaks first. "You're...gosh, you're—" He clears his throat. "Alessandra. You're Alessandra. I'm Harvey."

My heart clenches as he thrusts his hand toward me and then frowns at it with flushed cheeks. "I'm not sure about the protocol for this type of thing."

Before I know what I'm doing, my hand is in his and I'm shaking it lightly. "You can call me Aly."

"Aly. Right, yeah. It's a beautiful name." His smile is awkward but genuine as our hands drop. "My wife, Sandra, has gone out to get a pie from the bakery in town. Mart—my dad tells me you live above it."

My dad.

An unexpected sense of fulfillment hits me. Three lives changed massively today, and if my journey has helped reunite a father with his son, then at least the trials and heartache I've experienced weren't in vain.

Harvey showed up. Not for me but for his dad, proving that hope is never lost.

"My friend Quinn owns the bakery. You'll love her Danishes." I point to the sofa. "Can I join you?"

"Please. Please." He gestures for me to go first.

We sit a healthy distance apart, both our postures rigid and unsure. I go to speak, when Harvey blurts, "Are you happy? Healthy?"

His question catches me off guard.

He winces. "Is that the wrong thing to ask? Sandra said that was important. Honestly, I'd be lost without that woman. My car keys go missing at least twice a day." When he looks up, his face is apologetic. "Sorry, I'm a little nervous."

Harvey and Martin might share features, but they're nothing alike. Where Martin is stoic, Harvey is clumsy. It's endearing and quickly puts me at ease.

"I'm very happy. I've had a wonderful life, raised by two people who have loved me unconditionally since the day they brought me home. I've wanted for nothing. And apart from an emergency appendectomy at fourteen, I'm fit and healthy."

He exhales. "I'm really glad to hear that." Then his gaze drops to his fisted hands, and without being asked, he offers an explanation. "I was very young when I met Rebecca. My mom and I were visiting my aunt in Ringwood and we met at a house party. My aunt moved that winter and I never heard from Rebecca after that." His eyes flutter closed as he takes a breath. "I want to be honest with you, had I known she was pregnant...Well, I can't be certain what decision I would have made. I'm cursing myself for ignoring my dad's calls and letters now, but you have to understand, it had nothing to do with you. We have a complicated history.

"The moment I found out, the first thing I wished for was that you had a good life and a family that cared for you. Knowing that's the case brings me a lot of comfort. I don't know much about you, but from what my dad has shared, you're a pretty incredible young woman. A credit to your parents, I'm sure. They'd agree with me when I say our children's happiness is intrinsic to our own. It's clear they've raised a beautiful daughter." He leans forward, eyes sparkling. "If it isn't too much, I'd like you to pass on my thanks to your parents. For raising and loving you when I couldn't."

Something slides down my cheek. It's then I realize I'm crying.

"I can do that," I whisper as he hands me a tissue.

"My dad said you might have some questions about family history and medical records? I don't have anything on me, but I can get that information for you." He grabs a notepad and pen off the table and peers over at me, waiting.

In and out. That's what I'd said over two months ago when I first arrived in Sutton Bay. Once I had my answers, I'd leave.

After hearing Harvey's sincere words, witnessing his misplaced regret, and seeing what a lovely man he is in the short while we've been sitting here, those answers don't feel so important all of a sudden.

"How about today we get to know each other?" I offer.

The pen drops to the floor and his eyes spring wide. I'm worried I've overstepped, but then his surprised expression morphs into a smile. "Yes. Yes, that sounds good." He crosses a leg over the other and gets comfortable. "Tell me about your-self, Aly."

booth

"I REMEMBER YOUR DAD."

My head whips in Harvey's direction, a forkful of apple pie hovering an inch from my mouth. "You do?"

He nods. "Yeah. It was before he opened the restaurant. He was older than me, but we went to the same school. My mom even taught him. I'm sorry to hear about his passing."

I drop my chin. "I appreciate that."

Aly, Martin, Harvey, Sandra, and I sit around the large oak dining table in Martin's kitchen, sharing a freshly baked pie from Quinn's bakery. Aly "officially" introduced me to Harvey, and we've spent the last few hours chatting. It's mostly been Aly and Harvey getting to know each other. Martin and Sandra, like me, are content watching this new bond slowly knit together. A patchwork of new and old.

I've kept my emotions under check, but what I'm finding hard to control is the pride threatening to blast out of my chest over the woman sitting next to me. Aly smiles when I squeeze her thigh under the table, and shit, I need to kiss her so bad.

"He'd be proud to know you're carrying on the family business." Harvey glances between Aly and me. "Must be strange having your girlfriend as your boss?"

There hasn't been a drop of awkwardness this afternoon.

Until now.

Aly and I share a look.

Sandra nudges Harvey with her elbow and whispers, "I'm not sure that was the correct thing to say."

Fortunately, her joke moves the conversation along and we're not forced to explain our situation. Unfortunately, he wants to know more about my job. "You've worked there since you were a teenager? Have you always wanted to be a chef?"

Worn often, my smile slides on easily. "Always. Couldn't imagine doing it anywhere else but the place my dad founded."

Aly stiffens. It's subtle, but I'm a scholar for her and her body. Well versed in the way her eyes shine when I call her beautiful. The erotic noises she makes when eating. The wrinkles between her brows when she's fighting off a snarky comment.

Right now, her tense shoulders say she wants to speak up. To correct me.

Guilt riddles me over the fact I still haven't told her about Pedro's offer.

Thankfully, we move on to the next topic and before long, the sun begins to set.

Everyone is tired, but as I wait for Aly by my truck, watching her and Harvey say goodbye, I notice a change about her. She's always graceful; movements fluid and practiced. Now, there's an added eloquence to her, like an immovable blockade has finally shifted.

I'm close enough to catch the last of their conversation.

"Here's my card with my work and personal cell. I'm sorry we have to get back so soon," Harvey says regretfully. He's a nice guy and I'm sure he would stay all evening getting to know Aly if he could. "But if you ever want to call, text, or email, that's fine."

Aly flips over the small rectangular card in her fingers. "Thank you. I hope you have a safe journey home."

"And you," he returns.

Before Aly turns away, he stops her. "Would it...Could I hug you?"

Blinking rapidly, I watch as she struggles for a response. She isn't shy when it comes to human touch, but this has taken her by surprise. It's taken *me* by surprise.

Harvey shakes his head. "There I go again with my big mouth. I'm so—"

His apology evaporates when Aly wraps her arms around him, squeezes once, then pulls away.

I'm not witnessing a bond between father and daughter. That's never been Aly's intent. Instead, I observe two people, not lost, but who have found their paths unexpectedly crossing. Only they know what's next, but from Harvey's warm gaze and Aly's serene expression, this won't be the last they see of each other.

We drive back separately to her apartment, and when we're standing on the sidewalk outside the bakery, she takes a hold of my hand and tugs me up the stairs. Behind closed doors, Aly collapses into me, and when my T-shirt grows wet, it's then I realize she's handed over her trust to me absolutely. Mind, body, and soul bared.

Her tears slice me down the middle, but they aren't sad.

She's releasing everything she's built around her. All the disappointment, animosity, and doubt.

"I know, beautiful," I whisper into her hair. "You did so good. Let it out."

Her sobs quake her body. My hands rub up and down her back as I carry her to the sofa. With a shaky breath, she peers up at me, eyes shining and cheeks flushed.

"You good?" I ask.

She nods, cupping my jaw. "Thank you for being there." She looks into space over my shoulder. "I can't believe how nice he is. Do you think it went okay?"

God, this woman. So confident and striking, but it's her vulnerable side that has my heart skipping a beat.

I rest my hand over hers as she idly plays with the ends of my hair. "I don't think it could've gone any better. He's a fantastic guy. I'm happy for you. And Martin."

"Yeah, me too. They have a way to go, but I hope this is the first step in them reconnecting." Breaking our gazes, she reaches into her coat pocket. "I'm going to call my parents, they'll be waiting for an update."

"Yeah, of course." I go to stand, but she grips the hem of my T-shirt. "Where are you going?"

I point down the hallway. "I was gonna hang out in your bedroom until you're done."

She frowns at me like I'm stupid. "No. I want you here."

Turns out, I am stupid.

My heart fractures in bitter realization as she stares up at me, all doe eyed. I've fallen so deep for this intelligent, remarkable, beautiful creature that I feel the heat from the center of the earth.

And seven days is all we have left.

I trace the edge of her jaw while pushing that bitter feeling away. "My favorite place to be."

We settle back on the sofa, her back to my chest, as she calls her folks.

"Mama," she croaks.

"Thisavré mou," Lydia's concerned voice sounds through the phone. "Your father is here. We are listening. How did it go?"

She tells them everything. There's crying. Sighs of relief. Even some laughter. Aly trembles against me as her mother soothes her in Greek. It's hard to comprehend the emotions running through her, but not once does my hold on her slacken.

After saying goodbye, my arms remain banded around her. Letting her go isn't going to be easy. We stay like that for what feels like hours until she wriggles in my lap.

"Can we cook?" Her voice is raspy.

I chuckle. "Yeah, baby, we can cook. What are you in the mood for?"

She nibbles on the corner of her lip, humming as she thinks. "How about..."

How about we fall in love?

The thought pops into my head, makes camp, and refuses to leave.

The room sways.

I want to cook for Aly as she sits on the kitchen counter, legs swinging, while she tells me about her day. I want to find her in my bed after a long shift. I want to watch her paint in nothing but those silky pajamas. I want to rile her up just to kiss the frown off her face.

I want her mornings, days, and nights.

I want to *tell* her I love her.

No. Not want. *Need.*

Need or want, that future isn't on the cards.

"Do you have any tuna left? I'd kill for some tartare." Her happy voice sweeps away the miserable realization.

"I'll make you whatever you want."

Later, after we've had dinner and I've cherished her body until our limbs give out, I lock away any and all ideas of a life together. The sound of the key turning echoes in my skull, keeping me awake until the early hours.

CHAPTER FORTY-EIGHT

booth

It's our last *today*.

The past week has passed us by at breakneck speed.

We've tried to soak up every waking second, minute, and hour together when work allowed it. With the restaurant experiencing a sudden spike in bookings and her preparing for the project in Berlin, our time together hasn't been what we hoped.

Tonight, responsibilities are forgotten.

Nothing but she and I exist in the four cedar walls of this cozy sanctuary.

As per her request, we spend one last day at The Nook.

It hasn't snowed since she met Harvey, and slowly it's thawing. The drive up is quiet, yet peaceful, the crackle of the radio keeping us company as we navigate the winding roads. When the familiar A-frame cabin appears through the windshield, it all becomes very final.

I kill the engine, but neither of us makes a move.

"It feels full circle," she murmurs. "A lot happened the first time we stayed here together..."

A knot lodges in my throat. All I manage is a nod.

We unpack the truck, put the food in the fridge, and start a fire.

There's no discussion about what we do next. We just do it—our minds and bodies in sync. Aly unpacks a small easel and paints in front of the window while I pore over the instructions of my newest LEGO set. There's something comforting about sharing a space with someone, not talking, but finding solace in their presence.

That's how it is for the next couple of hours until a light touch on my shoulder has me looking up.

Aly jerks her head, asking for me to make space on the sofa. I shuffle back, and she snuggles into my side, a blanket hiding our entangled limbs.

I wish we existed in a circle.

With no end.

Infinite todays together.

After spending weeks without acknowledging the ticking clock, it stops today.

She rests her cheek on my chest, fingers tracing small patterns on the back of my hand as it rests on her hip. "I've never struggled to find the right words before, but when I search for the words to thank you, my mind pulls blank after blank."

Our fingers weave together. "You have nothing to thank me for."

Her gaze burns into the side of my face. My favorite little frown is aimed my way when I glance down. "That's just it. Everything you've done has been so selfless. Even when I was awful to you, you kept your promises and showed up for me. Relationships have been difficult for me in the past because of my defensive nature, yet nothing scared you off."

The pulse on her wrist matches the tempo of my heart as I raise it to my lips. "You fucking terrify me, Aly."

Her frown deepens.

"The feelings I have for you petrify me. There's no control-ling or ignoring them. You stormed into my life, with your sharp tongue and silver eyes, and owned me from that day onward. Now that I have you, you're leaving." My forehead falls to hers. "Nothing about this is fair, but if anyone needs to be thanked, it's you."

"What did *I* do?" Her eyes fluttered closed, but I don't dare shut mine.

"You gave yourself over to me—piece by beautiful piece until a breathtaking mosaic rested in my palms. I would have accepted anything, but now I have a masterpiece to carry with me. Reminding me of our time together."

Her eyes fly open, panicked almost. "This isn't goodbye *goodbye*. I'll still keep in touch about the restaurant."

My laugh lacks all humor. It's not goodbye, she's right, but she'll be the *owner* again. Not *mine*. "That's the other thing that scares me."

She tilts her head.

Voice heavy with emotion, my head lowers until our lips are inches apart. "Saying goodbye to this. It splits me down the middle, knowing that tomorrow is the last time I get to kiss you."

Her lips purse. "Why is it the last time?"

"Aly..." My sigh blows through the wispy curls framing her face. Something ignites in my chest that she's putting up a fight.

"The distance was an issue at first, and yes, our schedules are equally demanding, but it could work. We could make it work." She rises to her knees, towering over me, hands resting on my shoulders. "What I feel for you doesn't scare me, Booth. It did at first, and that's why I pushed you away. But no one understands me like you, and I can't imagine you not being a part of my life." My body shivers as she drags her nails over my scalp, tilting my head to meet her sanguine gaze. "If I see an opportunity, I take it. And I want this." She pauses, pinning me with her stare. "Tell me you don't?"

"That's exactly it, Silver." She falls into my lap with a single tug. My next words are bitter, leaving an acrid taste in my mouth. "I want this—you—too much for it to not work out because I'm here and you're there. Eventually, I'd want you to stay and I can't ask that of you."

Her silence is telling.

"I dream about it—of a life together. I've run a million scenarios over in my head and if I thought there was even the tiniest chance you'd be happy here, fucking believe me, Aly, I would have asked weeks ago." The sad yet accepting look in her eyes obliterates everything I have left. "I'll never be the same after you, Silv. *Never.*"

She knows I'm right.

And fuck, if I've never wanted to be wrong so much in my entire life.

"Today then." Her voice is hoarse, like she's been screaming for hours. "We make the most of today. Give me one last memory to remember our time together."

So I do just that. With a jagged heart, my lips meet hers fiercely, drinking down her gasp like the sweetest nectar. She clings to me as we stand, already grappling with my clothes on our journey toward the bed.

Space is the last thing we need, so as her back hits the mattress, I fall with her.

That's all I do with Alessandra Argiros.

Fall.

"I'm taking my time first. Later, I'll give you what we both ache for." Grasping the hem of her sweater, I reveal the milky skin of her stomach and lay gentle kisses around her navel. "There's no forgetting you, but I'm going to make love to you like I'm afraid it's possible."

With a strong grip on my hair, she leads me back up her

body and captures my mouth before mumbling, "Love me now. Fuck me later."

Love me now.

My heart protests in my chest, screaming, *I'll love no one the way I do you.*

But I love her too much to ask her to stay. Letting her go is all I can do.

We strip each other bare. Her sublime body stretches out underneath me. The gentle curve of her breasts, the dark curls surrounding her face like a midnight halo, and the silent gasp she makes as I drag my fingers through her slick center are things I will remember when I'm six feet under.

"Always so wet and ready for me, baby."

She reaches between us to grasp my cock and brings it to her entrance. Her back arches when my tip grazes her already swollen clit. "Only you. Only ever for you."

A primal surge threatens my control. I tamp it down, savoring every second as her tight heat draws me in until I fill her to the hilt.

"Ah, fuck, Aly. *Fuck!* How does it get better each time?" I groan against her throat.

"Because it's us. You know me. My body. But right now I need you to move. *Please.*" That single word, whispered like a prayer, is my undoing.

I push her knees to her chest, driving deeper. With our eyes level and heartbeats in tune, we move in lazy synchronization, rocking together slowly. Her nails score down my back with each thrust. It's unhurried as we build up to the crescendo.

I've never been a man of faith, but if I were to follow a religion, it would be *her.* No god, but a goddess. *My silver goddess.* I'd pray for her presence to bless me and worship at her altar daily.

As her walls grip me and her cries increase until she's

panting desperately against my skin, I know nothing will ever compare.

"Give it to me, Alessandra," I demand, hand stroking up her sides until my fingers lock around her jaw, keeping her gaze on mine. "Give me those sweet little noises that I'm going to dream about."

Suddenly, she triggers, her head thrown back in ecstasy as she rides out her orgasm. She clings to my shoulders, chanting my name. I'm quick to follow as I spill deep inside her, filling her so perfectly until our combined releases leak onto my thighs.

It's not long until we're losing ourselves to each other again. This time, we don't savor. We take. We receive. We give ourselves over completely.

It's fucking euphoric, yet all I can think is I have the woman of my dreams in my arms and I'm about to let her slip away.

CHAPTER FORTY-NINE

alessandra

Waking up in Booth's arms is heaven.

Leaving them is hell.

I'm rudely dragged from my deep slumber when my phone buzzes across the room.

My arms and legs are stiff. Not from sleep but from the ravenous and sensual way Booth took control of my body last night. The ache is welcome. I twist out of his hold and stare down at his sleeping form. He looks younger like this; brown hair disheveled with sleep, one arm slung over his face, lips parted as he snores softly.

My hand strokes down his cheek before I stand and walk toward my bag.

Each step is cumbersome. The thud of my feet hitting the solid floor is a bitter reminder that today is it.

When I pull out my phone, the screen is blank, but the vibration continues. The noise is coming from Booth's cell. Wanting to check it's no one important, I flip it over, and the caller ID has me doing a double take.

Curiosity might kill the cat, but why is Pedro—the executive chef of the Silver Goddess—calling him? As I stare at his phone, the call drops, but a text quickly follows. My finger hovers above the four digits I know to be Booth's passcode.

It's a huge invasion of privacy. One that would make me livid. Which is why I return the device and head to the bathroom instead to run through my morning routine. I return to the main space to find Booth stirring awake. "Morning, beautiful."

I'm so lost in my denial that today is our last, I almost forget about Pedro's mysterious call. Whatever suspicions brew in my brain, he can easily put to rest.

"Why is Pedro calling you?" I ask calmly.

Like a shot of caffeine into his veins, his eyes turn to saucers, voice stricken. "What? When did he call? What did he say?"

"I didn't answer." I move closer until our knees touch, him sitting and me standing. "Your phone was vibrating—I thought it was mine. How do you know him?"

He sighs heavily. "It's nothing."

I gesture over his rigid body, muscles straining tight. "This doesn't look like nothing. Talk to me."

Rough hands skim up the backs of my bare thighs as he drops his forehead to my stomach. "*Please,* drop it, Aly. I'm telling him no."

We don't push one another, but he's keeping something from me. He can be mad at me later, because I need an explanation.

My hands bracket his face, raising his gaze so he can't avoid eye contact. "What do you have to say no about?"

His shoulders slump in defeat. "A job. He wants to meet in New York to discuss the launch of a new restaurant. He's looking to bring someone on board for six months to assist."

This doesn't add up. His body language and flat tone shouldn't pair with the news he's revealing. Not just any news. Something he's always dreamed about.

"Wait? He wants to work with you? And you're saying no?"

He stares at me like I'm deluded. "Of course I am."

I step back, and his arms drop to his sides. Nothing makes sense. "*Why* would you turn it down?"

Booth rises, in nothing but tight gray briefs that should be distracting, but I can't seem to tear my gaze away from his dithering expression. "Are you serious? I can't just up and leave. It's not even permanent. Your dad was kind enough to put in a good word with Pedro, but c'mon, I'm hardly qualified."

"My dad doesn't blow smoke up people's asses for the sake of it. He obviously saw something in you. You want to say yes, it's written across your face. So why aren't you giving it a shot? You shut down whenever I try to broach the topic of you leaving Our Place." I'm aware my voice is rising, but my irritation is difficult to contain. "I'm not stupid, Booth. You hate your job."

Pain flashes on his face. "I don't have a choice."

My eyes narrow. "The choice is all yours. No one is stopping you. You're wasting away in that restaurant. I promised myself I wouldn't say anything, but I can't hold my tongue anymore. That night in your house when you told me about your dreams, the excitement and passion in your voice were unmistakable. I've never seen you like that before."

His chest rises and falls rapidly. "My family is relying on me."

My hand lands over his heart. The next words I speak are harsh, but I hope the touch reassures him they're spoken with care. "Your family wants you to be happy. They'd be sad to lose you, but they'd be devastated if you lost yourself. Lost sight of your dreams. You think you're good at hiding your emotions?"

He doesn't answer.

"You're not. Johanna sees the truth. Florence does. Your brothers. And so do I." His troubled gaze falls, the tempo of his heart thumping hard against my palm. "You didn't even correct me when I said you hate your job."

Realization dawns on him.

"Why didn't you tell me?"

When he reaches for me, an excuse on the tip of his tongue, my hand remains firmly on his chest, stopping him.

"Why didn't you tell me?" I repeat.

Booth stays calm. "What was the point? It's a silly daydream that would never happen."

That hurts. My chest aches because he didn't want to tell me, but also from his self-deprecation. "Right. So you were never going to tell me, is that it?"

"Aly, are we really arguing about this?" His eyes drift to the cuckoo clock. "I'm not spending the last few hours we have left together fighting. What's the big deal?"

Frustration laces my veins. My arms rise at my sides. "The big deal is that you don't trust me enough to tell me that *my* family's business offered you a job."

That riles him up. "You're kidding? Of course, I trust you. I wouldn't be here if I didn't."

"Apparently not enough to share that tidbit of information." I shake my head. "I get you're scared. Truly. But can you honestly stand there and tell me you're going to be happy in five, ten, twenty years?"

"It's not about my happiness," he mutters, voice weighed down with so much it's hard to pinpoint a single emotion.

Worry creases his brow when I remove my hand and step back. "Trust works both ways. I was protective of mine for good reason. When I was ready to give you it, I handed it over wholly. But you haven't given over all of your trust to me, or you would have talked to me."

His head falls back and he groans. "That's not fair."

My bag thuds at my feet as I pull out today's outfit. "It isn't fair. What you're doing to yourself isn't fair. And do you know what I've just realized?"

He waits for me to fill in the blank.

"You don't trust yourself, let alone me. You don't trust your family. Not the way they expect you to."

He falters, mouth hanging open as he searches for his argument. It doesn't come. When he notices me changing, he shakes himself out of his stupor. "Where are you going?"

I slip on a pair of black cigarette pants and a fitted cream sweater. My movements are rigid, but if I stop, I'll want to touch him. "I trust you more than I've ever trusted anyone. You cracked me wide open, took a hold of my trust, and protected it like the most precious thing in the world. I'll never be able to repay you for what you've done for me during my time here."

Panic has him snatching my purse off the bed, clutching it to his chest. "Your flight isn't until this evening. You can't go."

"I was always going, and I think it's best that I go now." I reach toward him. "Please don't make this harder than it is."

"Silv, c'mon. Why are you doing this?" His tone is pleading, but it's the sadness in his eyes that guts me. "You promised me all of you. You're still mine for a couple more hours."

My lip trembles and I bite down hard to stop it. "You had all of me." With him momentarily stunned, I pull my bag from his grip. "But you didn't give me all of you, and that hurts, Booth."

In the blink of an eye, my bag is flung back on the bed, and I'm encased in his smoky scent. Booth's arms band around my back, holding me prisoner in my favorite cage. "Please, Aly. Don't leave like this."

His shattered voice is a kick to the chest. "I have to. You know this. We agreed." I return his embrace, hugging him so tight his breath catches. "If you ever learn to trust yourself, I hope you find the courage to leave too. It doesn't mean you don't love your family or are risking your dad's legacy. Being selfish is brave."

An ocean-sized space sits between us when I break away.

"I'll never forget my time in Sutton Bay. Or you, Booth Sadler."

He collapses on the bed. Eyes and body crushed.

Because I can't help myself, I bend and press my lips to his cheek, fingers following.

"I'll text you when I land in New York." My fingertips stop at the corner of his mouth. They hover over where those godforsaken dimples sit.

"You'd be amazing at whatever you put your mind to. I wish you saw that."

I collect my things, order a cab, and use the bathroom. All the while, Booth sits on the bed, motionless and silent.

When I emerge, he's gone.

And sitting next to my paints and brushes is a tiny bouquet made entirely of LEGO.

CHAPTER FIFTY

booth

I woke up refreshed this morning. Sleeping beside Aly is incomparable. My body takes comfort in her proximity.

Now, it screams in protest at the distance between us.

The second my boots hit the creaky floorboards of my porch, exhaustion sweeps over me.

It's too much effort to change or turn on the heating. I have just enough energy to make it to my bed before collapsing face-first into the rumpled sheets that smell like her.

An intense force punches me in the chest. Thankfully, it also knocks me unconscious, and sleep takes over.

I'm not sure how long I'm out.

When my front door bursts open, my backside meets the floor as I fly off the bed. Angry footsteps storm my way.

"You've always been an idiot, but this really takes the cake!" Towering over me, Graham scowls down and points an angry finger in my direction. "What the fuck is wrong with you?"

Groaning, I crawl back onto the bed and return his scowl. "Ever heard of knocking?"

"No. Not when I find out from the girls that my little brother's a colossal idiot with his head so far up his ass he's failed to see what's right in front of him."

He's pissed and talking a lot. Both of which are completely unlike Graham.

And because it's so out of character, I get nervous and crack a joke.

"You're just jealous my tush is better than yours."

He picks up a magazine from my coffee table, rolls it up, and smacks me upside the head.

"Hey!" I rub at my ear. "What the fuck are you going on about?"

"The girls were waiting outside the bakery to say goodbye to Aly."

The mention of her name makes me cringe in shame. Not wanting him to notice I'm hanging on by a thread, I stand and move into the kitchen. "That's nice of them."

"Yeah, really nice." His footsteps echo behind me. "What wasn't nice was to hear from them that my talented, charismatic, skilled brother turned down his dream job. With no explanation."

I freeze. "She told them."

"Yeah, and I'm glad she did." A firm hand grasps my shoulder and forces me to turn around. "She told them because she cares."

Graham isn't mad anymore. He's disappointed.

In me.

A running theme with everyone I interact with today.

"Why didn't you tell us?" he asks.

I'm too tired to argue with him. Legs leaden with regret, he follows me over to the sofa and I tell him exactly what I told Aly. When I'm finished, he reaches for the magazine again.

My arms fly up to protect myself. "Cut that out, you prick."

Dropping his weapon, he studies me over the rim of his

glasses, then falls back against the sofa. "Did we pressure you into staying?"

My neck cracks with how quickly it whips in his direction. "What? No."

"Then why did you stay? Why take over from Gloria after she retired if this isn't what you wanted?"

I shrug, like the answer is obvious. "Who else would do it? Dad trusted me, and without him here anymore, I had to keep my promise."

His gaze darts around the room in confusion. "What promise?"

A chill breaks out over my skin at the memory. To a dreary Thursday afternoon. It was raining, not heavily, but that fine mist that soaks you in seconds. A sea of black outfits surrounded me. Heartbreak and devastation worn by everyone.

We didn't have a burial for Dad. It wasn't what he wanted. Instead, we scattered his ashes at Piper Beach, overlooking the bay, and watched as the tide washed them away.

When the waves kissed the tips of my shiny black dress shoes, I made a silent promise.

"The day we said goodbye to Dad." It's impossible to look at my brother as grief clenches its claws around my heart. "I promised him I would watch over the restaurant. I'd never turn my back on my family. It's what he would have wanted."

Painful silence stretches between us. I'm worried I've pissed him off again, but when I glance at Graham, he stares at me with a broken expression. "Booth." His tone is hushed. "He would have never expected that of you."

The ache in my chest makes it hard to speak. "Yeah, well, we'll never know, and it's too late to break that promise now."

I'm used to Graham's quiet. He's processing the anvil-sized information I've dropped. I turn my hands over, inspecting the small scars marring my skin. All from years of keeping a promise never spoken.

There's a rustling of paper, then a white envelope lands in my upturned palms.

Scrawled in handwriting I would recognize anywhere, is my name.

My heart stops.

"I don't think you're an idiot. Most of the time. But I think what you're doing is idiotic." He taps the envelope. "Dad would think so too. He'd be heartbroken to know you're holding yourself back." Graham's words wrench at my insides. "I, of all people, know how terrifying it is to put yourself out there. If I hadn't taken a risk a few months ago, do you know where I'd be?"

I swallow the lump in my throat and shake my head.

"I'd still be wallowing in self-pity and pining after Quinn. But I took the risk, and fuck, if it wasn't the best decision of my life. She saved me." Emotion wells in his eyes. There's no arguing with him there. "Aly has a right to be upset. She trusted you with the rawest parts of her and you held yourself back. Believe me when I say turning down this opportunity will be the second biggest mistake of your life."

My voice cracks. "And the first?"

There isn't an ounce of indecision in his words. "Letting Aly go."

Feeling like I'm going in circles, my eyes clamp shut to stop the room spinning. "She *had* to go. That was always the plan."

"She did. And the only thing stopping you from following her is *you*." My eyes ping open. "I'd be sad to see you go. We all would. But it'll be difficult to forgive you if you stay."

My shoulders shudder as I suppress the anguish threatening to break free. "I'm scared."

Suddenly, I'm wrapped in a brotherly embrace. Graham's big arms squeeze a sob out of me as he holds me tight. "Being scared is good."

Graham's arms lock around me as I work to regain myself.

When he pulls back, he glances down at the envelope clutched between my fingers. "I don't know what it says or when he wrote it, but his timing is always impeccable."

"What do you mean?"

Heartache laces his smile. "Pat found four letters stuffed away in a closet at Mom's. One for each of us." He swallows before staring longingly at the paper in my hands. "Pat read his after the news about the restaurant broke. He gave me mine after Quinn and I took some time apart. And I'm giving you yours now."

Another envelope appears from his pocket, and he doesn't need to explain who it's for or who will be delivering it.

Florence.

My heart clenches. "How will I know when to give it to her?"

"You'll just know. As much as I wanted to hand you yours months ago, something tells me now is the perfect time." He stands, leaving me frozen, and peers down at me knowingly. "When you're ready, we're all ears, but at the end of the day, we love you and want to see you happy."

With one final hug, he leaves.

I toy with the sharp corner of the envelope, unsure if I'm strong enough to read my dad's words.

My hesitation lasts all of five seconds before I'm tearing through the paper and unfolding the letter.

Booth,

Third born and first to show me you don't have to take life so seriously.

Your outlook on life and ability to read people have always astounded me. You always know if someone needs to laugh or a shoulder to lean on. As you get older, I hope you never lose that.

As I'm writing this, you've just graduated college, top of your class, and you're on the way to being a culinary genius. When you told me you wanted to become a chef, I knew in years to come I'd be bragging to my friends about my hotshot son and the fancy restaurant he creates masterpieces in.

I'm so excited to see you spread your wings. You're a brilliant young man and the same will be said about your career.

If only I possessed the same loyalty you have when I was your age. You might be the goofball always cracking jokes, but you're wise beyond your years. I've watched you grow from a boy to a man. It hits me with a sense of pride so powerful every time I walk into Our Place's kitchen to find you working hard behind that pass, but I know greatness has its limits and you haven't met yours yet.

You're not made for greatness, you _are_ greatness. And you are one of my greatest gifts. Whether it's within the walls of Our Place or thousands of miles away, I will never stop cheering you on. If you decide that this career isn't what you want anymore, I don't care. I just hope you never lose sight of what's important.

Your happiness.

Raising you has brought me endless amounts of happiness and I'm so lucky to call you my son.

Don't forget to reserve a table for your old man.

With all my love,

Dad

A broken, shaky breath leaves me. I drop the letter, not wanting the steady flow of tears to smudge the inked words. My chest heaves, feeling like it's about to cave in on itself.

It's not dated, but if it was written shortly after my graduation, he passed away a few weeks later. Right after I came to work at the restaurant full time.

I sweep my hair back off my forehead and stare up at the ceiling.

Graham was right. While my dad never once used this word when he spoke to any of his kids, he'd be disappointed if he saw me now.

My fears are of my own creation.

The overwhelming pressure I've felt over the years was created by me. It festered until it was easier to use it as an excuse than to face it head-on.

I'm tired of burying my head in the sand because it's the safest option. But there's just one thing holding me back.

I trust my dad's words. Trust Graham. But the fear of betraying my family still lingers.

There's a woman out there who inexplicably handed herself over to me, and I wasn't worthy. But I will be. I'll prove to her I am. But I can't do that until my dreams are reincarnated and my fears a thing of the past.

Then I'll give her my everything.

I just hope she accepts me.

HUFFING UNDER MY BREATH, I STOMP BACK AND FORTH ACROSS the parquet flooring of the restaurant. "Sixteen hours I had to wait for this meeting and they're late."

My mom, George, Graham, Quinn, Florence, and Dex all share a look.

"What?"

Silence.

"No, seriously, what's wrong?" My feet don't stop moving.

"Sweetheart," my mom says sweetly. "How do I say this nicely? You're—"

"You're pissing us off!" Florence interjects, earning a scowl from our mother. "What? He is. Sit down, Boothy, you're making me uncomfortable."

I slump onto a chair and throw my hands up in exasperation, about to argue, when Patrick and Johanna flounce in like they have all the time in the world. "Finally! What took you so long?"

Pat glances down at his watch. "We're three minutes late." He eyes our friends and family around the table. "This looks cozy."

Jo offers me a sympathetic smile as everyone chats among themselves and takes the empty seat next to me. She squeezes my forearm. "How are you doing?"

Pushing down my anxiety, I manage a weak smile. "I'm okay. I think. I just need to get this over with."

She nods in understanding. "I get that." She shoves her index and thumb in her mouth and whistles loudly, silencing the room. "Booth has something he'd like to say!"

All eyes flick to me.

"Right. Thanks for that," I mutter sarcastically, then clear my throat. My fingers tap on the table, reciting the speech I've practiced all morning over in my head before swallowing down my nerves. "I want...umm. I wa—*shit.*"

My voice cracks, throat closing over. *Fuck,* I can't do it. I can't let them down. White spots flash in my vision as I press the heels of my hands into my eyes.

There's a light tap on my shoulder and I glimpse up to find Jo smiling at me. "You have my blessing to be selfish."

"W-what?" My stomach drops to the soles of my feet.

"And mine." My head whips toward Patrick, his deep voice assured and clear. "You've always had my blessing and I'll be proud of you no matter what you decide."

"You already know my vote," Graham says. "You deserve this."

"Ditto. We want you to be happy." Quinn beams over at me. "Just promise I can come play in your fancy new kitchen."

"I can't wait to visit you at this swanky new restaurant," George exclaims.

Dex points at me with a serious look. "Booth, if you don't take this opportunity, I will make your life hell." There's a lot of cheer to his threat.

Florence sniffs, and at the tears shining in my little sister's eyes, my resolve is close to snapping. "Honestly? I'll miss you like crazy, but I will haunt you until the end of time if you turn this down."

I'm overwhelmed by the wave of support and love, striking me at all angles.

It's my mom's wet lashes and the way she clutches Patrick's hand tightly that makes me worry I'm about to make the wrong decision.

"Booth Elias Sadler," she begins, and I prepare myself. "I have loved you since the day they placed you in my arms. I have loved you through every cut, scrape, and graze. I have loved you through your darkest hours." She reaches across the table until our fingertips brush. "And I will love you when you're living your dream in New York. Or halfway across the world. Wherever you are, we will *all* love and support you." When a tear rolls down her cheek, disappearing into the smile lines around her mouth, I about lose it. "If your father were here today, he would be the loudest of us all, cheering you on every step of the way."

It's useless. Absolutely fucking useless keeping it together when my family has robbed me of my words and bombarded me with their blessings. One after the other.

"Fuck." I swipe at my cheeks. "My speech was really good too."

"Yeah, but we're sick of hearing your voice." Patrick chuckles.

"Fucker." I laugh through the tears. Breathing deeply, I scan everyone's faces. "You all know about the job in New York then?"

They all nod.

I scrub a hand down my face. "You don't know what it means to have you all backing me. I...I was worried you'd all be disappointed or feel I was betraying the restaurant."

"Booth," my mom whispers. "Your life might have started here, but it doesn't have to end here. City life will suit you." She levels me with a serious look. "But before anything else, you owe a certain lady an apology."

Twenty-seven, and I still shit my pants whenever my mom berates me.

Gaining Aly's forgiveness is going to be hard. This was a walk in the park compared to earning back her trust. For the last twenty-four hours, I've been haunted by her frayed expression. She wasn't even angry, which is worse. So much worse.

My mouth hangs open, about to beg my family for advice on how to win her back, when the front door opens. We all turn to find a young guy holding a manila envelope staring at us impatiently.

"Patrick Sadler?" he calls.

Pat stands, caution written over his face. "Yeah, that's me."

"Uh-oh, he's getting served," Flo snickers.

"Oh, no. I only do that on Tuesdays. This is a special delivery. Important documents or something." He glances at the whitewash walls and fishing gear hanging from the walls. "I just go where they tell me."

Patrick takes the envelope, signs the handheld tablet, then locks the front door. He tears open the seal on his return to the table and pulls out a stack of papers. His eyes scan over the documents. His face flat, but right as he goes to sit, he halts, hovering above the chair.

"Holy shit," he whispers. "Holy fucking shit. This can't be real."

"What?!" Jo scrambles to look over his shoulder, then her face mirrors his gobsmacked one. "No way..."

"No way, what!?" Florence cries as I shout, "Stop being cryptic!"

Patrick blinks slowly at the paper clutched in his shaking hands. My anxiety is about to blow through the roof. "Booth, I think you're going to have to do more than grovel to Aly."

My chair scrapes against the floor. "Is she okay? What's going on? Fuck, Pat, just tell me."

He shakes his head. "She's fine." Calmly, he places the paper flat on the table. He pauses, then lets out an almighty belly laugh as he taps at the signature scrawled at the bottom of the page. "Aly is absolutely fine. She's also no longer the owner of Our Place."

A chorus of gasps echo around me, but the ability to speak has been robbed from me.

"Who is?" Graham asks quietly.

Patrick's gaze tracks around the table. "We all are."

alessandra

"MISS, DID YOU HEAR ME?"

"Huh?" I drag my gaze from the small oval window. "I'm sorry. What did you say?"

The blonde flight attendant smiles down at me patiently. "I asked what you'd like to drink after takeoff?"

"Oh. Umm…water is fine. Thank you." My brain is too fuzzy to come up with anything better. It wouldn't taste right, anyway. A bitterness has lingered on my tongue since I left The Nook yesterday.

My belongings were shipped back to New York two days ago, leaving me with a small suitcase, packed in a hurry because I couldn't stand to stay in that apartment for a second longer. There were reminders of him at every turn. The kitchen counter where I'd watch him cook. The sofa where he'd sit and build his LEGO. The bed we spent countless hours discovering new ways to pleasure the other.

I'd said goodbye to Martin before we left for The Nook. We promised to keep in touch and I've already penciled in a visit for after my trip to Germany.

I was barely keeping a tight seal on my emotions as it was,

then I plowed right into Johanna, Quinn, and Florence on my frenzy out of the apartment. Just thinking about that interaction makes my heart heavy.

"I thought I saw you sneak past," Quinn teased, but her face dropped when she took in my bag. "You're leaving already? I thought your flight wasn't until this evening?"

"Oh, I'm catching an earlier one." I couldn't look at them, and stared solemnly at the bakery window, wishing I had time for one last croissant.

Their suspicion was obvious. Johanna and Quinn kept their observations to themselves. Florence, not so much.

"I hope you're better at lying when you're pitching to a room full of suits." She folded her arms and cocked a hip. "What did he do?"

He being Booth, I presumed.

"Nothing. He's...at the restaurant," I said hopefully.

"Nope. Just came from there. Try again," Florence challenged.

Their faces dropped at my wobbly exhale.

"Oh, Aly," Jo whispered. "What happened?"

My composure crumbled. There weren't any tears, but I spewed everything on the sidewalk outside Just Brew It until my mouth dried up and jaw ached.

To my surprise, they didn't press me to give him another chance or make excuses for him. They each hugged me good-bye, making plans to meet up once I was back stateside, and helped me with my bags.

It was watching the three of them wave at me through the window of my rental car that had the first tear falling. Since then, they haven't stopped.

I arrived in Sutton Bay tough like marble and left soft as a cotton ball, all thanks to Booth Sadler. Along with my trust, a piece of my heart remained in a fishing town in Maine.

It was stupid, because he knew my answer, but a small part

of me wished he'd asked me to stay. If only to prove that my feelings weren't one sided.

Staring out at the dark gray runway as the plane taxis, I muffle my cries into my palm as sudden realization hits me about what those feelings mean.

In my heart of hearts, I love Booth Sadler.

He tore through my walls, witnessed me at my worst, and cherished every single second we had together as if it was his mission in life.

He would have loved me deeply, passionately, and fiercely. With no limits, of that I'm certain.

But without his trust, would it have been enough?

I refuse to play a game of "what if," and instead, allow the tears to fall freely until my temples ache, throat stings, and heart splits in two.

New York feels empty.

Over eight million people, block after block of bumper-to-bumper traffic, chaotic sidewalks—and the loneliness has never been so strong.

The only saving grace is my parents.

They rallied around me when I landed at JFK, fussing over me like I was a little girl again. For once, rather than brush off their attention and put on a brave face, I embraced it. It felt unnatural at first, but slowly the turmoil inside my head lessened.

It's shocking I had tears left to shed after the flight. I cried into my mother's lap while my concerned father stood by. Not wanting to go to my apartment, I curled up on their sofa and slept.

That was two days ago, and even through my fretful sleep, Booth infiltrated my dreams. It was cruel. My brain remembered every tiny detail about him, but my heart was bruised because of him.

I texted him as promised, though I wasn't sure he would reply.

Aly: Just landed.

Dimples: I know, I tracked your flight. Say hi to Lydia and Daniel for me.

Aly: I will.

Dimples: I hope you have a good today.

How did I respond to that?

Since then, he hadn't texted or called, and neither had I.

The hammer hovered above the nail of our coffin. Waiting to finalize the end.

When the email notification confirming the documents had been safely delivered to the restaurant dropped in my inbox, I wanted to throw up.

Our Place was in a much better position than it was last year, and I was serious when I told the girls they didn't need me anymore. A well-established, wholesome, family-run restaurant needed help, and I did that.

It gave me Martin, Harvey, and a man I was so utterly in love with, it physically hurt. But it wasn't mine and neither was Booth. It belonged to the Sadler and Thomas families, not me. So my final parting gift was to hand over the keys.

It didn't mean I'd never step foot in Sutton Bay again —Martin was there. But now I had zero reason to see Booth. It would have been too painful.

I'm staring vacantly out the window of my parents' Greystone when my mom floats into the living room.

"Enough," she declares and claps her hands.

My brow quirks in surprise. "Enough of what?"

She swats my feet off the sofa and tuts before squeezing in next to me. "Enough wallowing." Her face softens, and she brushes my hair off my shoulder. "I'm proud of you for taking a break from work, but there are better ways to get over this."

I cringe. Asking my dad for time off work and to delay the Berlin trip felt like an all-time low.

My dad's response: "It's about time you did something for yourself."

Even with my parents' support and time to digest everything, I was crawling out of my skin. I didn't mope, it wasn't in my DNA, yet my body had molded itself to the sofa and I wanted nothing more than to disappear beneath a sea of blankets.

"Mother." I dismiss her studious gaze. "Please let me rot on the sofa?"

She gasps, slapping a hand to her chest. "Dreadful, Alessandra. We do not rot. We Argiros women, we thrive. You will start at dinner tomorrow." She's so confident despite my resounding groan.

"Mama, no. I don't want to leave the house," I plead and drag the fur throw up to my chin.

"Dinner is here, so no excuses." Her expression shifts, smiling down at me with such warmth it thaws the block of ice in my chest. "Oh, thisavré mou. I promise it will be okay. That boy loves you so—"

Voice hoarse like I've swallowed razor blades, I stop her. "Please don't. Not today. I'll be okay, and dinner sounds great, but please let me have one more day to be bitter, angry, tired, and heartbroken."

She's desperate to argue by the way her lips pinch together.

My exhausted brain sighs in relief when she holds her tongue, kisses me on the cheek, and leaves me to drown in self-pity.

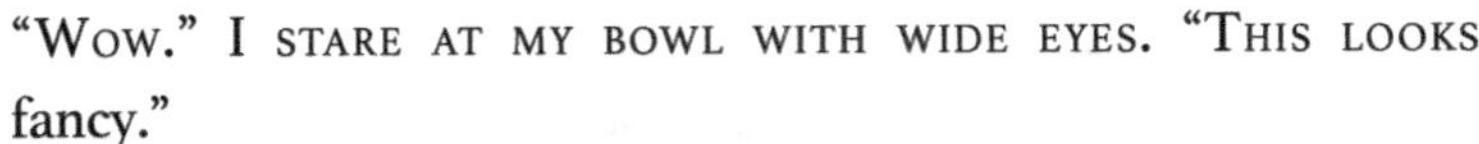

"Wow." I stare at my bowl with wide eyes. "This looks fancy."

When my mom said we were having dinner at home, I expected something quick and easy. Instead, my soup starter looks like something right out of a Michelin star restaurant. It might be blended-up vegetables, but as the creamy, aromatic flavors hit my tongue, I'm in heaven.

It's impossible to hold back my moan.

Veronica, my parents' housekeeper, appears pleased I'm ingesting something other than Cheetos. "You've outdone yourself, V. What is it?"

The middle-aged woman chuckles and plucks a small menu from her pocket. "I wish I were this talented. It's 'smoky sweet potato soup.'"

The next spoonful is already being shoveled into my mouth, making her laugh and my mom to *tsk*, muttering something about table manners under her breath. Dad just looks happy to see me eating.

It's only when our bowls are cleared that I recall Veronica's words. "Wait, what did she mean? Who cooked this?"

Mom blots at her mouth regally. "A friend of ours recommended a private chef to us. I thought it would be a nice change. Are you enjoying it?"

"It's amazing. You put in a lot of effort for Tuesday night dinner..." My curiosity vanishes when the next course is presented.

I'm salivating at the sight of my favorite dish and beam over at my parents, who watch me in apt fascination. "You know I'll never turn down tuna tartare."

Without waiting for their response, I dig in, my noises of appreciation the only sound around the table.

Suddenly, my heart pangs with sadness as I'm reminded of the heated stare Booth would pin me with whenever I moaned over his incredible cooking. He knew it, but most of the time, I played into it just to torture him.

My knife and fork hover above the juicy, fresh cubes of tuna and ripe avocado.

I miss him so much.

"Excuse me a minute, I need to visit the little boys' room." My dad excuses himself.

I push my food around the plate, feeling both full and empty.

To my mother's credit, she doesn't chastise me. Her hand settles on my arm, squeezing once before she stands.

"Where are you going?" I ask as she walks toward the kitchen door.

"I am going to fetch more wine." She nods at my plate. "Keep eating, you'll feel better."

Alone with my thoughts, and a meal that holds too many memories, I push back my chair and reach to clear my plate when my mom returns.

"Are you a vegetable? Because you make my heart skip a beet."

Silverware and porcelain crash to the table.

The hairs on my arms stand to attention and my breath hitches.

How am I so clueless?

I'm convinced this is a dream until I turn toward the doorway where that soothing, baritone voice came from.

My eyes lock with dazzling blue, and the world tilts.

Pressed, white chef shirt, snug black pants, red bandanna secured around his mop of brown hair, and the crooked smile I never stood a chance against.

"What are you doing here?" I whisper, fingers trembling over my lips.

Booth's features soften as his gaze sweeps over me. "I'm your chef." He gestures down his torso. "Isn't it obvious?"

My chef.

"You're here?"

He steps closer and my heart gallops in my chest. "Of course, my girl lives here. She's a big-shot investor. The most stunning woman I've ever seen in my life. Fierce as fire, and strong as the ocean. But...I'm a little mad at her."

My smile drops. "What did she do?"

Smirking, he nears closer until there are only several inches between us, and leans casually against the dining table. "She's always calling me out on my shit. Loves pushing my buttons and giving me a hard time. I fucking love it. But a few days ago, she didn't do that. Instead, she showed me patience and didn't pressure me when I needed it most."

"She sounds smart." My hands twitch at my sides.

He lets out a low whistle. "The smartest. Usually. The thing is, if she'd have used that big, beautiful brain of hers, and bullied me into doing what I was too scared to do, she would know that I called the executive chef of the Silver Goddess and agreed to meet with him tomorrow. She would also know quitting my job isn't the scariest thing anymore."

My eyes blow wide. "You quit? What about your family?"

A subtle smile pulls at his mouth. "Do you want to know what scares me now?"

He reaches out and brushes a frizzy curl away from my face, completely dismissing my nonsensical questions. That single touch unravels me, and a tear trickles down my cheek.

I lean into his warmth, reveling in the rough skin on his hand. "What?

When he bends down and inhales against my hair, my knees threaten to buckle.

A strong hand cups my jaw, dragging my misty gaze up. "That she might never know how insanely in love with her I am. How every day with her opened my eyes to a whole new world and made me a better man." His lips press to my forehead as he murmurs, "I'm sorry for holding myself back—I was an idiot, so blinded by a promise I made long ago, that I lost sight of what's important: happiness. And you, Alessandra Argiros, have made me the happiest man alive, with your cute frowns and secret smiles. I could live without oxygen, food, and wealth, because it's fucking pointless if you're not there with me. That's all we need, Silv. You and me." He pauses, and my heart thunders at his pleading eyes. "I'll move heaven and earth to make this work, Alessandra. Just say the word."

"But what about work? I'll be in Germa—"

He cuts me off. "Distance means nothing to me, baby. So long as I have you, that's all that matters." His lips brush over mine. Not quite a kiss. "I love you, Silver. And I know you love me."

Laughter bursts from me, along with more tears that he quickly wipes away. "What makes you so sure?"

"Because your sharp edges are there for the world to see, but your soft ones are just for me. I get all versions of you and I'm going to spend the rest of my life cherishing every one of them." With the tip of his finger, he raises my chin. Without a shadow of a doubt, this man is my future. "Now tell me."

I don't make him wait. With my next exhale, I breathe my words against his lips. "I love you, Booth."

One. Two. Pop. Pop. His dimpled smile is a sight to behold. "I know. Now kiss me, woman."

So I do. I kiss him like it's the first and last time. He kisses me back with equal need, licking and sucking into my mouth hungrily.

I give; he takes. He gives; I take.

Booth buries his face into my neck and sighs so happily. "You handed over the restaurant."

Anchoring him to me, I loop my arms around his shoulders. "Are you mad?"

"Livid, baby." His chuckle deceives him. "But you were a terrible boss. Fraternizing with the staff. Scandalous."

I roll my eyes. "I should have fired you months ago."

"Too late now."

We go in for another kiss until we're breathless.

"Hey, Silver?" he whispers, grin shining down on me to warm my face.

"Yeah, Dimples?" I ask and poke the little dent in his cheek.

"I can't wait to spend all my todays with you."

My smile matches his.

Equals in every sense of the word.

Finding Booth was unexpected. Loving him was inevitable.

Our future together has just begun, with a hundred new beginnings right in front of us.

ALESSANDRA

FOUR MONTHS LATER

"Alessandra, if you don't stop staring at me like that, we will never make it inside," Booth growls beside me. We're parked outside Shirley's, gussied up, ready to celebrate Johanna and Patrick's upcoming nuptials.

I tilt my head, an angelic pout on my lips. "I'm looking at you like I always do."

He points at my face. "And that's the problem. It's my kryptonite and right now I want to fuck you on the backseat, Jo and Pat's rehearsal dinner be damned."

Eyes blazing, he reaches for my hips over the console, but I wriggle away. "I can't be late, I'm in the bridal party."

Joy pulls at the corners of my mouth. When Jo asked me to be her bridesmaid, I thought she was joking. It was during my first visit back to the States. Booth and I split our time together alone, with my parents, and in Sutton Bay.

"What did you expect? We're going to be sisters." Was her response.

Then I remember the man next to me, and because I love to screw with him, I lower my voice. "Haven't you always wanted to fuck one of the bridesmaids?"

The horn blares through the small parking lot as Booth's fist thumps against the steering wheel. "You cruel, wicked thing."

"You love it." I chuckle.

He nods in defeat. "I really fucking do."

When I landed at JFK, jetlagged up to my eyeballs, it was only when I spotted Booth by the luggage carousel that my energy levels soared. We hadn't seen each other in weeks, and when I catapulted myself into his waiting arms, it felt like a lifetime.

The time apart has been tough.

Every video call, text message, and email has kept us going, but it was nothing compared to the real thing.

While I was away, working endlessly to finalize this new investment in Berlin, he was in New York *finally* living out his dream. He'd put in so many hours at the new restaurant he helped Pedro open, and I have it on good authority a permanent position awaits him.

Soon, we'd be together in one place, permanently, and I was counting down the days.

Just before I first departed for Germany, we flew out to visit Martin. Since then, we've spoken almost every week, and after the wedding, we're headed to Green Bay to visit Harvey and Sandra. It will also be the first time I meet his son—my brother —Luke.

"C'mon, Dimples. Let's get moving." My hand grips the door handle, but a firm hand on my thigh stops me. I turn to find Booth's wary gaze. "Hey, what's wrong?"

He takes a deep breath. "Sticky kids are out of the question. But..." Booth doesn't shy away from speaking his mind, apologetically and passionately. So this moment of hesitation is out of character.

"But what?"

The warmth of his touch leaves my thigh to take a hold of my left hand. "With Pat and Jo getting married, it made me realize we've never discussed..."

"Marriage?" I finish, cheeks straining to not react.

We haven't, he's right. There was little talk about children because we made that very clear early on that wasn't what either of us wanted. But getting married? We've somehow bypassed that subject.

My confident, charming goofball has the audacity to blush.

I let go of the handle, twist my body, and lean across the truck. "Do you want to marry me?"

Whatever response he had, dies. His eyes blow wide and mouth hangs open.

With the tip of my finger, I snap his jaw shut. "Cat got your tongue?"

That does the trick. He shakes himself from his stupor, and before I can blink, he pounces on me and drags me onto his lap. Voice gruff, he whispers against the sensitive spot between my shoulder and neck. "Yeah, Silv. Yeah, I do want to marry you. I want to see you wear my ring. See it glistening as I watch you paint. Feel the cold metal against my cheek as you fall asleep. Watch it sparkle as your ruby-red nails wrap around my cock."

All humor vacates my body. An innate need to experience all those things overwhelms me. "I want that too." My brow furrows, which he finds amusing, and he kisses the wrinkled skin. "Are you proposing?"

He barks with laughter. "No, baby. You'll know when I propose." He glides his hands up the outside of my thighs, calloused skin scraping deliciously against my skin. "Fireworks. Music. Maybe a flash mob."

I punch him in the arm, earning me another deep belly laugh. "You're ridiculous."

His smile widens. "Ridiculously in love."

"So, marriage, huh?" My fingers comb back his messy hair. "Think you can handle me?"

"Nope. But where's the fun in that?"

As quickly as his sentence ends, my lips are on his. I'm about to cave and suggest we move to the backseat when a blur of movement catches my eye through the rear window. Booth doesn't stop, his kisses journeying across my jaw. I try not to react when I spot Florence storming across the parking lot of Shirley's. Closely followed by Dex, who stalks behind her, his steps determined. When he reaches her, he spins her around, and *oh*.

"What are you looking at, Silv?" Booth grumbles. When he goes to turn, I distract him and smash my lips to his.

The moment his tongue strokes mine and his heady taste fills my mouth, all is forgotten.

Our lips move lazily together, feeding the hunger we can never quite fill.

It's a challenge not to strip bare and lose ourselves completely, but that's the thing; with Booth, I've never been lost.

He found me, wandering aimlessly for truths and answers I wasn't sure I'd ever find, and since that day forward, the path in front of me has never been clearer.

Our days are filled with so much love that distance and time mean nothing.

Because at the end of it all, he's mine; I'm his.

And that, is all we need.

***

Thank you so much for visiting Sutton Bay! I hope you enjoyed Alessandra and Booth's story.

Want more from them? Read their bonus chapter on my website. www.ronniemathews.com

393

acknowledgments

Aly and Booth, what fun you have been! This story fell out of me, and even though it brought me to tears a number of times, I was grinning at almost every chapter.

As much as this story came easily to me, it was written during a tough and challenging time in my life. Perhaps I have these characters to thank, but I know deep down that my husband, sister, parents, and friends kept me going as they cheered me on.

I'm so lucky to have an amazing group of alpha and beta readers who, without fail, keep me in check, treat me with care, and help me create beautiful stories. Albany, Christana, Courtney, Erin, Jules, Lauren, Magali, and Tabitha; please don't ever leave me.

A special thank you to Christana. For taking the time to share your own experiences and for helping me handle Aly's story with the utmost care. So grateful to have you on my team and to call you a friend.

Katie, my very own Agony Aunt—or Dead Abby (not a typo). Thanks for being the person I can turn to when author life gets wild, despite our little islands being thousands of miles apart.

Ginsa, buddy reading with you while drafting and editing kept me sane, even though we gravitate toward the saddest, most heart-wrenching books.

Paisley, you're my CMOS Queen and I hope you never stop sending me ridiculous reels.

Mel, once again, thank you. Aly and Booth's whimsical, winter love story has been brought to life thanks to your talents.

Caroline, thank you as always, you absolute darling.

Phoebe, you have been a god send the last few months with your beautiful edits. Your continuous support for my stories means the world to me.

To my street team. You know who you are, and I am forever grateful for you loving my stories the way I do, and celebrating them with the world.

Finally, to my readers. If this is the first time you're reading my stories or you've stuck around from the beginning, thank you from the bottom of my heart.

Ronnie Mathews writes small town, swoon-worthy stories with lots of feels and delicious spice. If she isn't writing or reading, you'll find her in the kitchen or out with friends and family trying to balance being an ambivert. She lives in the North West of England with her husband and black Labrador, Jake.